March To November

BYDDI LEE

ISBN-10: 099076950X

ISBN 13: 978-0-9907695-0-7

Library of Congress Control Number: 2014915764

SEANCHAI BOOKS

Published by Seanchai Books

Cover images copyright © 2014 by Seanchai Books.

Author photograph by Lech Naumovich Photography

For Allan

ACKNOWLEDGMENTS

Thank you to Joe Connolly, for helping me research burning buildings and Fire Service procedures in Belfast.

Thanks are also due to Deidre McCrory, Erin Forestner and Karla Consalvi, the brave souls who read the first embryonic draft and still encouraged me to keep going. Thanks to the members of the Monday Night Writers for helping me with story development and all things writing. To the Potluckers – my writing sista's – thanks for your roastings, the laughs, and the support, and most of all for helping me to polish off my baby! Thanks also to my editor, Karen Gentzler.

Cathy Thrush, without your design expertise and creativity, I would have had to labor a lot harder to bring this book into the big bad world. Thanks for all your above and beyond the call of duty hand-holding.

To my very first baby sitters Christal Neiderer, Helen Cassidy and Mareese Keane, the friends I trusted to be my beta readers. Thank you for being gentle!

A huge thank you to my Mum and Sister for always believing that I could do it and never telling me to catch myself on and get a real job! Thanks to my Dad for passing on his story-telling gene, and for watching over me from heaven.

This book would not have been possible without my husband's support and encouragement.

Friday, March 3rd

CHAPTER ONE

Tracey turned her kayak with a wide sweep stroke, stretching her torso forward and straightening her arm against the drag of the water, adjusting her balance with her hips and thighs so she didn't capsize. She made a conscious effort to engage her back muscles as she pulled the stroke through. The paddle made a satisfying swoosh as it tracked an arc through the water from bow to stern, nose to tail. Although she'd been kayaking for nearly two years, she still couldn't think of her boat in technical terms.

Her brother Dermot had treated her to kayaking lessons for her twenty-fifth birthday. It was the best present she'd ever received. She'd been taught never to kayak alone, but it was relatively safe here where the River Lagan flowed flat above the weir at Shaw's bridge. There was a steady traffic of joggers and cyclists who used the towpaths, where in bygone days horses had dragged barges to the port in Belfast.

The appearance of a lone figure around the corner coming towards her sent a spike of adrenalin through her gut. She thought she recognized that distinctive swagger – the shoulder plunging into the stride made by the corresponding leg, hands jammed in pockets, his head bobbing from side to side. His lower body seemed unable to match the pace, so that his stance pitched forward. Oh God, could it be her ex, Kieran Quinn?

Her heart hammered. Tracey squinted and strained forward, desperately hoping she was wrong and trying to focus more sharply, but the figure was too far away. It could be Kieran, but an evening stroll by the river was not his style. Perhaps he was coming to buy drugs. It would be dark soon. She shuddered, recalling the words he'd spat at her when she had ended their relationship.

"Don't think you can get rid of me that easily. I know where you live, and I can punch my way through that door again if I have to," he had said.

The man kept his head down and his shoulders hunched as he slouched past. He didn't look towards the river, and Tracey, at the far bank, couldn't really identify him with any certainty.

I'm overreacting. Whoever that is doesn't even know I'm here. She inhaled deeply, her breath visible in the cold air as she exhaled. Kayaking was meditation to her. Usually she could zone out on the river. But she couldn't get Kieran out of her head. Why the hell had she stayed with him for eight months? In the beginning, things were sweet. He had a steady job. He took her out on the weekends. Then one day he arrived on her doorstep covered in blood and drunk out of his mind. Most of the blood belonged to him, but he was too drunk to remember what had happened. Over the next six months he had gone on benders more and more frequently.

Tracey pulled her paddle through the water rhythmically, building up speed. The river whispered as it slid past her boat, droplets landing across her spray-deck, sparkling briefly before soaking into the black neoprene. The earthy smell of the water mixed with the tang of her wetsuit created a scent Tracey had grown to love. Her heartbeat steadied.

Her muscles were warm, but her hands felt frozen, clenched around the paddle, her skin marbled grey and lilac. The cold day snatched heat from bare skin. Once she hit a velvety, warm bath every cell in her hands and feet would tingle painfully back to life.

She trailed her paddle in the water, slowing the boat and steering it to the wooden platform of the jetty. If that was Kieran, she needed to get loaded up fast. At that moment she envied the joggers who could just stop when they were done and jump in their cars and go. She still had to carry the damn boat to the car and strap it on the roof-bars.

4

Tracey felt vulnerable hanging on with her fingertips to the grey, splintering wood. She took one last look at the flecks of light dancing on the water and scanned the far bank. It was empty all the way from where she had just turned at the bend, as far as the bridge downstream that lead to the car-park, except for a couple of cyclists with their heads down who were spinning their way across the bridge. She exhaled a breath she hadn't realized she'd been holding.

Grabbing the strap of her spray deck, she pulled, popping it open. Cold air flooded the cavity of her boat. Steam rose from her damp neoprene-clad thighs. A half-inch of water slopped around the bottom of the kayak, dampening her bum so the skin felt puckered and soggy.

Tracey put a hand on either side of the kayak's opening where her hips touched it. She pushed down and slid out of the boat as if she were slipping off a pair of jeans. She steadied herself. If she went too quickly now, she could end up in the river between the boat and the shore. She tried to ignore the urgency that rose up within her. With one arm, she grabbed the jetty and hauled herself further out, crawling until she could get her bum under her, keeping her feet in the boat, preventing it from moving off with the current. Then she reached down, grabbed the boat, and swung her feet ashore.

Standing up, she dragged the boat out of the water. Still casting glances along the towpath, she turned the kayak upside down and see-sawed it clumsily over her knee to empty the water. A honk from the river drew her attention to a family of ducks.

Shit, shit, shit! There he was again, on her side of the river now. He must have crossed on the footbridge upstream.

She hefted the yellow kayak onto one shoulder, using her buoyancy aid to pad out the contact between the hard plastic and the bone. Hooking her toes beneath the paddle shaft, she raised it to within reach of her hand. With the boat balanced, she looked up. He was getting closer and looking her way.

The sun, on its way to the horizon, popped out from under a cloud. The sudden brightness dazzled her, forcing her to lower her eyes. Tracey examined the ground in front of her, avoiding sharp stones, and hurried awkwardly up the hill to the parking lot.

Goosebumps rose on her scalp as she approached her car. Parked beside her blue Honda Civic was a white Subaru WRX. The passenger door was black. It had been replaced after Kieran pounded his mate's head against it during a fight.

The shadows lengthened briefly before the sun disappeared again as she hefted the kayak onto the roof rack of her car and pulled at the straps quickly. Fingers stiff, she fished the keys out from under the wheel arch, stashed there in case she capsized and lost them on the river. The bikers she'd seen earlier jumped into their cars and made off, leaving her in the parking lot with only two other empty cars.

Tracey flung open the door of her car and pushed her dry clothes off the driver's seat. Usually she'd get changed, but her nerves rattled too much to take the time. She spread the towel out so that she wouldn't soak the seat too much with her damp bum.

She had just turned the key in the ignition when a knock on the window made her jump. Tracey looked out at the thin, pallid face of the man with whom she had once been intimate. Her stomach pitched into her throat. Kieran placed a hand on the roof of the car and twirled his other hand in a circle. She took a deep breath and wound down the window.

"Well, hello stranger," Kieran said, flooding her car with the reek of alcohol. His sunken, bloodshot eyes darted from her to the corners of the car park and back. Stubble darkened his jaw.

"So what brings you all the way up here?" she said. She bit the inside of her lip. Stupid! Now he had a conversation point.

"Oh, you know," he said. "Seeing a man about a dog." He hunkered down and placed both hands on the couple of inches of window pane that hadn't gone down, leaving greasy fingerprints. The cuffs of his blue shirt were grimy, but further up, his arms filled the fabric as it stretched over his biceps. Despite the drink, Kieran kept his body in good shape. He was firm and muscular, and for a fraction of a second, Tracey felt the old chemistry kick in. He'd been a talented lover – when he was sober. Tracey's brain took charge despite her body's treacherous urges. This man should have a warning label.

She looked at his face as he spoke again, licking his lips before twisting them up into a grin. She could see where his yellowed teeth met his gums. "So, how ya been?"

"Fine, fine."

"Seeing anyone nowadays?" He steadied his gaze on her. Her stomach dropped.

"No," she said, and then wished she'd thought about that answer. What the hell - there was never a right answer to his questions.

"Ah, poor wee Tracey. How about a night out with me tonight? You know? For old times' sake." He wiggled his eyebrows up and down.

Tracey's hands tightened on the steering wheel. "I can't. I've got plans, sorry."

"Am I not good enough for ya? Just for a drink?" His eyebrows pulled together low over his eyes.

"It's not that. It's just, em, I have plans made, with friends." She hated the tremble in her voice.

"Oh, aye? What friends?" One eyebrow arched.

"Look, I have to go, Kieran." Tracey tried to sound assertive, the way her counselor had shown her in role-plays, but her stomach contracted. She revved the car.

Kieran reached in and tried to snatch at the dangling key fob, but missed. His face was right up against hers. The sour stench of his breath nearly made her gag. She pushed with both her hands against his shoulder, and he moved back a little.

"Oh, feisty!' he sneered.

"Back off, Kieran." Adrenaline frayed her thoughts. "Get away from the car. I'll tell Dermot about this. You might just get another visit, and it won't be so gentle next time."

"You wee bitch," Kieran said, slamming his hand down on the roof of the car and making Tracey jump. She lifted her phone from the shelf beneath the car radio.

"One call, Kieran," she threatened. Kieran stepped back. Tracey stood on the gas. An arc of gravel spun out from behind the wheels as the car sprang forward. She heard another thud impact the car, and as she looked in her rearview mirror, she saw Kieran giving her the fingers, his mouth moving and his face contorted.

Tracey turned left onto the main road and drove up to the Sporting roundabout. As she waited for her turn to enter, she checked her mirror again. The white Subaru had turned left too. Was Kieran following her? She jigged in her seat, urging the traffic to give her a break. She launched into a gap in the stream of cars, causing another driver to blast his horn. She didn't care as she sped away, driving north towards the University area.

Tracey picked up her phone, her gaze flicking from the road in front, to the rearview mirror and back to the phone. She called her brother, Dermot.

"Please pick up. Please pick up," she said out loud. "Shit!" It went to his answering machine.

The Subaru was three cars behind her. She couldn't go home now. She still lived with her mother, who suffered from self-diagnosed "bad nerves". Another visit from Kieran would not help!

When her father died six months ago, Kieran drank all the way through the wake and missed the funeral. The day after they buried her father, she had dumped him.

Later that night Tracey and her mother woke to a relentless hammering on the door. He screamed obscenities at Tracey and threatened to kill her. Afraid to face him, they watched from an upstairs window, clinging to each other in terror as Kieran smashed his fist through the door, splintering bone and wood alike. By the time he had broken through, a police car had arrived, and he'd been carted off.

To prevent a repeat performance, Dermot had threatened Kieran. Tracey's mother refilled her valium prescription, and Tracey went to counseling.

She'd have to drive to Dermot's house. Even if he wasn't home, there was no chance that Kieran was going to risk meeting him. Kieran had been there with her before and would recognize the street.

As she turned onto Dermot's street, the Subaru drove on past the intersection. Awash with relief, Tracey's hands trembled. The adrenalin that had aided her flight now overwhelmed her. Her joins felt loose and fluid, and ever so slightly out of her control. Her blood seemed effervescent in her veins, as if they pulsed with bubbles. She parked in front of her big brother's house and burst into tears. Digging into her handbag, she found a raggy tissue and blew her nose. No point going in looking like this.

But it was too late. The door opened, and a tall blond man stood in the doorway. Pearly light poured out into the night, giving his outline a glow. He bent down and gave the woman next to him a peck on the cheek, then walked out into the front pathway. The woman watched after him, glancing over at Tracey's car. She cocked her head forward and waved. Crap! Her sister-in-law, Molly, had spotted her. Now she had to go in and explain why she was here, with big red eyes and dressed in a wetsuit.

Molly moved forward, her blond curls dancing, and grabbed the man's hand, dragging him towards the car.

"Tracey! This is my cousin, Tommy," Molly said, pulling open the car door. She did a double take at Tracey's attire before continuing. "He's moving back here from London to set up his own business."

"Tracey, lovely to meet you again," he said. Perhaps the glow was just the streetlight shining from behind him, but to Tracey, he was radiant as she looked up at his smiling grey eyes set above high cheek bones and a square jaw. His full lips parted in a smile to show even, white teeth. Molly's cousin Tommy – the one that got away.

"Nice to meet you again too." Christ! Why was she talking like a character out of Pride and Prejudice? Her cheeks burned.

"So you two know each other?" Molly said, looking from Tracey to Tommy.

"Yes, we met," they said together. Tracey stopped talking.

"At your wedding," Tommy continued. Tracey squirmed a little more. She remembered how they'd danced all evening, shared a sweet lingering kiss during a slow dance. They'd connected - or so she'd thought. He'd promised to call but never did.

She wished she was not sitting in smelly neoprene. The wetsuit did little to hide every bulge and curve. She got out of the car quickly, hoping that if she stood up, she'd looked less like the Michelin man.

"I was just kayaking," Tracey said, hoping that he'd think her red eyes were caused by the wind or by getting water in them.

"Cool," Tommy said, smiling and nodding. He hadn't changed in eight years. His eyelids had that sleepy closed lid look when he smiled. Her body reacted, and her brain scrambled. Holy crap! Why did she have to bump into him looking like shit? Was the universe laughing at her? Sweat trickled down Tracey's back.

"I just …," She nodded towards the house. "Is Dermot home?"

"He is. He's watching the soccer" Molly said, her pale blue husky-dog eyes searched Tracey's. "Are you okay?"

"I, well… It's just…"

Tommy put his hands in front of his chest, palms out, fingers splayed.

"Sorry to interrupt, but I really gotta go," he said. Gratefully, Tracey smiled at him. For a moment their eyes locked, and a jolt of pleasure fired through her.

"Nice meeting you again, Tommy," she said. The connection severed, and he turned and walked away from them. Tracey admired the round bum in his jeans. She felt Molly's arm slip through hers.

"He's a lovely guy," Molly said, watching after him. She squeezed Tracey's arm against her side. "You could do worse."

"Believe me, I have." Suddenly overwhelmed with self-pity, Tracey burst into tears again. Molly guided her into the house. Dermot was parked in front of the television. Molly lifted the remote and turned down the volume. He looked up as if to protest, but when he saw Tracey he stood up and walked over to embrace her. Tracey clung to him and cried.

"Ugh, you're all damp." He pushed her away but kept his hands on her shoulders. He lowered his head so he could look right into her face, his black eyes gleaming out from beneath the dark "v" of his eyebrows. "That bastard Quinn again?"

Tracey nodded. A sob escaped her, and she sniffed it back in.

"Did he hurt you? I'll fucking kill him!"

"No, no. Seriously, I'm okay. I told him I'd send you after him again if he came near me, and he backed off. But, well I just called because I, well, he followed me." Tracey was just glad to know that someone gave a shit about her.

"I could pay that fecker Kieran a visit later."

"It's too dangerous." Molly said. "You've already pretended to be in the IRA to scare him."

Tracey agreed.

"Wait a wee minute. I didn't 'pretend' anything. I can't help it if Kieran assumes that anyone waiting for him in a dark ally in a black leather jacket with a baseball bat is in the Ra," Dermot insisted.

"Well, dah! It's not like you were playing baseball with it," Molly said. "How many Irish baseball teams do you know of?"

Despite her distress, Tracey had to smile. "Look, I feel better now. Let's just forget it," she said.

"You need to stop seeing these losers. Pick a nice guy, someone who'll treat you right. What about our Tommy? He's a great fella, good craic too."

"You know, honey, that's exactly what I said too." Molly's face glowed as she looked at her husband. Envy sawed into Tracey. How nice to be smugly married and playing with other people's lives.

"Now, don't you two start acting cupid!" Tracey said. She'd never told them about kissing Tommy at their wedding. What was there to tell in the end? She continued, "I'm still running away from the last one. My counselor says…"

"Counselor? Bullshit!" Dermot blurted.

Tracey stopped and glared at Dermot.

Molly put her arm around her sister-in-law, rubbed her shoulder, and said, "Dermot, don't be like that! If counseling helps Tracey, then you should be glad. I wish you'd consider going too."

"No fecking way!" He ran his hand through his hair, which flopped back into the same place it had been. "Sorry, Tracey. If it helps you though, knock yourself out."

"It does." Tracey sniffed. The counselor had given her a new way of looking at things.

"I just want a normal life," she had told the counselor. "I don't want to be worrying about what or how much someone drinks. I want to be able to plan things in advance and know they won't be ruined because some drunken bastard has screwed it all up."

"You need to break the mold. Do you see any patterns in the men you date?" the counselor had asked.

"Yeah, they all drink too much," Tracey said, surprised it hadn't occurred to her sooner. Then she realized something else and added sourly, "Just like dear old Dad!"

"Perhaps that has been your version of 'normal'?"

"Well, I want a saner 'normal'," Tracey said.

"Then you need to increase your expectations. Aim higher," her counselor had said.

The "to be or not to be counseled" argument was not one Tracey wanted to get into again. She shifted towards the doorway.

"Tell you what," Dermot said. "Why don't you give me a lift over to The Bot on your way home; I can watch the rest of the match there."

"In peace?" Molly scowled. Dermot sighed loudly. His fists slowly closed and opened at his sides. Molly shrugged and turned her back on him.

"If Quinn is still skulking about, he'll see me in the car with you," Dermot continued.

Tracey shook her head slowly. "Jeez, Dermot, when are you ever going to learn to drive?"

"Hey, driving's overrated. Besides, why should I? This way, I can always have a drink and never have to be the designated driver!"

Tracey and Molly both cast their eyes skyward and nudged each other. They'd heard it all before.

"Okay. But I gotta go right now. I really need to get out of my kayaking gear."

"Great. And Tracey," Dermot picked up his jacket from the hall stand. "Seriously, think about Tommy…"

"Oh shut up and come on! Bye, Molly, and thank you." Tracey gave her sister-in-law a quick hug and headed out to the car, followed by Dermot who fumbled into his jacket as he walked.

Thinking about Tommy hadn't gotten her anywhere in the past. He might be the most gorgeous man she'd ever seen, but he'd had his chance and blown it. As the counselor had said – raise those expectations. She wasn't going to let anyone treat her like crap ever again.

Friday, March 3rd

CHAPTER TWO

Tracey Duggan. Tommy added her to his list of good reasons for coming back. She was a real woman, not one of those dolled up city girls he was used to seeing in London. He wished he'd called her after the wedding, but there'd been no point. A storm had swept through Tommy's life, leaving him bereft and defeated. He had run away from it all.

Tommy opened the door to the rental house. It was small but good enough until he got his business established and could afford to buy something. His dog greeted him in a flurry of fur and slobber.

"Alright, Wolfie, alright," Tommy said. He pushed the dog's big paws from his chest and made him sit.

"Are you hungry?"

The dog's forehead puckered and his ears pricked up. The expression, so human, made Tommy laugh. This mutt, the size of a Great Dane with Border Collie markings had come with the ground floor flat he'd rented when he first went to London. His previous owner, moving overseas, had been about to put the nine-month old pup into the dog shelter when Tommy called to view the place. Keeping Wolfie solved two problems at once, providing Tommy with companionship that helped alleviate those first homesick months in the Big Smoke, and giving them both a place to live.

Now, Tommy was back and lucky to find a Belfast rental without a pet clause, although Molly had agreed to keep Wolfie if it had been an issue.

Tommy spooned out the dog's food and watched as Wolfie gobbled it up in five seconds flat. He looked up at Tommy and pawed the empty bowl.

"No!" Tommy said, hunkering down beside the dog, "Ya silly big mutt!"

The dog slugged him with a wet tongue right across the mouth.

"Yuk!" Tommy wiped his face but the smell of dog food lingered. "You're all I've got big lad." He scratched the dog's head and the dog collapsed in a pile on the floor, rolled on his back and waited to get his chest scratched. Tommy did the needful, squashing the temptation to feel sorry for himself. After all there was Molly; his only other really close family. They were more like brother and sister than cousins. They were born months apart and neither of them had siblings. Their mothers, sisters and good friends, had brought them up together. They'd shared cots and buggies until they were too big to. After that they usually shared punishments. Molly had always been there for him.

Unlike his father.

"Got to get this over with, Wolfie." Tommy stood up. The dog squirmed around scrambling right side up again. He whined as Tommy lifted his coat.

"No! Stay," Tommy lifted his keys as the dog looked up, doleful. "You're in charge, big lad."

Wolfie flopped down on the floor, his eyes glued to Tommy's every move as he exited.

***

South Belfast had changed in subtle ways since Tommy had left. The ceasefire had allowed wealth to trickle into the suburbs. The new shops and businesses on the Lisburn Road impressed Tommy with their contemporary style. It was a slice of London, with all the craic of home.

Moving through the familiar streets brought a sting of loss. Tommy hadn't been home since the day after his mother's funeral eight years ago. It wasn't that his father had kicked him out as such, but he couldn't stay in this city, let alone that house with that man. London lacked the judgment Tommy had once faced in Belfast. His job defined him, but he loved doing what he did. Now that he'd come home again, he hoped that this new, more cosmopolitan Belfast had moved away from its narrow-mindedness.

Tommy parked on the street in front of a large box hedge that enclosed a grey semi-detached house. The front lawn and flowers, once so carefully tended by his mother, had been ripped out and concreted over. It didn't surprise Tommy. Even so, he approached the front door still half expecting to see the curtains twitch and his mother's face appear at the window. How could she not be here anymore? Tommy longed for a conversation with her. Sometimes she appeared in his dreams. Healthy, from before the cancer had ravaged her. But the curtains were still and the house shrouded in stealthy gloom as if it, too, keenly noted her absence.

The doorbell still sang out the same "Avon Lady" chime. A yellow glow lit up the fan light, and from inside Tommy heard the shuffle of feet and the bang of a door. The front door opened and his father stood before him.

"Tommy!" There was a brief flash across his father's face. Was it pleasure? Then it was clamped down with a puckering of the forehead. "It's been a while."

"It has." And there it was. Probably the only thing they would agree on.

Tommy's father, Sean O Brian, had once been a tall, burley man. Now he was stooped over and wizened, too old for his age. Grey wispy hair had replaced his once golden curls. He still wore a three piece suit and leather shoes even around the house, but his shirt looked grimy and a faint sour odor floated around him.

"Come in. Don't just stand there."

Tommy followed his father through to the living room. The house hung in limbo. Except for the film of dust that coated everything, his mother could be in the kitchen. He sat down on the sofa and watched his father settle into the same old chair he'd sat in for nearly half a century. Those years had worn the beige velvet smooth where Sean's hands rested. Sean cleared his throat with a noisy rattle. For a minute, unspoken words hovered over them. Tommy wasn't sure how to begin.

"D'you come back on the ferry?" Sean asked.

"Yes."

"How was it?"

"Calm. You know, nothing special."

"Are you back to stay?" Sean asked.

"Yes. I've rented a wee two-up-two-down behind the University."

"In the Holylands?"

"Yes." The Holylands was a grid of streets that all had biblical names. Silence settled between them again. Tommy battled with impatience. Finally he spoke.

"So you re-did the garden?"

"It got too over-grown." Sean rubbed his chin. "I wasn't as good at the gardening as…" He shrugged. "You know what I mean?"

Tommy fought the urge to yell, "No I don't know! She loved the garden and you destroyed it." Instead, he bit down on the inside of his mouth and nodded. There'd been too much yelling in the past.

"Do you want a cup of tea?" Sean asked, getting to his feet.

"No thanks."

Sean looked disappointed and lingered in a half standing position.

"Well, unless you're making some," Tommy said. Sean stood up and shuffled out of the room. Tommy heard a switch clicking in the kitchen followed by the clink and clatter of cups and doors. He got up and followed his father.

The kitchen hadn't changed, except it looked more dingy and unkempt than when his mother had been alive.

"I don't have any biscuits or anything," Sean said. "If I'd known you were coming…"

"No, it's fine."

"Here." Sean handed him a large envelope from a corner shelf. It had a dusty cobweb stuck to it.

"What's this?" Tommy asked. The envelope felt heavy, full of documents.

"The deeds to the cottage in Donegal. Your mother made me promise to sign it over to you."

Tommy felt heat in his eyes. He licked his lips.

"But don't you want it?"

Sean shook his head. "I never liked the place. I only went there for her. It's all yours now. I haven't been since. . ." His shoulders drooped a fraction, and he shook his head slowly before he turned his back to Tommy and lifted the kettle. Steam rose as he wet the tea.

He lifted two cups, nodded at the milk jug and sugar bowl, and then walked back towards the living room.

Tommy took a second alone to breathe deeply. He didn't want to unravel in front of his father. That would be too upsetting for both of them.

In the living room his father settled back into his chair and Tommy sat down.

"And what are you working at now?" Sean asked.

Tommy braced himself.

"I've bought a business in town."

His father looked up, his face brightening.

"Really?"

Tommy lifted his head slightly.

"I saved hard in London. It wasn't easy but it was worth it, I hope."

"My son, a business man." Sean sat up straighter and had a faraway look for a second. Then he asked, "So what are you selling, son?"

"It's a salon." Tommy set down his cup as he spoke.

"Hairdressing!" Sean hissed. He ran his hand over his face. "So you're still a poofter then?"

Tommy clenched his teeth. A wall of glass broke in his chest. His father would never change.

"I told you before. I. Am. Not. Gay."

"Then why don't you get a real job? When I was your age I was building houses, not poncing around cutting women's hair! Even if you aren't gay everyone will still think that you are." He hacked out a cough.

"So you still care more about what people think than about your own family!" said Tommy.

Sean sat straighter and narrowed his eyes.

"It was your mother who wouldn't tell anyone about her cancer – not me."

Tommy snorted. "Yeah, only because of your Victorian attitude! She was afraid to admit she even had breasts, never mind a lump on one of them."

"You're refusing to see the truth, and you know it!"

"Pot, kettle, kettle, pot," Tommy said. He took satisfaction from the puce color rising in Sean's face.

"This is a different thing entirely," said Sean. "She wasn't running around pretending to be a pervert!"

"Jesus Christ, Da! Being Gay is not being a pervert," Tommy said incredulous.

"I knew it!" Sean sprung to his feet. "You are a homo. Why else are you sticking up for the filthy bastards?

"Because you are wrong in every fucking way! You won't even listen to me."

"What's that like, eh?" Sean sneered.

"This is totally different. You disowned me over nothing. A job! A hairdressing job for God's sake. It's not like I was joining the police. But then you'd like that, wouldn't you?"

"Don't be ridiculous," Sean said. "What would your mother say, eh?"

"She'd be proud of the fact that I've bought my own business, with my own hard earned cash. Families are supposed to support each other."

"Support goes both ways," Sean said.

"What do you mean by that?"

"Nothing."

"No, you meant something."

"How do you think I feel, with the whole world thinking my son is gay?" Sean said.

Tommy stood up. It was back to the same old script with his Da playing the same bitter, awkward, old bastard as usual.

"Here's who I am regardless of what that says to the world." Tommy turned and walked out.

His Da could just go to hell. Why the fuck had Tommy visited him at all? He'd had this notion that his father might have changed. That he'd welcome him back, kill the fatted calf. Fat chance!

Tommy had never been able to understand how a loving father could change almost overnight and become the tyrant he now was. It seemed tied up with his career choice, yet how could something so simple unleash such venom? Tommy wondered if salvaging his relationship with his father would cost him his career. Or would his father just find another excuse to blame Tommy for the shithole Sean had sunken into since his wife passed away?

As Tommy opened his car door, he realized he still clung to the deeds for the cottage.

Saturday, March 4th

CHAPTER THREE

Molly lay in the hinterland of sleep, that smoky area with softened edges where dreams linger before the day begins. She pictured a pile of presents at the foot of her bed, as thrilled as a kid at Christmas, though she knew it ridiculous to expect this fuss for her thirtieth birthday. She couldn't imagine anyone doing this for her, not even her husband, Dermot – especially not Dermot.

Molly had set up a pile of presents at the foot of the bed for him on several of his birthdays. She often sprung surprises for her friends' birthdays. She treated the people around her like she wanted to be treated, hoping that one day they would take the hint and surprise her, bring her back to the childish exuberances that adults so loftily leave behind. Molly wanted to hold on to the magic. Birthdays should echo the magic of that first day you come into the world. Maybe her parents cried when she was born - her mother exhausted, hair stuck to her head with sweat, kissing baby Molly's forehead tenderly; her father holding his tiny daughter in his awkward, bumbling way, terrified that he'd drop her. Her birth-day. A day all about her.

Her mother seemed to take vindictive delight in letting her know that it hadn't been like that.

"When I saw you were a girl I just didn't know how to tell your father. He was so disappointed you weren't a boy," her mother, Aileen O'Kane, said often throughout Molly's life but never within earshot of Molly's gentle father. Molly had worked all her life to make it up to her Dad, to make him proud of his daughter and only child.

Four months after Molly's birth, Aileen's sister gave birth to a boy, Tommy O'Brian. As they grew up, this golden haired boy-cousin could do no wrong in Aileen's eyes, whereas she would take every opportunity to point out her daughter's faults.

Molly shoved the specter of her mother to the back of her brain and rolled over. The bed beside her was empty. He hadn't even kissed her before slipping out like a dirty sleepover. She felt translucent, as if someone might look at her now and not even see her. She stared at a strip of wall that glowed where sunlight leaked in from a chink in the peach curtains. The morning sun gave the room a comforting orange glow. Molly strode to the window and whipped back the curtain. As the sun blazed into the room, she decided to at least enjoy this beautiful morning, catching a contagious hope in the March sunshine as she squinted out the window. She loved springtime, when life bounced back against winter.

She turned and smiled as the bedroom door opened and Dermot struggled into the room with a tray.

"Happy birthday," he said.

"Ooh, lovely. Thanks, love," she said. He remembered. He made an effort. Her excitement resurfaced. The smell of bacon circled in the air, making her salivate.

She got back into bed, and Dermot settled the tray onto her knees, his head bowed in concentration, bringing him inches from her face. She lifted her hand to touch the softness of his hair, black and shiny, alive with luster. She loved how it flopped onto his forehead, giving him that aura of little-boy-lost.

"Have you eaten yet? Wanna share?" she said.

"No thanks, kitten. I've had mine. Need to let it settle before football," Dermot patted his tummy without making eye contact with her. The food turned to sawdust in her mouth. Why couldn't he just miss the football for one week to spend time with her?

"I thought we could do something together today." She struggled to keep the plea from her voice.

"Tell you what, I'll take you out to Mc Ginty's for dinner," he said, looking up, a sheepish smile stretching to his eyes, "I need to go into town this afternoon too…"

"Well, if it's to buy me a birthday present, don't bother!" Tears prickled at her eyes. *Dammit!* How pathetic to cry on her birthday.

"Ach Molly, I've just been so busy lately."

"You're always too busy. Football, golf, darts, horses. It's my birthday. Can't you miss football just this once?" She'd started now, and they'd both suffer from her words. "Dermot, it is just a silly game grown men play to make them feel part of the pack. It's not life and death you know." Her nastiness both satisfied and appalled her.

"You know I can't let the lads down," he said.

"But you can let me down?"

"This is different."

"Look, it's easy," she said, injecting authority into her tone. "Just call one of the team and tell them. Fuck sakes, that's what subs are for. Sure you'd be doing someone a huge favor, giving them their big break with P1 Athletic, wow, lucky fucker." She forced a smile hoping to pierce her sarcasm, desperate for him to turn this around and stop making her look like the bad guy.

"Please, don't start that. Besides, I thought you were going to take Fran shopping today," Dermot said.

"She knows it's my birthday. She said she'd be okay. That we should spend more time together!"

"Jesus Christ, you make her sound like a marriage guidance counselor! What the hell would she know about being married anyway?"

She pushed the tray away and stood up. "Well, she was married for twenty-five years before her husband died. She's lonely. And she's just looking out for us. You know that!"

"I know, I know. Sorry, but she should mind her own business. I suppose you bleat out our most intimate secrets to her!" Dermot said.

Molly's face grew warm. She looked at the eggs congealing as they cooled on the plate. True, she confided in Fran, probably far more than Dermot would like.

Outside a car beeped.

"That will be my taxi."

"What? But it's only ten. You said the match is at twelve. You don't have to be the first one there, you know. You'll look like the team geek, all super keen, sitting there in your stupid wee shorts," she called after him as he pounded down the stairs.

"Don't walk away from me!" she shouted after him. "I'm sorry. Please, wait! Just let's settle this…"

The front door slammed. By the time she reached the window, he had climbed into the taxi. Her eyes stung. Why did she always come across as the battleaxe and start the arguments these days? It was strange how they had rowed less when times were tougher — back when Dermot was tormented by his father's behavior.

The day stretched ahead of her, empty. She needed something to fill her time, like the way a baby would. It would glue Dermot back to her. But Dermot had said not yet. He needed time for himself. He'd protected and raised his nine siblings, something that never failed to amaze her. His alcoholic father had sucked so much of his childhood from him, and after his father's death last year, Dermot said they should have time to play, be free. He told her they should wait before starting a family, but he didn't say for how long.

Molly understood Dermot's position, to a point. The very first time she met him she'd been an excited sixteen-year-old walking with her best friend, Tracey Duggan, on their way to the Community Club Disco off the Falls Road one summer evening. At a few of the houses they passed, people sat outside their front doors basking in the last rays of the day. Molly didn't know anyone having come from across town, but Tracey greeted several of the women as they passed by. The turned up a side street and could hear Alanis Morissette's *You Outa Know* playing. The beat made Molly hurry her pace. She didn't want to miss anything, but Tracey stopped abruptly and spun around.

"Walk with me, quick!"

Confused, Molly looked up and saw a man staggering towards them. Even as she turned, she glanced back at him over her shoulder. His crumpled suit jacket, out of place paired with grubby jeans, and stubbled chin gave him a disheveled cast. He stopped, pushed his face forward and squinted.

"Tracey, 's'at you?" he said reaching out his hand. "Come 'ere ya wee bitch."

Tracey grabbed Molly by the hand and dragged her along. Molly, frightened by the man's tone, stumbled after her. Just before they got to the corner she turned back to see if the man was following. He stopped in the street and yelled incoherent words at them. She turned back to Tracey but not before Molly had noticed the darkening stain on the front of the man's jeans. She felt grimy just witnessing the man pissing himself. They rounded the corner at top speed and crashed headlong into a young fellow not much older than them. He had to hold onto both girls so that the threesome didn't topple. He smelt good, aftershave with a twang of fresh cigarette smoke. To Molly it spoke of sophistication, a man of the world. She found herself staring at the most gorgeous dark brown eyes she'd ever seen, peering out from under a floppy fringe of jet black hair.

"Oh God, Dermot," Tracey was saying, "Dad's coming. And he's pluethered again." She burst into tears.

"That's your Dad?" Molly asked, horrified. Dermot pulled Tracey to him in a quick hug, her head only coming up to his chest. When he let her go she searched her pockets for a hanky. The look of concern on his face went directly to Molly's heart. With this high drama, and him looking like a movie-star, she could be starring in her very own film. But then she remembered the stained jeans and heat reddened her face. She stepped back.

"It's okay. I'll bring him home. What kind of form is he in?" Dermot said.

Tracey sniffed and blew her nose. "I'm not sure. I ran. I just didn't want everyone at the disco to see."

Tracey looked down, and Molly almost felt the shame rippling from her.

"So, he'll be here any minute," Dermot said as he stepped to the corner and popped his head around the wall. "Ah, for fucks sake!"

Dermot disappeared around the corner. Tracey's blue eyes, topped with blue eye-shadow, opened wide as she looked at Molly. Together they went round the corner and saw the drunken father lying snoring on the footpath. Tracey walked up to Dermot who was going through his father's pockets. He pulled out a wallet and opened it, whistling softly through his teeth.

"He must've had a win on the horses. A big win. He managed to drink himself to oblivion and still have money left over. Here." He handed Tracey a ten pound note. "Have fun you two. Ma will appreciate the rest. I'll get Da home."

Tracey grinned and pocketed the money.

"Won't your Dad be mad that you took it?" Molly asked.

"Nah. He'll think he drank it." Dermot clicked out of the side of his mouth and winked at Molly. That was the moment she fell in love with him, and so with sixteen-year-old logic in play, she ignored him for the next two years until he mercifully noticed her at last.

Now, even after being married for eight years, her life focused on Dermot. He made every cell in her body sing for joy and her entire being glow when he paid attention to her. Not that that occurred very often and not without some maneuvering on her part.

Perhaps, she should have offered to go watch the soccer match. That way they would be spending the day together. She didn't relish the idea of standing at the sidelines in the cold by herself. This was a male domain. The guys didn't want their wives and girlfriends there.

As she glanced around the room she spied his football bag in the corner. Shit! Dermot looked after the team uniforms. Their argument caused him to forget all his teams' jerseys, shorts and socks. He'd most likely notice he'd forgotten the kit as soon as he went to get out of the cab, having to take another taxi to come get it. He'd be in a foul mood after wasting all that money. If she left right now, she'd catch him before they left to come back or at least see him on his way back, cutting short the taxi ride. She'd bring the kit down to the pitch for him. She'd make things right and save the day.

Molly jumped into her jeans and pulled a fleecy sweater over her pajama top. Scooping up her blonde curls, she secured them into a loose, messy bun on top of her head. She checked the mirror, deciding that she didn't look like she'd just gotten out of bed. Finally she scribbled a note and left it on the front door in case he got back before she could catch him.

The streets of South Belfast were quiet on Saturday mornings. Dominated by the Queen's University of Belfast campus, most of the residents were either students or recently graduated young professionals, still sleeping off their Friday night. Saturday didn't start until noon.

The air was fresh outside, kissed with cold. The sun's warmth, as promised through the bedroom window, was one of those cruel illusions that often happened at this time of the year. Molly ached for the warmth of summer. The leaves on the trees were budding, but the frisky north winds gave the sunny days a sharp edge and battered the early blossoming daffodils.

As she started up the red Citroen, she looked forward to seeing Dermot and healing the rift from their argument. After all, he was going to get her a present later. It wasn't as if he'd forgotten, and he had brought her breakfast in bed, though he did most Saturdays. How many husbands did that?

It didn't take long to reach the playing fields. He'd be thrilled that she had brought the kit bag. She could just imagine how he'd run out to meet her when he saw the car drive up. She could already see his eyes crinkle, the sheerest smile brush his lips. Just for her. Their hands might touch when she gave him the bag. A private moment in public. Just between them.

Molly saw no other cars as she pulled into the gravel parking area. A clubhouse, badly in need of a paint job, sat at the far end of the parking area. Molly trundled the car as close to the door of the clubhouse as she could, the wheels crunching the gravel.

She'd dropped Dermot off here many times, and it always buzzed with activity. She had never been inside the Clubhouse. In fact, she'd never even left the sanctuary of her car.

She grabbed the bulky bag from the seat beside her and got out of the car, locking it with the electronic key amid a flash of tail lights. Hoping that she didn't look too much of a mess, she approached the clubhouse.

Inside, there were changing rooms to the left and an untidy notice board on her right. At the bottom of the hall a door had a crooked sign that said "of ce". Her heartbeat quickened as she rapped the door. She always felt nervous amongst the football crowd.

"Yep!" said a voice from inside. She opened the door.

"Hiya! Em, I was wondering where the team is for the match today?"

"You wanna play?" The man's eyes disappeared into his piggy face as he laughed at her. She felt the palms of her hands moisten.

"No, no." She gave short laugh and flicked him a smile. "It's just that I have a kit bag for my husband, and he was supposed to be playing here. He left the house without it."

"No matches here love, hasn't been for a month now. They're putting in a new drainage system for the pitches, what with all this rain and all, they're not playable. They've been playing instead over at the Union pitches." He stood with his hands sinking into where his waist should be, his belly stretching the grubby blue jersey, pouring over the top of his belt. Five months pregnant, Dermot might say behind his hand.

"Oh thanks, I'll just bring this over to the Union pitches then. The match isn't until twelve, so I think I'll catch them," she muttered, turning to leave the office that stank of stale sweat, stale testosterone.

"What's the team called, love? The Union pitches don't let anyone but the university teams play till two," he said as she reached for the grimy door handle.

"P1 Athletic. They're in a league." She pulled the door open, her heart thumping.

"Oh, they've been playing there this month all right, but they don't have a match today, love. My son's on that team. He's away to watch Liverpool playing instead."

Swamped in confusion, she felt her stomach tip over.

"Thanks," she managed, forcing her legs to move her down the hallway out of the dingy building. The door slammed behind her as she left.

Saturday, March 4th

CHAPTER FOUR

Sheila opened the door to the reception area of the Beauty Spot, her nose twitching. The relaxing effect of the duck egg blue walls, lush sand-colored carpet and potted palms in the corners was ruined by the sting of citrus in the air. Sheila felt her jaw clench. Joan, the receptionist, should never have been hired. Her grey skin, grey eyes and brown hair lacked luster and lay pasted to her skull, her ears sticking out through its lankness. A white apron hung shapelessly on Joan's skinny frame. All of it engendered a sense of pity in Sheila that annoyed her.

"What did you put on that?" Sheila asked, pointing at an aromatherapy oil burner.

"It's orange oil. It...it's supposed to be uplifting," Joan said.

"God!" The word snarled from the back of Sheila's throat. She blew out the flame and picked up the pot.

"Take that out the back and get rid of it. We want relaxation in here. Use the lavender and chamomile," Sheila snapped. Joan flinched as Sheila handed her the pot. Her meekness aggravated Sheila even more.

"Your client is here," Joan said softly, nodding in the direction of a slim twenty-something blond, sitting on the cream leather sofa flicking through magazines. She scurried out the door.

"Hi," Sheila said, as she slipped behind the desk and checked the desk top schedule. "You're Tracey Duggan, and you're down for a leg wax. Right?"

"Yup!" Tracey smiled.

Despite Tracey's blonde hair and fair complexion, Sheila saw the family resemblance in Tracey's high cheekbones scooping down to full lips with that Angelina Jolie dimple. Lips like that were so kissable. Sheila cleared her throat and showed Tracey into the cubicle.

Sheila pasted a strip of wax from Tracey's knee to her ankle, savoring the sweet smell that rose from the disturbed wax. She applied a strip of fabric over the top of the wax, stretched the skin at the ankle with one hand and using the other, ripped the cloth from the skin. It came away with a satisfying, sucking "swaaap" sound and Tracey yelped. About ten more "swaaaps" to go. Sheila smiled.

The procedure only took about fifteen minutes, though it must have seemed longer to Tracey.

"If you come more regularly, it won't hurt as much," Sheila advised.

Tracey nodded. "I know. I know," she agreed, "it's just plucking up the courage to come at all, if you pardon the pun!" Sheila smiled her "client smile."

The bell above the outside door tinkled as Tracey opened it to leave. The sounds of traffic sloshed into the salon, out of place in the calming aroma of chamomile and lavender. As if a sound could drive away a smell.

Sheila took her break alone in the coffee room, so called because it had a sink and a fridge. Along one wall a couple of cheap white kitchen units housed their mugs and coffee fixings. The countertop, once white and clinical, was now stained and cluttered with half opened cartons of wax, bags of cotton wool and a jumble of beauty products. Sheila hated the way the coffee room had turned into the holding area between the store room and shop front.

When Sheila had her own salon, it would be pristine all the time. Each month, she squirreled away a proportion of her wages, amassing a tidy sum over ten years. She reckoned she'd be able to go out on her own comfortably in about five years.

She sat with her elbows resting on the table, toying with the tepid cup. The tan liquid swirled, gently wafting the smell of coffee up to her. She took a slug, and then set the cup down as the door to the room opened and Elaine, Sheila's co-worker and best friend, entered amid a bluster of crackling plastic shopping bags.

"Hey, what did you do to poor Joan?" Elaine asked, "She's out there quivering at her post and asking me if the place smells okay now. She says you shouted at her?" Elaine dropped the bags in a heap in the corner and reached for a mug from the draining board.

"I didn't shout at her," Sheila said, rolling her eyes.

"Well, did you raise your voice?"

"No. I, well, okay maybe a wee bit," Sheila admitted, "but the idiot was burning orange oil. Way too much of it, too. It was stinging my eyes and the clients were lying on the floor gasping like your old goldfish that used to jump out of its bowl!"

They both laughed.

"Ach, be nice Sheila, she's just a bit daft is all," Elaine said, her big green eyes, heavy with black eyeliner, were soft and pleading.

"So what's in all the bags?" Sheila asked.

"Well," Elaine said, pushing a lock of her ginger hair behind her ear, "I thought I'd get started buying stuff for the trip to India."

"But we haven't bought the tickets yet!"

"Well, that's a formality. We're still going, aren't we?"

"Of course we are," Sheila said. With her savings so on target she didn't mind splashing out on a holiday every so often. Besides, Elaine had been banging on about going to India for years. She believed in reincarnation, claiming that she had once lived in India 300 years ago. Sheila wondered if Elaine had her green eyes, red hair and freckles in her other lives as well.

"Great. Oh and I need to lose some weight. I bought the clothes a little on the small side. Will you come swimming with me?" asked Elaine.

Before Sheila could think of a good excuse not to, Elaine piped up again.

"We could go tomorrow. I'm sure your period is finished by now."

Realization fell hard and violently in Sheila's chest. *Her period!* She had used that as her excuse last week but had totally forgotten about it.

"What's wrong, Sheila? You look like you've seen a ghost."

Sheila didn't know where she found her voice, but she managed in a strangled bleat, "I think I've eaten something that disagrees with me."

She jumped up from the table and made a dash to the toilet down the hall. She locked the door against the world, creating a space to think.

Her period was six days late. She had never been this late before. *Shit.*

Just the thought of it made her stomach lift momentarily, like going over a humpback bridge in a car.

Pregnant – no way!

She insisted they use condoms because she wasn't sure where else he'd been dipping his wick. She couldn't be pregnant. A current of fear rummaged through her gut, squishing her heart. She focused on controlling her panic as she caught her next breath, in through the nose, out through the mouth. Her heart rate slowed. She fought for control.

A draught of aloneness swooped over her, bringing Sheila back to her school days. She saw herself as she was then, the most reviled girl in the class, the memory sharp and merciless.

The other children had surrounded her. She stood with her back to the school wall, her heart racing, fearing this new brand of torture. Suzy O'Cane stepped forward, her hand shot out and she tapped Sheila on the elbow. Sheila retracted. In unison, like a collective beast, the children laughed hungrily, swarming forward. Suzy wiped her hand on the girl next to her.

"Ugh – I've got it now!" the girl squealed as if contaminated with some horrific disease. She held her hand up and ran at a clutch of kids who scattered, screaming. Sheila would have preferred a punch. That way she could have at least hit back. Instead, she stood frozen against the wall in her patched clothes and scuffed shoes holding back the scalding tears that lay behind her eyes. Even the teachers seemed to sniff at her presence. Sheila felt a keen injustice at this. Her clothes may have been tatty but they were clean. In those days, being born out of wedlock in small town Ireland was enough to leave you covered in crap.

The knock on the toilet door made Sheila jump.

"Sheila, are you OK?" The concern in Elaine's voice soothed the raw edges of Sheila's thoughts.

"I had a bad kebab last night," Sheila answered, knowing that the quiver in her voice lent weight to her fib.

"Poor pet! I have a free slot," Elaine said, "go you on home and I'll take your next client."

"Thanks so much. I owe you one." Sheila unlocked the door and Elaine wrapped her up in a hug.

"Go and take care of yourself. We'll be able to cover for you. I'll call you later to make sure you're okay." Elaine pushed her in the direction of the lockers. Sheila was too worried to feel guilty about lying to her friend.

Oh God – pregnant... Her cycle was usually so predictable she could plan around it. Her heart thumped, drumming up tension behind her eyes.

She left the Beauty Spot and headed straight to the supermarket. In a daze she picked up a dual packet of an early pregnancy predictor kit, terrified she'd bump into someone she knew. As she drove home, the package seemed to hum in the bag beside her.

As soon as she got home, Sheila took the test to the bathroom. Hands shaking, she picked at the cellophane, trying to gain purchase, snagging a corner and ripping it open. Once free of its plastic, she opened the box and emptied its contents onto the bathroom countertop.

As she peed, she prayed for that first twinge, a cramp, a drop of blood on the white porcelain or smeared into the toilet paper as she wiped herself dry.

She waited on the test's results for three long minutes. Nah, she thought, not me, this couldn't happen to me, and certainly not with *him*. He was supposed to be strictly for fun. She didn't do serious. But serious was catching up with her now. She held her breath as first one blue line appeared. Her scalp prickled as the second line bloomed bright, clear and very, very blue. There was no ambiguity about this test. Repeating the test delivered the same result. Even so, she couldn't believe it.

She flushed with heat. Sweat popped on her upper lip. Her stomach lifted and Sheila flew to the toilet to throw up. Even as she hung over the bowl, shattered, her nose assaulted by the sting of urine mixed with the scorch of vomit, she wondered had her mother felt this dread when she'd discovered she was pregnant with Sheila?

She hated to think so. She was in exactly the position her mother had preached so hard to her about as a teenager.

"Men only want one thing Sheila. Once they get it they're gone," Maria said one afternoon shortly after Sheila had started her periods. She spoke urgently, this message the most important thing she had to pass on to a confused little girl.

"They will all tell you that you are beautiful," she said, "Unfortunately, you are. It's going to be hard to find a man who will love you for what you are inside. Your beauty is your curse." They sat in the dim kitchen, and Sheila watched the raindrops slide down the windows on the outside, gliding past the rising condensation on the inside, the two bodies of water never meeting. Her mother seemed so dumb. Sheila hadn't even a friend then, never mind a boyfriend.

It wasn't that she'd had her heart broken like her poor embittered mother. Sheila had just never opened her heart. Guys didn't hold her attention very long. Everyone had a flaw that she couldn't get around. She didn't believe in Mr. Right – just Mr. Right Now.

Should she tell him? What could he do anyway? He was already married. Though she never asked, she didn't think he had any children.

Still, as a graduate of the Maria Mooney School of love and life, if anyone could bring up a kid, she could. She would simply end the relationship and be done with it. And why not? He'd never leave his wife. They never did. But the child support would be very handy. She would need the money to claw back her dreams of opening her own place.

Sheila looked at herself in the mirror as she washed her hands. Her eyes flashed and she fought to find the cool, calm person she had learned to put on show from a very young age, starting with making Father's Day cards in school. She could still remember her soft little-girl hand holding the red crayon and drawing a big heart on the outside, like a Valentines' card.

The other children in the class worked hard on their cards too. There was a buzz of excitement that Friday when the teacher announced that they could take the cards home to their fathers. But Sheila made her card knowing her father would never see it. She had nowhere to send it. Inside it said, in her lopsided, little-girl writing, "Happy Father's Day from Sheila." The words copied down dutifully from the blackboard, when really she'd wanted to write, "Daddy, where are you, and why did you leave us?" That stinging question, which her mother had refused to answer, still haunted the corners of her heart.

She would tell him. She'd at least attempt to give her child something she never had: a father. She hoped Dermot would see it that way too.

Saturday, March 4th

CHAPTER FIVE

It felt like the school bell had finally rung. Freedom for the rest of the day, and Dermot was determined to take full advantage of it. He'd guessed it would be difficult to get away but he'd underestimated how much. Molly had really laid it on thick. He smarted at how she put down his team, his commitment to them, to football and him keeping fit. She should be glad he wasn't out drinking all day, wasting their money on booze. He wasn't perfect but at least he'd be coming home sober. There were worse things than a bit on the side. What Molly didn't know wouldn't hurt her. He needed a break from her constant nagging.

Perhaps it was the lack of drama in Molly's early life, growing up in a nice normal family, that had her thirsting for theatrics now. Relentlessly, she conspired to be the focus of his attention. She blew everything out of proportion. She seemed to thrive on other peoples' sagas, wallowing in the drama of a broken relationship or a deadly diagnosis, regaling Dermot with gory details he didn't want to hear. Why did she have to be the fountain-of-all-gossip on each of her friends' heartbreaks or triumphs?

She didn't just glory in the dire and disastrous, he'd give her that. Glory of any sort warranted celebration. She even had a birthday party for Wolfie, the damn dog. She was the queen of over-the-top.

But he hadn't noticed that about her until it was too late. At the start, he'd only seen how cute and bubbly she'd been. She embraced mischief, or at least let him think that. But one minute he was devising ways of getting into her knickers; the next they were walking up the aisle. It didn't take long after their wedding day for the rot to set in. Her gusto, which at first attracted him, wore him down now. Her overpowering neediness quashed all his desire.

The taxi driver pulled into a parking lot and stopped.

"Four-seventy-five, mate," said the driver.

Dermot could see the black Ford Ka parked in the corner. The Big-Lad sprung to life immediately, making it uncomfortable to fish the change for the cab out of his jeans pocket. He pulled out a fiver, handed it to the cabbie and waited on his change.

"Thanks, mate," Dermot said as a hand appeared at the passenger side window and dropped two shiny coins into Dermot's palm. The driver didn't answer but pulled off, spinning gravel from his back wheels.

Dermot sauntered over to Sheila's car. He knew he was a looker. While Molly followed him around the house like an annoying puppy, Sheila was so cool she was on the verge of being offhand with him. It was the chase that kept him interested, and boy, was he interested. He could hardly fold himself up to get into the car.

The scent of Sheila's perfume mingled with the smell of the Yankee candle air-freshener dangling from the mirror. If it wasn't broad daylight he'd jump her there and then. But something was in the air today. He had barely closed the car door before Sheila spoke to him with more of a chill in her voice than her accustomed loftiness.

"Put your seat belt on," she said. Dermot sighed as he reached around fumbling for the belt.

"Yes Mum," he said.

"What?" Sheila snapped her head around to glare at him.

"Hey, calm down, I'm just teasing," he said.

"Why didn't you just get the taxi to drop you at my apartment instead of dragging me all the way down here?" she asked.

"It's far too expensive to take the taxi all that way," he said.

"Well, it's high time that you got up off your ass and learned to drive."

The Big-Lad deflated. Women had a huge problem with him not knowing how to drive. He was scared to learn. Not so much frightened of the driving itself but of looking like a right eejit driving slow with the 'L' plates up. He didn't want to make those strange noises beginners made whilst changing gears, and he couldn't bear the embarrassment of stalling. He could opt for an automatic car, but then he'd be slagged about driving a dodgem car. Dermot wanted to be cool, to drive fast with confidence without the awkward beginner stages.

They traveled in silence until they were back at her place. Women were so strange. The affair, only six weeks old, still bore the hallmark of fresh and insatiable lust. Last week, Sheila had been all over him. She couldn't get his clothes off him fast enough, and they'd shagged right there in the kitchen, up against the stainless steel fridge. Just thinking about it made him hard again. She'd taken him into the bedroom for round two, and he'd been shattered for the rest of the day. Thankfully, Molly thought he'd played too hard a game of football.

This time, sitting in the kitchen, as she made them both a cup of tea, Dermot looked at the fridge. The hand prints and sweaty butt-cheek smears had been polished away. It looked like an ordinary, innocent fridge, the kitchen like a show-house kitchen. Dermot liked that about Sheila. No clutter, no fussy tack.

She handed him a cup and a coaster. That meant she wanted them to drink it in the living room. No coaster, no cuppa. The living room was all cream: cream carpet, cream leather sofa, cream walls. Stark as it was, Dermot liked it for its plainness. They sat in their usual places on the sofa and Dermot reached for Sheila, his desire peaking.

"Jeez Sheila, what's up?" he said, as she lifted his hand from her thigh with one finger and thumb as if it were diseased. "I've already had a shitty day so far."

"Well it's definitely not PMS," she said in a measured tone. Dermot smiled. This really was the perfect woman. She didn't even suffer from PMS. Man, he really had lucked out.

"So, what's up then, Sweetie?" he asked. She looked at him with those big brown eyes, so dark he could hardly see where the pupil began. They looked like they were perpetually dilated, perpetually aroused. This belied the flinty set of her lips pressed tightly together, curling slightly at the corners like a too-puckered smile.

"What I'm trying to say is that I won't be having PMS this month, Dermot," she said, "nor will I for another eight months or so." She hesitated.

"Why not?" Dermot asked. She gave a long sigh, shaking her head, making him feel dumb.

"I take it you weren't much good at biology in school?" She arched one eyebrow. He looked blankly at her, clueless.

"I'm pregnant."

Dermot reeled, his stomach flipping over. He felt sick.

"Fuck! Are you sure?" he said, his heart clanging. This wasn't real. It couldn't be. He'd used condoms even though she claimed to be on the pill. Somewhere, someone had made a mistake.

"Yes, I'm positive."

"No, no, I mean are you sure it's mine?" Fuck, why did he say that? He just needed a get-out clause. If he could just think of all the angles, there was bound to be a way back to normality, like the undo button on his computer.

"You bastard!" She jumped up. "How dare you? You're the one who has the rep for cheating. Just get the fuck out. I never want to see you again. GET OUT!"

Her face contorted, and Dermot could see a battle for control. A battle Sheila lost, as first her mouth trembled, her chin wobbled, and then the rest of her face crumpled. Tears streamed down, dripping off her chin, a flash flood. Her gleaming eyes darted wild and frightened. Her loss of control and her sudden acute vulnerability calmed the chaos of Dermot's panic. He was horrified at what he had said, yet perversely pleased that he had punched through her veneer, although the dig about his fidelity still stung.

"Oh, my God, Sheila, I'm so sorry." He felt like a total shit. But now that he was in this deep, he didn't know where to turn.

Sheila was sobbing now, her surrender complete. Not only did he feel the burden of responsibility, he resented it. Sheila ruled their time together. His only contribution was being present, escaping the clutches of his wife and home life, as if that were his gift to her. Sheila called the shots and here she was, helpless and behaving as lost as he felt. Large uncontrollable shudders shook her shoulders. He needed to make her stop crying.

"I was just shocked, am shocked. Really, I didn't mean to say that. Look, let's just sit down and calm down." He took her hands, partly to steady her and partly to prevent her from hitting him. Gently, he sat her on the sofa. He watched in amazement as she took a deep breath, gave her shoulders a shake, straightened her spine and arranged the mask on her face. She pulled her features together like she was sucking everything in.

"What about an abortion?" he said. He thought that abortion was still illegal in Northern Ireland, but she could go to England. He didn't even know anyone who'd had an abortion. It wasn't done, or at least wasn't discussed, the topic even more taboo than sex, even gay sex.

"Oh believe me I've thought about it. I suppose the nuns did a good job on me convincing me that life begins at conception. I can't get past that it's already a person." Sheila stopped and stared off into space. Dermot noticed that she referred to this "living person" as "it" but said nothing. Did she want him to change her mind? Did he want her to change her mind?

Sheila shrugged.

"No, I just can't do it. For now, I'm keeping it. If I change my mind it will be because I want to, nothing to do with what you want. I don't care what you say," she continued, her face set again. "If you don't want us, you can leave us. Don't feel like you need to decide right now. You've got at least nine months to decide." Her voice regained its strength, her serenity reinstated. Relief infused Dermot, allowing him to breathe again. She continued, "I'm telling you about the baby because it is your right to know. You *are* the father." She paused and stared at him. He nodded and hoped she didn't notice as he gulped, afraid to speak.

"I know you are married and you...we didn't plan this. I can look after myself, but I would like you to consider helping me...us...*it* financially. I don't expect anything more of you, Dermot."

Sheila looked down at her hands clasped together in her lap. Dermot could see her knuckles were white. She wouldn't make eye contact with him. Dermot was struck by how brave she was. She had thought about this and was willing to go it alone rather than abort her baby. Dermot was glad that discussion was off the table. Tempting as it was to clear up this mess, he didn't want to be the type of man who would kill his own child. He wouldn't think about it now. He wasn't sure he could trust himself not to fantasize about how easy a solution it would have been.

"What about Molly?" he said, thinking out loud.

"You need to make that decision. Do you love her? Do you want her? It's really not my problem." She lifted her head and looked straight at him, but her face remained impossible to read. What was she hoping he'd say? She was giving him an out. Did he really want to be a father? Okay he didn't need to decide right now.

Dermot cut his visit short. He took the bus into town. Thank Christ he remembered to get Molly a present. Something bland, too expensive and she'd get suspicious, too cheap and she'd complain. Then he'd go home and pretend he'd been out to training. Pretend everything was normal. Pretend he'd never heard of Sheila Mooney nor fathered her child. He had to keep Molly in the dark until he figured out what he really wanted, a demanding wife or a hot mistress with a kid, his kid, in tow.

Saturday, March 4th

CHAPTER SIX

Outside the clubhouse, Molly took a deep breath and slowly exhaled. What the hell was going on? She got into the car, put the key in the ignition but didn't turn it. Staring blindly ahead, she sat with her hands on the steering wheel.

No matches today. Why had Dermot lied to her? What could he be doing that was so bad that he would not tell her about it? Could he be secretly gambling, or drinking? If so, why would he do either secretly when he already did both quite openly? Unless he'd forgotten there was no football and had headed straight into town. But it had too much of an air of premeditation. He'd have brought the team kit if he'd simply forgotten. Molly felt sure that Dermot knew there was no football. Besides, she'd have met him at the pitches. She had been only minutes behind him. So where did he go?

The question sneered at her as she drove the short distance home. If it wasn't alcohol and it wasn't gambling, as he was far too tight to risk losing money, could he be meeting someone else? Could there be another woman? She clutched the steering wheel to stop her hands from shaking. Dermot wouldn't do that to her. He was a family man. He'd worked hard to keep his family intact during the bad days with his dad. He wouldn't risk losing her, would he?

Molly's breathing felt quick and ineffectual. She couldn't bear to follow this line of thought, but the idea of waiting until Dermot got home to ask him where he'd been drove her crazy. She took a deep breath and talked to herself in the rear view mirror.

"Stop over-reacting, you silly goose." The sound of her voice, strangely normal, made her relax. The only thing she was sure of was that Dermot was keeping a secret.

As she pulled her car into the street she lived on, she spotted Tommy's car parked outside her house. *Crap!* She'd forgotten that he was coming over to do her hair. Tommy could keep a secret, maybe Dermot was even confiding in him. But why would he confide in Tommy and not in her? Oh God! Maybe he had cancer or something awful. He might be secretly going to the hospital, but not on a Saturday. She could ask Tommy, but she could not put words to this, not yet. She parked behind him and waved.

Unfolding himself out of his car, Tommy waved back as he stretched his lean frame. He dragged his hands through his fair hair, pulling it back from his face, only to flop back exactly the way it had been.

Molly wondered where he got his tan at this time of year. Probably from walking the dog still trapped in the car. It jumped around, rocking the hatchback.

"Awh, let Wolfie out. He looks clean today. We'll let him in!"

"He should look clean," Tommy said, struggling with a lead attached to a wriggling mass of fur. "I took him to get groomed, and the place was terrible. I'm gonna phone the RSPCA."

"Why? What did they do?" Molly said, dragging her concentration to focus on her cousin as she donned her "happy" face.

"They're cruel to the animals!"

"No! Did they beat them?"

"Oh! No. But they bathed them in cold water!"

"No!" Molly said, trying not to laugh. Tommy had a knack of cheering her up even if he didn't know how much she needed it.

"I know! Poor Wolfie won't be going back there again," Tommy said as he scratched the dog's ears. Wolfie thumped his tail in agreement.

"Thank God for that. Anyway, come in, come in. Do you want a cuppa?" Molly opened the front door, getting knocked to the side as Wolfie pushed past her, dragging Tommy with him, and causing a logjam in the entrance. Laughing, they made it to the kitchen, and as Molly filled the kettle, Tommy set a grocery bag on the table.

"Can I feed Wolfie here?" he asked fishing a couple of cans of dog food from one bag. "I was afraid he'd get so stressed at the groomers he'd throw up."

"Lovely," Molly said and grimaced. "Go ahead. There's an old bowl in the bottom cupboard you can use for him." She felt a little nauseous herself, more from worrying what the hell Dermot was keeping from her, than the mention of Wolfie's ailment. What if Dermot was doing something illegal? What if he'd joined the IRA? But why would anyone join the IRA during a ceasefire? Besides, Dermot didn't give a hoot about Irish freedom so long as he had a roof over his head and food on the table. But did she really know what he cared about these days?

"So, Happy Birthday, doll! Big three-O then, eh?" Molly jumped as Tommy burst into her thoughts. "I'll be watching out for those grey hairs now." Tommy put the bowl on the floor. Wolfie dived into it.

"Sure I've had grey hairs since I was thirteen."

"God that's right! I dyed your hair orange, remember?"

"How could I forget?"

Drugs! Maybe Dermot was doing drugs? But then, wouldn't she have noticed *something*? Didn't it change people's personalities? And their bank account would show him withdrawing money to support a drug habit. Oh God, maybe he was a dealer.

"Molly, earth calling Molly," Tommy said waving his hand in front of her face.

"Sorry." Molly reigned her thoughts back in. "So can I go straight?"

"Ha ha," Tommy said, "You're worse than Dad with the gay references."

"No, my hair, ya berk!" She could see how Sean might think Tommy was gay, but Molly knew he wasn't. He just was not swayed by peer pressure or convention. Even she thought him a little light in the loafers, but that was just Tommy. It didn't make him gay, and even if it did, she'd love him anyways.

After they finished their tea, they got down to the serious business of Molly's hair. Molly tried to concentrate on what Tommy said as he touched up the roots, trimmed the ends and blow-dried her curls straight until it looked like a sheet of golden silk. Her mind never strayed far from the Dermot mystery.

"Thanks," Molly said, taking in her image from as many different angles in the mirror as she could. "How much do I owe you?"

"Birthday pressy," he replied. "So what are you doing tonight?"

"Dermot is taking me out for dinner to McGinty's. Do you want to join us for a drink?"

"I might. But I don't want to be a gooseberry. Oh here, a bunch of us are going to the cottage in Donegal for St Patrick's Day, weekend after next. Dad gave me the deeds."

"That's wonderful. See, he does love you," Molly said.

Though basic, the cottage had an open fire and a wonderful view. They'd shared many a good weekend up there over the years. Even when Tommy was in London, Sean had let Molly and Dermot use it. Sean was a difficult old man, but Molly rubbed along nicely with him. She reckoned she was about the only one.

Seeing Tommy's closed face, Molly reached out and patted his hand. She didn't know what to say.

"You and Dermot should come - it'll be good craic," Tommy said quickly.

"Yeah, I'll talk to Dermot about it. But he has football. . ." She tailed off. She could feel her blood rushing to her face. Should she tell Tommy? What would she say? No, best leave it between herself and Dermot.

"Sure you can come without him. Orla and some of the other girls, the old gang from college, will be there. You can share with them."

"I'll think about it." Sweat flushed over her at the thought. She couldn't go away and leave Dermot alone if she suspected him of cheating.

"So you saw Tracey last night. Ever think of rekindling that flame?" she said trying to take her thoughts off Dermot.

Tommy rested his chin on his hand and narrowed his eyes.

"What makes you think there was a flame?" he asked.

"Oh, I saw you two at our wedding. You guys were lost in each other. Locked at the tonsils, so to speak."

Tommy laughed and drew his hand across his mouth as if fastening a zipper.

"So what happened to the lovely Tabitha? Come on, spill it," Molly persisted. Her pulse had returned to normal and she didn't feel like throwing up any more.

"We had fun for a while. She even moved in with me, but it just didn't work out."

"I'm sorry," Molly said.

"Don't be. It's not like I had my heart broken. She dumped me, but I think I was relieved. I wanted to come home, and the timing was right. We're still friends. Besides, Tabitha, like, what kind of a name is that? Dad would probably think I was dating a cat!"

"So, Tracey?"

"You are persistent, aren't you?"

"Well, it might help win your Dad around, too."

"Hardly the basis for a relationship."

"Relationship? That sounds serious."

"Ach, would you stop! She's a lovely girl, and that's all I'll say on the matter." Tommy pushed back his chair and stoop up.

"I hear she'll be in Fibber Magee's tonight," Molly said.

"Oh! Excuse me," Tommy said as he reached for his ringing phone.

As he chattered away, Molly cleaned up the kitchen and glanced at the clock. It was nearly five o' clock. Dermot would be home soon. Panic rose in her chest. She couldn't bear to confront him. One minute things were so normal, making tea, teasing Tommy, and the moment she thought about those empty football fields and Dermot's lies, her heart rattled around in her chest.

"Gotta love ya and leave ya!" Tommy said, picking up his box of hairdressing accoutrements. "Wolfie, come on boy."

Wolfie uncurled from his place in the corner, stretched and yawned to reveal a long pink tongue. A quick sneeze and snuffle, then he trotted to Tommy and stood patiently, wagging his tail leisurely, while Tommy clipped his lead on.

"Sure, I'll see you later," Molly replied, getting up and following him to the front door.

"Well, actually, that was Orla. There's a bunch of her mates going out tonight, so I thought I might just go with them, seeing as how you're all sorted with Dermot," he said.

"Where are they going? Fibber Magee's?" Molly suppressed a grin and waved until the car left the street.

No matches here love…

She shivered and stood at the door of the house, rubbing her arms.

"Happy birthday, child dear." The voice beside Molly pulled her out of her reverie.

Fran stood up from behind a rose bush. The old lady smiled and walked over to the fence. She wore a blue nylon housecoat over her tweed skirt and peach twin set. Fran always dressed as though she were going out to work even though she had been retired for many years. Molly never saw her in trousers or pajamas and a dressing gown.

As Molly leaned in for a hug, she smelt the familiar scent of lemon verbena, Fran's favorite hand lotion.

"I love your hair. Is it for your big party tonight?" Fran said.

"What party?"

"Oh no! Oh dear, dear, dear!" Fran shook her head. Her eyes watered. "Nothing, child dear, nothing. Please, forget I spoke. I—I get mixed up all the time. You know I do."

"Okay, Fran," Molly said. "Don't worry about it." Molly put her arm around Fran's shoulder and gave her a squeeze. "It'll be our wee secret." Fran's eyes crinkled in a smile.

Molly patted Fran's arm, took a deep breath and grinned. Her world had just turned from dark and heavy to bright and breezy. *A party* – that she wasn't supposed to know about. It was her thirtieth birthday after all. Of course he told her he was playing football today so that he could do final preparations for the party. That would explain why he hadn't had time to buy her a present.

God, she felt daft! McGinty's had a big function room upstairs. They had been to a few parties up there before. It held sixty or eighty people, sitting at tables or dancing on the wooden floor in front of the DJ.

Tracey and Tommy's plan for Fibber Magees was an obvious decoy. No wonder they hadn't included her.

Oh, thank God, thank God. How could she have thought any of those awful things about her Dermot?

Excitement wriggled through her and a cozy joy took hold. She definitely did not want to spoil the surprise. Was Fran coming to the party too? Molly considered asking her, then realized that Fran would feel really bad if she thought that she had spoiled the surprise. Molly insisted on filling the coal bucket and putting the washing into the tumble dryer for Fran before heading back to her own house. She'd have to hurry up and get ready. That's why Tommy had insisted on doing her hair today. What a sly fox!

"Thank you, child dear. Here's a little something for your birthday. It's not very much." Fran handed her a little pink package and a card as she left. Molly hugged her saying "Thank you," and ran through the sprinkle of rain that had started, back to her own house.

Molly loved opening presents. Inside, a silver butterfly pendant hung from a silver chain. She tried it on in front of the mirror in her bedroom, touched by Fran's generosity.

She hurried back up to the bedroom and replaced the kit bag in case Dermot came home early. That would let the cat out of the kit bag. She went back down to the kitchen and noticed the grocery bag left behind by Tommy.

"That nit-wit," she muttered happily to herself as she tidied away the cans of Pedigree Chum, rabbit flavor, humming Michael Jackson's version of "Happy Birthday" to herself. Birthdays were all about being made to feel really special, being spoiled. How sweet of Dermot to arrange a surprise for her. He really did love her after all.

Saturday, March 4th

CHAPTER SEVEN

Tracey got out of the taxi in front of the Europa Hotel. She passed a huddle of tourists looking up at the building. A Texan accent drawled, "The guide book says this is the most bombed hotel in Europe."

"Looks in pretty good shape to me," said one of the women, "If it's good enough for President Clinton, it's sure good enough for us."

It amused Tracey how people seemed to enjoy this fact about the Europa Hotel. Few commented on its excellent location and luxurious décor.

She crossed the road to Robinson's bar. People bustled around, dressed in their party clothes, smiling, anticipating a good evening. Tracey walked to the back of the pub, over the geometric black and white tiles, shiny and ready for the inevitable beer that would be slopped on it, making it tacky. To her right, the carved wooden bar gleamed, and staff busied themselves stacking glassware and changing kegs. A couple of old men sat locked in conversation. Another sat by himself at the end of the bar staring off into space. Two younger men with pints of lager in their hands stood along the back wall beside a door with a stain glass inset. They looked at her. One caught her eye and smiled. Tracey looked away and pushed open the heavy door, walking into the part of the building known as "Fibber Magee's."

Fibber's was decorated to look like the inside of an old Irish grocery store, complete with fake cuts of meat hanging from the butcher's section. A traditional Irish bar section had an open fireplace with merry flames crackling in the grate.

Tracey found Orla sitting alone by the fire. She wasn't hard to spot. Orla, on the plumper side of curvy with a fondness for wearing tight tops over her large bosom, advertised her craft as a hairdresser by wearing the biggest hairstyle in the loudest color considered in vogue. Sometimes her appearance bordered on frightening. Tonight she wore a hot pink, gravity-defying boob tube that toned in nicely with her maroon hair.

Orla had arranged several chairs around a table. The bar would be busy later.

"Hiya," Tracey said greeting Orla with a hug and air kiss. "Who else is coming?" She sat down on a chair opposite Orla and peeled off her jacket.

"Kate and Geraldine are coming down later," Orla said. She picked up an enormous purple handbag with clunky brass chain handles. It almost swallowed her entire arm as she rummaged around in it.

"And Tommy O Brian's coming too." Orla's face disappeared into the mouth of the big bag.

"What? Tommy, Molly's cousin? The snogged-me-and-disappeared-off-the-face-of-the-earth Tommy?"

Orla looked up and shrugged. "Jeez, it's been eight years, like. Get over it." Orla pulled a fat wallet out of the bag. "How 'bout I buy you a drink? What you having?"

"A pint, but don't think you're getting off that lightly," Tracey said.

"Look, he's lost touch with all his old buddies…"

"Well judging by his telephoning skills, that's no surprise."

"And, well, he offered me a job in his new salon." Orla's grin split her face.

"That's brilliant!" Tracey clapped her hands. She knew Orla hated her current place and that she and Tommy had studied hairdressing together. "Okay, I suppose I can forgive you, but no matchmaking, okay?"

"Okay, okay, shut up now. Here he comes." Orla stood up and made a drinking motion with her hand. Tommy gave her the thumbs up, and she headed for the bar.

Tommy's collarless white shirt and stone colored canvas trousers, effortlessly smart, showed off his tan. His sun-kissed glow spoke of time spent outside. It was fresh on him, clinging to him like a smell. Lean and long of limb, he moved gracefully toward the table. His eyes crinkled at the corners. A smile lingered.

The evening brightened up for Tracey, though she was loathe to attribute it to Tommy's presence. As his smile sparkled upon seeing her, she felt invigorated and alive as if, suddenly, she mattered. So as much as she wanted to gripe about the fact that he had never called her, she pushed it aside. It would only make her look petty. Better if he thought it hadn't bothered her. That way she'd salvage some pride.

"So how are you settling back into Belfast?" she asked as he sat in the chair next to her.

"Great, actually. The work starts this week refurbishing the salon. Should be ready for customers in a few weeks," Tommy said. "And how are you keeping? Are you still working at Grafton House?"

"God, no, that was a hundred years ago. I'm a Personal Assistant to the owner of Stockton's," she said, wondering why she hadn't just said she worked in an office, like she usually did when asked the same thing. She was impressed that he'd remembered that she'd worked at the old folks home, Grafton House. She'd been the bookkeeper there.

"Stockton's?"

"They outfit bars and hotels mostly. Someone has to choose which old bottles to put on shelves like that." She pointed to a collection of dusty bottles.

"Perhaps you could help me out with the salon?"

"What are you looking for?" Tracey sensed his enthusiasm as he sat forward and planted his hands on the table.

"Well, it's down by the docks, so I'm gonna theme it after the Tall Ships. You know with sails and rigging. Gets it away from being too girly. I want men to go there too. I'm thinking of calling it 'Clippers'." He ran his hand through his hair and sat back, as if waiting for the idea to soak in.

"I like it. It's a clever pun," she said. "Sure, give me a call, and I'd be happy to help." Tracey could have bitten off her tongue. The last time she'd asked him to call, he never bothered. She didn't know why it still bugged her so much. Before the moment stretched to outright awkward, Orla stepped in between them, allowing Tracey to hide her flaming face from Tommy.

"Clippers, eh?" Orla said setting down a tray with three pints of Guinness. "I quite like 'Hair Peace'."

"Aye, but if the cease-fire broke it would sound kinda dumb," Tommy said.

"Well, here's hoping it doesn't," Tracey said lifting her drink. "Cheers!"

As they wiped away their creamy moustaches, Orla pointed to the corner where a couple of men were tuning up fiddles. Tracey recognized them as the session band "Harpin' On."

"I've a wee surprise for ye," Orla said, blushing. "They've asked me to play with them tonight. Just a wee session in the bar here, not a full-on gig." She played the bodhrán, an Irish frame drum. Tracey loved the urgency that a bodhrán lent to the music, whipping the pace to a frenzy, lulling it to a heartbeat then whirling the tempo again.

"That's fantastic! *Maith thú*, Orla," Tracey said, congratulating her in Gaelic.

"Jeyes fluids *agus* mahogany banisters!" Tommy said, speaking nonsense but making it sound like Gaelic in the way he ran the words together. Orla laughed and punched his arm as she got up and walked over to the band.

Tracey watched her, wondering what the hell to talk to Tommy about. Where were the other girls? Shouldn't they be here? As Orla sat down with her musician friends, she flung Tracey a wink. Tracey felt her face flame. That wee bitch! She'd set her up. Indignant, yet surprisingly pleased, Tracey threw Orla a scowl then turned to Tommy, determined not to make an eejit of herself.

"So," Tracey said, scanning the seating area of the bar, "Are Dermot and Molly coming out tonight?"

"No," Tommy answered, "Dermot's taking her out for dinner."

"Wow, Dermot's gone all rose-mantic."

"I was surprised too," Tommy admitted. "You know how Molly loves a big shindig – I thought Dermot would have organized a party for her thirtieth."

Tracey sat back and took a sip of her drink. He had a point but she didn't care for the critical tone he assumed about her big brother.

"Well, you know our Dermot." She shrugged. "He's a great guy but he's just not big on the frills. Why didn't you do something for Molly's birthday?"

"Me?"

"Aye – you. Or at least her family," Tracey said. "Didn't her dad manage Nelly's Cellars before he retired? He could've gotten a deal there."

"Wait a wee minute there." Tommy straightened up and then leaned forward resting his elbow on the table, pitching himself towards her slightly. "It's the husband's duty to do these things, not the father's. You're being unfair to Molly's Dad. Did your parents organize Dermot's thirtieth?"

Tracey snapped her head round to look into his face. She opened her mouth, closed it and shook her head. No point telling him that her Da had been on a bender for that entire week, while her mother had been practically comatose with valium. That had been her father's last binge before his liver finally packed in. Tommy wouldn't understand. He came from a normal family.

"Well, it hardly matters now," she said. As she turned away from him he placed his hand on her forearm, its warmth reaching deep.

"Molly's probably having a ball. You know how mad she is about Dermot." Tommy's Adam's apple bobbed and his cheeks pinkened. He looked young and vulnerable. Tracey felt sorry for him. He probably knew through Molly and Dermot that her father had died around then. He looked at her, his head tilted to the side and his brow furrowed, like a contrite Golden Labrador. She smiled and patted his hand.

"Totally insane," she said.

"Who's insane now?" said a voice from behind. Tracey snatched her hands back as Kate and Geraldine descended upon the table. The pair were dolled up to the nines, scanty dresses, high heels and make-up applied with a trowel. They looked great. Tracey wished she'd worn something a little less casual than her black jeans and purple top. She couldn't decide if she was glad of the distraction they provided or if she wanted Tommy all to herself.

As the girls got themselves settled in, Tracey glanced around the bar. Her blood ran cold as she noticed an old mate of her ex-boyfriend, Kieran. After that awful run-in yesterday in the parking lot, she really did not need a repeat performance, especially not in front of Tommy. Her eyes scanned the room, checking that Kieran wasn't around, and she realized she'd been holding her breath. She felt haunted by him, expecting to see him everywhere she went.

"Everything all right, Tracey?" Tommy's voice brought calm to her again.

"Yep, great." She nodded, flashing a smile.

"Oh here comes Orla now," Tommy said as he clapped his hands together. The girly gesture irritated Tracey. It made her cringe the way he could be so effeminate sometimes. Imagine going out with him and everyone wondering if he was secretly gay? Tracey watched him, his face beaming with pleasure for Orla as she beat the bodhrán. The tickle of irritation gave in to admiration as she observed Tommy's heartfelt enjoyment of the music, evident now by his more normal clap to the beat and tapping of his feet. He was a nice guy. Why couldn't she let it go at that? Apart from the fact that he couldn't use a damn phone, she had little else to fault him with. He confused her. One minute she wanted to kiss him, another she wanted to shake him.

The evening took off. Music spun around them, swinging through the low lighting and twirling through the smell of sweat and booze. Tracey sang till her throat hurt. The fiddler played an instrumental. His body writhed around the instrument, and it infected her too, tapping her foot, jigging her shoulders. Bewitched, she joined the dancers who had pushed back the tables and chairs, orderly at the beginning of the night, now a disheveled circle.

Tommy smiled over at her. She had been stealing glances at him all night. He was definitely growing on her. She sat down from her dancing, looked over at Tommy and drank him in. He had the most beautiful mouth, full pouting lips that she wanted to kiss. She longed to place her hand on his arm just below his elbow and feel the soft fuzz of the downy hair there and the ripple of the muscle that lay beneath.

Tracey leaned over to Tommy.

"It's my round. What are you having?" she said.

"Just water."

"Really?"

"I'm going hiking tomorrow. I don't want to spoil my day with a hangover."

"Where are you going?" she asked. She liked that he did something at the weekend rather than lie around with a hangover.

"The Mournes hopefully. But I haven't decided yet. I'll wait and see what the weather's like. If it's miserable, I might just have to settle for a few rounds of Botanic Gardens."

"Are you going by yourself?"

"Me and the dog, so far. Do you hike?" Tommy shouted as the music started again. Was he going to ask her to join him? Would *she* be too hung-over?

Just then she saw Kieran pushing through the flaying limbs as he struggled through the tangle of bodies ceili-swinging to the music. Her hopes of going unnoticed were dashed as he looked straight at her and grinned with his lips pressed tight together. Tracey jumped up.

"I better go to the bar before it closes." She wriggled through the crowd hoping that Kieran would give up or be too drunk to remember that he'd seen her. She didn't want another confrontation, especially not in front of Tommy. Her heart hammered and her hands shook so much that she dropped her purse. A dancing foot kicked the purse across the floor, and it skittered down a hallway towards the staffroom. Tracey ran after it, glad she hadn't lost sight of it in the chaos.

She swooped down, scooped it up and turned to go back into the main area of the bar. Kieran blocked her path.

"So, Tracey, just you and me again," he snarled. "Romantic isn't it?" As he stepped towards her, she stepped back, only to find herself backed up against a fire exit. One push and they'd be outside, alone in the dark. She could not bear the sour stench of his breath as he leaned towards her.

"Leave me alone!" she cried.

"Oh, I don't think so. Anything could happen to you all alone," he sneered as he reached behind her and pushed the door open.

Saturday, March 4th

CHAPTER EIGHT

For the rest of the afternoon Molly pondered on the emotional roller coaster that had hurled her through her birthday. First she'd been delighted with breakfast in bed, then annoyed at Dermot for leaving her to "play football." She cringed at how she had thought him capable of any of the myriad of foul things her imagination had conjured. But she smiled as she remembered Fran's words, "...your big party tonight..."

At six-thirty Molly stood in front of the mirrored wardrobe. She wore a black satin Basque with delicate white flowers embroidered over it, teamed with a flirty black skirt. On one foot she wore a high-heeled leather boot. She bent at the waist and rummaged in the bottom of the wardrobe for the elusive other boot.

"Now that's a sight for sore eyes!" said a voice behind her. "You don't get many of those to the pound!" Dermot patted her bum as Molly stood up with the boot, her hair disheveled and a flush to her cheeks. Dermot's words and playful tone made her feel pretty, fresh and happy. She looked up into his eyes, so dark brown they were practically black, stood on her tip-toes, lips pursed for a kiss. He met her lips and smiled a slow smile that sent heat coiling from her waist to her kneecaps. She sent her whole heart shining from her eyes as she smiled at him, then breaking the spell, he stepped back as if off balance.

He hesitated briefly before pulling a large envelope from behind his back. He lowered his eyes, "Happy birthday!"

"Oh thanks. Can I open it now?"

She gave him a hug. She breathed him in deeply.

"I. Love. You." She punctuated each word with a kiss, her hands sliding into the back pockets of his jeans, pulling him closer to her.

"I better make a move," he said, disentangling himself from her. "Can you get me a clean shirt?"

Him and his obsession about his shirts, her brain flashed. You could tell that he didn't have to do the laundry. Dermot didn't like to use the tumble dryer. He said it cost too much. In winter damp clothes hung constantly in the house. Molly often secretly used the tumble drier before Dermot got home from work.

"Tommy called round earlier," Molly called from the depths of the closet. "He wants to know do we wanna go with him to Donegal, weekend after next?"

"After that last trip, I'd wanna know is there gonna be toilet facilities this time?"

"Oh God, I hope so!" She handed him a shirt. The water pipes in the cottage had frozen over the New Year's holiday, so the toilet wouldn't flush, and they had decided to "make like a bear" in the woods out the back. They nicknamed that area of the bog "The Turd World." The neighbor's dog had rolled in something that smelled like human poop, and Dermot had teased Molly that it was hers.

Dermot wagged a finger at her.

"It wasn't mine!" Molly said.

Dermot grinned and narrowed his eyes. "How can you be so sure? Was it the color? Texture? What?"

"Taste, I think!" she chuckled.

"Yeeeuuck!" both of them chimed together. She came round beside him and reached her arm around his waist, gazing up into his smiling face.

"I think they got the toilet fixed, but we should bring a big shovel just in case. Oh, and ban the Guinness!" she said. "So can we go?"

"We'll see," he said. The playful atmosphere turned chilly.

She pulled away. How could they connect so fully one minute, then stare at each other across a deep chasm the next? She could go to Donegal with Tommy by herself, but she knew she wouldn't enjoy it without Dermot. He was fun when he wanted to be - the life and soul of the party!

Even his wedding speech had begun "I'd like to thank Molly for having me." She had beamed with pleasure as she anticipated hearing him say something nice about his new wife.

"But not as often as I may have liked!" he continued. The smile froze on her face, but the crowd loved it! He was regular stand-up comedian, though his mother refused to speak to him for the next few hours. Later, he told Molly that he had cracked the joke not expecting so many people to get it, amazed that the hall had erupted like it did. He pointed out that the best comedy duos always had a fall guy. Over the next eight years she found herself the butt of his jokes with increasing frequency. Most times she enjoyed the attention.

Molly opened her envelope. "Birthday greetings to a dear wife," written above a big teddy bear. Inside, he had signed it just with his initial. Another smaller envelope contained a thirty-pound gift voucher. Feeling pathetically let down, Molly tried to regard this as part of the surprise. Perhaps he wanted her to think that he got her a present that required no thought or consideration. After all, she had to bear in mind that he had been running around all day. She set the card and voucher down on the bedside table.

"Are we driving or getting a taxi tonight?" Dermot shouted from the bathroom.

"What? And then I couldn't have a drink on my own birthday?" Molly seethed.

"Well, we could park the car in one of the side streets and walk back for it in the morning, or take the bus up."

There was that "we" thing again. She didn't quite know where he got the "we" from. Thirty-seven and he had never learned to drive! Who does that now? True he grew up in the city and didn't need a car. A family as large as his, with an alcoholic father, couldn't afford a car, but perhaps in his twenties he could have made some effort to learn.

A taxi both ways cost too much. Perhaps it was selfish of her to expect Dermot to pay all that money. After all, he may have had to fork out a lot of cash for this bash of hers tonight.

"Ok, I'll take the car up," she conceded.

***

A blast of damp heat hit Molly and Dermot as they walked into the bar area of Mc Ginty's. Seven-thirty was early for the bar to be so packed. Molly scanned the bar as they walked through to the restaurant area near the back but did not see anyone she knew. The dark maroon walls and black ceiling would have been oppressive were it not for the high polish of the wood of the bar, benches and tables, and the brass trimmings reflecting the light. Several old men sat up at the bar staring at the big T.V. in the corner. The screen displayed a green background, and the speakers emitted the crowd noise associated with sports viewing.

She felt alight with expectation. Everyone would be waiting upstairs. She hoped that Dermot would take them straight up and not hang around down here too long. Despite her excitement, Molly felt hungry.

Dermot led her to a table near the toilets. It was the only one still set up for dining and their only option. Ammonia stung Molly's nose every time the toilet door swung open.

"What do you wanna drink, Kitten?" asked Dermot, getting up again to go to the bar.

"I'll just have a Diet Coke to start with," she replied. She anticipated it would be a long night, and she wanted to pace herself. The rumble of her stomach confirmed the wisdom of her decision.

***

Plates scraped clean and glasses empty, Molly itched for Dermot to make the next move upstairs to the party. During dinner, Dermot, not overly chatty at the best of times, seemed quiet. Molly asked him about his week at work and he updated her on the latest office gossip. They drifted in and out of discussion of what was happening in the soaps and the news. Bland topics that couldn't scratch Molly's mental itch – the party upstairs! She tried not to wonder who would be there. She willed herself to live in the moment. Enjoy dinner with her husband.

Any minute now, Molly expected Dermot to concoct some story to lure her upstairs. Then she spotted Veronica Daly and her husband, Philip, come in through the side door of the bar. Veronica was the other P1 teacher in Molly's school. She still had a coat on, but where it gaped open, Molly could see Veronica was dressed up and wearing impossibly high shoes. She carried a large paper shopping bag. The kind that people put presents in. Veronica looked around the bar quickly. She spoke to Philip, who nodded and followed her on in.

Molly could not wipe the grin off her face. These guys were late to everything. If Dermot saw them he'd be furious that they were risking spoiling the big wow factor upstairs.

Veronica dashed over to the toilets without noticing them. Philip stood at the door, pushing buttons on his phone. Molly wished he'd go on upstairs. She didn't want Dermot to see them and get stressed. She pulled her chair in to the table at an angle, so that Veronica could sneak past her when she came out of the toilets. Molly tried to concentrate on her conversation with Dermot.

"Well, hello there," said Dermot, looking past Molly. She turned to see Veronica totter over to them. "You're looking well tonight. Where are you off to?"

"Hi, Dermot. Hi, Molly." Veronica's face was bright red.

Molly felt sorry for her. It was mean of Dermot to put the poor woman on the spot like this. "We're on our way to Mam and Dad's wedding anniversary meal and I…" She cleared her throat. "I needed to nip in here on the way to use the bathroom." She gave a nervous giggle and flicked her brown hair out of her eyes.

Great cover story. Bravo. Molly nodded, wishing she could stop grinning.

"Why don't you join us for a drink?" Molly said.

"Sorry, we're late as it is. See you on Monday." Veronica flapped her hand, then ran to the door, grabbed Philip by the hand and bustled him out with her.

"Do you mind if we don't stay out too late, Kitten?" asked Dermott, fidgeting with his empty glass. "I'm bushed after the match today, and we have a big training session tomorrow to prepare for next week's league in Leeds."

"What? You wanna go home now?" Molly said, confused. Maybe he was just kidding. "Isn't there something on upstairs tonight?"

"Nope, sure, they lost their license for up there."

Oh God, that's right! How could she have forgotten? And why would all her friends sit waiting upstairs while they ate down here? What a desperate fool she'd been.

Somewhere in the abyss of her heart, a penny dropped. Its splash echoed through her brain, ringing at her thoughts. Reason battled through, like a fat lady pushing up the aisle of a bus. His lies about the football. His lack of thought for her present. He hadn't even complimented her straightened hair today when he came back from town. When was the last time he had volunteered a kiss, or even told her, unprompted, that he loved her?

The Knowing crashed in and there was no turning back. She couldn't ban it from her thoughts. She didn't want to face this. It wasn't happening. *The cheating bastard!* She had no proof. If she confronted him now he'd deny it.

Dermot stood up and turned his back to her as he lifted his jacket from the back of the chair.

"Ready to go, Kitten?" His voice slammed into her psyche.

Molly sat with both hands on the table in front of her, knuckles whitening as they curled into fists. She shot out her right hand, punching Dermot's empty glass right off the table. It shattered at his feet. He jumped.

"What the fuck?" Dermot bent down to pick up the broken glass. "Ow!" He dropped the fragment and held his finger up to his face.

As he peered at it, Molly felt a grim satisfaction as a trickle of blood dripped onto the napkin in front of her. Three drops of red making a clover shape on the white paper.

"You're so clumsy. Come on. I want to go home and get a band-aid for this," he said and sucked his finger.

Molly clamped her jaw together. She folded up the napkin and popped it into her pocket. She wanted his blood all right. Hatred spread like venom through her. She watched him walk to the door of the bar. He turned and looked at her.

"Come on," he said, then looked down at his finger and wiggled it towards her. "I'll live."

When he laughed, Molly felt herself unraveling. She loved him and hated him all at once. She wanted to scream at him, beg him, beat him, hold him, smother him with kisses and scratch his eyes out. She pressed her hands to her temples. *Move – don't let him know. Don't let him insult you anymore by denying it.*

She gripped the table and stood up robotically. With eyes cast down, she pulled on her jacket. She watched herself as if she were outside her own body going through the motions –pushing in her chair, following Dermot out to the car, getting in and driving home. Something stronger than herself controlled her body.

She needed time to think. If she gave in to believing he was cheating, she would explode into tiny fragments of pink flesh splattered all over the inside of her car. Insanity tugged at her. Behind her eyes a storm broke in her head. She heard it in her ears and felt it under her skin.

Beside her, Dermot played with the radio, jumping from station to station until he found a song he wanted to hear. Molly didn't hear any of it. Dermot seemed oblivious to her. Something shut down in Molly, leaving her too tired and weary to fight it. She only felt the Knowing seeping into her soul.

Saturday, March 4th

CHAPTER NINE

Tommy watched Tracey as she walked to the bar. Her black trousers hugged her figure, enticingly outlining her pert bum. Her high shoes forced her hips to sway slightly as she walked. When she bent over to pick up something she'd dropped, her silky purple top rode up just enough to give Tommy a glimpse of the waist band of a black lacy thong, provoking a tingle of pleasure.

Just then a man with short, brown, greasy hair stepped up close to Tracey. Tommy experienced a dart of jealousy that was quickly replaced by alarm when he saw the expression of horror on Tracey's face. As the man shoved her out the fire door, Tommy sprang to his feet.

Tommy pushed past the tables and sprinted for the door. He arrived in the alleyway in time to see the man pressing against Tracey, who was backed up against a stack of kegs, one of many that lined the alley. Her hands were planted on his chest and her elbows locked. She twisted her head away from her assailant's face.

Outraged, Tommy grabbed the man's shoulder and spun him round. The man staggered violently and nearly lost his balance.

"What the fuck do you think you're doing?" the man snarled, taking another unsteady step back.

"You okay, Tracey?" Tommy said.

She nodded.

"'S none of yer fucking business. Fuck away off, before I make ya." The man squared his shoulders. He was about the same height as Tommy, but he was very drunk. Tommy liked his odds. He wanted to hurt this scumbag. He planted his feet, held his hands palm up about hip level and forced a deliberate smile.

"So make me."

"No, Tommy don't!" Tracey cried.

The man pulled an empty bottle from a crate beside him and in one swift movement smashed the bottle off a metal keg and lunged towards Tommy. Tommy stepped back but the man was faster and more coordinated that Tommy had given him credit for. The jagged glass swung past Tommy's face in a downward arc as he twisted out of its way. It caught him just above the elbow, ripping the shirt and scratching his left forearm enough to sting and draw blood. Tommy heard Tracey's cry of alarm, more a squeak than a scream, but it seemed distant as fury flooded him.

Having missed his mark, Tommy's assailant pitched forward, dropping his weapon, and sprawling in the alley. He pushed off the ground, and Tommy kicked, catching the man square in the face. The crunch echoed in the alleyway, followed by the man's gargled squeal that jolted Tommy back to himself. Bile burned his throat as he stared at the man on the ground. The man shrieked as blood gushed from between the fingers covering his face.

"Jesus Christ, Tommy, you broke his nose!" Tracey took a step toward the figure on the ground, then stopped. She seemed stunned, conflicted. The man struggled to his feet swaying towards Tracey. Tommy moved between him and Tracey. The man glared at him.

"I'll fucking get you for this, you bastard." He looked at Tracey. "You comin'?" He patted his thigh as if summoning a dog.

Tracey backed away from him, shaking her head. Tommy put his hand on her shoulder. She shrugged it off but didn't take her eyes of the man.

His face twisted as he snarled, "Watch your back, Tracey. You can bet I'm watching yours." He dabbed his mouth gingerly on the cuff of his shirt. He peered at the blood smeared on the sleeve, then hawked up from the back of his throat and spat a mouth full of blood that landed at Tracey's feet. She swore and jumped back as he sneered. Then he turned and lumbered away with an uncoordinated swagger.

"You know him?" Tommy peered at Tracey. Her chin wobbled slightly as she nodded and lowered her face into her hands for a moment. She looked up at Tommy, lost, woeful, her blue eyes brimming with tears. He wanted to pull her to him in a big hug, but she was already moving away from him.

"He's my ex-boyfriend."

"What? You went out with that guy?" Tommy couldn't pair this lovely girl with that cretin.

"Well, don't get on your high horse about it," she snapped back.

"No, I didn't mean anything, It's just he's so, so... And you're, well you're, you know..."

"Jesus, Tommy, anyone ever tell you have a way with words?"

"What I mean is, aren't you way out of his league?"

Tracey laughed bitterly.

Tommy frowned. His best shirt was ripped. He was bleeding. He'd just broken a guy's nose, and now she was laughing at him.

"What's so funny?"

"You. You and your little Walton's world."

"My Walton's world?" Tommy was totally confused. His arm stung but not nearly as much as his pride. Hadn't he been the hero and saved her? Wasn't she supposed to swoon and fall into his arms?

"Tommy, everything in your world is cut and dried. Nice parents in a nice neighborhood. You get to go to college, finish your training in London. You don't drink too much, you wear the right clothes, hang out with a nice crowd, have a nice flat, start a nice business. It's all so fucking easy. You think you can stand there and tell me I'm going out with guys who are beneath me." She turned and pulled the handle on the fire door, but it was locked. She kicked it. Then she turned and shoved a stack of crates filled with bottles. The whole thing rocked then settled, but before Tommy could draw a sigh of relief the topmost crate toppled off the far side emptying bottles against the alley wall and smashing to the ground.

"Are you fucking insane?" Tommy hissed and grabbed her arm. He pulled Tracey, running down the alley to where it joined the main street. She shrugged him off and strode off down Great Victoria Street.

He ran after her, catching up in a few easy strides. She marched on, ignoring him. He caught up again, this time stepping in front of her.

"What was all that about? I don't think fighting off the bouncers would be as easy as getting rid of your boyfriend, you know?" he said.

"He's not my boyfriend!" Tracy stepped around him and kept walking. It was closing time and all around them the pubs were emptying. It was the time of the living dead in Belfast and no one was going to notice one more couple having a drunken row. Tracey stepped into the street waving at a cab barreling along with its light off. It honked its horn, and she sprang out of the way, swearing at the driver as she did.

Tommy decided that she was too upset and too drunk to be left alone.

"Christ," he muttered, gritted his teeth and went after her.

"Wait." He was surprised that she stopped. She stood with her hands on her hips, her chin out, eyes narrowed.

"What now?" she said.

"Let's just get you home, okay?"

"I don't need your help."

"Why are you being like this?"Tommy snapped, his anger rekindling.

"Fuck it, Tommy, I thought you were different? But you, you bust his nose. And he was lying on the ground when you kicked him." Tommy felt his face grow hot. It was shameful. How could he justify it? He was bloodied, and he'd lost control. But he wasn't sorry. One good stab from that broken bottle and it would have been a totally different story. He looked at Tracey's white face, her lips pressed tight, and her eyes blazing blue. She trembled, maybe suffering from shock. That episode in the alley had been pretty ugly. A shiver ran down his neck. He was probably reacting to it also. He took a deep breath.

"Different? What do you mean different?" Tommy tried to keep his voice soft.

"Forget it." Little spots of pink blossomed on her cheeks. She started walking again. Tommy fell into step beside her. She seemed flustered, embarrassed maybe. So she was shook up from her encounter with Kieran, but why was she so strange with him? He thought they got on well, at least before he'd bust her ex's nose.

"Where do you live?" Tommy asked. "I'll walk you home."

"It's too far. Why would you care?"

"I just don't want to read in the Belfast Telegraph about something happening to you and have it on my conscience." Irritating as it was, her fury ignited a flame in Tommy that flicked deliciously in his loins. He considered pulling her to him, pushing her against the wall and kissing her, but that would leave him no better than the arsehole he'd just pulled off her.

"It's too far to walk. I have to get a taxi." She watched another cab race by, full of people.

"We'll never get one here," he said, taking in the scores of people lined up at the taxi ranks. Most taxis weren't even stopping, having been filled farther down the street, outside the Europa Hotel and Robinson's.

"I'll phone for one," Tracey said, searching her hand bag.

"Nah, they'll only come to a house address at this time of the morning," Tommy said. Even if the taxi was coming, they would have to wait out here in the cold for an hour. She shivered. It was a balmy Belfast night for March, probably hitting about six degrees Celsius.

"Let's phone from my place," Tommy suggested. "No funny business." He couldn't help smirking as she scowled.

"Where is your place?"

"Palestine Street," Tommy said.

"Fine, I'll book one now to be at your house in half an hour." She twisted around to glare up at him as she pulled her phone out and punched at the keypad.

Tommy felt that he'd won that round. His arm throbbed and he looked at his shirt soaked from the elbow in blood. The wound itself had scabbed over and he'd stopped bleeding. It was only a scratch really, but a cab driver would never stop for them with him so bloodied.

It struck Tommy that she seemed to see his life as this perfect bubble. On one level, it pleased him, and yet it seemed unjust. He had his fair share of challenge and pain. They'd both lost a parent. She'd suffered from the life hers had lived. He'd suffered from the death his had died. How could he compare the suffering?

Tommy wasn't sure what to talk about as they set off. It was simpler to say nothing. Normally it took twenty minutes at a good pace to reach Palestine Street from the city center. He could hear her breathing beside him, not out of breath, but the pace brisk enough to get the heart pumping. She swung her arms, and the beat of her shoes set a strong rhythm to their march. An hour ago, he'd have welcomed the idea of taking her home, back when she seemed sane and rational, back when her arched eyebrow could lift more than his spirits. Now Tommy was relieved that Tracey didn't want to hang out at his house.

"Does Kieran know where you live?" Tommy asked.

She stopped and looked up at him, her eyebrows drawn together in worry, blue eyes framed by long dark eyelashes that distracted him so he couldn't think what to say next. She looked beautiful. Under the street lights her hair shone golden and her skin glowed. He savored her proximity, smelling the faint waft of her perfume, flowery and clean, mingled with the sweet undertone of musk. His body reacted to her against his will.

"He does, but I don't think he'll come round the house. He's more of an opportunist than a premeditator."

"Jesus, that's pretty nasty stuff. Promise me you'll be careful." They started walking again and turned into Palestine Street.

"Why Tommy? Are you looking for another drunk to beat up?" Tracey said.

"Listen, I bled for you tonight. You could at least thank me."

"I never asked you to. You men are all the same. You think a show of aggression is gonna make me all weak at the knees? Go fuck yerself, Tommy. Stay out of my business. It's pretty obvious you consider it sordid and beneath you."

"I never said that!"

"You didn't have to. It's written all over your face."

Tommy raised both hands and ran his fingers through his hair from the temples back. He felt his temper spiral.

"You are fucking impossible, Tracey. I'm just trying to be helpful. I thought I was being nice. Maybe you'd have preferred me to let that ballix give you one in the back alley. Maybe that's how you like it?" Her gasp halted him.

Tears spilled down her face as she turned away from him. Crap! It wasn't him saying those obscene things. He was the fucking good guy!

Behind him a horn blared, making them both jump. The Taxi was sitting outside his house. Tracey ran up the street to the car.

"I'm sorry," Tommy shouted after her.

"Oh fuck away off," she called over her shoulder as she reached for the car door handle and tugged the door open. Tracey jumped into the taxi, slamming the door. She wound down the window as the cab moved off, passing the spot where Tommy stood.

"You were quite the hero. Thank you." Her voice dripped with acid.

Sunday, March 5th

CHAPTER TEN

Dermot woke up with a start. He knew he'd been dreaming, but as he opened his eyes to the morning sun the dream evaporated, and he was left with the sensation that something was not quite right. Then he remembered his impending fatherhood. It was all he could think about since Sheila told him yesterday. When the first rush of adrenalin had worn off, sometime during that boring night out with Molly, he realized that he was curious about what being a father would be like. Now, as he yawned and stretched his way to a new day, he realized that he'd most likely made his choice.

The other side of the bed was empty. Molly was up already. Good job she hadn't been drinking last night. At least she wasn't here in the bed asking that dumb question "Penny for your thoughts?"

She always took the hump if he claimed to have no thoughts.

"That's impossible. You have to be thinking something. How can you be thinking nothing?" she'd say.

How could he explain that he was thinking about Sheila, the mother of his child? In the past he'd just said he wasn't thinking of anything. Usually that was true. Anyway, his thoughts were his private property. She'd retaliate by threatening to keep her thoughts to herself. He wished she would. He didn't really care what Molly thought these days.

Dermot pulled the duvet round him, contemplating another wee snooze, hoping that if he thought hard enough about Sheila and the episode against the fridge he might dream about it. Lust seeped through him with a delicious tingle to his groin.

Downstairs the vacuum cleaner roared to life. What the blazes was Molly thinking of? Dermot sat up, furious that his precious Sunday morning lie-in was being so rudely interrupted. He got up, berating himself for not having gotten her drunk last night. At least it would have kept her ill in bed.

He went to the bathroom to shave. He had to search to find his razor. The bathroom cabinet was stuffed full of various half used bottles of women's crap. God this was ridiculous. He needed space.

Did he really want to be a father? There was a flutter in his chest before he took a deep breath. It was daunting, but at least if Sheila was capable of looking after a child by herself, then he wouldn't have as much to do. It wouldn't be the same as when he was growing up. Two wages, one baby and no alcoholics. It couldn't be that bad. Dermot enjoyed Sheila, even when they weren't in the sack. They could spend time together just doing nothing, like if he wanted to watch football on her pay-per-view. She'd sit beside him reading a book, waiting for the football to end. That felt nice: companionable.

As quickly as he could, he shaved, showered and dressed. He splashed on aftershave, grimaced at the sting, and then admired his look in the full-length mirror. Would his baby look like him? A mixture of him and Sheila would be a right stunner. Boy or girl? He didn't care so long as it was healthy, so long as it didn't get into drugs or alcohol, like his dead beat family. Would their genes be passed down? He wasn't an alco or a druggie, neither was Sheila. Junior would be fine. More than fine. Dermot was surprised to feel proud of the kid already.

The vacuum cleaner powered down, leaving a mild ringing in his ears.

Dermot called a taxi from the phone by the bed.

"What time will you be back?" Molly asked, suddenly beside him.

Dermot jumped.

"Same as usual," he said.

She stared at him for a prolonged moment, then blinked before saying, "Fine, I'll have dinner ready for six then." Her tone strange, removed.

Outside a car beeped.

"There's the taxi. Better go!" Dermot practically skipped to the front door. Just as he opened the latch, Molly's voice droned from behind him,

"Don't forget your kit bag."

He turned around to see Molly standing one arm extended, dangling the kit bag from her finger tips, her face like stone.

"Oh," he spluttered, "Thanks. Thanks Kitten." He grabbed the kit bag and smiled, but her face remained flinty.

"Wanker," Dermot thought he heard Molly say, as he turned away.

"Pardon me?" he snapped back, surprised.

"Nothing." She stared blankly at him.

Christ Almighty, definitely PMS. He then sprinted down the path to the taxi, avoiding a row. He wanted to be in a good mood when Sheila met his cab in the shopping center car-park. Losing Sheila now was not really an option. Suddenly, he feared the thought of never seeing her again. He surprised himself. Holy shit! He loved her. This was about more than choosing fatherhood. He had never wanted Molly's kids. If they were as demanding as their mother, he'd end up in the nut house. Sheila never made demands on him. She gave him space to be himself. Sheila was always calm and serene, never bothered if he couldn't make a date. Molly was too hyper. She was always trying to block out his time, tell him what to do, emasculate him. Sheila made him feel like a real man. While Molly irritated him most of the time, Sheila soothed him. It wasn't his fault he turned to someone else. Molly made it easy for him to choose Sheila.

He couldn't wait to tell Sheila. She was there waiting for him in the usual place. She looked good in a black v-neck top. He helped himself to an eyeful of her cleavage. Wouldn't her boobs get bigger when she was pregnant? The Big Lad liked the thought of that and sprung to attention. Sheila's face was closed. She was probably nervous; worried that he'd turn her down. He grinned, bubbling over inside with excitement. He kissed her, looked deeply into her eyes for a moment, but decided to break the news in the house rather than here in a parking lot. She might be overcome with emotion or, better still, lust.

As they closed the front door behind them, Dermot put his arm around Sheila's waist. The hallway was small and warm, the radiator on the wall piping hot. The cream walls were bare, without even a picture. Marble floor-tiles in hues of cream, beige and mushroom gleamed, reflecting the glint from the mini chandelier lampshade, Sheila's only concession to décor in this space. It was classy and uncluttered, like Sheila, Dermot thought. Then immediately he wondered what it would feel like to have those tiles cool against his back and buttocks as Sheila sat astride on top of him. Just thinking about it turned him on.

"I've got good news." He kept his voice low, throaty.

She tilted her head to the side.

"I could do with some good news. What is it?"

"Sheila, I've thought long and hard about this," he began. "I want to be a father to our child. A good father."

"Are you sure?" she asked.

He was disappointed that she didn't seem more thrilled. Perhaps she couldn't believe her good luck. He followed her into the living room, casting a glance back at the hall floor before he answered her.

"Yeah, definitely. It's all I've been able to think about."

"Since yesterday afternoon," she said. The corner of her mouth twitched upwards. Dermot had that irritating feeling that she was mocking him but wasn't sure why.

"This is a really important decision, Sheila, of course it's all that I can think about," he said, slightly wounded. "I'm choosing you, and our baby. Everything's going to be all right."

"That remains to be seen," Sheila said.

Dermot hugged her to him. She relaxed so that the contours of their bodies folded together. He felt aroused. As he ground into her slowly, kissing her neck, he murmured, "I love you, Sheila."

She stiffened and pulled away.

"What?" She started at him.

He cleared his throat and reached for her hands with both of his. He felt himself blushing and was thrilled that she could reduce him to feeling like an awkward teenager. The buzz of the chase, he loved that.

"I know that I don't love her," he began. "I love you. Sheila, only you. And our baby, of course." He placed his hand on her tummy. Sheila pushed it away.

"You're sure?" she asked. He was sure he saw her chin wobble. It was all so much more than she'd probably hoped for. He knew she'd be overwhelmed.

"When do you want me to move in?" he asked in a soft voice.

"We don't have to decide right away," Sheila said turning away, walking into the living room and sitting down on the sofa.

"Well, we could wait until the end of June before we tell Molly," he suggested. "That way she would be off work and have time to deal with it." He tried to ignore the bad feeling that sprouted in the pit of his stomach.

"Anyway, it's for her own good," He said. Sheila arched an eyebrow, and the corner of her mouth twitched. Dermot didn't want her agreeing with him too much. He swallowed hard before trusting himself to speak again.

"It's only fair to give Molly the opportunity to meet someone else too. Someone who loves her better than me. She'll see that in time. Leaving her will be an act of kindness in the long run. Molly will get over this. Some melodrama of her own would do her no harm. She loves the drama."

Sheila said nothing. Dermot felt that his speech had hit the nail on the head. They'd both feel better now. He wished he could move in straight away, forget all about Molly and just start his new life now. He didn't relish keeping it a secret for four more months.

"When's the baby due?"

"End of October," said Sheila. "Plenty of time. You don't need to move in yet."

"But…" Dermot began.

"For Molly's sake," Sheila interrupted. "It will be a lot for her to deal with. You know, losing you." She smiled and reached for Dermot's hand.

"Yeah, she'll be devastated," Dermot agreed, sitting down beside Sheila. "Feck it! She'll get over it, comfort eat for a month and then devise some plan for coping and moving on." He squashed the bad feeling deep down where he couldn't feel it anymore. In the meantime, it was going to be a rocky ride. Breaking the news to Molly would be grim. But not as grim as living with Molly, knowing Sheila was out there with his child.

His child. The thought kicked him full in the consciousness. *His child.* He was surprised by how *fatherly* he felt. Yes, staying with Sheila was the honorable thing to do.

***

Dermot's mouth watered at the smell of chili that that greeted him when he arrived home from Sheila's house on Sunday evening. Molly was obviously on a cooking spree again. Dermot put on the television and found a soccer match before going to find a beer.

In the kitchen, pots hissed and bubbled on the hob, and Molly was hanging clothes on racks over the radiators.

"Woaw something smells good!" he said, jocularly. "Jeez, Molly, the clothes will stink of the chili."

"Well, shall I tumble dry them then?" she asked, her face void of expression.

"No, too expensive, what about outside?"

"Forecast is for rain." She clipped back, "Do you want rice or chips with your chili, or sausages?"

"Sausages?"

"Never mind, private joke," she said without laughing.

"Huh? Well, chips then?"

"Deep fat fryer's broken. Do you want to run up to the chippy? Exercise would do you good," she stated.

Christ, she was dry tonight. Still it was better than having her nag at him. She probably still had PMS.

"Nah, rice is fine. Have I time for a shower?"

"Suppose showers at the playing field are still broken," Molly said.

It was strange how she brought that up. Women were obsessed with these stupid little details. Half the time the lads didn't bother after football at all if they were in a hurry to get to the pub. A good spray of cheap deodorant did the job. Women loved that manly aroma!

"Yeah, they are," Dermott mumbled, confused by her attitude. Something about her question niggled at him, but he was unable to focus on the thought. Hunger did that to him. He was looking forward to his dinner. He inhaled the smell, his mouth watering. He decided that the shower could wait until the morning. There was football to watch.

Molly didn't make him chili often. Why did she bother to cook it for him when she was so off with him right now? She could be very weird. He used to love her selfless gestures. He had enjoyed feeling pampered and precious. Now he felt claustrophobic. How had that soured so badly?

Dermot wolfed down the chili. Molly seemed to be in a world of her own, and he was content to eat his food quietly in front of the telly, mulling over his afternoon with Sheila. He considered asking Molly how her day went, and then decided that he didn't really care.

He wondered why he didn't feel guilty eating the food that Molly had prepared, while spending the whole meal thinking about the baby he had planted in another woman's womb. Some things just were meant to be. It was out of his hands now really.

Sunday, March 5th

CHAPTER ELEVEN

Tracey woke up mortified. How could she have spoken to Tommy like that? Why had she been such a bitch? She'd been shocked when he'd kicked Kieran in the face, but by Christ, she'd been really glad that he'd shown up. A chill ran up her spine when she considered what might have happened if he hadn't. She'd acted crazy. Why couldn't she just have had a lovely evening in Tommy's company? Kieran blighted her life.

Tracey opened the curtains of her bedroom, squinting in the cool morning light. The sky looked exactly like her emotions, pewter and turbulent. She felt groggy. Thirst focused her efforts as she pulled on her dressing gown and headed downstairs. The tap water tasted like elixir, and she glugged down a half a pint in one go. She refilled the glass.

"Good afternoon, Tracey," said a voice behind her. Tracey glanced at the clock on the wall before she answered.

"Mum, it's only ten o clock." Tracey drank more water, slower this time.

Carmel Duggan wheezed as she sat down at the kitchen table, its yellow Formica top rubbed to a white patch at her end. In the center, a bowl of sugar, a bottle of HP sauce and a bottle of ketchup huddled around an ashtray. Carmel pulled the ashtray towards her.

"Did you empty this?" Carmel asked.

"Yes, it stank," she said.

"Ah Jesus, I had a half a ciggy in there." Carmel stood up. "Did you throw it in the kitchen bin?"

"Oh gross, don't go bin-hoking. Have you none left? I'll run up to the shop and get you some."

"Ach, that would be great love."

Tracey went upstairs, pulled on some clothes and grabbed her purse. By the time she got back down to the kitchen, Carmel was sitting in a fog of blue acrid smoke.

"I thought you'd none left," Tracey said.

"I never said that." Carmel shifted position, crossing her legs and blowing out a stream of smoke. Tracey coughed and waved her hand in front of her face.

"But you were going to let me buy you more…"

"Never look a gift horse." Carmel smiled, smoothing the wrinkled skin around her lips.

Tracey stared at her mother, this skinny woman with short dark hair and a face like corduroy. Her eyebrows - drawn on now since the hairs lost the will to re-grow after years of ruthless plucking - pushed her forehead into deeper ripples.

"What?" her mother hacked out, the word forming the beginning of a cough.

"Nothing. I'm going for a shower."

"But what about my ciggys?"

Tracey ignored her mother and went back up stairs. Her mother drove her nuts most of the time, and she dealt with that. She could move out now that she was working. Carmel claimed she'd be lonely. She'd be afraid of someone breaking in. She worried about getting sick and no one there to help her. What if she fell down the stairs?

You're lucky I haven't pushed you down the damn stairs!

Tracey stood in the shower and tried to find that place in her head where tranquil waters flowed. Despite her frustrations with her mother, Tracey did try to be kind to her. The poor woman had had a hard life. Tracey thought it sad that the people who should have loved her mother most had treated her so badly, starting with the man she'd married as a teenage bride. Even her own kids tried to avoid her. Out of the ten of them, it was only the two eldest, she and Dermot, who even bothered with her.

76

Carmel had cried when Dermot married Molly, claiming that he'd have made a great priest and that he was breaking his mother's heart. She got over it. He was soon reinstated as her most favored child. She got over the fact that Tracey hadn't joined the convent rather more quickly. The others had flown the coop, settling elsewhere. Jackie, the youngest, had moved to London when he was sixteen and hadn't even come home for his father's funeral. They rarely heard from him now. Tracey had little contact with any of them except Dermot.

Carmel had a nasty streak that could turn people against her. *Just like me last night.* This idea frightened Tracey. Was she destined to turn into her mother? Crikey, she was twenty-seven and still living at home. She wished she could talk to Molly, but she didn't want to admit that she had seen Kieran again, though Tommy would probably tell her. Nor did she want to admit how nasty she'd been to Tommy. She wasn't sure if he'd tell Molly about that. He'd not been lily white in that whole exchange either. Most of all, she didn't want Molly to guess that the whole reason behind it all was that she really liked Tommy. She liked him too much. But he'd already made it clear that he thought she was socially way beneath him, tarred with the "Kieran" brush. Was that why she'd been such a bitch to him? Pushed him away before he could shun her?

She couldn't talk to Dermot because he'd want to go after Kieran again. Tracey felt a stab of envy. She had no one to confide in, no one of her own. Loneliness wrapped around her as solidly as the towel she used to dry herself. Molly and Dermot were so lucky to have each other. Molly just didn't realize what it was like to be single and not have that special someone to always be on your side, to fight your battles alongside you. *Fight.* Her stomach curdled as she thought of the sound of Kieran's nose breaking. Maybe fighting was overrated.

More stomach churning was the memory of Tommy's face when she had sarcastically called him a hero as the cab pulled away. He'd looked so defeated. And he'd been right, to a point. Kieran had a broken bottle. He'd played dirty first. Why hadn't she seen that instead of getting mad?

Tracey did not want to be that nasty bitchy person. *Her mother.* She had to break this pattern, and it wasn't going to be easy. First, she'd have to try to put right her behavior from last night. Tracey swallowed the lump in her throat. She was going to have to apologize to Tommy. But how? She didn't have his number and she couldn't ask anyone for it. She knew where he lived, but could she really turn up at his house unannounced? Perhaps if she just bumped into him somewhere, like in the park?

She glanced out the window. Was the weather sufficiently bad to keep Tommy from going to the mountains today? He had mentioned last night that if the weather was bad he'd just walk in Botanic Gardens. It was near his house, and she could do with a walk too.

Excitement rose within her at the thought of seeing him again. It was quickly followed by panic. What would she say? She'd just be honest, play no games and speak from the heart. She was sorry, she'd been wrong and she hoped he'd forgive her. She took a couple of deep breaths and realized that she was smiling as she caught a glimpse of herself in the bathroom mirror. It felt good to have a plan, to have some control. Scary too. What if he didn't show up? There was always plan B. She could present herself at his house. And what if he had gone to the mountains? She didn't want to think about that. It was too close to failure.

Feeling new energy, Tracey hurried to get out of the house. She pulled on a grey woolen sweater and a matching beanie. A big red scarf lifted the color scheme and made her feel brave. She pulled on her hiking boots, overkill for a walk in the park, but they were cozy and comfy.

"I'm away, Mum," she called as she passed the kitchen door. The air was blue-grey with cigarette smoke.

"Where are you going?"

"Mass," Tracey lied, knowing it would keep her mother happy.

She drove past the Kings Hall and down Balmoral Avenue. The last time she'd driven this route was when she'd gone to kayak at Shaw's Bridge, where she'd run into Kieran. That was only two days ago. Then she'd seen him again the next day, last night. Had he followed her? Her blood pulsed faster as she checked her rear view mirror. Balmoral Avenue was empty behind her, the beautiful houses tucked behind their hedges of privet and stone walls. It was a far cry from her street, where the front doors opened straight onto the footpath with only a doorstep to break the stride of those who entered.

She turned left onto the Malone Road and drove down to the University Area. It was quiet on this lazy Sunday morning. She parked in Elmwood Avenue, beside the Students' Union. The trees that lined the street had begun to bud. Every so often, the sun broke from behind a cloud, and the street glowed lime green in the fresh foliage.

She walked towards the main building of the University, the Lanyan Building. It sat castle-like with its red-brick turrets, serene against manicured lawns. Tracey turned right and headed to Botanic Gardens. Her nerves jangled as she walked past through the gates. She couldn't decide what would be worse: Tommy being there or Tommy not being there. To her left, the white framed glasshouse stood looking rich and regal. She wondered if it was open today. Usually the less ornate tropical ravine greenhouse to her right was open. It would provide a place of shelter if it rained.

She walked around a plastic bag that littered the footpath. She thought about picking it up, hating to see rubbish lying around, but she wandered on down the path. Feck it. Today it could be someone else's problem.

As she looped around the main lawn, a huge dog bounded from behind her and out into the expanse of grass. He looked so vigorous and happy with his tongue lolling from his mouth and tail wagging that Tracey was drawn to watching him. Behind her, his owner flung a ball far into the field of grass and the mutt raced after it. He brought it back slobbering and ran behind her. She turned her head watching as the dog ran up to a man sitting on a park bench. Tracey looked again.

Tommy! Her heart sped up as panic engulfed her. She'd thought she was prepared but she'd expected to have to sit around and wait a while. She swung away from him and kept her head down. Thankfully, she had her hat on, and she didn't think that Tommy had seen her. She had to apologize, but she wasn't ready. Shit! Maybe she should just get it over with. A quick straightforward apology like, "Sorry for my behavior last night. I hope your arm is better." She could be back at her car having done the right thing in ten minutes flat.

She could just leave. Walk away from the whole thing and let things settle down. She might not bump into Tommy for another eight years. She could see the gate to the park only about twenty yards away. If she kept going, Tommy would never know she'd been there, engrossed as he was, playing with his dog.

And I wouldn't have fixed a damn thing!

She had to apologize, even if just to prove to herself that she was changing things. She knew she had to do if she were to move on from this shitty life she led; to not turn into Carmel — wizened, bitter, and disgusted with herself.

She gathered her courage around her as if gathering a billowing skirt and turned back into the park. She could still see Tommy with the dog. Tracey took three deeps breaths to try to calm down and then she walked towards the big blond man and his bouncing dog.

"Hello Tommy," Tracey began. Tommy spun round. His face flashed to a smile, then it went pale, the smile frozen in place.

"Hi," he said and ran his fingers through his hair, looking around. The silence stretched, and Tracey rushed in.

"Listen, I'm really sorry about last night. My behavior was awful, ungrateful, just awful. I'm sorry." She stopped, realizing she was repeating herself. Tommy's mouth fell open as if about to speak, but he just breathed in again and closed his mouth.

"How is your arm?" she said. She desperately wished he'd say something to help her out. She struggled to keep calm. Her nerves were bouncing in all directions.

"Em, fine," Tommy stammered, touching the arm above the elbow before he threw the ball. The dog raced across the lawn after it.

Tension dripped in the air between them, oppressive, suffocating Tracey. She swallowed.

"That's good, that's good," she said. "I just want you to know that…" She shoved her hands into her pockets to stop them from shaking and blinked hard, tilting her head back. Her humiliation would be complete if she cried. "Just that, I'm not proud of my behavior last night, and you deserved better. Thank you for saving me from Kieran." She heard the waver in her voice. She prayed that he'd say something.

"I'm glad you're okay. But I'm not sure what you want from me now. I wouldn't have done anything different," Tommy said. The warm man she talked and laughed with last night in the bar was gone.

"It's important to me that you know why I reacted the way I did," she said.

"Why would you care what I think?"

"Because I value your opinion," she said trying to keep her words as honest and simple as possible.

"You didn't seem to value it much last night."

Christ, he was stubborn.

"I'm sorry. I'm horribly embarrassed, but I can explain." She watched the dog come bounding towards them with the ball in his mouth, slobber flying. The dog took one look at Tommy and kept on running towards Tracey. Just as he was skidding to a halt, he stepped on the plastic bag Tracey had ignored and went sliding, frantically trying to stop. His momentum swiped Tracey's legs out from under her, bowling her over the top of the dog. A yelp, a mad flurry of limbs, and the dog got up. He proceeded to lick Tracey's face as she sat in a heap.

"Wolfie!" Tommy cried as he crossed the gap between them and hauled the dog off. He put out a hand to help Tracey up. She straightened up her legs and felt a sting across her knees. She looked down and saw that her jeans were ripped and her knees were grazed. Her tears spilled over their lids. To her added horror, she couldn't stop herself from crying, sobbing. The dog whined.

"You're bleeding, let me help." Tommy's voice was full of concern. It warmed Tracey despite the sting of pain and humiliation. Gently, Tommy put his arm around her and guided her to the nearest bench. He scolded Wolfie and made him lie down. The dog whimpered and thumped his tail. *Poor dog.* Tommy clicked the leash onto the dog's collar. The dog raised its eyes in a mournful look, then thumped its tail hard once again

"I'm okay, really." Tracey bit her lip. She burst into another rounds of sobs.

"Hey, hey, it's okay," Tommy said. "Please don't cry." His gentle tone made her unravel.

"It's just that I did think you were different from the other guys, Tommy." She might regret this later but right now she just wanted to get to the truth of the matter. She took a deep breath and looked up into his soothing grey eyes. "My father used to come home drunk a lot and yell at Mum. He'd break things and push her around. You know?" Tommy nodded. Tracey realized that he was holding her hand, and with his other hand he was giving her a hanky. She accepted it and dried her face. The worst was over. She felt steadier now.

"Anyways, Dermot was only ten the first time he stood up against Dad. The drunken bastard knocked him unconscious with the first blow. But that didn't stop Dermot the next time. As he got older he could take the beatings better, and Mum was left alone. We all were. Dermot took it for all of us. He never actually hit back at Dad. He just tried to stop him."

"And when I kicked Kieran it reminded you of your Dad?" Tommy said in a low voice.

Tracey nodded. Neither of them spoke for a while, but this time there was none of the tension strung between them. A breeze shuffled the leaves above them, and a woman pushed a stroller past them.

Tommy broke the silence.

"I'm sorry too. For my words, Tracey. They were cruel and cutting. Words can damage too. I'm really sorry." Tommy looked sad, as if he were talking about more than the words he'd spat at her last night. As if he'd suffered the wounds that words could inflict. Tracey wondered who had hurt him, surprised that this golden man could have anyone in his life who would want to hurt him. To inflict pain verbally, you had to have a connection to someone. That was why his words had hurt her last night.

"So, I'll accept your apology if you'll accept mine?" Tommy continued. A smile haunted the corners of his mouth. Christ, how she wanted to kiss it. She was close enough, but one screw up a week was enough.

"Agreed," she said. Relief rolled around her. It had been a good idea to come. She felt wrung-out but wholesome.

"I think Wolfie has some apologizing to do, too," Tommy said. The dog thumped his tail and flipped his tongue out quickly to lick Tracey's hand. Tracey grinned.

"It was hardly his fault someone was a litter bug, eh Wolfie?" She lifted her hand and scratched him behind his ear. The dog rolled his head to that side, closed his eyes and groaned with pleasure.

"Still, we should really get you new jeans." Tommy looked at the holes at the knees.

"No, really, these are old. I was going to make them into shorts for the summer anyways. Seriously, don't worry." Tracey stood up, trying not to wince at the sting. Tommy put his arm around her waist, allowing her to lean her weight on him. She felt warm and safe. The dog followed quietly behind.

"I could put some salve on that. The house is close by," Tommy offered.

"No thanks, I'll be fine," Tracey said. Everything was perfect as it was. She didn't want to outstay her welcome or screw things up by throwing herself at him.

"Will you be okay for driving?" Tommy asked. He was so sweet. Tracey's heart filled. Then she realized that there was no point. He was out of her league.

"I can drive. It just stings a little. The car's just outside the gates, in Elmwood," she said.

"Can I ask you something? Just don't get mad…" Tommy began.

Tracey sucked in a breath but nodded anyway.

"What did you ever see in that guy Kieran to begin with?"

"Kieran was alright before he got into drugs. No rocket scientist, but he seemed decent at first. And a good laugh. We had fun. It wasn't serious. At least not on my part," Tracey added. "But he started taking all sorts of drugs, and he changed. He became really paranoid and possessive of me. He wouldn't let me talk to any other men. It was ridiculous really, you know, childish jealousy." She wondered, was that enough of a warning for Tommy to be careful? Though from what she'd seen last night, it was evident that he could handle himself.

Tommy didn't reply and they walked the rest of the way in silence, but Tracey felt comfortable enough with that.

Tommy helped her into the car. Sitting down was particularly painful as the raw skin rubbed against the inside of the jeans.

"See you sometime, maybe with Molly and Dermot?" Tommy said in through the open window.

"Yes, I'd like that." She waved and then put the car in gear. Just then, a white Subaru pulled out from a space just across the street and about thirty yards down. Tracey gasped when she saw the black passenger door. Tommy was already at the crossing, heading back the way they'd come, to get back into the park. Her heart pounded.

Please don't let Kieran see Tommy.

The Subaru reached her car, slowed down briefly and then sped off, spinning its wheels. Tommy glanced up as it drove past. Wolfie barked, and Tommy's attention was drawn to the dog.

A shiver ran up Tracey's spine. Should she have warned Tommy or maybe she really needed to go to the police about Kieran? Things had changed now in Belfast, but it was still not pleasant to involve the police. Perhaps she should have followed her mother's advice and just joined the convent. At least her knees couldn't feel any worse.

Sunday, March 5th

CHAPTER TWELVE

Lying awake through the black night drained Molly. Every time she closed her eyes, she pictured Dermot making love to someone else - someone prettier, thinner and sexier. Wracked by spasms of anger, she could only think of Dermot with venom. She'd show him. Life was going to get very tough for Dermot Duggan.

Early Sunday morning, she got up and went downstairs. Her mother always told her that housework cured any heartache. Molly chose vacuuming. Dermot had requested that she not vacuum whilst he was in the house. The noise bothered him. Fucking *bothered* him! Ha, why not run the tumbler dryer too. She put on a load of washing. When she finished her vacuuming, she could hear Dermot moving around upstairs, getting ready for his supposed Sunday training session.

She followed him in her car when he left in the cab twenty minutes later. He never looked back, confident in his deception. Was he really that stupid? Or more to the point, did he think she was so dumb that it required no work to deceive her? If she'd been a bit slow on the uptake until now, well, things were about to change. By God, she was going to show Dermot she was no fool.

Molly followed the taxi until it pulled into a supermarket car park. The Sunday morning traffic was light, allowing Molly to pull over on the street in a spot that gave her a good view of the parking lot.

Dermot got out of the taxi and got into a black Peugeot 206 that had seen better days. An involuntary gasp escaped her as he nonchalantly kissed the female driver. It wasn't a simple kiss on the cheek either. He looked at her face before he kissed her. *The way he used to kiss me.* Molly blinked back the tears.

It was risky to follow the Peugeot, but Molly burned with curiosity. Who was she? Where did she live? What was so special about her? Was she skinny?

Following as close as she dared, Molly tracked them to a block of apartments on the outskirts of town. He's too tight to pay the taxi fare to here, Molly thought venomously as she watched Dermot follow a slender, black-haired woman to the door of a ground floor apartment.

Molly felt her blood pulsing in her head. She stared at the dark woman, appalled by her beauty, scared by the sleek physique. She could see why any man would run after her. Hurt lodged painfully in the centre of her chest. The apartment door closed. From the outside it looked normal, benign, like a body hiding cancer before the tumor bulged.

Molly's breaths came short. Her eyes squinted as she drove to the end of the street and turned left. She drove nowhere in particular, just moving, automatic and numb.

How dare he do this to her? Did everyone else know? She wanted to scream at him, claw at him, and rake her nails down his face. She'd been there for him—always! Did that bitch care for him like she did? Did she wash his clothes and drape them all around her home to dry? Did she cook him meals that only he liked? Did she fucking love him?

Jesus Christ, he could have given her all kinds of diseases, consorting with tramps like this.

Her control over her life took a nosedive in a plume of red smoke.

"I'll get you back for this," she said aloud. Her fingers tightened on the steering wheel, her knuckles white. As if the car had guided itself, she found herself at home. She went through the motions of letting herself in. In a daze, she walked up the stairs and eventually found herself staring at her reflection in the bathroom mirror, not even sure how long she'd been there. How could she look so normal, in light of what she had found out? Shouldn't her face be red with rage and her hair wild and unkempt with despair? Even her eyes looked calm as they locked her heartbreak behind them. To see her right now, no one would ever know the turmoil she was in.

Beside the sink, the toothpaste lay with the lid off, paste puddled in a minty mound. *That arsehole couldn't even respect her wishes and put the cap back on!* She should dump him. Kick him out and see what he'd do then. Fear clutched at her. No, he'd run to that tart, and then she'd have lost him completely. Molly didn't want to lose him. *Pathetic or what?*

Exasperated, she clutched the tube of toothpaste and squeezed it down the sink Molly washed it down with both taps on full blast. Just enough left for tonight and she'd make sure and get to the bathroom first in the morning. *Maybe not quite so pathetic.*

Back in the kitchen she flicked on the kettle and took the carton of milk from the fridge. She'd toss that in the morning too. She'd make that bastard suffer little by little.

As she waited for the kettle to boil, she wandered through the kitchen, idly opening cupboards, not sure what she was even looking for. She stopped when she found herself staring at the cans of dog food that Tommy had left behind yesterday. It felt like years ago, like looking back at her childhood. Only yesterday her life had been so different, teetering on the edge, sure, but today, nothing but despair.

She opened the fridge. The bag of red hot chili peppers she'd bought only on Friday were still there, too cheerily bright on the bottom shelf. She didn't even like chili. She made it especially for him and had to wear gloves to protect her fingers from the peppers' heat. She looked around the kitchen and saw wet clothes still in the washing machine from earlier, his clothes that she laundered every week. She picked up one of the chili peppers and crushed it into the crotch of a pair of boxer shorts. She felt the heat in her fingers but didn't care. One after another she ground chili peppers into all his underwear she could find. Perhaps she wouldn't run the dryer after all.

Seeing the pile of crushed peppers on the counter top, she reached into the cupboard and took out a tin of dog food. She heated a dollop of oil in a pan and then chopped two of the chilies, some onions, some garlic, and added them, with salt, to sizzle in a large pan. Molly put the underwear back on the radiators to dry. The smell of chilies infiltrated the house. She mashed up the dog food and added it to the pan, surprised that it didn't smell worse. She hid the empty cans in the wheelie bin in the backyard, pushing them as far down as she could reach. Back inside, the aroma of chilies filled the kitchen.

As the chili bubbled and plopped in the saucepan, Molly began to hope that the situation would improve. Yes, she was hurt, but she was going to fight for her marriage. It wasn't pathetic. It was brave and strong, and she was a good Catholic woman. He'd made a mistake many men made. In fact, some men did worse things. Look at Dermot's own father, coming home drunk and beating his wife and his kid. For better or worse, she'd vowed, and she was willing to forgive. Once things came to a head with Dermot and the air cleared and the affair was behind them, things would get better, much better. This would give her leverage to make some demands. Perhaps she would be able to get Dermot to quit football as a kind of penance, a way to show her that he was committed to them. She would come out of it all looking like the merciful, forgiving wife. Well, of course she was merciful and forgiving. She loved him.

In fact, some day they might even laugh about this. Someday, when they were both very old, she amended the thought, with no teeth and no hair: very, very old.

Molly heard Dermot's key in the front door. Through the open kitchen doorway, Molly watched him walk straight into the living room and turn the TV on. He flopped down onto the sofa as he flicked the channels, stopping eventually on a soccer match. The tinny sound of the crowd roaring and the commentator's whiney voice filled her ears. She clenched her teeth.

He should be coming in to say hello to me, to kiss me and ask about my day. She was unbalanced by his physical presence, the smell of his aftershave mixed with his sweat, the stubble on his chin, his shirt sleeves – crumpled cotton where he pushed them up above his elbow, too lazy to roll or fold them – like unmade beds.

She couldn't tell anyone, not even Tommy. Not yet. It would be too humiliating. There was no need for anyone to know until she had it all figured out. Not until after she confronted Dermot, though she wasn't sure when that would be because she found it hard to stand up to adults. She had no problem with her pupils. It was as if she donned an assertive cloak when she dealt with them. Thirty kids no older than six were a tough taskmaster, but Molly had a talent for connecting with the little ones. Several of her little boys had already proposed to her. The beauty of working with kids was that they didn't give you much time to dwell on your own problems. Some of her little ones had huge problems of their own. She often wondered how such little folk could survive some of the upheaval they experienced in their short lives and still manage to laugh and play. If they could do it, so could she.

"Dinner's ready. Shall we eat at the table?" Molly asked.

"I'll have mine here," Dermot said, without even looking at her. She walked past the set table, lifting a fork in her free hand and gave him the plate of chili.

She watched him take the first bite and swallow it, his dark eyes never leaving the screen. She walked back to the kitchen, saying nothing.

His sudden roar made her jump and turn around. Dermot lurched forward, punching the air with his fork. On the TV screen, a footballer ran around with his shirt over his head. Molly's heart-rate steadied.

She wanted to say, "Stop! Don't eat the chili!"

He might say, "Why? It smells great."

Perhaps she would follow up with, "No don't eat it. I'm so sorry. It's made from dog food, and I made it because I know... I know about your affair..."

He'd jump up, switch off the telly, and say "Oh my God, Molly, I'm sorry – she means nothing to me. I don't know why it happened. Forget the chili, I'm taking you out to Deans, we'll talk this all through. Just please forgive me. I love only you." He would move towards her and they'd embrace.

As she stood in the kitchen putting together her plate of salad and imagining their exchange, tears sprang to her eyes. *Fuck him, as if he'd bring you to KFC, never mind Dean's!*

Molly shook her head. As she sat down to eat by herself at the table, she looked over at Dermot. His black hair glinted with blue in the lights cast from the T.V. There wasn't much of the chili left on his plate. She felt ridiculously giddy, enjoying having one up on him. Funny how much she could love him and hate him in the same instant. Either way, she couldn't imagine life without him.

Monday, March 6th

CHAPTER THIRTEEN

After a night of tossing and turning, Dermot woke up feeling wretched and weary. It was Monday. He had to go to work. Bored by the weekly routine, he often felt that he had been destined for better things than sitting behind a desk all day, managing project schedules for a construction company. He'd probably earn more money as a builder or skilled tradesman. Maybe he'd need to, now that he was going to have to support a child.

He hated his job, but he made enough income for a comfortable living, a couple of pints at the weekend and sure, what more did he want? Dermot hummed *Tell me why I don't like Mondays* under his breath as he rolled out of bed.

He pulled on some underwear and sauntered into the bathroom. Molly left as he entered, flashing him a bright smile. Opening the bathroom cabinet he reached in for his toothbrush and toothpaste. No toothpaste. A twisted and clearly tortured for the last drop, empty tube lay in the bin.

"Molly, where's the toothpaste?"

"In the bathroom cabinet." Her voice floated in from the bedroom.

"It's empty. Is there any more?"

"Well, did you buy any more?" she answered.

Frustration ripped at him. He was about to reply that she knew he never did the shopping, but if he complained about Molly not doing the shopping properly, she might say that he could do it in future. He couldn't be bothered lugging all those crackly plastic bags from the supermarket, handles breaking and stuff falling out. OK, put up and shut up, he reckoned. He'd just get some chewing gum in the corner shop on the way to work.

Molly had already left the house by the time Dermot came down to the kitchen. Chili smell still clung to the room as Dermot poured himself a big bowl of Muesli. If he didn't have his muesli his whole routine was knocked off. Constipation would set in and he'd have stomach cramps by lunchtime.

The milk carton was empty.

"I don't believe this!" he said through unbrushed teeth, taking the carton out of the fridge and slamming it into the bin. He hated when the empty carton was put back in the fridge. Usually Molly was good about these things. It was as if she was setting out to annoy him today.

With a constitution well on the way to becoming clogged up and breath smelling like a dog had solved *its* constitution problems in his mouth, Dermot left the house, slamming the door behind him. He walked to work every day. It was less than a mile away, and there was a shop conveniently located halfway between the house and the office.

By the time Dermot reached the shop, something was definitely not right with him, and it wasn't his bowels or bad breath. Initially, he felt a decidedly unpleasant buzzing sensation around his genitals. Thinking that he simply needed to rearrange the ensemble, he put his hand in his pocket and ruffled around. The commotion brought relief and flames simultaneously. Dermot began to feel clammy. Had he picked up something nasty again? It had been so humiliating going to the doctor the last time.

At the till queue, Dermot attempted another furtive fondle via his trouser pocket. A burning sensation rippled between his legs, and a groan of pain escaped him. Abruptly, a voice behind him shrieked, making him jump.

"Oh my God! You are disgusting. Quick, Annie, call the police." A tiny wrinkled creature was spitting at him. "People like you are sick. Get out now or we'll call the police."

Flustered and embarrassed, Dermot left the shop filled with angry old ladies who continued to berate him even as he crossed the road. He was bathed in sweat, felt terrible, and had no hope of getting chewing gum unless he took a detour. All he wanted to do was stand waist deep in freezing cold water.

Fifteen minutes into his working day, Dermot tried to figure out how he could block the sink in the toilets and fill it with water. Of course, something as simple as a plug did not exist in the men's toilets. Fortunately, on this floor the sink was inside the same room as the actual toilet bowl, so the door could be locked and give him sanctuary. If it had just been a row of sinks and stalls, like downstairs, there'd be some explaining to do when his colleagues came in and caught him soaking his meat and two veg in the sink. The idea even made Dermot grin as he stuffed toilet roll down the plughole.

The cool relief was bliss, but work had to be done. Delicately Dermot patted himself dry with toilet roll then got dressed. He had a short-lived respite. No sooner had he sat down than the heat fired up again. The rest of his working day consisted of frequent trips to the toilet. He felt tortured, trying to decide whether or not he should go to the doctor. The pain wasn't so bad that it would force him to undergo that embarrassment, so he reckoned he'd give it a day or two first and see how things went. In the meantime, he could buy some ointment at the chemist – maybe chamomile lotion – that was good for lots of things.

He wondered where he could have picked this up. Not from Molly, confident she didn't sleep around; they'd not been having sex much in the past six months anyway. He'd had other flings in the past but was keeping all the action for Sheila now. He figured she might have given him something. If so, would it hurt the baby, handicapping it somehow? Had she been sleeping around and given this to him? Was it really his baby after all?

Monday, March 6th

CHAPTER FOURTEEN

Teaching kept Molly's mind off her worries, and before long it was time for the children to go home. She had the empty classroom all to herself to prepare for the next day. The gerbil cage was starting to smell a bit. Another task to add to her list of things to do.

Angie, the gerbil, was an easy catch. Molly grabbed her quickly and put her into the spare cage, where the little rodent stood quivering, her big eyes blinking. Then Molly lifted out the fluff and paper that Angie, who kept a very messy home, had strewn throughout the cage. Molly scraped up the feces and sawdust mixed with gerbil food that covered the floor.

It reminded Molly of muesli. Anger ignited at the base of her throat. Bloody Dermot had to have his muesli every morning and not just any old muesli either. She, like the mug she was, had to drive to the other side of town to a health food store that sold the only kind that he'd eat. It just had to have the toasted flax seeds in it – seeds that looked just like this damn Gerbil shit. Ha! Muesli – she'd give him some fresh muesli all right. An idea formed. She couldn't resist getting a little Ziploc plastic bag and putting a couple of scoops into it. She sealed it and popped it into her handbag telling herself that she might never use it, but the thought of having more secret revenge eased the stabbing behind her ribs. She emptied the rest into the bin, added clean sawdust, food and water, and returned Angie to her cage.

The gerbil ran around sniffing, and then settled down to tearing paper, contented.

After a quick Google search, Molly was satisfied that Gerbil poop wasn't likely to poison the bastard. She powered down her computer and left the classroom.

***

Later that evening, Dermot arrived home from work and went straight upstairs to have a bath. One look at Dermot was enough to tell Molly that something was tormenting him, and she knew what that something was. She surprised herself with the wickedness she possessed, but it was nothing compared to the wickedness he had perpetrated against her.

Molly cooked dinner and called Dermot down. He sat at the table, and she served up the left-over chili from the previous night whilst she had another salad. He wriggled around in his seat, trying to get comfortable.

She smiled at him, trying to look as benign as possible. Then she put on her most docile tone of voice.

"What's the matter, pet? You don't seem to be able to settle."

"Nothing, nothing," he replied tersely.

Molly watched him change position a couple of times. It crossed her mind that he had not mentioned his discomfort and wondered if he had ever caught something before and hidden it from her. She squashed down her rage as she spoke, trying to sound nonchalant.

"What about some music? Red Hot Chili Peppers perhaps?"

Putting the disk into the machine, she struggled to keep the grin off her face. She liked the twisted justice. The more he thought he caught something nasty, the more he would try to conceal it, so he'd never think to ask if she was sabotaging his underwear. Maybe he'd even stop sleeping with that slut. There wasn't much going on in the marital bed these days anyway, so it didn't matter to her. She wanted to hurt him as much as she was hurting, or even better, hurt that bitch he was sleeping with. Bitch, bitch, bitch! Itch, itch, itch!

Tuesday, 7th March

The worry started eating away at Molly, literally, making her clothes feel looser. Having a curvaceous figure, Molly always aspired to lose weight, but she had a weakness for chocolate. Molly rejoiced at the prospect of dropping a dress size. This would help in her plan to draw Dermot back to her and keep him there. Some new, smaller clothes were needed. She had to pick up Fran's blood pressure prescription anyway, so she decided she would hit the shops on her way home from school on Tuesday.

It wasn't called retail therapy for nothing, she thought, as she browsed through the rails, caressing fabrics and comparing colors. She was feeling better than she had all week. Still - it was only Tuesday. She needed to think about when she would approach Dermot. It was hard to wear the mask, but she needed to think carefully about her approach and what she would demand from him.

"Hi Molly!" A voice broke into her thoughts from across the rail.

Molly looked up and smiled. Tracey approached and embraced her. The two girls looked more like siblings than Tracey and Dermot did, nearly mirror images of each other except for the eyes. Tracey's were a shade of blue darker, twinkling with the smile that lit up her face.

Not only Dermot's favorite sister, Tracey and Molly were bosom buddies, having more in common with each other than either had with Dermot. Molly considered suggesting a coffee so she could tell

Tracey about Dermot's infidelity, but quickly shied away from the idea. It was just too hard to hang words on the deed.

"Hi Tracey, what's up? Have you the day off work?"

"Oh God, no, this *is* work. The boss needs an outfit for a grand opening on Thursday, and I've to come up with something."

Tracey cast her eyes to the skies. She worked as a Personal Assistant for some executive type, and her job description seemed to cover a vast array of areas. Molly thought it seemed like a fun job, though she realized that she only felt like that because Tracey's positive attitude and boundless energy would make any job appear attractive. Luckily for Tracey, her boss hated shopping, but she could send Tracey to shop for her because Tracey was of a similar build.

"Let's team up and make it an expedition," said Tracey.

It all seemed so normal. Molly found it easier to breathe. Telling Tracey would spoil this. Instead, she painted a smile on her face and said, "Sure!"

The girls hit the shops with a mission. They carried clothes to the fitting rooms by the dozen, so that as Tracey pointed out, they only had to undress once in each shop. Molly noticed the fitting room staff grimace to see them coming loaded down with merchandise.

The shops were quiet, and they had the fitting rooms to themselves. They decided to pile into the large cubicle, usually reserved for wheelchair users, so they could chat without having to shout at each other.

"What did you do for your birthday? Dermot said he was taking you out?" Tracey asked as she pulled a dress over her head.

"Oh, we just went to Mc Ginty's for something to eat," Molly replied, relieved that Tracey couldn't read her face.

"What? That brother of mine needs a good kick up the arse sometimes," Tracey said. "I'd have loved a big night out for you, but Dermot sounded like he had a secret planned just for the two of you, so I didn't want to get involved."

Oh, he had a secret all right, thought Molly bitterly, but she put a bright tone in her voice to divert Tracey's attention.

"So what did you end up doing at the weekend then?"

Tracey pulled the last dress from her head and stood with tousled hair. Her face flushed red. She couldn't quite look Molly in the eye.

"What? What? Tell me. You met someone?" Molly said.

"No." Tracey blushed deeper and fidgeted with the top she was about to try on. She eventually said, "I don't really want to talk about it." She turned her back to Molly. So Dermot wasn't the only one with secrets.

For a moment Molly felt her bitterness extend to Tracey. Fine, don't share, she thought. Maybe Tracey knew about Dermot's tart. The hairs on the back of Molly's neck tingled. Could Tracey keep that from her? She shoved it away. Tracey was keeping something from her for sure. She loved Tracey nearly as much as she loved Dermot and couldn't bear to lose both of them.

Suddenly the changing room felt too small, its jumble of clothes in the corner untidy and depressing. These were the clothes that no one wanted. Molly pulled on her own clothes as fast as she could.

"I have to go," she said. She had to get away from Tracey before she exploded and the whole ugly mess came out.

"But we just..." Tracey began.

"See ya." Molly pushed through the door, still buttoning her jeans.

Molly's hands shook as she drove home. She felt insane. How much longer could she bottle this up? Would it be better if she confronted him tonight? They'd probably have a rocky night thrashing things out, but maybe Dermot would be so repentant that he'd cancel his football trip to Leeds next weekend. Ha, as if she'd let him out of her sight again. Maybe they could go to Donegal with Tommy and be a proper couple again. Yes, tonight it would have to be. Optimism infused her. It was going to be all right. Soon.

When Molly dropped the tablets off, Fran looked her in the eyes and asked, "Are you all right, dear?"

"Fine, fine, great actually." Molly tried to sound bright and cheery, unable to bear telling Fran what was playing on her. It would make it too real, and Fran had a way of making Molly face facts. She couldn't handle that.

"How was your birthday?" She asked, reading Molly as if her thoughts were displayed on a ticker board.

Molly nearly choked, managing a glib, "Grand, just lovely."

Molly sensed that Fran knew there was more and loved her for backing off, leaving Molly with her pain and confusion. She had no words for Fran to describe how she felt.

Alone in her own house next door, Molly tried to focus her thoughts on what to tell Dermot as she sorted the laundry. She paired all Dermot's socks and went to his drawer to put them away when she found the envelope with his tickets for Leeds. As she lifted them out to set the socks in, something fluttered out of the envelope and dropped on the bed.

She stopped, stricken, unable to breathe. There were two tickets!

One ticket bore his name, and the other read "Sheila Mooney". And they weren't going to Leeds. Molly felt the bile rise in her throat. They were going to Euro Disney.

The bastard! Fury stabbed her, a physical pain in her chest. She gasped for air, suffocating as the reality dawned on her. He was taking that bitch away with him.

He had hardly ever taken Molly any further than Dublin, unless she had nagged at him for ages to go on holiday, and now instead of bringing her with him for her birthday treat, he was taking that tart he was banging on the side.

Frenzied, she ripped the tickets into the smallest pieces she could. It didn't take long and her rage was still foaming, smashing against the inside of her head like storm waves on a pier.

She heard Dermot come in the front door and pound up the stairs straight to the bathroom. The shower went on. He must have been with the slut this evening. Dermot never used to take this many showers and certainly not at seven thirty in the evening, unless he was going out. And by God, she vowed, he was not going out tonight!

Molly ran downstairs to the kitchen. She paused a moment, waiting while the water got good and hot upstairs, and then turned on the hot tap. She could hear Dermot above her in the bathroom cursing as his water went cold. Anticipating that he would turn on the hot tap higher, she swiftly turned off the hot tap and blasted the cold. Upstairs, Dermot yelped. Downstairs, Molly grinned maliciously. Dermot got out of the shower.

He was dressed by the time Molly followed him into the bedroom. Her nerves stretched and sung, buzzing in her head as she fought to gain control.

"The affair has to stop," she said, quietly and calmly, despite feeling her blood pounding at her temple.

He blanched. His dark eyes flew wide open, shocked, and then they clamped down. She could see that he too fought for control.

"What do you mean?" he stammered. He stood statuesque, hands on his hips, defiant despite the quiver in his voice.

"Don't try to deny it. I know about her. I know that you are seeing another woman. You were planning on going away with her this weekend. Here's your tickets!" She flung what looked like a fist-full of confetti at him. Gratification filled her as she watched horror flood his features.

"You silly bitch!" he roared, his eyes blazing, control lost. "Those fucking tickets cost me six hundred quid."

"Should have got an e-ticket then." She smirked. "Nope, you're grounded this weekend, Darling. No football and no floosie!" She nearly enjoyed this.

He thundered around the room cursing, trying to pick up the tickets. He'd lost control whilst she kept hers —intact—a victory. Now she only had to threaten to throw him out. Then he'd start pleading, and telling her he was sorry. She'd negotiate some very strict terms that involved him spending much more time with her and less at football or other extracurricular activities. She felt empowered.

"Fuck off you stupid bitch. I'm leaving you!" he said.

His jaw clenched, his black eyes blazed, ripping into hers. Suddenly she was flummoxed. This wasn't going as planned. The husband always chooses the wife. How many stories were there of how silly women were to fool around with married men because the mistress would always be the one hurt? They were the ones left alone, not the wife, not her.

"You can't," she said through gritted teeth, grappling for poise. "You're my husband; you're married to me. You'll get over her, and we'll have counseling and get this back on track. We love each other too much to let this come between us."

"I don't love you anymore."

The sentence hung in the air between them. To her it seemed that neither one could breathe, that neither one believed the words had come to the light of day. Even so, he looked relieved, but that harrowing sentence dumped Molly on the doorway of a nightmare.

"You can't mean it," her voice little more than a whisper.

"I'm sorry to tell you like this," he said more gently now, his voice soft though his eyes still flashed flinty. Hope sparked in her, sputtered and died. "But I have to. We are having a baby."

Reality swung out from under her. She was falling. Down, down, faster, faster – and yet there she stood in front of him.

"What? What? But you always. . . " she managed to say.

"It's different with her."

Molly searched the black depths of his eyes, longing for answers to questions she couldn't bear to formulate. She couldn't believe it, couldn't believe that her heart still beat. That time hadn't stopped. She drew in a breath. How long had it been since she had last done that? It was simply so much effort now. She couldn't believe that she had been doing it all her life and only now noticed that she breathed. Then pain hit her. It seared her chest right behind her sternum. Her heart ripped open.

She conceded defeat, barely aware as Dermot grabbed his jacket, brushed past her and left the house. She sat down on the bed, numb with shock. He was gone. It was over.

Tuesday, 7th March

CHAPTER FIFTEEN

The door slammed behind Dermot as he made a hasty exit. The night hung around him, cold with moisture. He shoved his hands into his jacket. His heart raced. He thought he'd been clever. Stress rocketed through him. The tickets! What a vindictive bitch.

He looked up and down the length of the empty street, then took his hand from the jacket pocket and gave his groin a scratch. It still stung. Scratching didn't really help. He stuffed his hand back into his jacket pocket and hoped that he had given that bitch a dose of whatever it was. All that money and the tickets were in shreds. Sheila would go ballistic. *Sheila.*

He hadn't banked on moving in with her so soon, but he didn't think she would mind. She was mad about him. He had that effect on women, and he couldn't help it any more than his Dad had been able to help being an alcoholic.

Hardly aware of where he walked, Dermot arrived at a taxi depot and went in. The office smelled of stale cigarette smoke and alcohol. There were stains in the concrete floor in the corner. No wonder the place stank of urine. The guy behind the Plexiglas informed him, through grunts and a nod of the head, that a taxi waited for him outside. Dermot sprinted out, eager to escape the stench.

Dermot gave the driver Sheila's address, then settled back to mull over his next move. Molly was entitled to half of everything they owned. He'd have a chat with his mate, Ronnie, who was a solicitor. It had amused Dermot in the past when Molly and Ronnie had had rows about the law, especially about his defense of people that he knew were guilty. Molly despised Ronnie and could not see the funny side of his often quoted advice for when one was caught red-handed: "Deny, deny, *deny.*"

Dermot thought grimly that he should have done just that earlier tonight when Molly had confronted him. "I'm just too honest to be a solicitor," he thought.

He would now have a baby to support. Sheila didn't make a great deal of money as a beautician. He might lose out financially, unless he could get his thinking cap on and quick.

Thankfully, Sheila was in. He didn't have a key yet. It was cold outside and at least a ten-minute walk to the nearest pub. Dermot pulled on a mask of joviality as Sheila swung open the front door.

"Surprise!" he chimed as he put his arms out for her.

"Dermot! What are you doing here?"

"Aren't you pleased to see me?"

"Well, of course I am but, well, it's just, I wasn't expecting you tonight. But it is a nice surprise. How did you get away? What did you tell Molly?"

"I told her I was seeing you, and that you were pregnant, and that I was leaving her for you," Dermot said, following Sheila through to the living room.

"Ach, Dermot, seriously, quit acting the wag. What *did* you say?"

"Honestly, Sheila, that's what I told her." Dermot took both of Sheila's hands so that he was facing her and said in a more gentle tone of voice, "The truth's out, Sheila. I couldn't help it. I'm all yours." He moved to embrace her, but she backed off.

"What's wrong?" Dermot thought she'd be thrilled, but Sheila turned white. She looked positively appalled. Shock, he reasoned, and joy too, in that weird way that women can cry when they are happy. The way they did on Miss World.

"Jesus Christ, Dermot!" She breathed the words so that they sounded more like a low hiss.

"What?" Dermot felt impatient for his hero's welcome, "I thought you'd be pleased. I thought this was what you wanted?"

"It's just so sudden! How did she take it?"

"Who?"

"Christ-of-almighty. Molly! Who'd you think? The Queen of fucking England?" Her sharpness wounded him.

"Why do you give a fuck about Molly anyway? You weren't too concerned about her when you were letting yourself get impregnated by her husband."

"You bastard!" she snarled, her eyes narrowing.

Crap, he thought, why did he say things to Sheila to try to provoke a reaction? Why couldn't he just be passive – like when he dealt with Molly? He couldn't afford to offend Sheila right now. He needed somewhere to stay.

"Oh God, I'm so sorry," he said, watching her face for signs of forgiveness. "It was awful," he said, aiming for pathos. "We had a terrible row, and it all just spilled out. It's been so hard. I haven't been able to get you out of my mind."

"It's just so sudden," she said, and then added softly, "Molly must be devastated."

Remorse battered weakly at him. He banished the picture of Molly's defeated eyes.

"Really, what did she say?"

"Not much. I left before she had a chance to say too much." Dermot couldn't really recall what she had said; he had been too infuriated about the tickets. "She found the tickets for the weekend." Dermot hesitated slightly, thinking of the tiny pieces of paper she had reduced them to. "She ripped them to pieces. She was furious."

"I'm not surprised, are you? Her husband has just told her he's having an affair and a baby with another woman. How'd you think she'd be? Happy for us?" Sheila's sounded decidedly sarcastic. She should be berating the bitch for ruining their trip.

"Shit, whose side are you on?"

"God, Dermot! Don't be so bloody childish! It's the electronic age! I'm sure you could get the damn things reissued or something," Sheila said.

"I suppose. But they probably charge me something to do it."

"See if you can get them refunded. I don't feel like going now." She placed her hand over her stomach.

"They're not refundable. I took the cheap deal," Dermot mumbled.

Sheila rolled her eyes up and shook her head as they rolled back down. "Well she did us a favor then. So where did you move to?"

"Ach ya know, it was all so quick. I haven't had time to figure it all out yet." He couldn't understand why she was so rankled. He looked at her sheepishly. "Can I stay here till we come up with a plan?"

Sheila frowned and opened her mouth as if to speak, then closed it, her head turning slowly away.

"It's late. And cold," Dermot said, "and I've nowhere else."

"There's your mother's house," Sheila said, tilting her head to one side, folding her arms and leaning back against the wall.

"Ah God, that would be torture. She's a head case, and she'll go ballistic, and I'll have to listen to her crying and going on and on…"

"Okay, okay. We'll start here for tonight and we'll figure the rest out tomorrow," she said, interrupting him.

He grinned, and she reached out and tousled his hair. He breathed a sigh of relief and kissed her, pulling her down to the sofa with him. Eventually, as the kissing became more intense, Dermot began to squirm. He pulled away, and Sheila looked askance at him . He was too embarrassed to tell her that he might have an STD, unsure where he had picked it up.

He'd had a one-night stand about seven months ago at a stag do for one of his mates in Edinburgh - some wee lassie from the Scottish Highlands who was at University. She and her mates had invited some of the lads back to their digs for drinks and some drugs after the pub. Dermot didn't do drugs but had gone anyway because the girl was cute, and he reckoned he was in with a chance. The flat was a mess. Dermot thought that three girls should have cleaned it up better. The girl, whose name Dermot couldn't remember, said she smoked marijuana and snorted cocaine on occasions. At least she didn't inject, Dermot thought at the time. He had his standards. Even so, he knew he should have been more careful.

Now, he was itching like a colony of fire ants were in his pants, leaving him too uncomfortable for any sex. He'd have to say something to Sheila. A half truth might accomplish the same end, but without the fallout.

"It's just that I've got a bit of a groin strain after footy, and well, things are a bit tender in that region. I'm not sure if I'll be able to perform," he said, his face growing hot.

"I did a massage course for beauty therapy. I'll see if I can ease it out." Before Dermot could object Sheila opened Dermot's jeans buttons and slipped her hand down inside his boxers. Dermot smiled. He enjoyed the sensation, but as he grew more aroused, the stinging got worse, and he pulled her hand out. Sheila looked at her fingers.

"That's weird!" she said, "It tingles!" She sniffed at her hand making Dermot even more self conscious.

"This is weird," she said. Dermot squirmed as Sheila lowered her head to his groin and inhaled.

"Phew, that reeks," she said.

"What? How do you mean?" Dermot was flummoxed. "I showered before I came over and put on all clean clothes – I can't be smelly already."

"Clean undies too?"

"Absolutely! Molly had them folded and in the drawer."

Sheila began to laugh. "How long did you say Molly knew about us?"

"Well actually, she didn't say. Why?"

"When did you last eat chili?"

"Chili?" What an odd question. "Last night."

"Did you cook it?"

"Nope, Molly did, why?"

"Have you ever cooked it for yourself?"

"Yeah, loadsa times."

"Let me guess. Dried chili powder not the real chili peppers?"

"Yeah, so?"

"If the chili peppers are hot enough they can make your skin burn. I always use gloves. I think she used some in your underpants! That's not groin strain, love. Face facts: You're hot stuff!" Sheila doubled over laughing.

"That bitch!" Dermot couldn't see the funny side. He had suffered agonies since yesterday morning. He jumped up, peeled off his jeans, and then tore at his underpants. Free at last, he aped around the room fanning the big lad.

"What do I do now? It's still hot!"

"Well, I always used to eat ice cream after hot food but…"

Dermot rushed into the kitchen opened the freezer and taking the ice cream, stuck his throbbing —for all the wrong reasons — member into the hard frozen ice cream.

"That's not going to work, Dermot. The ice cream is too hard. You need to let it melt. Give it over to me." Sheila turned on the hot tap. Dermot moved to give Sheila the ice cream tub, but stopped as if turned to stone. Horrified, he didn't dare move.

"Sheila. It's stuck. My willy's stuck to the ice cream!" His voice rose in panic. Sheila started to chortle again.

"Shit! Shit! What do I do? What do I do?" The ice on the outside of the tub was starting to melt as it warmed beneath Dermot's hand and became slippery. Dermot howled in pain as the ice cream tub slid from his grasp and fell to the floor, tugging his penis briefly, then letting it go as it claimed a small but painful layer of skin.

Dermot stood squealing, naked from the waist down, with a piece of his foreskin still attached to the raspberry ripple.

Sheila stared at the tub on the floor, shook her head and said, "Oh dear! What a waste of ice cream!"

Tuesday, 7th March

CHAPTER SIXTEEN

Tommy loved all the new and exciting changes taking shape at his new salon, Clippers. The walls, painted in shades of blue and grey, broke up the large main area into sections. Sail cloths hung from the ceiling, creating individual booths for each client. Mirrors shaped like port holes gave a general nautical feel, despite the shiny hair driers and wall of sinks towards the back. Theme balanced well with function.

He held a hand mirror up to the back of his client's head and angled it so she could see the wedged bob he'd just cut and styled.

"Oh my God, I just love it," she said.

Tommy placed her somewhere in her forties. She'd come in with mid-length hair, split ends and inch-long pepper-pot roots that gave way to a faded blonde.

"You did exactly what I wanted," she continued. "I'm so glad that you talked me into this color." She ran her fingers up through the back of her cayenne locks. "It's so rich and young looking. And this style will be so much easier. Thank you. Thank you so much."

Tommy thrived on this, another satisfied customer, another woman feeling better about herself. He hoped her joy would last at least six weeks until she needed the roots touched up. He walked her to the reception desk, cleverly shaped like a crow's nest from a ship.

An artistically arranged pile of rope and netting hid the till from the customer's view.

He'd love to show the salon to Tracey. As PA to a bar outfitter, she might have some more ideas for décor. Feck it! The décor looked fine. He just wanted an excuse to talk to her. Tommy had always rated how much he wanted to go out with someone by how much he thought about her and how those thoughts played on him. It perturbed him that he couldn't get Tracey out of his head. She had that combination of "little girl lost" and "Amazon warrior." She'd looked so defeated when she'd fallen over the dog on Sunday, yet she'd had the courage to seek him out and apologize to him. That took a lot of guts. The memory of her voice, trembling a little as she spoke about her violent father, tugged at him. He'd wanted to scoop her up into a hug and protect her forever. He wanted to make her happy again. Watch her face as she smiled. Touch the soft golden curls that tumbled down onto her forehead before she'd tuck them behind an ear. He couldn't stop thinking about her, her sweet, flowery smell, the way her nose crinkled at the corners when she was about to say something she knew would be funny. Something about her vulnerability attracted him and scared him at the same time. Maybe he feared hurting her more? So far that is all he seemed to have accomplished. His stomach flipped when he thought about what would have happened had he not been there on Saturday to drag that ape off her.

Pull yourself together man, he thought, rubbing his hands together, *time to get back to business*. He'd just closed the till, depositing the client's check, when his phone rang. The display showed Molly.

"Hi, Molls. How are ya?"

"Tommy?" Molly's voice was distraught, "Oh, God, Tommy!" She broke down into sobs, unable to even form words. The sound clattered down the line to Tommy.

"Christ, Molly, what's wrong?"

"It's Dermot," she gasped between sobs. Christ! Had he died? "I can't... It's just. Oh, God. Please, can you come over? Now?"

Adrenalin coursed through him.

"Yes, yes. I'll be right there. Do you need to call an ambulance or anything? Is he okay?"

"I don't need an ambulance. It's just... It's something else. no one's hurt, but please come quick. I can't tell you on the phone."

Molly broke down crying again, and Tommy couldn't make any sense out of her garbled words. He grabbed his jacket and keys and ran to his car.

"I'll be right there. Hold on, Pet. I'm coming right now. Don't go anywhere. Actually, go into the kitchen and put the kettle on. I'll be there in five minutes. OK?"

"OK. Just hurry please!" Molly sounded so lost.

What the hell had happened? He couldn't drive fast enough. The streets of Belfast were crammed with traffic. His tires squealed as he took off from traffic lights, and horns blared at him as he dodged in and out between the other cars.

Molly's front door opened as Tommy reached for the bell.

"What's wrong?" Tommy asked, frightened now. "Where's Dermot?"

"He's at his... He's not here. He's gone." Molly whispered.

"What? Gone where?" Tommy could hardly hear Molly.

Christ, had Dermot been lifted by the army? But that wasn't how things went now. Tommy hoped so anyways.

"Molly, what happened?" Tommy raised his voice, and she looked up startled, as if she'd forgotten about him.

"He's left me." She broke down into sobs.

Tommy hugged her to him before letting her go and guiding her into the living room. Molly curled herself up into an impossibly small ball and sat on one end of the sofa, staring into the empty fireplace. She seemed catatonic with grief.

"Do you want to tell me what happened?" he asked her gently.

She shook her head. "I can't. It's awful. He's gone. He doesn't l-l-love me." She started to blubber and talk at the same time, leaving Tommy at a loss. He couldn't get any sense out of Molly. So they'd had a row and he'd left, but what the hell had her in such a state of shock? Anger and frustration flared.

"Molly. Listen to me. Did he hurt you? Did he hit you?"

"No."

"So you had a row?"

She nodded and sniffed, gulping as she breathed out.

"Molly, he'll be back. You'll sort it out."

At this point she broke down and wept. Tommy felt helpless as he held her, rocking her as he would a small child.

"We need a game plan. Do you want me to talk to Dermot?"

Molly stopped crying and huffed in a couple of deep breaths as she shook her head. "He might listen to Tracey," she said.

Tommy sat up straighter.

"She's Dermot's favorite sister. She was my best friend." She finished in a whisper.

"And there's no reason why she still wouldn't be. Do you want me to call her?"

"I think she might know. I was talking to her this afternoon, and she was really cagey. I felt like she was keeping something from me," Molly said. A fresh wave of tears ran down her face.

"Give me her number, and I'll call her," Tommy said, wiping tears from her face.

His nerves hummed as he waited for Tracey to answer. He couldn't wait to hear her voice, yet he worried that she'd known about this beforehand. He wanted to believe she didn't. Hopefully they'd get to the bottom of it. Perhaps Molly just over-reacted.

He heard a soft, enquiring, "Hello?"

"Hi, it's Tommy, Molly's cousin." Too perky, he thought. *Calm down, you're not sixteen.*

"Oh, hi. How are you?"

He could hear a smile in her tone. His heart lifted only to be beaten down as he spoke his next words, his tone more muted. "I'm good. Where are you?"

"Downtown, what's up?"

"I've some bad news."

"What is it?" she asked.

"I'm at Molly's house. Something awful has happened. Dermot's left her." Silence seeped from the other end.

"Hello?" Tommy said.

"Yes, yes I'm still here. What do you mean 'Dermot's left her'?"

"That's all I can get out of her. She's in a state. Could you, would you come over. I really need help."

"Oh, my God," Tracey said. "Dermot's, like, left? Like as in gone-to-the-pub-for-a-pint left or divorce left?"

"I think it's the second one. Honestly Tracey, she's absolutely devastated. I've never seen Molly this upset before. I don't know how to handle it. It's like she's catatonic. She just sits on the sofa staring, or else she's crying. I'm sorry Tracey. It's such an awful shock."

Tommy heard her sniff. God how could he ask her this next question? His stomach turned to water as he said his next words.

"Molly was wondering, had you been talking to him in the last couple of days? Has he said anything?"

"Oh my God! No, no, Jesus Christ, like I'd keep that from Molly. She's my best friend. Is that what you think of me? Bloody hell!"

"God, no!" Tommy said. "But Molly just wondered…"

"Does she think I knew something? Is that why she ran out on me this afternoon? What a fucking mess! I'm coming right over." She hung up.

Was she going to arrive all fired up again? Tommy felt like the messenger about to be shot. His mind raged at Dermot, but he wasn't sure how to handle Tracey. Nothing new there.

Tuesday, 7th March

CHAPTER SEVENTEEN

Tracey hung up the phone. She blew out through her mouth directing the air upwards lifting her fringe off her forehead. She wanted to kill Dermot. A pulse throbbed below her right ear. How could he leave Molly? Especially now, with their father gone. And Tommy and Molly thought she knew something about it. She took a deep breath, in through her nose and out through her mouth, but her heart still raced. She felt queasy.

She wanted to go in to Molly's with guns blazing, declaring her innocence and ignorance of the matter, but she pulled her reins in. Molly needed her now, not more aggravation. She could hardly blame her for being suspicious. If the person who is supposed to love you the most in the world can do this, then what are others capable of?

It took Tracey less than twenty minutes to drive to Molly's house. She walked from her car to Molly's door, fast heels clacking on the pavement. Their sound made her feel purposeful.

Tommy opened the door for her, his tall frame filling the doorway. She looked into his grey eyes and saw a storm pulsing there, yet his face remained calm, and a smile lingered over his lips. Tracey's eyes felt scorched, and her chin wobbled as she tried to speak. For a moment they stood looking at each other—wordless. Then Tommy gathered her up in a hug. Instantly, she felt better. She soaked up strength from his embrace. He smelt of the ocean, of fresh air, of life.

She squeezed him back, and then pulled apart to look up into his face before speaking quietly and urgently.

"God I needed that," she stammered.

Tommy smiled, flushed pink and stood back giving her back her space. "Where is she?"

"On the sofa. Hasn't moved from there all evening. I've never seen her so withdrawn. I think she's in shock," Tommy said, opening the living room door and ushering Tracey through from the hallway.

Tracey entered the living room and saw Molly solidified onto one spot on the sofa. She seemed waifish, curled up on the dark red cushions, her skin translucent white in contrast to the color around her, as startling as blood on bandages. Her hair hung matted and tangled around her face, nearly hiding her mottled, white and flushed cheeks. Even though raw red, her eyes were as startling as ever, like a Husky dog's eyes. The iris, outlined with a navy blue rim, faded through a clear pale blue to nearly white by the time it reached the dark contrast of the pupil.

"What's going on Love? What happened?" Tracey asked.

"I thought you knew? Earlier when I asked you about the weekend, and you went all strange."

Tracey looked over Molly's head at Tommy. He pursed his lips together into a straight line and nodded slightly. He got it. He believed her.

"Molly, I swear, I've no idea what is happening with Dermot. Do you want me to ring him?" Tracey asked.

Molly nodded and sniffed again.

Hands trembling, Tracey found Dermot's name in her phone and hit the green call button.

"Hey, little sis."

Anger flared in her at his breezy tone.

"What's going on? I'm at Molly's," Tracey said.

"Oh that." His tenor shifted down a gear. "So she called you?"

"Is it true?" she asked.

"What did Molly tell you?"

"Dermot don't play games. Are you leaving Molly?" She felt sickened by the very words.

"Yes."

"What? Why? Why would you do that?"

"There's someone else," Dermot said.

Tracey felt the breath leave her body. She looked over at Molly. They made eye contact, and Molly shook her head slowly, her eyebrows pulled together, her forehead furrowed. She suddenly looked a hundred years old. Tracey moved out to the hallway pulling, the door closed behind her.

"How the fuck could you do this?" Tracey hissed at Dermot. "What brand of idiot are you? Molly's your wife. Come home, you moron."

"Look. I'm leaving Molly because I got…because Sheila is pregnant. It's complicated. No, actually it's not. We love each other." Behind Dermot's words, Tracey could hear her father's voice weaving a necklace of lies.

"Oh for God's sake, Dermot," Tracey said, spitting his name, "you're married to Molly. You love Molly."

"Not any more. It's different with Sheila," Dermot said. "We're soul mates."

"Soul mates? Soul mates, my arse. Don't make me laugh!" Tracey shouted. "That's rich coming from you. Mister 'I don't do squishy touchy feely, too-good-for counseling.' I thought you didn't believe in crap like that?"

"That all changes when you find yours."

"Bullshit! That's just what Dad used to do – changed the rules to suit himself. As if we weren't all messed up enough with his shenanigans? Now that he's dead, are you going to take up where he left off?" Tracey stopped.

Dermot kept quiet.

"Dermot – are you still there?" Tracey asked. She knew how those words could punch a hole in him, but she needed to make him *see*.

"Yeah," he said.

"Look, we need to talk this out rationally. Find out why you did this," Tracey began.

"No," Dermot interrupted, "just because you've been going to some shrink, you think that we just all need to sit down and talk. Talking won't fix this."

"So you agree it needs to be fixed?"

"No – it's fixed already. My shitty marriage is over. I should've left Molly years ago. She'd drive anyone round the twist. I'm not the bad guy here!"

Tracey felt bristles of anger prickle her. She bit back the "Fuck you!" retort and instead said, "It's a counselor, not a shrink, and I think we all needed one after what Dad put us through. Maybe if you had talked to one you wouldn't be in this mess."

"Aye, and if my aunt had balls she'd be my uncle!"

"Oh, come on Dermot. This is serious. Molly is devastated!"

"Ach, Molly is always up to high doe about something. You know what she's like. I can't take her anymore. She's too much. Fecking drama queen all the way. You've said so yourself," Dermot said.

Despite the element of truth to that, Tracey dug in to prevent Dermot using it.

"Dermot, you knew what she was like before you married her. You accepted her eccentricities when it suited you. She's the same as she's always been. She has lots of energy, but the upside is she's always positive. She's always on your side, always fighting for you, supporting you. It's all about you. She doesn't deserve this."

The other end of the line went quiet again.

Tracey hoped she'd hit a nerve. She went in for the kill. "She was with you through the tough times. She's cleaned up piss, vomit, blood, and supported every stance you took with Dad. She deserves more. *She* deserves that baby."

"No," Dermot said, "you just don't understand. She enjoyed all the drama and chaos Dad's binges brought to our lives. Sure, she'd tend his wounds or change his clothes, but she thrived on it. Then she'd want to talk it all through – over and over again. She still tries to. She says it helps to bond us. Fuck that! I want to forget it all now the bastard is in the grave. Time for something new."

"Oh, like a new woman? A new baby?" Tracey said, bitterness dripping from the words. She felt heavy. Defeated and disappointed. Like his father before him, it appeared that Dermot just looked out for number one, tearing apart lives and making up excuses. She felt helpless and angry, furious, in fact. Just as she had started to rise out of the ashes that her family had swirled about them, he threw her a whole new bucket of crap to deal with.

Almost pleading, she continued, "Please, just come back to the house, and we'll sort this out. Maybe you both can get counseling. She'd benefit from it too."

"No, Tracey. It's none of your business."

"It *is* my business. This affects all of us. Not just Molly. What will Mum say?"

"Look - I'm not going back. It's over. Get used to it!" Dermot hung up.

Tracey fought back the brewing tears as she considered no more "Molly and Dermot". She wrapped her arms around herself, lowered her chin to her chest and squeezed her shoulders up to her ears. Hearing a sound, she looked up.

Tommy stood in the doorway. He must have heard every word she'd said. A shadow fell over his features. Tracey's stomach flipped over.

"So now you know," Tracey whispered.

"Shit, I was hoping it was just her interpretation of a lover's tiff," Tommy said quietly. "What a ballix!"

"Look, I'll try to talk to him again, but…" Tracey stopped talking as Tommy's frown deepened.

"Dermot's a waste of space. Molly's better off without him."

She didn't want to make this stand, and especially not now, but she continued, heart thudding, "He *is* my *brother*, Tommy. I've got to try to fix this."

"It's too broken now to be fixed," Tommy said. Little muscles flickered at his temple as he clamped his mouth closed.

"This isn't the time for this conversation. It's about Molly, now."

"I'm sorry. Okay?" His face relaxed a little, his brow furrowed.

"Okay," said Tracey but her heart sank. This wasn't the end of the Dermot debate. An ugly and malevolent sensation lingered as she tucked the topic away and took a deep breath.

Tracey went back into the living room and ran to Molly. They burst into tears as they folded into each other in a hug.

"How could he do this to me?" The words sounded wispy, ethereal. Molly repeated them until it sounded like a mantra. "How could anyone do this to someone they love?" Molly sighed so deeply it ended with a hiccup. "I can't bear it. I actually feel physical pain. Here." She pointed to her sternum. Molly started crying again, and Tracey, speechless, looked at Tommy. His face grew drawn, his grey eyes darkened with a blend of anger and pain.

"Cuppa tea?" Tommy offered, the chirp in his tone forced and unnatural.

Molly nodded. Tommy went to the kitchen. Putting on the kettle provided the answer for every emergency in Ireland: births, deaths, and ended marriages. Tommy returned with the steaming mugs of fresh tea into the living room and set them on the coffee table. Tracey held Molly's hand, massaging it while Molly recounted the miserable details, her voice dull and flat and her eyes bearing a lost, beaten cast that wrapped Tracey in sadness.

"I'll stay with you tonight, Molly," Tracey said, "I don't think you should be alone right now. Tomorrow, we'll phone the school and tell them you aren't coming in. Then we'll get you a doctor's appointment."

"What do I need a doctor for?"

"You may need something to help you sleep, and he can write you a sick line if you need more time off work."

Molly sighed and nodded.

"I need to get back for the dog," Tommy said, standing up to go.

Molly looked at him as if waking up from a trance and then nodded.

Tracey's heart dropped, but she knew that they didn't both need to stay. The burden just seemed lighter with Tommy there.

Tracey walked him to the door. "Call me if you need anything, okay?" he said.

"Okay, and thank you," she said.

"I'm sorry for eavesdropping earlier. I was just. . . I needed to know."

"I know. I know. I just wish you hadn't heard some of that stuff."

As he looked at her, his eyes softened. They seemed to lighten and expand and in that instant, the world held just them. Tommy placed his finger gently on her lips.

"I understand," he said softly.

He bent forward and replaced his finger with his lips. They pressed gently on hers and for a second she was too stunned to react. Then she wrapped her arms around his shoulders and pulled him to her. His arms snaked around her waist. Heat rushed through her body. She felt suddenly strong and invincible, as if he had imparted a shield against fragility. She wanted to cling like this to him forever but pulled back to hold his face between her hands. The heat ebbed away, leaving a fortifying glow. He smiled, soft ridges of skin forming at the corners of his eyes and lips.

"I'll come over tomorrow morning to let you away to work," Tommy said, stepping back, searching his pockets and pulling out his car keys.

"No, no, its fine Tommy, you go on to work. You can't just drop everything. I've some time owed to me, and I think it's more a women's thing, but come round later, and we'll have dinner with her. Try to keep her occupied. It's going to be a very rough ride," Tracey said. Her mind screamed at her: *tell him to stay!*

"If you have time, call by the salon and give me an update."

Tracey felt oddly thrilled with this invite.

"I'd love to," She said. He grinned, bent forward and quickly kissed her cheek, then whisked around and strode down the path to his car. She stood at the door, waving him off as he turned out of the street.

She felt lonely all of a sudden, as if Molly's situation reminded her how fragile relationships could be. She didn't want to lose her brother any more than Molly did. And now that she had Tommy in her life, she wanted to keep him there, more hugs, more kisses, all of it, if she could just figure out how.

Saturday, March 11th

CHAPTER EIGHTEEN

"How is anyone expected to do this for the rest of their lives?" thought Sheila, exhausted as she listened to the gurgle and whistle of Dermot snoring. She normally anticipated a sleep-in on Saturday mornings. The day outside glowed bright, the sun already up. Devoid of sleep, irritation seeped through her, followed by fear. Did she really want some big man messing up her sleep, not to mention her apartment? She'd no idea where to put all his stuff. Sheila hated clutter and never even kept bookshelves. The less paraphernalia in the place, the less cleaning up she had to do.

Dermot had wrought havoc on her well-ordered apartment. He left coffee cups lying about and jam-jars with lids off or loosely put back on so that when she lifted them by the lid, the jar fell. What a mess. He always left a newspaper behind when he came around, too. She didn't read them, hating the awkward, ungainly bother of turning the giant pages. They left black smudges all over her cream furniture. Dermot never noticed that she constantly cleaned up after him.

She'd been annoyed that Dermot complained about his shortage of clothes, but was too cowardly to go around to his own house and face Molly. The morning after they'd discovered the chili in his underpants, Sheila made him wear an old pair of hers, insisting that he buy new underwear on his lunch break. The chilies were just too toxic, even after going through the wash.

He did make her laugh, though, when he climbed out of the car that morning and quipped, "Sheila, I just can't wait to get home this evening and get your knickers off."

Sheila looked over at him as he lay oblivious beside her in the bed. He could be very funny at times, but he still bugged the shit out of her, sitting each evening for the rest of the week in Sheila's pink fluffy dressing gown, waiting while his socks, shirt, and sometimes trousers went through the washer and dryer. He amazed Sheila by grumpily admitting that it was the first time he'd ever had to wash his own clothes.

Sheila also found Dermot's constant company in the evening a challenge. It was the early days, she reminded herself. A few disputes were inevitable. Some couples argued over things like leaving the lid off the toothpaste, but she had never imagined that someone would be so lazy as to not replace a flip top lid.

Passion still lingered. Dermot knew exactly which buttons to push, and now, chili-free, he was willing and able to push them. At eight-weeks pregnant, Sheila was not quite as willing. Morning sickness, inappropriately named, hit her in the evenings, not severe, but enough to leave her feeling tired and groggy. She went to bed early most nights.

She should wake him and see if he'd push those buttons now. She was a morning person in more ways than one. Her temptation to snuggle over to his side of the bed diminished as phlegm caught in his throat, turning his snore into a snort. Umm sexy…

She wondered if she'd be able to keep up yoga whilst pregnant. She'd miss the trip to India with her friend Elaine now. What the hell would her mother say about the baby? Random thoughts hammered around in her head, whirling together as if flung around in a food blender. The images hazed and bled one into another as Sheila slid into a light doze.

Dermot's big arm landed across her, ripping her from her reverie.

"Der-mot," she whined, "Get off me!"

Dermot snuffled and rolled the other way, giving her back her space.

"Sorry," he muttered, still dripping in sleep.

"Let's get up," Sheila said, sitting up and swinging her legs over the edge of the bed.

"Huh?" More gurgles merged into snores.

"Up, up, up and away." In one swift movement, she hoisted the duvet off the bed as she stood up, exposing Dermot's naked body to the chilly air. He wriggled into a ball, pale and pathetic, a far cry from the sexy man who had first seduced her. Disgusted, she flung the duvet into a corner, far from Dermot's grappling hands. She pulled back the curtain. Dermot shrank back, hands shielding his eyes, crouching like a victim of torture.

"Give over," he said, groping around for something to cover himself.

"Breakfast in ten minutes," Sheila called from the doorway. "Be there or it goes in the bin."

Sheila felt like screaming when she went into the kitchen. It looked like a poltergeist had passed through. Drawers lay open and cupboard doors swung on their hinges. A trail of dirty dishes led from the counter, covered in crumbs of toast, to the coffee table in the living room.

The smell of frying bacon guaranteed that Dermot would show up in the kitchen. For someone who had slept so much, Sheila thought he looked a bit rough first thing in the day. A morning person by nature, she woke early and usually ate breakfast long before Dermot struggled out of bed. Now, he sat at the kitchen table, his hair sticking up on one side. Dark stubble lined his jaw and darkened his face all the way up to his cheek bone. He poked at blears in his eyes. Even so, Sheila couldn't help admiring the shape his muscular arms made under his tee shirt.

Sheila gave him a cup of coffee made from beans she had ground only minutes beforehand.

"That should clear out the cobwebs," she said.

Dermot grimaced after the first slug.

"What? Don't you like it?"

"Well it's very…em…very strong."

"But I thought you liked it strong?"

"Yeah, well it doesn't taste like the coffee you usually make."

"Oh, the instant coffee." She nodded sagely. "So, you're telling me you're a coffee Philistine?"

"How do you mean?"

"This is fresh ground, top of the range, handpicked, fair trade, organic coffee." She bowed with a flourish of her hand. "And you just don't appreciate it."

"I don't appreciate being tossed out of bed at eight on a Saturday morning and then getting poisoned with this." He shoved the mug away. Coffee slopped out over the top and pooled on the counter.

"Piss off, Dermot. Don't be such a gaunch! You land here and just expect me to fall into your crappy little lifestyle. I hardly slept the whole week, what with you snoring and wrecking about the bed. I'm not going to waste my day off in bed watching you sleep."

"I snore?" Dermot looked surprised. "Molly never complained."

"Well, go on back to her then," snapped Sheila. "At least then I'll get a decent night's sleep."

"Ah, Sheila, I'm sorry. Don't be like that." He stood up and wrapped his arms around her.

She surprised herself by cuddling against his chest and inhaling his musky scent.

"Let's do something nice today. Newcastle, the beach?" he said.

"In March?"

"You've got a coat, haven't ya?"

"Suppose so." She looked up at him, grinned and pecked him on the end of his nose. "Let's eat up and go. Don't want to waste the day eh?" She smiled prettily, allowing him a glimpse of the flirty woman he first met.

"Ok," he said. "Let's do it."

***

The pebbles on the beach clattered underfoot as Sheila and Dermot made their way to the water's edge. Slieve Donard rose to their right from the ocean's edge in an upsweep of dark land topped by a rounded dome, silhouetted against a brilliant blue sky. The sun sparkled off the ocean, sending out flying daggers of light that pierced the eye and mesmerized all at once. Like a gaudy salesman, the sun did not deliver the warmth it promised.

Sheila shivered slightly and zipped up her jacket. The turn of events in the last five days surprised her. Having a baby was one thing, looking after Dermot, another.

After the ice cream incident, Sheila had felt a twinge of disgust for him. How could he be so dumb? And if he thought he caught something nasty, when did he intend to tell her? The way he'd treated Molly didn't say much about him as a person either. She tried to figure out what role she wanted Dermot to play. She couldn't decide if she wanted, or needed, a live-in Dad.

All she'd really thought about for the long term was financial support. But the baby needed a father for sure. Could Dermot fulfill that role? Dermot made her laugh though. Childish and lost at times, he had a little boy's heart. She hoped she'd have a little boy. Being a woman was so much harder.

Sheila smiled up at Dermot, thankful he could not read her mind. He in turn, watched, agog, as a group of adults shuffled down the beach behind a uniformed figure who held hands with two of the older people.

"Don't stare, Dermot," Sheila admonished gently, "I think they're patients from that psychiatric hospital up the road. Look, there's the nurse."

Some of the patients were pulling off their shoes and socks. Laughter drifted across the beach. Sheila and Dermot sat on a huge bleached out log left behind by the tide. Dermot reached down and began to take off his shoes.

"What on earth are you doing?" asked Sheila.

"Going in for a paddle."

"Are you insane? It's freezing."

"Shhh. Mind your language." Dermot nodded in the direction of the patients.

Sheila's cheeks burned. She looked around to see if any of the group nearby had overheard her.

Dermot straightened up and began to navigate his way delicately over the stones. The waves hurried into the beach with a whoosh and rattled the pebbles as they retreated.

Squinting against the sharp light, Sheila watched Dermot approach the water's edge and gingerly dip a toe into the water, only to pull it up quickly and yelp.

"Whoa, that's freezing."

"Well, I did try to warn you." Sheila giggled.

Dermot returned to the water's edge. He pulled his head back and air whistled out through his teeth as he exhaled, flapping his arms against his sides.

"It's just a matter of getting used to it." He grunted as he took another step deeper. An extra big wave crashed in and curled around his leg as far up as his knee, making him squeal, "Jeeezus!"

"Why bother?" Sheila said, unable to grasp the concept of putting so much effort into something so futile.

"It's nice, really. Refreshing." He gingerly inched further into the water, down the pebbled beach. "Try it."

"No way! Oh, look, saved by the bell." Her mobile phone beeped to tell her she had a text message. Elaine wanted to know her schedule for the week.

Sheila sat on the log and concentrated on writing the reply. The glare of the sun reflecting on the screen made it difficult to see the words, giving Sheila a headache as she texted.

She pressed send and looked up, staring off into the horizon, unable to decide where exactly the sea met the sky in the grey hazy distance.

She scanned back along the beach looking for Dermot, searching at first for a lone figure but not finding one. Then to her surprise, she picked out his tall, dark figure surrounded by the patients from the hospital.

Dermot and three others were walking in water up over their ankles, moving slowly and peering down into the sea. Dermot appeared to spot something in the water and moved quickly to pick it up. One of the patients jubilantly grabbed the object from Dermot, looked at it for a second, and then shoved it into his mouth. Dermot started toward him, hands gesturing wildly, and then he dropped his hands as if defeated.

Sheila watched Dermot and the patients slap each other on the backs in a farewell gesture as the nurse started to round the patients up. Dermot made to move towards Sheila when the nurse asked Dermot, "Where do you think you're going?"

Dermot shrugged and gestured towards Sheila.

"I'm with her," she heard him protest.

"Nothing to do with me." She grinned, holding her arms out, palms upward.

Dermot gave her a mock evil eye.

The confused nurse began apologizing once he realized that he had one patient too many.

Breathless from laughing, Dermot ran up to Sheila on pebbles that rattled out from beneath his feet. His cheeks flushed red from the snap of the air. His black eyes glinted above his sparkling white smile. Sheila felt a rush of affection for him.

"Gonna leave me for the loony bin?" he challenged.

"I reckon it's the place for you. That guy is a professional. Knew a looper when he saw one."

"You'll suffer for that." Dermot grabbed her at the waist and began to tickle her ribs through her jacket. Squirming, she pleaded for mercy.

"No, no, I hate that. Stop. Please stop it!" She forced a straight face and said in an urgent tone. "The baby! Mind the baby."

Instantly Dermot let go.

Sheila stumbled and quickly stepped back to gain balance.

"Oh, God, are you okay?" Dermot sounded urgent and anxious.

Sheila felt guilty for using the baby as leverage. She looked up into his dark eyes, brimming with concern for her, and wondered at the power she now held over him.

"What were you doing anyway?" she asked, befuddled by her thoughts.

"Oh, that poor guy lost his false teeth."

"His false teeth? In the sea?" Sheila said, amused. "And he put them straight back in?"

"I know. I tried to stop him, but I was too slow. He was so happy to find them. Poor thing."

They laughed companionably as they walked hand in hand back up the beach.

She had never noticed this caring streak in Dermot before. It intrigued her. Perhaps he might be worth having around full time after all.

Sunday, March 12th

CHAPTER NINETEEN

Dermot needed his clothes. He thought of phoning Tracey to ask her to pick them up, but he wanted to avoid another lecture. Sheila had insisted on having some time on her own in the apartment. She chased him out, telling him that he should get his clothes or at least buy new ones. Sheila must think he was made of money, and she never even offered him a lift. The look of distaste she flashed him when he'd asked her to drive him would've been enough to freeze the balls off a brass monkey. Boy, she was feisty, but he admired that. She stated her case and left it, rather than nag on and on like Molly did.

By comparison, Molly seemed like such a wimp. Just like his mother: weak and whiney. His mother had let his father walk all over her, and Molly did the same with her friends. It disgusted Dermot. He'd often told both of them to stand up for themselves and not be such mugs. If you welcome that sort of treatment, you really couldn't expect people to treat you any other way.

It was only late afternoon, but already the March day was losing its warmth. Chimneys atop the red-bricked terrace houses spewed smoke. The smell of the burning coal wafted in the air.

Dermot strode down the street, hands shoved in pockets, collar up and shoulders hunched up around his ears. He hesitated in front of his own house. Dark now, without the curtains pulled shut, the black windows stared out at him like the eyes in a giant, skeletal face.

The gate clanged against the wall as Dermot pushed it open with more force than needed. It hung there, vibrating, before slowly swinging closed again with another clatter behind him. He dug in his pocket for his key, but before he found it, the front door latch clicked and the door swung open.

"You're back?" Molly said, and her voice lifted in hope. She peered around the door.

"I came for my clothes." He moved past her and made to go up the stairs.

Molly's limp hair hung in flat, greasy curls around her face. Dark rings beneath her eyes told of sleepless nights and made her white face look hollow and unnatural. Disturbed by how pale and ill she looked, Dermot couldn't believe that he was solely responsible. She might be coming down with something. Hopefully, it was just a cold or flu, nothing serious. Christ, what would people think if he left her, and her sick with something terminal?

"Are you OK?"

"Not really, Dermot," she said softly, receptive to his concern. Her anxious eyes searched his face, beseeching. This irritated him.

"So, what's up?" he said, his words callous but his tone innocent.

"Oh, nothing much," she said. "My husband is just threatening to leave me." She looked for his reaction.

He felt stung by her mocking attitude.

"Ah, Molly, I'm not threatening to leave you."

Molly's features relaxed, and just as she began to smile, Dermot added, "I have left. I'm not coming back."

Molly stepped back as if struck.

"You can't leave me. I'm your wife. We're married. You promised to always stay with me. You promised it in front of God."

"Oh, for God's sakes, it's over. I just came back for my clothes."

"Look, Dermot," she said, as if explaining something complicated to a young child, "have your fling with this woman if you really must. Get it out of your system. We'll get help, counseling."

Christ, thought Dermot, what woman would ever say that to any man? How pathetic. He needed to cut himself loose, so he said firmly, "No, Molly it's over. Dead. Kaput. Sheila is having my baby, and she needs me."

Molly's face closed in. Dermot sensed defeat battling with pride as she struggled, unsuccessfully, not to cry. Her mouth contorted as she spoke.

"You just can't go. You are such a prick sometimes, Dermot, but I've always done everything your way. I've cooked what you like to eat, watched the TV you like to watch, even went on honeymoon where you chose. Port-fucking-stewart! I did everything you asked of me. I gave you my best years - my youth. You owe me."

"You said you liked Portstewart," he said, indignant. How dare she belittle him? That honeymoon cost him a fortune.

"For a Sunday drive, not a two week honeymoon at the Hotel of the Damned." she yelled.

"Very apt for the marriage of the damned, don't you think?"

"What more do you want? Blood? You've taken everything else." She sobbed, frothing with fury.

"I just want the fuck out."

He stormed upstairs and into their bedroom. Like a rocket out of control, he flew around the room, pulling his kitbag from the bottom of the wardrobe, dragging with it a plethora of old plastic bags filled with old dusty trainers, golf balls and dirty towels. Flinging the kitbag on the bed, he began filling it with clothes from the hangers in the wardrobe. Some of the hangers stuck inside the clothes, making it hard to pack them.

Downstairs he heard Molly rattling about. He wanted to get as far from her as possible. He couldn't cope with her hurt. Or his guilt. He felt as if she accused him of being like his Da. He wasn't like him. He just wasn't.

Molly came charging up the stairs and into the room behind him. In his peripheral vision he could see she carried a blue plastic bottle. Suddenly, she reached round him, taking him by surprise, and poured something into the kitbag on top of his clothes. The smell of bleach sung out from the bag.

"Fuck, Molly," he roared as he grabbed her hand. "You bitch!"

All sympathy vanished as he tried to save his clothes. She struggled against him, but the bottle swung up, the bleach soared from it in an arch into the air and landed across her face. Squealing with pain, she raised her other hand, too late to protect her eyes.

Dermot dropped her arm in horror as she curled into a ball screaming, "Water, get water, oh God!"

He raced to the bathroom and grabbed the toothbrush mug, filling it with water. It still had grey gunge in the bottom, but speed was more important than hygiene. He sprinted up to Molly and doused her eyes with the water. She squealed, barely able to open her eyes.

He forced himself to think straight. Get her to a hospital. But how? He didn't drive. He picked up the phone at the side of the bed and pounded out Tommy's mobile number. The call seemed to take an eternity to connect. Molly managed to fumble her way to the bathroom, splashing in the sink, still crying.

The phone rang about four times.

"Hey, Molly," Tommy said. Pleasure rang in his voice "How are _?"

"It's not Molly, it's me, Dermot."

"What the hell do you want?"

"Molly needs a lift to casualty."

"What the fuck have you done to her, you bastard?"

"I didn't do anything. It was an accident. She got bleach in her eyes."

"Shit!"

"Can you give us a lift to the hospital or not?" Panic crept into Dermot's voice.

"Shit, shit, shit. I'm out on Cave Hill with the dog. It will take too long for me to get to the car and then across town to get to you. Call a cab. I'll meet you at the City Hospital. And hurry the fuck up." Tommy rang off.

The taxi company answered on the second ring and said they'd be there right away.

Somewhat relieved, Dermot ran to the bathroom to see how Molly was doing.

"It feels like my eyes are on fire," she sobbed. "No matter how much water I put on them it's no better."

"Can you see anything?" Dermot sensed Molly calming down as he spoke more gently.

"I can open my eyes but it's too sore. It's all blurry. The light hurts." She leaned into Dermot. He felt the dampness spread from her wet clothes to his sleeve.

He moved away from her, saying, "The taxi will be here any minute to take you to the hospital. Have you any cash to pay for it?"

"In my bag, on the coffee table downstairs."

The taxi beeped outside. Dermot helped Molly down the stairs, feeling uncomfortable when she put her arm around his waist and snuggled in close. He grabbed her handbag as they passed the living room, giving him a chance to put some physical distance between them, and then he took her hand to guide her to the taxi.

"What happened to you?" asked the driver, as he pulled out into the traffic.

"She got bleach in her eye," Dermot said abruptly.

"My cousin drank bleach when he was four," the driver said. "The doctor told him to drink milk. Did ya put any milk in yer eyes luv? That might work."

Molly made a noise that could be interpreted as a no, but the driver didn't wait for an answer.

"I once got a grain of sand in me eye. Oh, boy, did that hurt. I had to go to the doctor, and they had to freeze the eye, and I had to wear a patch for a week. It was great actually. I was only ten, and I got loads of sweets and sympathy." He continued to regale Dermot and Molly with tales of horrific injuries that he or other members of his family had suffered over the years.

Dermot tuned out the drone. Agitation clawed at him as he sat in the taxi. Molly's sniffing and hiccupping made him clench his teeth, his jaw muscles strung so taut he developed a headache. Finally, the driver said, "Here ya are luv." He pulled up to the door of the hospital.

"That'll be eight twenty." He looked at Dermot for payment.

"Oh, hang on a sec," said Dermot, as he searched for Molly's purse in her bag. Molly fumbled her way out of the taxi and stood on the pavement as he paid the driver with a ten. Dermot pocketed the change. The cabbie drove off.

They waited in the casualty department for a mercifully short few minutes. The triage nurse assessed Molly and shunted her to the top of the queue. Still sniffing and pathetic, Molly was whisked in to see the doctor, leaving Dermot to sit in the waiting room.

A large TV screen blared above the receptionist's sliding glass panel at one end of the room, and a Coke machine hummed at the other. Beside it, another machine dispensed snacks. Dermot marveled that anyone could eat with the stench of hospital disinfectant in their nostrils.

Rows of brown plastic chairs faced the TV. At the other end of the front row from Dermot sat an overweight lady with a pushchair. He couldn't tell if the woman was a patient or waiting for one. She looked grotty and unkempt. He looked away, afraid to catch her eye. A child he guessed to be about four years old, with dirty blond hair and an equally dirty face, ran amok around the waiting room. Green snot ran in two lines from his nose to his top lip. Every so often he flicked out his tongue and caught the dribble. Sometimes he sucked the runny green tracks back up into his nostrils with a loud snort.

Dermot felt queasy just watching the child. It reminded him what kids were like. His mind flashed forward to this time next year. He knew he should feel dread at the prospect, but even this snotty terror in front of him didn't tarnish his image of the new baby, his new baby.

Dermot stood up. He wasn't needed here anymore. Molly was in capable hands, and Tommy would arrive soon. Good job he'd kept the change from the taxi. He'd need that to get the bus back and salvage his stuff in peace.

Outside, Dermot jumped on a bus, leaving the hospital grounds just as he spotted Tommy's car arriving. Relieved that he missed bumping into Tommy, Dermot realized with a tinge of regret that he was frightened of his old friend now.

Sunday, March 12th

CHAPTER TWENTY

Tommy's mind raced as he locked the dog in the car. He sprinted from the car-park to the casualty department, his brain spewing out fuel that fed his fury towards Dermot. It wasn't enough that the fucker broke his cousin's heart and destroyed her life, now he had assaulted her.

If he's blinded her, I'll kill the bastard.

Even though night had dropped down with a chill, he arrived at the hospital doors with a film of sweat breaking on his forehead and dampening the small of his back. He peeled off his jacket as he followed the signs to casualty.

As he entered the waiting room, he wondered why Molly and Dermot were not there. He approached the receptionist. She concentrated on paperwork, leaving Tommy standing at the desk. He tried to slow down his heart rate by focusing on the flakes of dandruff nestled against her scalp in the parting of her hair, white and stark against the dark brown.

"Name?" she finally asked looking up.

"I'm looking for Molly Duggan."

"And you are?"

"Her cu-brother."

She arched an eyebrow.

Tommy forced a smile. "I just want to know if she got here and if she's okay."

Years dropped from the receptionist as her forehead smoothed, reminding Tommy how taxing a casualty workers job could be.

"She's with the doctor right now. We'll know how she is shortly. You can take a seat in the waiting room until your cu-sister comes out." She lost another ten years as a smile brightened her lips.

He calmed down slightly he wondered if he should ring Tracey. He knew how exhausted she was from running between work and Molly all week. They'd both decided to give Molly some time by herself. Look how that turned out. No, he'd ring when he at least knew what to tell her. No point putting Tracey through needless worry.

Tommy sat down in one of the brown plastic chairs. A grubby four-year-old ran up to the chair next to him. Tommy smiled at the kid. The child, shy at first, flicked out his tongue, licking the snot on his top lip, and stood staring at Tommy.

"Hey, wee man," Tommy said, wishing he had a hanky. "What's your name?"

The child looked down and swung one foot out to the side, rocking with the momentum.

"Billy," he muttered.

"That's a cool name. Billy." Tommy nodded, repeating the name as if savoring it. The child responded with a wide grin.

"And how old are you, Billy?"

"Billy, stop bothering that man," called a fat woman from the end of the row.

"Oh, it's okay," Tommy answered. "I don't mind."

"Well, I do," the woman said. "Get over here, you."

Billy's smile vanished. He hung his head and slunk back toward the fat woman whose attention returned to the TV.

Billy looked over his shoulder. Tommy winked. Billy beamed a quick smile before he sat beside the woman and watched the TV with her.

The time ticked by slowly. The six o' clock news rattled out of the telly. Not much happened in the news today, and no bad thing, though it didn't offer much in the way of distraction. Today's big story reported a local celebrity's divorce. The next covered politicians in Stormont who bickered about some bylaw that would either prevent or allow a visitor centre at a local beauty spot. Tommy didn't care, so long as the news stayed unexciting.

Boring news meant no shootings or bombings, a far cry from the days when the news held a body count each day. Tommy hoped those days were long past them, and he felt sure the majority of the people who lived in Ireland and Britain shared his sentiment. If only people didn't ache so much for revenge, hold on so tight to grudges. If only they could simply forgive and forget.

Ha! Twenty minutes ago he would have cheerfully killed Dermot. Forgiveness eluded even those who preached it. Tommy considered the resentments he held onto. His father would not give in, and Tommy certainly couldn't meet him halfway, creating a deadlocked situation. Molly and Dermot provided yet another example of stalemate, and Molly, poor Molly, with a mother whose sharp, critical tongue had carved out a young woman so afraid of failure that she couldn't dump a prick like Dermot. A hopeless shadow flitted over Tommy briefly.

Molly came into the waiting area with a huge white patch over one eye.

Tommy jumped to his feet. "What the hell did Dermot do to you?"

"It wasn't his fault. I was...," She looked at her feet before continuing. "He came home to get his things, and I poured bleach on his stuff. I got some in my eye."

"Jesus, Molly, he's no good. Let him go."

"Don't say that," Molly said through gritted teeth.

"You don't need him."

"Don't tell me what I need. Where's Dermot?" She looked around her wildly. "Did you say something to him? Did you tell him to leave?"

"No, but I would have. I thought he was with you." Tommy swallowed back his anger.

"He was. I left him here. Maybe he's gone to the canteen for tea?" Hope echoed in her words.

"Seriously, Molly?" Anger flushed through Tommy. He pushed it away, took a deep breath, and said evenly, "I've been sitting here a good forty minutes now. Don't you think he'd have come back by now?"

"Maybe not, maybe he's hungry. He wouldn't leave me here alone."

What planet was she on?

"Molly, he called me. He knew you wouldn't be alone."

Her chin puckered, and she pressed her lips tightly together. Maybe it wasn't the right time for tough love. He'd talk to her when her hurt subsided.

"Let's take a look in the canteen then," he said. He set his hand on her shoulder, turning her to face him. "Are you okay?"

"Yeah, yeah, I'm fine." She brushed him off irritably. "We could all have a cup of tea together and get this mess cleared up."

Really? A cup of tea and a chat would clear up this mess? Tommy bit his tongue as he fell in step beside her. His heart stung for her. He couldn't do a damn thing about her suffering, and that annoyed him. They stopped at the end of the corridor, picked up the directional arrow and followed it.

"So, what did the doctor say?" asked Tommy.

"He says I was very lucky. It was only in one eye and they washed it out. Look!" She pointed at her once navy, now tie-dyed, cotton top. "I'm still soaked from Dermot panicking and throwing the water over me. But it's okay now. Still stings like hell, but I've got ointment, and I'll be sensitive to light for a few days. He's given me a week's sick line for work. So that's the good news." She forced a smile at him.

Tommy used the kerfuffle of holding open a swinging door to avoid eye contact.

The canteen rang with the clatter of metal pots, cutlery scraping plates and the shuffle of chairs. Staff sat in groups, chatting. Visitors mostly sat alone, staring into space as if stunned. The smell of cooked onions saturated the air. Steam from all the bodies and cooking clashed with the cold windows, condensed and dripped down to puddle on the windowsills.

Molly stood on her tiptoes and scanned the room. Her breathing quickened as she failed to pick out Dermot. She wrapped her arms around herself, gulped in a mouthful of air and then, with her head lowered so Tommy couldn't see her face, she said, "Let's go. Maybe he went home."

Tommy didn't think it likely. For the first time ever, he saw a streak of cowardice in Dermot. Feeling disloyal to Molly, he couldn't help but think her foolish. She would be much better off without Dermot, if only she would wise up to the fact. He followed behind her as she walked out of the hospital, weighed down by defeat.

They walked to the car and got in, their silence only broken by the dog's excited barking. Even Wolfie's gargantuan welcome seemed to fail to bring her any joy. As Molly's hurt level escalated, so did Tommy's feelings of utter helplessness. He gave up attempting to say the right things to her.

Wolfie sat in the back seat with his head on Molly's shoulder. Every so often his tongue would flick out to lick Molly's cheek. It reminded Tommy of little Billy, and he smiled to himself.

"What?" Molly said, bursting in on his thoughts.

"What what?" said Tommy, enjoying the familiar routine they often played out with each other. Molly smiled a little, recognizing the script.

"Whaddya mean what what? I said 'what' first!"

"You said which 'what' first?"

"What witch are you talking about?"

"Talking, talking, you talked first!" Tommy said. They could go on inanely like this for ages. They'd made it up as children and had kept adding to it during the years.

"No, seriously Tommy, what made you smile?" Molly asked.

Tommy gave in to her curiosity. "In the waiting room there was this kid. His nose was so runny it looked like his brains had melted in his head and were leaking out his nose."

"Yuck. Was it green?" Molly asked. She taught four-year-olds, so she'd be well used to the slime that a kid could produce.

"Yeah, a sort of yellowy green."

Her laugh delighted Tommy. He loved her sense of humor, usually innocent and bubbly, but with a streak of black humor that could catch someone off guard.

"I bet that's why Dermot didn't stay," she mused, "he'd be so grossed out by that!"

"I don't get how a guy who reared so many brothers and sisters could have survived that, being so squeamish," said Tommy, trying to divert attention away from the fact that Dermot had left.

"Oh God, I know! Do you remember the time the wee Westie threw up in the park in front of us, and Wolfie ate it, and Dermot threw up too?"

"Yeah, and I had to practically sit on Wolfie to stop him from eating Dermot's puke too!" Hearing his name, Wolfie turned and licked Tommy up the side of his face.

"Stop it, Wolfie. I know where you've been!" Tommy cried, wiping his face down with his sleeve. Wolfie's tail thumped the window behind him as if wagging a grin from the other end.

Tommy pulled up outside Molly's house. All the curtains were still open, the empty darkness gaping behind them, but a light, carelessly left on in Molly's bedroom, glowed out into the street.

Tommy guessed that Molly thought Dermot must still be there from the way she flung open the car door without even checking to see if he had a hold of the dog. Both Molly and the dog poured from the car together.

Tommy jumped out of the driver's side, calling Wolfie to heel. Reluctantly, the dog went to his owner, crouching in submission as he neared him. Tommy secured the big mutt to its lead and walked into the house behind Molly, wishing he could control humans as well as he could control his dog.

Molly charged halfway up the stairs before Tommy even got to the front hall. He closed the front door behind him, then closed Wolfie into the kitchen before he followed Molly up into her room. He found her standing at the doorway, staring at the wreckage in the bedroom.

Dermot had emptied the bleached clothes from the kitbag onto the pretty peach bedspread which now had huge white splotches all over it. The bottle of bleach lay where it had fallen on the terracotta carpet. The remains of the bleach had pooled out, lightening a spot about the size of a saucer to mustard yellow. Footprint shaped mustard spots led off in random directions from the main spill.

Drawers lay open where Dermot had emptied their contents. Wardrobe doors swung revealing spaces where clothes had once hung. One bedside table sat bare.

Molly sank to her knees. She began to rock back and forth, crying in long wailing sobs that reminded Tommy of the women of old, keening at gravesides. Downstairs, Wolfie joined in with a heart-rending, spine-tingling howl.

"The bastard!" Tommy said. "Molly, honey, don't. Please. This can all be cleaned up, and we can get a nice rug for the floor to cover that. I'll get you a new duvet cover, pet. Any color you want. Sure that one's old."

"That was a wedding present!" she wailed.

"Shhh, now Molly, don't…" Tommy coaxed, kneeling down beside her and hugging her. "It will be okay, pet."

He rocked her back and forth, whispering encouragement and pleading with her to stop crying. After a while she stopped, though more from exhaustion than from trying to please him. Her tears made her eye patch soggy and dampened a spot on his shirt where those from the uncovered eye had fallen.

He looked down at it, then at her, and said, "God, I hope they got all the bleach out of your eye, Molls!"

She rewarded him with a snuffle.

"That's better," he said giving her another squeeze. "Let's go downstairs for a cuppa."

He helped her stand up and then followed her downstairs to where Wolfie greeted them with as much jubilance as if he hadn't seen them in weeks.

In the kitchen, Molly sat with her elbows on the table, her hands clasped together and her head resting on them. She said nothing and Tommy let her have some quiet time while he put on the kettle and looked for the tea bags.

Wolfie sat on the floor with his head on Molly's knee as if it weighed far too much for him to hold up by himself. He only moved to occasionally thump his tail against the table leg. Every now and again his eyes rolled up in his head as he looked up at Molly's face.

Tommy opened and closed several of the cupboard doors. He didn't want to disturb Molly, but eventually had to admit defeat.

"Molly, is there any more sugar? I think the bowl is empty."

"I'll get you some," said Molly, getting up and moving to a cupboard that Tommy had already looked in. She opened the cupboard door and stopped dead.

"Oh my God!" she gasped. "I don't believe it."

"What is it?" asked Tommy, dreading something else upsetting her.

Tommy looked at her bewildered. Her hysterical laughter frightened him. She seemed to have lost all control as she stood pointing to an empty space in the cupboard, tears of mirth rolling down the one side of her face from her good eye.

"It's Dermot," she said laughing with head-back, belly-laughs. "He even took his muesli!"

Thursday, March 16th

CHAPTER TWENTY-ONE

The doorbell rang. Molly walked slowly into the hall. Although it was now nearly noon, she still wore the old grey, oversized tee shirt and grey jogging bottoms that she'd slept in all week. She rubbed her hand down her face. The letter box rattled, pushed open from the outside, and wrinkle-swathed eyes peered through at her.

"Molly, let me in, it's raining out here," Fran said.

Molly turned the lock and pulled the door to the point where it always stuck. She readjusted her grip on the handle and yanked the door open.

"Child dear, look at the state of you," her neighbor said, pulling Molly into a hug. "Go jump in the shower. I'll put on the kettle. I brought some bacon butties." Fran lifted a plastic bag.

"I'm not really hungry," Molly said.

"Listen to me. You need to eat something." Fran shook her head. "When did you last eat?"

Molly shrugged.

"How's the eye?"

Molly touched her brow and shrugged again and said in small voice "Okay."

She'd taken the patch off her eye this morning, following the doctor's instructions to leave it on for four days. The patch left two fierce red squares, one above her brow and the other on the apple of her cheek. For a long time this morning, she had looked at her eyes in the mirror. If eyes were the window to the soul, what did these bloodshot orbs have to say about hers?

Fran strode through the living room to the kitchen, taking off her coat. Molly trailed after her, not caring about the stack of dishes in the sink nor the smell coming from the water they sat in. Fran pulled open the fridge, its light brightening the gloom a little.

"Jesus, Molly, what's all this?"

"It's just food Tommy brought round," Molly said. She sat down heavily on a kitchen chair, propped an elbow on the table and rested her head on her hand.

"Tommy?" Fran asked.

"Yeah, you know, Tommy. My cousin."

"Oh. Okay, okay, Tommy," Fran said, and rubbed her temples, stretching her hand across her eyes.

"You alright, Fran?" Molly asked, but didn't move from the table.

"Yes, of course I'm alright," Fran answered sharply. She lifted plates of food out of the fridge, peeling back the cellophane and sniffing them.

"Phew! How long's that been there?" Fran screwed up her face and looked round at Molly. "Well?"

Molly's eyes filled with tears. She dragged herself through each day. She didn't want to eat and could barely swallow water, so why cook or even shop? Since Molly saw no point in leaving the house, why bother getting showered and dressed at all? Tommy called every day, brought food, cooked the food, filled the fridge and begged Molly to eat it.

"I can't. I just can't eat," Molly said. Tears flowed down her cheeks unchecked. "My mother was right. I should have seen it all coming."

Molly scrunched her eyes closed and brought her hands to her face. She sat trembling.

"Like, how long had Dermot been having his affair? Had I been throwing myself at him for hugs, kisses or worse, and all the time he had really been thinking of that black-haired woman?"

Fran moved to her side and put her arm around Molly's shoulder.

"Hush, child dear," Fran murmured, rubbing her hand up and down Molly's arm.

But Molly cringed, thinking about times when, as his wife, she walked around naked in front of him, even danced, laughing at her wobbly bits, in the way that a confident wife would do with her loving husband.

Fran cleared her throat. "When my Anthony died, I wanted to lie down and die too. But life's not like that. We don't have the choice in these things. You need to buck up – get angry, stop lying down and taking all this."

Molly looked up at Fran, astonished, but Fran stared into some space above her head.

"I got so angry. Angry at him, for jumping in the fecking Lagan. Bloody eejit, could hardly swim the length of himself." Fran's voice sounded cold. "I hated that little girl. I hated her parents. I blamed them for her falling in the damn river in the first place. And I hated all the years we'd lost. All that time I wouldn't be able to share with Anthony."

"I'm so sorry you lost him, but at least you know he loved you," Molly said quietly.

"Aye, well...."

"Dermot doesn't love me anymore," Molly said. The words nearly choked her. "When did he stop? Why didn't I notice? How could it feel the same when he didn't love me as those times when he said he did love me?" She stopped talking, exhausted. Had he ever loved her? And if he didn't, how could she have been so blind as to love him and get nothing in return?

He used to make her so happy. Happy enough that she didn't care that he had given her a zirconium engagement ring instead of a diamond and that they only went as far as Portstewart on Honeymoon. These material things were never important. It was their love that had mattered.

"I feel so stupid, Fran." Molly hung her head.

"You aren't the first or the last woman to be duped like this. You have to pull yourself together. So you couldn't keep your pooch on the porch. You'll just have to train the next one better."

"There won't be a next one." Molly had never looked at another guy since the day she'd bumped into Dermot at the tender age of sixteen.

"Ach, time enough for all that, Child dear. Have you been sleeping at all?" Fran asked.

Molly sighed and shook her head. Each night, she lay sleepless in her bed, her mind frenzied, longing for the bliss that sleep promised. But it proved false; as soon as she drifted off, her dreams would continue to torment her.

She had dreamt last night that she and Dermot had gone to a ball. Everyone she knew had gathered, the women all in beautiful glittering gowns, the men in tuxedos and bow ties. She wore a beautiful silver gown and knew she looked stunning. Every time she turned to look for Dermot, she just caught a glimpse of him disappearing through a door or around a corner. Eventually she found him. He commanded the dance floor, twirling a faceless black-haired woman in a dark red gown. It had a long train, and when the woman stopped rotating, her dress seemed to pool out behind her like blood. The puddle of blood grew until it spilled to where Molly stood rooted to the spot in horror. She opened her mouth to scream but no sound would come out.

Suddenly she'd bolted awake. The silence of the room pounded in her ears, sweat slick on her body, and for a moment she was unable to move, as if still paralyzed by the horror. She had cried then, lost, lonely, but mostly scared of feeling this terrible pain forever.

"Right, then – we need to get you to a doctor and ask for some sleeping tablets," Fran said. "I'm making the appointment right now." She reached for the phone.

Each morning Molly had vowed to see her doctor, but she passed through each day so numb and listless that she never quite got round to booking an appointment. Then the night came, and the same incessant thoughts would rage.

Molly felt that the whole street, indeed the whole world, knew what had happened, convinced that if she went even so far as the corner shop people would be whispering about Dermot leaving her.

Yes, she had definitely thought about going to the doctor – she just couldn't get past the front door.

"Tomorrow morning at ten. Perfect!" Fran hung up. "Appointment's made, child dear, and if I have to march you down there myself, I will."

Molly looked forward to escaping her pain.

Thursday, March 16th

CHAPTER TWENTY-TWO

Tracey took a deep breath and stopped outside the door of the hair dressing salon. She was doing this for Molly. Yes, she wanted to see Tommy again, and he had invited her, but this was purely a mercy mission, for Molly's benefit. *Right?*

Nah. She knew better than to lie to herself. She missed Tommy, longed for another fix of him just to get her through the next week, like an addict needing one more hit.

She and Tommy had both been so busy looking after Molly and juggling work that she's seen little of him. She played their kiss over and over again in her head. She needed more, needed to see him again, if not alone, at least without Molly.

Tracey resented giving up her time with Tommy to tend to Molly and she despised herself for that. Molly needed her, but Molly's depression sucked Tracey into a dark tunnel of despair. Tommy shone brightly at the end of that tunnel. She longed to get to know him better. Where would it all end? In tears, most likely, but here she stood at the door of the salon.

A bell tinkled as Tracey swung the door open. She loved the fresh blue paintwork teamed with gray that captured the ocean and made Tracey feel like she could be standing on the deck of a large and lovely yacht. The clever use of seagoing props, like tiny anchors on the walls that doubled as coat hooks, gave the place a fun but practical feel.

Orla worked with a hairdryer and brush on a client's hair in one of the booths sectioned off by white sailcloth. She wore her own hair, a rich mahogany color today, in a French braid off to the side. It finished in a perky bun behind her ear, and it looked quite demure by Orla's standards. She gave Tracey a nod over the noise of the dryer and put five fingers in the air.

Tracey flushed as she mouthed back, "Tommy?"

Orla grinned, winked and nodded towards a door at the back of the room. A blush flamed Tracey's cheeks as she walked through the salon, wondering if Orla knew about her and Tommy. She hoped not. Orla could be about as subtle as a spark in a methane refinery.

In the large, airy back room, Tommy stood adrift amidst a sea of cardboard boxes. Tall and tanned, wearing a blue and white striped polo shirt, jeans and a pair of navy canvas shoes, he looked as though he'd be right at home on a real yacht. His smile crinkled his eyes at their corners when Tracey entered the room, his grey irises a calm place for her to focus.

"Well, hello," he said, moving towards her, his arms outstretched. "Glad you could come down. Sorry about the mess - I'm still trying to unpack stock. Apart from that, what do you think of the place?"

"I love it," she said, leaning in for a hug.

He kissed her cheek as they hugged in a loose embrace and then kept one arm across her back as they stood slightly apart. Energy from his touch fizzled against her skin.

Now, standing here, Tracey didn't know where to start or what to say. She brushed her hair back from her face and tucked it behind her ears. Perhaps she should get her hair done.

Tommy cocked his head to one side and frowned.

"Is everything okay?" he asked.

Tracey felt secure again as his arm dropped around her waist and drew her against him in a squeezed half hug. He walked to a chair, opening a chasm between them that gave Tracey vertigo.

"Grab a pew," he said as he picked up an elongated chrome figurine from the chair. He pulled a wooden footstool up alongside Tracey and sat on it, placing the figurine carefully on the table behind him.

Tracey sat down. The difference in the height of their seats brought her eyes level with his and her lips less than two feet from his lips. She wanted to touch him, inhale him, kiss him. Butterflies tumbled in her stomach, and she pushed those thoughts away. She needed to concentrate on Molly. On anything really, other than those cool, grey eyes and those tender lips so close to her.

"With me, yes," she said. "But I'm worried about Molly. I saw her on Monday and Tuesday, but now. . . She won't answer her phone. I went round to the house yesterday, and she didn't answer the door, but I'm sure she was there."

"Did she tell you she ended up at the emergency room on Sunday night?" A muscle flicked at Tommy's jaw.

"Dermot told me."

"Oh, I'm sure you got his version all right." Tommy's face closed.

Tracey's heart hammered. She couldn't bear another row with Tommy.

"Tommy, please. Don't start about Dermot. I don't want to defend him anymore than you would want to. I'm his sister. I can't help that. Please don't take your frustration with him out on me. No amount of me berating him or sticking up for him will change a damn thing." Tracey reached up and laid her hand gently along his jaw. Stubble rubbed her palm. She stared into the grey eyes, took in the tanned skin, his slightly parted lips. She ached to connect with him and get behind that shutter he'd pulled down over his face.

"I want to get Molly back on her feet. Let's help each other do that, not fight with each other, okay?" Tracey said. She gazed at him, trying to beam her heart out through her eyes.

He ran his fingers through his hair, exhaling.

"Jeez, Tracey, I'm sorry. But I just don't know where to start with Molly. I'm at my wits end. She won't eat, and I don't think she's sleeping either. She's a mess. Is this normal? A grieving thing or something?"

"I don't know. It's the first time I've seen a marriage break up at such close quarters. She'll need time to work through it. I've tried to talk to her about seeing a counselor, but she equates that with seeing a shrink, and then she gets tetchy with me. She thinks I'm suggesting she's nuts."

Tommy shook his head slowly and stood up.

"Well, she's just getting over the shock of it, I suppose. It's only been what? Less than two weeks. I suppose if she bounced back already we'd have more to worry about," he said.

"I think she needs a diversion. We need to take her mind off what's happened. Show her that life goes on," Tracey said.

She watched Tommy pace in the small space in front of her as he thought. Five steps each direction, his arms folded and his head bowed.

"After Mum died, I yearned to be outside, in the mountains, the wilderness, somewhere where I could feel the wind blowing all the crap away," Tommy said.

Tracey could picture him standing on a mountain top with the wind blasting his fair hair across his face. He had his head back and arms outstretched; the sun would be setting behind him, of course. Tracey sighed.

"So did you get that, the wind and the wilderness?" she asked.

"Well, kind of. If you consider the Larne-Stranraer Ferry wild?" Tommy gave her a wry grin and raised an eyebrow.

"Let's take her somewhere. Not the ferry to Scotland though," she added hastily. "She might get seasick."

"What about Donegal? I was planning a trip up there soon, and my family has a cottage there. You should come too. It might take the edge off Dermot not being there. What do you say?" Tommy sounded excited. He stopped pacing and stood in front of her.

"Great idea. When?" *A trip with Tommy.* Yes, it would be great for both her and Molly too.

"As soon as possible I think, since the salon isn't officially open yet, so I've got the time. Are you busy this weekend? Tomorrow is Friday – that's a bit of a rush but maybe Saturday? I'll ask Orla and a few others to come too, so Molly won't feel like the third wheel. Even one night might help."

"Okay," Tracey said. "Let's do it."

Tommy pulled out his phone and started pushing buttons.

"So what is that?" she asked pointing at the figurine as Tommy put his phone down beside it.

"Oh that." Tommy reddened and cleared his throat. "It's an award I won in London a couple of years back – Hairdresser of the Year."

He held it in his hands and kept his head down, looking at it with a crooked half smile.

"Wow! That's a pretty big deal. Your parents must have been so proud of you."

"Well, Mum had already passed away."

"How long ago did she pass away?" Tracey asked, shifting towards him.

"Eight years, next month."

"I'm sorry." Tracy looked down, putting her hand over his.

Tommy flipped his palm up and held her hand. He pulled his bottom lip in with his teeth, pressing the blood out of it, and released it. Tracey watched the color rushing back into it.

"It's okay though. It comes to us all – the death of a parent. But I do still miss her."

"I'll bet your Dad was proud of you though," Tracey said.

Tommy barked a sharp laugh.

"Not quite," he said. "He never wanted me to be a hairdresser. Said it was a soft job for a man. He asked me if I was 'Queer' and wouldn't believe me when I said no. I'm not homophobic, but as far as my dad is concerned – 'if I'm not agin 'em I must be one of 'em.' His words."

Tommy looked straight at Tracey. His grey eyes seemed darker, almost stormy.

"He'll come round," she said, but his expression pulled at her heart.

Tommy let out his breath.

"It's been eight years. We're polite strangers. Even when Mum was dying, he couldn't bury the hatchet. Except in my back." Tommy pulled his gaze away and stared at the award before speaking again.

"When I first started training, he refused to tell anyone at his golf club that I was going to be a hairdresser. He told them I was doing carpentry. I didn't even know this until this one day his golfing buddy's wife met me downtown and asked me if I did homers.

"'Sure,' I says, 'what would you like, a cut and blow dry, some highlights?'

"'No,' says she, 'I was thinking of a sideboard for the dining room.'"

Tracey couldn't stop the snort, despite her sympathy for Tommy. She pulled her hands up to cover her mouth. She could not hold it in. Her shoulders shook even as she tried not to laugh.

She felt Tommy moving beside her. She kept her eyes down, afraid to look up and see the anger in his face. She tried to hold her breath and think of something really sad, but she couldn't stop the giggle that erupted again. She geared up to apologize but heard Tommy laughing. He stood shaking his head, with one hand rubbing his eyes, but definitely laughing.

"Maybe you just need to prove to your Dad that you aren't gay," Tracey said, relieved.

"But why the hell should I? Even if I was, he should accept me for what I am; he should still love me. He's wrong. It's that simple."

"It's never simple. People, parents, love – none of it is ever simple. Did you guys ever get on well?" she asked.

"Sure, he was a great dad. Solid, everything was all about us." Tommy swallowed. "When I was young, long before I started hairdressing, we'd all go to the seaside, hike the Mournes. You know, that sort of thing."

Tracey didn't know that sort of thing at all, but she nodded.

"I'm just suggesting that you accept him for what he is. So he's a bigot. It's not your job to change him. Accept him for that. Just tell him the truth," she said.

"I've tried that, but the old bastard won't believe me." Tommy sighed. "I don't want to lose him, I've already lost Mum."

"Introduce him to your girlfriend." Tracey felt sweat on the palms of her hands. What was she saying?

"Really?" Tommy squinted his eyebrows together.

Tracey felt the heat rise in her face as she nodded.

"I might scare her off. She's new and quite skittish." His eyes sparkled at her.

"That's inconvenient. Maybe you could take them both out to dinner? You should do it quick in case she doesn't stick around. You know... if she's that... 'skittish.'" Tracey couldn't believe she had the guts to say these things; she rarely got to the "meet the parents" stage, but something fresh sparkled in her chest as she spoke.

"Good plan! But I don't envy the girl." Tommy set the award on a shelf. "Besides, I don't think the ould bastard would even..."

Tracey walked up to Tommy and placed her finger on his lips.

"You don't know 'til you've tried." Standing on tiptoe, she brought her lips up to where her finger had rested and kissed Tommy. He lifted her up and sat down in the chair with her on his knee. Heat flickered through her as their lips parted and the tips of their tongues tentatively searched for each other. The bell in the front of the salon tinkled, and they stood up quickly, flushed and slightly out of breath. Tommy pulled the hem of his polo shirt down and grinned, shrugging his shoulders. Definitely not gay, at least not judging by the toot in his flute, thought Tracey. They locked eyes for a timeless second, then Orla opened the storeroom door.

"That's your client, Tommy," she said.

"I'll be right there," Tommy said.

Orla let the door thud closed.

"So maybe I'll set up dinner with my Dad for next week," Tommy said. "So he can meet my girlfriend?"

Joy and alarm rushed through Tracey at once.

"Are you asking me to meet your Dad?" she said slowly.

"Too soon?" Tommy asked as crimson crept up his cheeks.

"Not just that but…" She floundered for a better way to say it. "What if I screw up? He sounds scary."

"He can't get on with me any worse than he already does, so you won't do any damage on that score. And I'll be with you every step of the way." He wrapped her up in his arms again. Tracey absorbed his comfort.

"Feck it. Let's do that too then!" she declared, gripped by fierce abandon as she launched them into another spine melting kiss.

Friday, March 17th

CHAPTER TWENTY-THREE

Molly hated the surgery. The contractors had converted two old Victorian houses into a health centre by knocking down the walls at the landings of the staircases and joining them together. Molly found the place a confusing maze and often got lost or ended up sitting in the wrong doctor's waiting room. Today she hoped she'd found the correct place. She sat on a grotty plastic chair and idly thumbed through a two-year-old magazine with its cover missing.

Molly felt that everyone who saw her could tap straight into her brain and see what had happened, that her shame emanated from her in tangible waves. She welcomed the small mercy of the empty waiting room,

After the compulsory NHS forty-minute wait, the doctor called her in. Dr. O' Hara, a slightly overweight woman in her fifties, wore a dark green polo neck that stretched over her ample bust and did nothing to disguise the spread of her belly that spilled out over her black pencil skirt. She had her long, straight brown hair scraped back and held with a comb on each side so that Molly could see the grey roots at her temples. Molly didn't know her doctor well, but as soon as she sat down, wings of panic beat within her.

"How are you today, Molly?" the doctor asked, swiveling her chair so that her body faced Molly even as her eyes scanned the screen on her desk.

"My husband left me, and I can't sleep." It sounded dumb to Molly, so vacant of the pain and horror it held for her.

The doctor showed no surprise or emotion, except for concern. She nodded, clicked the mouse a few times and then faced Molly. "This prescription should help you sleep," she said, as the printer on the desk spat forth a small page. She handed it to Molly. "And I'll give you a sick line for two weeks."

It seemed all very nice and simple.

"Do the tablets stop dreams?" Molly asked.

The doctor's face softened. She shook her head, and Molly sensed her sympathy.

Yes, it was simple, but not perfect. Never perfect.

"Would you like to see a counselor?" she asked.

"No," Molly said, indignant. She wasn't crazy, just sad. "Thanks anyway," she added softly.

Robotically, she left the surgery. Outside the pavement was dry. Litter and leaves chased each other in eddies between garden walls and hedges. The pharmacy sat at the top of Botanic Avenue, a busy street behind the University. What if she met someone she knew? The pharmacist knew her. Would she want to chat?

She trudged forward in a cloud of surrealism. She'd never before wanted to avoid anyone, never mind everyone. She hardly knew this creature that existed in her body. Keeping her eyes down, she passed Dukes Hotel. Laughter spilled out onto the street like a taboo drug. People started celebrating Saint Patrick's Day as soon as the pubs opened, but Molly had nothing to celebrate this year.

The pharmacy seemed warm and hushed in contrast to the bustle and whizz of traffic outside. Relieved to see no line of people waiting on scripts, Molly handed hers over. The pharmacist worked away at the back of the shop. Molly sat on the chair usually reserved for old folk.

"No alcohol with these, okay?"

Molly jumped. The pharmacist's voice sounded loud and intrusive. She strode out from the back and placed the bag on the counter.

"Not even today," the pharmacist continued with a grin.

Molly mumbled, "Okay," as she paid with her credit card. She had the sensation that she'd been caught doing something wrong.

Fine hairs on the back of her neck bristled and sweat dampened her armpits.

She picked up her package and turned to go.

"Happy Saint Patrick's Day," the pharmacist called after her.

What the fuck is there to be happy about?

Molly dragged herself home. In previous years, she would have spent most of the St Patrick's Day partying, but today she sat, as she sat most days now, mute, on the sofa staring into space, barely noticing the passage of time. At least today she had been to the doctor's and could look forward to a good night's sleep. She hoped.

Molly took her tablet on Friday night. For the first time in nearly two weeks she escaped from her torment and slept without dreaming.

Friday, March 17th

CHAPTER TWENTY-FOUR

What a damn fine idea. Tracey had suggested it, after all, so she sounded willing to be labeled as his girlfriend. Now Tommy just had to get his father to agree to come to dinner with them.

He had come in early to get hair product out of boxes and onto display shelves. Technically the salon was closed for Saint Patrick's Day. When he'd gone to the alley with some empty boxes, he noticed an illegally parked car blocking him into his parking space. Tommy circled the car. It pissed him off that the driver had blocked him in. He left a note on the car's windscreen to let the owner know that he would call the police if he found the car there again. Fair warning.

Tommy took being stuck as a sign from the universe that he should finish unpacking. He turned on the sound system and selected a Bruce Springsteen medley. Satisfied at how well the new sound system played, he turned the Boss up loud as he happily pottered away, until his stomach told him it was lunchtime. He knew his father would be getting home from Mass around now, a good time to call, if there were ever such a thing. He turned down the music and lifted the phone.

His father picked up on the third ring.

"Hello, Dad," Tommy said. He heard his father clear his throat.

"Yes."

"It's me, Tommy."

"Yes. I know. I only have one child. Who else would call me Dad?"

Christ, he's not making it easy!

"I just wanted to say Happy Saint Patrick's Day."

"Huh!"

Tommy wondered why he even bothered.

"And, em, I was wondering if you'd like to come out to dinner next Wednesday."

"Well, I don't…"

"To meet my new girlfriend," Tommy interrupted.

"Girlfriend?"

"Yeah." Tommy slammed down the heat of resentment flaring in his chest.

"That's a turn up for the books," Sean said. "Don't go putting on a show on my account."

Resentment burned violently to rage, making Tommy sick to his stomach.

"Actually, I have nothing to prove to you. It was her idea. She thinks we should be part of each other's lives." Tommy stopped himself from adding, *but then she hasn't met you yet.* Sharp words, so tempting to throw at the awkward old ballix, would not help.

Keep it true, keep it simple.

"And… so do I," he continued. "Do you want to come or not?"

Tommy waited for a response.

It felt like forever before he heard his father's voice again, subdued to almost a whisper.

"Yes. Yes, son. I - I do."

"Great, I'll pick you up at six."

"Hmmm. Alright then." His Dad said gruffly before hanging up.

Tommy's hands trembled as he put the phone down, and he noticed a patch of sweat growing cold at the small of his back. He recognized a small yet significant victory. His Dad may not quite be killing the fattened calf, but Tommy knew he'd chipped through some of the old man's armor.

Tracey had made everything so simple. He liked her honest approach – no playing games, no hard-to-get, no getting freaked out at labels and time frames. And maybe, with her help, he might salvage something from this wreck of a relationship he had with his father.

Tommy locked up the salon and walked round to his car. The illegal parker had left, but as Tommy approached he saw that the headlights were broken and the front dented in. *That arsehole!* There were flecks of white paint on the black paint of Tommy's car. The idiot must not think much of his own car to ram it into someone else's, or else they were so bloody stupid that they crashed into a stationary car in an alleyway from a full stop. Drunk from celebrating St Patrick's Day, Tommy reckoned. He decided to call the police, just in case he needed it for a claim report for the insurance.

The police switchboard shunted Tommy through to three different people before he eventually got someone to take the details.

"Do you have the license plate of the car that ran into your car, sir?" said the police woman.

"No."

"Well, we can't do much, but if you can tell me the time it happened and describe the car, I'll take a note of the incident."

"Great. Thanks. It was sometime this morning between ten and twelve. The car was a white Subaru," said Tommy. "It looks like this guy's had lots of accidents. One of the doors had been replaced. It had a black front passenger door."

Saturday, March 18th

CHAPTER TWENTY-FIVE

A peach glow permeated the room through the heavy material of the curtains. Molly shrugged awake. As she opened her eyes, she stretched comfortably. Then she remembered, and the good morning glow vanished.

Like a specter hovering over her while she slept, despair dived into her. Molly groaned and turned on her side away from the windows. A metallic aftertaste clung to her mouth, a side effect of the sleeping tablet. She felt groggy. Sleep had been her only escape from the torment in her heart.

"Dear God, please let him come back," she prayed. "I'll go to mass every week. Work with the poor. Please help me."

She'd do anything to escape this grief, to go back to the way things were. She couldn't imagine how she would move forward from this stagnation. Helpless, she didn't know what to do. She held her breath, hoping that she would simply stop breathing. Escape the insanity-inducing pain in her chest. She'd had enough. She just wanted to slide away, just wanted it all to stop.

"Just take me now God, I'm ready."

As the reflex to breathe kicked in, Molly felt her own body betraying her. The rest of her life lay empty –ahead: an abyss, black and deep, and she stood on the edge of the precipice, looking through the gates of hell into empty space.

The phone by the bed rang so loudly she could nearly see the wave of sound radiate from it. Her heart quickened. Perhaps it was Dermot. Maybe he had come to his senses. The thought gave her enough energy to sit upright and reach for the handset.

"Hello?" she said her voice still croaky from her drugged sleep.

"Tommy here," Tommy said in a chirpy, no-nonsense voice.

She sank back on her pillows.

"Listen, I'll be round in an hour," he continued. "Please be dressed, a shower will help you feel better. Will you do that for me?"

"Alright, Tommy, alright." But she didn't sound convincing, even to herself.

"Can I bring Wolfie? He's wet." Tommy sounded apologetic. "I just gave him a bath."

Molly said, "No problem."

She didn't care.

She went to the bathroom, and as she sat there she decided to have a shower after all. She felt smelly, and if Dermot did call round, she'd repulse him if she stank to high heaven.

She examined herself in the mirror. She looked colorless. Her blond hair hung limply around her face, and her skin looked grey apart from where she still had two little red square sores. Her loose pajamas swamped her frame. In the past two weeks she had lost ten pounds. For the first time in her life, she was skinny.

Okay, a shower and get dressed. That had been the only two items on her to-do list for the past fortnight. Most days she didn't even accomplish that, but today she decided to grit her teeth and get on with it.

After her shower she felt fresher and somewhat physically revived. She put on her smallest jeans and a formerly tight tee shirt. Her tiny, waifish figure pleased her. She looked the way she knew Dermot liked girls to look, going by the famous women he openly admired. Molly didn't want to think about the not-so-famous women he covertly admired. The cloud loomed again, threatening to engulf her. The front door bell rang, dragging her back from the shadows.

She opened the front door to a smiling Tommy and a bouncing Wolfie. As she stepped back to let them through, Wolfie surged forward, dragging both humans up the hallway with him.

"Jeez Wolfie! Sit, Sit, SIT!" The dog stopped and cowered, and Molly burst into tears, flopping onto the bottom stair.

The dog immediately changed gears and crept up to Molly, whimpering and timidly wagging his tail. He nuzzled her cheek. Molly looked up, and Wolfie flicked her cheek with his tongue, catching a tasty tear. For the first time in two weeks she smiled a real smile of affection. She hugged the dog whose excitement level geared up again as if wound up by his thrashing tail.

She looked up at Tommy and he put out his hand for hers and pulled her to her feet. Wolfie ambled into the living room ahead of them, wagging his tail and clearing the coffee table of three newspapers, a couple of coasters and a box of tissues.

"You're dressed!" Tommy said. "That's a good start! Now you need an overnight bag." He bent down to pick up the things Wolfie had knocked over.

"What do I need an overnight bag for?"

"We're all going up to the cottage in Donegal."

Molly hadn't even thought about the proposed trip since Dermot left. She didn't want to go; she couldn't be bothered.

"We?" Molly asked.

"Orla, Carla and Mickey, and," Tommy blushed, "Tracey."

Carla and Mickey were old school chums of Tommy and Molly's who also happened to be childhood sweethearts. They started dating when they were fifteen years old and had never broken up. They finished each other's sentences and stole each other's punch lines.

"I don't think I'll go. I'll only bring the group down."

"Molly, we'll be even more down thinking of you here on your own."

"Ach, don't be daft."

"Please, Molly," Tommy said putting his hand on her shoulder. "For me?"

"I said no!" Gripped by aggravation, she shrugged him off.

"You have to come." Tommy flushed redder. "If you don't, Tracey will stay here with you. Please Molly, I know you've a lot to deal with and you probably don't want to hear this…" He ran his hand through his hair, flustered. "I really want to make it work with her. She's…we…"

"I know, I know." Molly felt discomfort for him. "You were never a 'female-with-pulse' sort of guy."

"Don't knock it. It's better than the "female-no-pulse" guy!" He nudged her.

He tipped his head to one side and raised his eyebrows. Molly's heart melted, so she smiled to herself. It didn't quite reach her lips, but she momentarily felt a bit better.

"OK, but Tommy..." She hesitated and then took a deep breath. "Don't expect too much from me. One night, okay?"

"Okay!" Tommy gave her a quick hug. "Thanks, cuz."

"I'll just get packed. Coming up?" Molly asked looking at Wolfie. He cocked his head as if pondering the question.

"I thought he wasn't allowed in your room," Tommy said.

"That was Dermot's rule," she replied. "And Dermot doesn't live here anymore."

Saturday, March 18th

CHAPTER TWENTY-SIX

Tracey checked the mirror one last time. A few wispy blonde curls escaped from her jaunty pony tail, framing her face in a softer, more romantic look. She put on a little make-up, but kept it natural.

She twirled to view her outfit from behind. These figure-hugging jeans always made her feel risqué and younger than her twenty-nine years. Her red canvas shoes felt so comfortable she could have been in her bare feet. A red jersey hooded cardigan that zipped up the front, over a white long-sleeved tee shirt, completed the outfit. She wanted to look casual and comfortable, at least more casual than she felt, though comfortable was easy around Tommy.

A car horn tooted; Tommy, right on time.

Inside the car, Wolfie hunkered in the hatchback with his head hanging over into the back seat. Molly scratched his ears. Pale and thin, she smiled a welcome. Tracey dumped her rucksack on the passenger seat.

"Gee whiz! How long are you going for?" Tommy teased.

"Well, you know what Donegal is like. A rain jacket. A spare sweater in case it gets cold. Another spare in case it rains and the first one gets wet. Spare jeans likewise. Coat, hat, scarf and gloves. Thermal underwear."

Tracey blushed as Tommy raised an eyebrow. She kept going.

"Something nice for the pub. And swim suit and shorts in case the weather is nice."

"It's Donegal." Molly clicked her tongue off the roof of her mouth and threw her head up. "It's never nice."

"The very weekend you don't bring the shorts is the one time it's going to be hot," Tracey insisted.

"Like when?" Molly said.

"Wasn't there a heat wave back in the eighties? We must be due another soon," Tracey said.

Tommy laughed. He looked gorgeous wearing jeans and a white tee shirt under a weathered brown leather jacket. It creaked when he moved, and Tracey caught a pleasant waft of the leather mingled with his spicy aftershave.

"Are we picking up Orla?" Tracey asked looking into the full back seat.

"No," Tommy said. "She's going up with Carla and Mickey."

"Carla and Mickey are coming? Are they bringing the terrible two?" Would she get Tommy to herself at all this weekend?

"Nope, thank God. The twins are wrecking granny's house for the weekend," Tommy said.

"Poor woman!" Tracey said. She shifted around in the front seat and looked over her shoulder at Molly, who nodded but seemed to only half listen.

"So, I said we should meet up in the hotel in Ballybofey," Tommy continued. "Is that OK? We could grab something to eat?"

"Sounds good," both girls said together and then laughed. Tracey liked seeing Molly smile again. What the hell was wrong with that brother of hers? Deep down, she recognized the family curse. Dermot took after their dad. The self-serving attitude seemed to endure in the male gene in their family. Tracey noticed it in her younger brothers as well.

Tracey watched the urban sprawl of Belfast give way to rolling green fields. The cloud cover broke, and patches of blue sky appeared as the car made its way to the border. Because it was the Saturday morning after Saint Patrick's Day, they travelled with little or no traffic on the roads.

Tommy played some Jack Johnson on the car stereo and had drinks and snacks to hand around. As they ate and chatted, Wolfie drooled elastic slobbers down the back of the seat. It took them an hour and a half to reach the hotel at Ballybofey.

Tommy took the dog for a quick walk and toilet break while the girls sat in the car. Tracey rolled down the window and inhaled deeply, closing her eyes with the pleasure of it.

"Turf," said Molly. "I love it too. That's how you know you're in Donegal. I haven't been up in ages. Dermot was always too busy with football." She stopped abruptly.

Tracey knew it hadn't been football keeping Dermot busy lately. She reached for Molly's hand and gave it a quick squeeze. She nodded towards Tommy and Wolfie loping their way up the lane towards them, Wolfie carrying a three-foot-long stick that thwacked off the grass.

"You've done really well today. You've been strong," Tracey said, and they exchanged a sad smile.

Tommy locked Wolfie in the car before they walked to the hotel. Tracey itched to grab Tommy's hand but instead linked arms with Molly. Tommy moved in step beside Tracey, his hands shoved into the back pockets of his jeans, his gait loose, sexy. Tracey wanted to just look at him, to watch the muscles in his thighs stretch his jeans, to capture it all, as if recording it for when he wasn't near. But she pulled her eyes away, not wanting to be caught gawking.

Massive concrete floor pots, four feet in diameter, stood on either side of the hotel door. Feisty daffodils, bobbing in the playful March breeze, nodded their heads in welcome. The warm lobby of the hotel contrasted with the fresh weather outside. Light oak paneling of the reception desk on one side and the bar area on the other gave a warm golden feel to the lobby. Polished granite tiles shone in multicolor in the sunlight that glinted through the stained glass patterns on the front doors.

They headed to the bar and chose a table near the fireplace, glad of the heat thrown out by the burning turf. As Tracey read the menu, Orla bustled in and made a beeline for them.

She had dyed her hair orange at the roots and pink at the tips for the weekend, backcombing so it stood high at the crown and flowed in a layered mane down her back. Chains that jangled as she moved ornamented her khaki combat gear. Under the open jacket she wore a tight animal print v-neck top that served up her ample bosom to its fullest glory.

"Hey guys," she said, greeting each of them with a big hug. "Carla and Mickey are parking the car. They dropped me at the door. What is that car park like?"

"Crazy," Tommy said. "Guinness everyone?"

They nodded. Tommy headed to the bar, and Orla sat down.

"Tommy told me about that bastard Dermot," Orla said.

Tracey held her breath as Molly's face flushed.

"I know he's your brother and all, Tracey, but you know what?" Orla turned to Molly. "This is the best favor he's ever done you. He set you free, babe. You're far too good for him."

Molly's eyes filled with tears.

Tracey's mind raced to paste the situation back together before Orla completely blasted her way through Molly's fragile composure.

"So, we're going to forget about that shit and have a great weekend," Orla bulldozed on as Tommy set a pint of Guinness in front of her.

"Happy Saint Patrick's Day," Orla said, raising her glass.

Tracey cast a glance at Molly. She caught her eye and flicked back a brief nod. Tracey exhaled.

Orla didn't mean any harm.

"Salt of the earth" they'd say in Belfast. Tracey was aware that Molly knew Orla only too well. This was her way of showing support. Molly grew quiet, but the tears cleared from her eyes as she took a slug of Guinness. They were still licking off their Guinness moustaches when Carla and Mickey arrived. They had a similar complexion: ginger hair and green eyes. Mickey stood a solid six feet tall in bare feet. Carla, a petite five foot three, boosted her height with platform wedge heels. Whilst Carla had a glossy mane of flaming red hair, Mickey's hair was thinning. He'd grown too tall for his hair, as he put it.

"Hey, started the boozing without us, have ye?" cried Mickey, grinning and patting his pot belly.

"Aha – two pints of Guinness?" asked Tommy.

"You bet. No twins, so we're getting our heads showered," Carla said.

"Getting off our heads more like," Mickey said, sitting down. "Hiya Tracey."

Carla moved to Molly, gently hugged her, and said "How are you?"

Molly dropped her eyes and mumbled, "Fine".

Mickey patted her arm and said "Just let us know if you need anything."

Molly nodded.

Tracey swallowed a lump in her throat, moved by the simple gesture. She wondered at how people offered their support in such different ways, brash confrontation contrasting with quiet sincerity. Perhaps Molly needed a taste of each.

"And Tracey, has that wanker Kieran stopped giving you grief?" Orla asked.

"Haven't seen him in a while. I think he's taken the hint," Tracey said, glancing around to check Tommy was still at the bar. "Let's not mention him in front of Tommy, okay?"

"Jaysus! Of course not. What do you take me for?" Orla said giving Tracey a shove with her elbow.

The Guinness went down smoothly, adding to Tracey's relaxed feeling. She should stop worrying so much, but Molly looked so vulnerable right now that Tracey couldn't help but feel protective of her.

An assortment of fish, burgers, lasagna and chips arrived at their table. They tucked into their food with gusto, except for Molly. Tracey noticed her pushing her food round the plate.

Tracey leaned in and whispered, "Come on Molls, you've got to eat. How am I going to share clothes with you if you're a size zero? Besides it'll ruin your modeling career. They won't hire the size zeros anymore."

"You think?" said Molly. She cast her eyes up, but a smile hovered on her lips. "Look!" She popped a chip in her mouth, chewed and swallowed.

"Good girl!" said Tracey. "And now one for Tommy?"

Molly pulled a face like a petulant child, then sighed and said "Oh, all right," and chomped on another. She ate about half of the food on her plate, more than Tommy had reported she had eaten all week. Pleased, Tracey polished off her own lunch and the Guinness too. They sat chatting in the afterglow of a good nosh up.

When the bill arrived, Orla reached for it but Mickey stopped her.

"Give it here," Mickey. "It's my treat. We are celebrating no kids with us this weekend."

"No way," Tommy said. "It's my turn. You got it the last time."

"No you wouldn't let me give you money for petrol. I'll get it," Tracey said.

"No, no please let me get it. You've all been so good to me recently. Please, I'd really like to get it this time. I insist," Molly said standing up and lifting her bag.

"No!" the rest answered in unison.

"We're getting it. Molly, you're coming to the loo with me," Carla said, taking Molly by the arm and leading her towards the toilets with Orla on the other side.

"God, look at the time," Tommy said, flustered. "The dog will be tearing the car apart. Will you tell Molly I'll pick you guys up at the door, Tracey? Come on Mickey; you must be parked near me."

"Okay, no bothers. See you there," Tracey said, following the girls to the toilets while Mickey and Tommy went to get the cars.

Full after her lunch, Tracey fought to keep her eyes open on the second half of the journey. She loved watching the landscape change from the lush fertile farmland of County Tyrone to the barren yet beautiful starkness of heather-covered, boulder-strewn mountains. It made her wish she could paint.

The roads deteriorated as the scenery became more stunning. The M1 had petered out to a dual carriageway and then to a one-lane road. Upon crossing the border into Donegal, the road became twisty and peppered with potholes. Tommy slowed down after they hit a massive rut that bounced the car, making Wolfie yelp as his head smacked off the ceiling.

Tracey liked the mutt but sometimes felt strangely envious of the attention Tommy lavished on him. She felt ridiculous being jealous of a dog. She glanced over at Tommy as he concentrated on the road ahead. She wanted to touch him, rest her hand at the nape of his neck, massage the shoulders that must be aching by now after the long drive. His cheeks bunched as a slow smile spread. He glanced at her, caught her eye and winked. She smiled, hoping that her foundation make-up covered the pink glow that heated up her skin.

"Nearly there." Tommy put on the indicator and turned the car up a narrow lane with grass growing up the middle of it. Molly and the dog yawned loudly in the back of the car. Tracey tried to quash the butterflies in her tummy. Where was she sleeping tonight? The possibilities made her tingle.

Her watch said six-thirty when they pulled up at an old stone cottage, high up a mountain road. The sky held the promise of rain, but breaks in the clouds allowed bands of sunlight to shine like spotlights onto the land below, momentarily lighting up tracts of scenery as the sunbeams moved across the landscape.

"If the weather's good, you can see Mount Errigal, Ulster's highest mountain," Molly said, gazing towards the clouds on the eastern horizon.

Tracey could see the ocean glinting in the west. Sunset bathed the mountain in bronze light and turned the sky crimson to reflect pink and mauve off the ocean.

Tracey loved the little cottage immediately. Recent renovations had replaced a small window on the back wall with a much larger double glazed picture window. She looked forward to sitting by the fire, sipping a Guinness and watching the parade of colors as the sun went down. It had only two actual rooms, with a loft and a small kitchen and toilet extension.

Wolfie galloped around the outside of the cottage, sniffing out his favorite pee posts and announcing his arrival with squirts of urine.

When they'd unpacked the cars, everyone reconvened in the living room in front of the fire. The dog sprawled on the mat, stinky-dog steam rising from his fur.

"Shall we eat out tonight, or in?" asked Tommy. "I know this great seafood restaurant and the pub has live music too."

"Let's eat out," Molly suggested. "This time I'm getting it, no arguments."

"Didn't you already get the lunch?" Tommy said, sounding confused.

"No, Carla grabbed me and dragged me to the loo."

"Yeah, I told Mickey to get it," Carla said.

"No, you didn't," said Mickey. "You said you were getting it."

"Shit! So who got it?"

Everyone looked at each other, mouths open, and eyes wide.

"Oh my God! How can we ever go back there?" Tommy said, his face bright red. "We've been stopping there since I was thirteen."

Molly began to giggle. "We'll have to go there on the way back and explain." She laughed as the others joined in. "No such thing as a free lunch."

"Nah," Orla said, "don't be such a Muppet. We got away with it. I say take the money and run."

Molly shook her head. "Too much bad karma. Besides, some poor waitress may have to foot the bill."

"Well, if it had that kind of an owner, I'd never eat there again anyway," said Mickey, folding his arms in disgust.

"Sure, we'd never know," Tommy said. "I'm going back regardless."

Tommy's honesty impressed Tracey, but he was such a bloody saint, it intimidated her. She didn't think she would go back and pay for something she had managed to wangle for free. The Duggans didn't get many breaks in life and took what they could when they had the chance.

Tracey wandered into the master bedroom and noticed that Molly had placed Tracey's rucksack beside Tommy's. Just seeing the two bags side by side gave her a tickle of excitement, but a tiny cottage full to the rafters with other people would not be a great springboard for a night of passion. They would have to rein it in for this weekend, she thought, as Molly and Orla chattered away with great clarity in the loft above her head. When she thought of lying all night beside Tommy, butterflies stirred not only in her tummy but lower down. At some point she might have to start plotting to seduce Saint Tommy.

Saturday, March 18th

CHAPTER TWENTY-SEVEN

Molly squeezed up the bench so that they could get everyone around one table. Conversation buzzed, the restaurant wall-to-wall with groups of people, chatting noisily over huge platters of crab, lobsters and prawns. A mixture of full, half-full and empty pint-glasses filled the tables. Staff charged around, carrying plates of food and balancing stacked towers of empty glasses up their arms.

"Isn't it great to have the smoking ban?" Orla said, her eyes following three guys from a nearby table as they headed outside.

"But you don't smoke," Molly said.

"I sure do, and if I go for one now I get those three hunks all to myself."

She lifted her handbag, clacking to the door in her high heels.

"She's a head case!" Mickey said. "She's more likely to frighten those three eejits than chat them up."

"Don't be so mean," Carla said, digging him in the ribs. "Looks like they are getting on just fine!"

Through the window they could see the four of them laughing, one of the lads lighting Orla's cigarette, shielding the lighters flame from the wind. Molly watched Orla nudge one of the men and throw her head back laughing. The men laughed too, but the guy she'd nudged stepped back a little. Orla turned her head and nodded vigorously as another guy spoke to her, then she slapped his arm, and they all laughed again.

Envy snaked through Molly as she watched Orla. She wondered what her own body language would say to guys. Probably something like, "Please, walk all over me."

Drinking her second Guinness, she felt the buzz kick in. Her friends could always out-drink her, and if she expected to last the night she needed to pace herself. She'd had some nice moments today and felt better than she had since Dermot left, but as alcohol loosened up her emotions, it made it harder to keep a grip on them. All around her, people were laughing and having a good time, but Molly felt like an observer, looking in through a window watching happy people eat dinner together in a cozy yellow light.

Around her, people naturally paired up. Of course Carla and Mickey, together since time began. She envied them their companionship. She forgot that she had ever felt like that around Dermot, yet he'd only left two weeks ago.

She wondered if she'd dreamt her marriage. The only evidence of it now existed in the photos, which she still found too painful to look at, and the wedding ring she still wore. She couldn't bear to take it off. When she did slide it up her finger, it left a trench in her flesh, just like a scar. Sitting in the boisterous restaurant, she missed him so intensely it made her catch her breath.

"Are you okay?" Tracey asked, setting another Guinness in front of Molly.

"Yes, yes, fine, just a hiccup!" Molly said, her voice sounding higher than she'd like it to. She patted her napkin to her lips but avoided eye contact.

Tracey turned her attention back to Tommy. Molly couldn't blame her. They were perfect for each other. They seemed to sink into one another's eyes, and they glowed in each other's company.

Molly couldn't remember a time like that with Dermot. Feeling cheated, she grappled with her reasons for loving him. Unable to give herself a good argument, she despised being consumed by such an intangible magic. Once upon a time, she led the charge in their relationship. Every time his father tore another lump of his heart out, she held him together, providing comfort and support. She witnessed firsthand Dermot's battered upbringing, his love and loathing of his father pulling him to pieces. When Dermot Duggan Senior died,

Molly hoped that Dermot Junior would find life easier. No longer did he have to search back alleyways for his father when he didn't arrive home, nor carry the stinking, comatose man back to his distraught wife.

However, Dermot, having no reason to depend on Molly for solace, didn't turn to her at all. This, she realized, had been the turning point. His father's dramas had glued them together, making Dermot need her. When she needed him, he recoiled. No matter what she tried to do to bring him back to her, they drifted apart. He had outgrown her. As this realization dawned, the injustice of it pierced her. She still needed him, wanted him, and loved him.

She finished her Guinness and decided not to have another. She didn't want to be hung-over, nor did she like the way her thoughts drifted. She stood up and scouted out the easiest route to the bar. She needed water.

Orla returned from yet another cigarette break bringing with her a whiff of cigarette smoke mixed with cold air. She stumbled against Molly before flopping into the bench.

"Same again?" Molly asked everyone, forcing a big smile. She wanted them to know she could do this. She could go on as normal.

"Nah," said Tommy. "I'm good."

Molly always liked the way Tommy would stop drinking after he had enough to feel merry. Dermot usually only stopped after he was too drunk to hold the glass.

"I'll have water," Tracey said.

"Yeah, me too," Carla said.

"Jaysus, yer some bunch to be out on the rip with," cried Orla. "I'll have a vodka and Red Bull."

"I'll have another pint. Here, I'll come up with you to help carry it down," Mickey said, getting up.

By the time they got back from the bar with the drinks, a group of musicians had set up in the corner, asking for requests. They began with "The Boys from the County Armagh" dedicated to the "birthday girl" from Armagh, amid a big cheer from a boisterous group in a back corner. The jovial music pulled Molly in, and soon she swayed and sang at the top of her voice with the others at her table. She had to work at it, but it was worth if it stopped Tommy and Tracey from worrying about her. For a while, she wasn't looking in through the window, though neither did she fully feel part of the scene.

When the musicians wound down, the bar emptied. Molly and the rest of the gang started the mile-long walk up the lane to the cottage. The stars glowed, tiny pricks of light against a pitch black blanket of sky.

Tracey linked arms with Molly on one side and Tommy on the other. She appreciated their companionship, and it moved her so much, she didn't trust herself to speak.

"The problem with these clear nights is how cold it gets," Tracey said, snuggling closer to Molly.

"It's beautiful though. Look, there's the starry plough." Tommy pointed at the constellation.

"No tha's the Big Dipper," slurred Orla from behind them.

"It's the same thing, ya big drunken eejit," Mickey said, catching up to them with his arm around Carla. "Big Dipper is what the Americans call it. When did you turn into a Yank?"

"Oh, fuck away off," Orla said. "I was there last summer. God, it was hot! I came home like a lobster."

No one spoke, saving their breath for climbing the short but steep part of the lane just before it reached the cottage. Molly noticed the burn in her thighs. By the time they reached the top she'd unzipped her jacket.

"We should go hiking tomorrow," Carla said, as they approached the driveway to the cottage.

"Not me. I'm going to be helping gravity keep the sofa down," Orla announced. She flung open the cottage door and let it bang against the wall.

Tommy tutted and muttered beneath his breath, "Orla's hammered."

Wolfie bounded out to greet Tommy, who rewarded him with a scratch behind the ears. The dog padded up to each of them and gave them a quick sniff before loping off into the darkness.

Once inside, the lights seemed garish and bright to her eyes.

"Let's go hiking too, before we go home tomorrow. I'd love to see more of the place," Molly heard Tracey say quietly to Tommy.

"Ah, come on, Orla, we should go too," Molly said, realizing how the endorphins from their brief walk had perked her up. *Hiking's what normal, happy people do.*

"Do I look like a hiker?" Orla asked, standing with her back to the fireplace.

"Awe, please," Molly said. "I don't want to be the gooseberry." She heard the catch in her voice and felt pathetic.

Tracey put her arm around her shoulder. "Don't say that. We'd love you to come."

"I know. It's just…without Dermot…"

"Sure you've been out with us before without that gobshite," Orla chimed in.

Molly felt Tracey stiffen and pull away.

Carla spoke from where she sat on the sofa, her voice low, "Orla, leave it alone. Now's not the time."

"And when is?" Orla asked, putting her hands on her hips. "Molly will be much better off the sooner she realizes what an arsehole Dermot really is."

"Tea any one?" Mickey asked, moving out to the kitchen.

No one answered him.

"Carla, she needs to know this," Orla continued.

"Know what?" Molly asked pushing away a suffocating panic.

"Look, let's all just go to bed now. It's late," Carla said standing up and staring at Orla.

"I have to tell her. It will help her see how much better off she is without him." Orla glared down from her three inch height advantage at Carla.

"Molly, go to bed. It's better if you do." Carla kept her eyes locked on Orla's.

"Orla, tell me," Molly said, nausea rising.

"Dermot tried to snog me one night, about three years ago." Orla broke eye contact with Carla to look at Molly.

"The bastard!" Tommy thumped his hand off the table.

"No," Molly cried. It was like she'd been punched in the gut. "You led him on! You, you, bitch."

"Fuck off! No way did I lead him on. He was drunk as a skunk."

Fury pummeled Molly.

"Well, he'd have to be. Look at you!" she screamed and jabbed her forefinger at Orla.

That slut always threw herself at men, Dermot couldn't help it!

"Jesus Christ, that's a bit low. I might not be Scarlett Johansson, but that randy fucker would poke a hole in the wall if the wall let him." Spittle sprang from Ola's lips. Her stature expanded as she towered over Molly.

"You liar! You're always after the men. I don't believe you," Molly said, backing away, her heart-rate blasting through her chest. "It's just the drink talking. You're plastered."

"Fuck you. At least I'll be sober in the morning. How can you be such an idiot about him? Are you blind as well as fuckin' stupid? Grow up Molly!" Orla roared.

"Why are you making this up? Just because you couldn't get a man to marry you, you have to prey on married men." Molly's head buzzed with hatred for Orla.

"I don't need a man, not one like that arsehole, anyways," Orla said evenly. "You're pathetic, Molly, fucking pathetic, mooning around after him. Where is your self-respect, woman?"

The tone of the words thumped into that part of Molly's brain that registered truth. She looked around her wildly, staggering back a little. Tommy reached her and hugged her to him.

Carla stood beside Orla and softly placed her hand on her arm. Orla's shoulders slumped as she deflated.

"Told ya," Carla said to Orla, then faced Molly. "I'm so sorry pet, but she's telling the truth. He tried the same thing on me too."

"What?" Tommy and Molly exclaimed together. Molly felt lightheaded, her world gone from beneath her. She could hear herself panting, gasping in the air, puffing it out in a rush.

"Does Mickey know?" Tommy asked.

"Yes," Mickey said from the kitchen doorway. "Oh, I had strong words with him all right. He's a letch when he's drunk, Molly, always has been. I'm so sorry pet."

Molly rolled her face into Tommy's chest, sobbing. His arms wrapped around her. She pulled away, fuelled by adrenalin. She could taste it on her tongue.

"I trusted you!" she spat the words at Carla. "All these years, and you never told me?" Screaming at them didn't help blast away the shards in her chest. Molly turned to Orla again. "You, especially you . . . Why not? You were supposed to be my friend…"

"I… we…," Orla started. Her face crumpled, and Molly watched the tears flood down her cheeks.

A dam burst in Molly's chest. This was Orla, her childhood buddy who had loyally defended her in many a schoolyard tussle,

Orla's friendship the backdrop of every stage of Molly's life, Orla the undefeated, who stood crying at Molly's harsh words. Shame pushed her fury aside.

"Why didn't you tell me?" Molly asked softly.

"We were just trying to protect you," Carla said. "You were already married. What would you have done? Left him?"

Molly shook her head. Her heart, dragged down deep within her, rasped against the splinters of her rage. He'd made her friends suffer too. She stung with fresh hatred for him. Or was that hatred for herself, for her own stupidity?

"I was afraid you'd... you'd... hate me." Orla's voice pitched up into a wail.

Molly's horrible words echoed in her head. Poor Orla, the butt of everyone's joke, feared that Molly would turn on her.

Molly flung herself at Orla, breaking into sobs to match Orla's.

"I didn't mean what I said. I'm so sorry," Molly cried.

"I really didn't throw myself at him, really, you know. I know what people think of me..."

"Shush, now don't say that," Molly said.

"I wondered, was it me. Did he think I was slutty and that's why he picked on me? I felt like shite, Molly, really."

Molly felt her friend's pain. That bastard had hurt her, made her feel bad, victimized even.

"But when I asked Carla what I should do," Orla continued, "She told me that he done the same on her, and she's not like me...definitely not tarty."

"Shush, don't say that about yourself." Molly regretted her cutting words. She tried to breathe evenly despite the truth churning her guts.

Catch a grip of yourself – It's not their fault.

"That's why Mickey talked to him, sober. Dermot never tried it again. If he had, we'd have had to tell you. We thought we'd fixed it," Orla said.

Molly tried to process all she'd heard. Dermot was a serial cheater, and she'd totally missed it. How could she trust herself again, never mind him? She hugged Orla as a fresh wave of grief hit her. A hand patted her back.

"Orla, maybe you should take her up to bed." Tommy's voice sounded close and concerned. "Will you be okay, Molly?"

She nodded, her face still buried in Orla's shoulder.

"Did everyone know except me?" Molly asked in a muffled voice. "Tracey, did you know?"

Tracey didn't answer.

"Tracey?"

Molly looked around the room at her friends. Tommy moved across to the front door. It hung ajar. Tracey was gone.

Sunday, March 19th

CHAPTER TWENTY-EIGHT

Tommy grabbed the torch that sat by the front door as he stumbled out into the blackness. Cold air sucked his breath away. He prayed that the batteries weren't dead as he fumbled with the switch. He ran out the driveway and onto the lane before a cone of light cut through the darkness.

"Tracey?" he yelled. His voice echoed off the hills. He remembered that Wolfie hadn't been in the cottage. He must be with Tracey. He whistled and heard a gratifying, "Woof" to his left. Tommy ran in the direction of the sound. A few seconds later, the light picked up Wolfie trotting towards him.

"Where's Tracey? Take me to Tracey."

The dog bounded in a wide circle around him.

Fuck! That must only work in Lassie movies.

If he went in the direction the dog had come from that might work, but it frightened him because he knew that an old well lay half buried in that direction beside a derelict stone cottage, abandoned during the Irish Famine. The walls around the well had crumbled to nothing more than a pillar of stones, and while the well itself wasn't deep, a person could break a leg if they ran into it by accident.

Fear prickled Tommy's scalp as he remembered the deep bog holes, abandoned, overgrown and scattered all over the place. Frantically, he swept the torchlight from side to side, trying to watch where he placed his own feet. If Tracey fell into one of those holes, she'd never be able to climb out. The sides were straight up and down, and the water would make them slick if she tried to grab a hand hold. He thought of her sliding below the tannin stained water.

"Tracey!" he yelled again, forcing his lungs to empty into his voice box. He was pitched into blackness as the torch suddenly died. He shook it. Nothing. He slapped it against his other hand, and it flickered on to a weak glow, barely able to make a splatter of light.

"Over here," she answered.

Thank God.

He swung to his left, and he heard her sniff loudly and blow her nose. The torchlight found her sitting on the windowsill of the dilapidated cottage. She jumped down as Tommy approached. He took her up in his arms in a bear hug. She clung to him.

"Are you okay?" he asked.

"Yes." She sounded like she was lying. "I had Wolfie."

The dog woofed again, and his tail swished against the long grass.

"Tommy? Tracey? Are you okay?" Mickey called from the cottage door, his voice amplifying and diminishing as the wind switched directions.

"We're fine!" Tommy called back. He watched as Mickey's silhouette stuck a "thumbs-up" above his head and then retreated into the cottage, closing the door and turning off the outside light.

"Hey!" Tommy shouted. He shrugged and turned back to Tracey. "They're all a bit worse for wear in there. Sense has left the building."

"It's not that dark once your eyes get used to it. You should turn off the torch too."

"Well, you can't say I don't carry a torch for you."

Tracey smiled and said, "The moon's about to come out. See the glow on the horizon there."

He saw a pinpoint of light grow larger and disappear. He knew well the three quick flashes, one long one.

"Do you mean the light house?" he asked.

"No, there." She moved his chin to adjust the direction of his gaze, her fingertips cold circles on his skin.

He squinted, but his pupils still hadn't fully adjusted.

"Did you know what Dermot was like, hitting on all Molly's friends?" Tracey asked, releasing his face.

"No! God no. I'd have done more than have a few strong words with him," Tommy said. "I knew he was a flirt, and the girls seem to like him, but this is too much. Did you know?"

"No way! Sure he'd treat his sister and his wife totally differently." Tracey looked up at Tommy. "I just can't get my head around this Dermot everyone keeps talking about. He's not the one I know."

Tommy didn't know what to say. He sat against the window sill beside her and put his arm around her. She leaned into him, but he felt her trembling.

"He's betrayed me too you know. I looked up to him so much. I really thought he was wonderful. And now..." Tracey interrupted herself with a shake of her head.

Tommy couldn't stick up for Dermot. He loathed him, especially now that his actions had hurt these two wonderful women.

"I'm so fucking mad at him." She spat the words out. She drew in a deep breath and sat up straighter, shaking her head, her hair bobbing against her chin. "But anger is so destructive. It will only hurt me in the end."

"You can't help the way you feel," Tommy said.

"True, but I can help the way I deal with those feelings," she said, calmer.

Tommy admired the way she handled her emotions right then, fighting the rage. He'd have just given in, hated with wild abandon.

"I keep telling myself people are not perfect. Dermot's fault is that he likes women. Lots of them, by the sounds of things." The angry edge returned to her voice. "He's not a bad person. I still love him. If Wolfie bit someone, wouldn't you still love him even though he'd done something bad?"

"Wolfie would never do that. Besides, dogs are much nicer than most people. Look at how loyal and trustworthy they are. They'd never run off leaving someone they love," Tommy said, his voice flinty, yet immediately despising himself for the dig.

Tracey inhaled sharply and looked up at him. Her eyes narrowed, and her lips formed a tight little line. She pushed herself away and standing up, took a step back from his grasp.

"Let me tell you about Dermot and loyalty," she said. "I told you already how he took beatings from my drunken father that were aimed at my mum." Tracey ran a hand through her hair, holding it at the nape of her neck. Wisps of it escaped and flicked around her face, dancing in the breeze.

Tommy wanted to pull her back to him but felt paralyzed.

"Not just that, "God this is embarrassing. I'm ashamed to tell you this . . . " Tracey hesitated.

Tommy braced himself for what might come. Tracey stood with her chin sunk to her chest. All he could see were the curls on the top of her head.

"When I was twelve, ra-ra skirts were the whole rage," she continued.

Tommy wasn't quite sure what a ra-ra skirt was, but he listened without interrupting her.

"Everyone had one except me. Mum hadn't much spare cash and Da drank that anyways, so I had practical clothes but no money for fashion. I was with a bunch of my friends in Top Shop one day, and we were all trying them on, even me, though I'd no hope in hell of buying one." She gave a deep sigh.

Tommy waited.

"Anyways, I didn't take mine off. I just put my own clothes on over the top. God, I was crapping it," she gushed, and lifted her hands to her face. "We left the store, and the skirt triggered the alarm. The security guard chased us, and we ran like the hammers. I thought I'd gotten away with it." She looked up.

Tommy could see light glittering in the pools of her eyes.

"You're probably disgusted. I'm a thief, for Christ's sake." She spat out the last sentence.

"You were just a kid," he said.

"Aye, but you never shoplifted? Nor Molly?"

"We . . . we pretty much got what we wanted. Not everything, but plenty. It's different." What could he say to make her feel better?

Her head drooped again. He felt terrible for her.

"Well, I'd have gotten away except the security guard drank with my Da. He'd seen me drag Da home a few times. He'd recognized me and told him. Da came home that night roaring drunk and mad as a bull. He grabbed me . . . " She faltered, and a sob escaped her.

Tommy put his arm around her.

"Shush now, it's okay, you're okay," he murmured into her hair.

"He had me by the throat against the wall, calling me a thieving bitch and yelling about how I'd let him down in front of his mate. In front of the whole bar," she snorted. "Like he'd never done that for himself." She gave a bitter laugh, frosty with the absence of mirth.

"I'd nearly passed out from lack of air when Dermot burst in. He was only fourteen. He pulled Da off me and yelled at him, telling him if he hadn't drunk all the money, perhaps I wouldn't have had to steal."

She looked up again with an expression that made Tommy's heart clench with sorrow for her.

Shaking her head, she continued tearfully, "I did have clothes. I didn't have to steal. It's not like I was going bare. I just wanted something trendy. Dermot knew that. He knew I was wrong, but still he stood up for me. Da beat Dermot so badly he couldn't open his eyes for two days, and he peed blood for a week. Da wouldn't let Mum take him to hospital either. Dermot missed a lot of school and got into trouble for that too. And it wasn't the only time he stood up for one of his siblings. He was always the only one who ended up getting beaten. He kept us safe." Tracey stood with her head bowed, looking down at her fingers twisting around each other.

Tommy's indignation evaporated. Who was he to complain about his father? Shame made his cheeks hot, and he felt his eyes tear up. He tilted his head up and swallowed, embarrassed.

"When anyone at school slagged off my Dad, Dermot would fight them. Poor Dermot was always in trouble because of his loyalty to his family." Tracey slumped back against the wall beside Tommy. "I spent years wishing I could escape my family. But what if Dermot had left us as soon as he could? Who would Da have beaten next? I'm glued into this family whether I want to be or not. But, bloody hell, why did Dermot have to be this lecherous fucker?" She thumped her fist down on the stone window sill. "Ow," she said, rubbing her hand.

"I'm sorry. I know Dermot had it tough, but I can't sympathize with him either. He's broken Molly's heart. What happened to him is no excuse," Tommy said.

"I know, I know. The trouble is I fucking agree with everyone too. But Dermot stood up for me when I was in the wrong. I should be sticking up for him, showing him loyalty no matter what. It's just... first my Dad and then that arsehole Kieran and now this. I just want one man in my life who isn't a complete wanker, someone I can trust, a hero figure," she sobbed. "Someone that I can rely on. Is that so much to fucking ask?"

She buried her face in his shoulder, and he held her. It seemed as if she wept for a lifetime of disappointment.

"If you let me, I promise I'll try my best to never let you down," he said gently. He felt a film of anxiety fall over him like a cellophane wrapper. What if he let her down too? No, never, he vowed.

She pulled away and looked up at him, her tear drops glistening in the moonlight. She'd been right about the moon. It slid up above the horizon, fat, full and florescent, exactly where she'd predicted. The vegetation on the bog shivered to life with an iridescent shimmer. Silvery light lit up Tracey's hair and threw her features into sharp relief, giving her an ethereal beauty that made Tommy's lower abdomen smolder.

"That's a big promise," she said.

"I mean it."

"I believe you, but remember, people aren't perfect," Tracey said. "But I will hold you to it."

She stood up on her tiptoes and pecked his lips, then gave him a playful punch on the arm.

"Thanks for coming after me. How's Molly and Orla? I left just as they had begun to make up. I didn't want to talk to anyone else about Dermot...except you, of course," she said as she looked into his eyes and gave him a slow smile.

His heart walloped him.

"They seemed to be making up okay. Look," he said, reaching for her hand. "We don't have to solve this tonight. I'll try to respect that he's your brother, and you love him, if you can understand that it's hard for me to forgive his...what can I call it? Imperfections?"

"I suppose that about sums it up, but you know it won't be the end of this," she said, snuggling against him.

"I know," he said. "But just as worrisome - what are we going to do about Orla's aspirations to look like Scarlett Johansson?"

Tracey let out a throaty giggle. She sounded sexy. Tommy swooped in for a kiss. Her fingers reached up and entwined in his hair as she held his head down to hers. The kiss deepened. Their tongues searched each other's mouths urgently. Tommy pressed against Tracey, and she ground back.

He slid his hand up inside her shirt, and she hissed. He'd forgotten how cold it was tonight.

"It's okay," she murmured.

Her hardened nipple topped her breast. A moan escaped her as his fingers encircled it and gently squeezed.

He felt her hands at his belt buckle. Although he wanted her to free him from his jeans, he pulled back.

"Ticks," he said.

"What?"

"Ticks, the place is full of bloodsucking ticks. Let's get in the car," he said.

"Good idea," Tracey said, grinning. "You're awful practical."

She started running, tripping and stumbling over the rocks and tufts of grass. Tommy, thankful he still had the keys in his pocket, caught up with her, laughing.

"Yep, I sure am!"

***

The wind on the mountain howled. The smell of bacon cooking forced his eyes open. But Tommy's biggest joy on awakening this morning lay wrapped up in his arms.

The previous night, after having sex in the cramped confines of the car, they'd crept back into the cottage and snuggled down under the big fluffy duvet, kissing and giggling at the snoring they could hear coming from upstairs. Tommy was sure he'd never get to sleep. Tracey swore she wouldn't either, but they made a pact to try and after a few false starts, disrupted by giddy attacks, Tommy could hear Tracey's breathing lengthen and relax. Once she had drifted off, he swiftly followed.

In the morning, she looked so beautiful lying there sleeping that Tommy was afraid to move and lose the moment. Her golden hair fanned across the pillow. Her cheeks were slightly flushed, her expression peaceful. Tracey's eyes flickered open, her face dimpling in pleasure as she saw him watching her.

"I really hope you didn't do that all night." She laughed and reached to kiss him.

"Mmm." He returned the kiss and then pulled back. "Why not?"

"Well for one, you'll be all cranky today from not having slept, and two, it's just far too freaky." She said "freaky" by drawing out the word in two long syllables and rolling her eyes.

Tommy drew her to him in a long kiss that left them both breathless. When they pulled apart, they lay gazing at each other. Tommy drank her in with his eyes.

From the kitchen came a series of clatters and bangs.

"Come and get it while it's hot," called Orla.

Tommy grinned. "It's a bit hot here too. You go first. I need to calm down a bit." He looked down.

Tracey's eyes followed, and then she looked up at him and smirked. He watched as she hopped out of bed and pulled a big woolly jumper and some socks on over her pajamas, disappointed that she hadn't gone the full hog and changed into her day clothes. He was impatient to see more of her but understood completely. Despite their passion last night, they'd had to wear something to stay warm. These old Irish stone cottages were always cold, especially if they were only lived in part time.

Tommy expected Orla to be too hung over to move, so he was surprised to hear her up already.

"How do you want your eggs?" she called from the kitchen.

"Unfertilized," answered Carla and Mickey as they made their way down the ladder from the loft.

Molly, hair scooped up in a bun, ran back and forth from the kitchen with the fried eggs cooked to each person's specifications.

Tommy raised an eyebrow at Mickey, who shrugged.

"You know women. Looks like they're best of friends now," Mickey said to Tommy out of earshot of the rest.

"Christ, those were harsh words exchanged last night," Tommy said.

"Ah, those girls go back a long way. They've no doubt said worse things about and to each other before," Mickey said, attempting to even out a flattened bed-head patch of hair. "God I'm thirsty. My head's busting and my guts are wild dodgy," he added, making a beeline for the table.

People are not perfect. Tracey's voice echoed at him from the previous night. Molly and Orla seemed to accept that, Tommy thought as he let Wolfie outside to gallop in the wind. Better than having him drool at them whilst they ate.

Through the picture window, Tommy saw foul weather. The few trees hardy enough to live on the mountain whipped about beneath a leaden sky. Even the long bog grasses all bowed the same direction. Mount Errigal could not be seen, and it seemed to Tommy that if he went outside, he'd only have to raise his hand and stand on his tiptoes to reach the sky, the clouds hung so low.

"At least it's not raining," Tracey said, joining him at the window and slipping her hand around his waist.

"How do you fancy a ride on a boat today?" Tommy asked.

She closed one eye and twisted her lips off to one side, making a little humming sound.

"Big boat or little boat?" she said.

"Big – a ferry. To Arranmore Island."

"That sounds good." She squeezed him. "Do we have to ask everyone?"

"Do you like cycling?"

She squinted at him again.

"Yes, but what..." She stopped as Tommy put his finger to her lips.

"There are two bikes in the shed. Only two. So, if we say we are cycling to the ferry, then the others might not come," he said.

"Oh, you've got it all figured out." She stood on her tip-toes and kissed his cheek. "Let's eat, then go."

Tommy followed her to the table where Molly was just bringing out the last of the food platters filled with bacon, sausage, potato bread, fried soda bread, mushrooms and eggs. The potato bread was crispy, golden – fried to perfection. The mighty Ulster Fry – heart attack on a plate – would keep their bellies full until dinner time. Tommy's mouth watered.

"There's beans too, if anyone wants some," Molly said.

Tommy shook his head. "Don't worry, Molls, there's plenty here."

Everyone agreed.

Molly sat down. Tommy watched her help herself to a plateful of food.

"So, what will we do today?" Orla asked. "The weather's too crap to hike. Seriously, like..."

"Why don't we go shopping in Dungloe today?" suggested Carla.

"Shopping in Dungloe?" Orla snorted. "What for? A few plastic leprechauns and an Arran sweater?"

"The Arran sweater wouldn't go amiss," Carla said, shivered and looked out at the bleak sky.

"Is there a pool and Jacuzzi at the hotel in Dungloe?" Orla asked.

"Great idea," Carla said.

"We were thinking of cycling down to Burtonport and taking the ferry to Arranmore Island," Tommy said. Mickey winked at him and Tommy gave him the stink eye. He wouldn't deny that he and Tracey were a couple, but it's not like he was expected to stand up and announce it either.

"Knock yourselves out – I'm for the Jacuzzi," Orla said. "What about the dog?"

"He can run beside the bikes. He'll love the exercise," Tommy said. "We can all meet in Dungloe later for a bite to eat before we head back to Belfast." He watched Molly. He felt a little bad about insisting she come to Donegal and then going off with Tracey for the day. She caught him looking at her.

"All I want to do is lie about in a pool all day. You don't have to baby me." Her husky-dog eyes gazed at him earnestly.

He wanted to hug her. To tell her she was his best friend and better than a sister could be. Instead, he pulled one of her curls hanging over her forehead so it straightened. He let go, and as it curled back up, he said, "Bo-ing!" They laughed. Tommy's heart filled at the sound.

***

With the wind in their faces, Tommy and Tracey freewheeled downhill all the way from the cottage to the ferry at Burtonport. Tommy's eyes were streaming by the time they stopped in the little fishing village.

"Why is there a big red spider on that building?" Tracey asked, tipping her bike to one side and planting her feet on the ground.

"That's a lobster," Tommy answered. Tracey turned her head to the side.

"Oh yes, I see it now." It was hard to miss the eight foot plastic lobster stuck to the wall of "The Lobster Pot" bar, but Tommy had never heard it described as a spider. He liked seeing this place through Tracey's eyes.

The road swung down past the bar and opened out on the right-hand side to a square that had two more bars in it. On the left, a large grey metal shed marred the quaintness of the town. The fishermen brought their catch here.

Straight ahead of them lay the harbor. Tommy could see the ferry approaching the ramp where its jaws would open. At least that was how Tommy had always seen the boat. It rolled out its tongue, and the cars drove out of its belly and onto land, like Jonah and the whale.

Tommy, Tracey and Wolfie boarded and stood at the back of the ferry in a slightly more sheltered outdoor spot, watching the cars load up.

"Molly seemed perkier this morning, considering..." Tracy said as she stood with her back to the rail. Her hair fluttered around her face, flung forward by the sea breeze, then blasted in another direction a second later.

Tommy watched her hair, mesmerized. Now that he had her alone, he didn't want to talk about Molly - and definitely not about Dermot. He shrugged, then nodded.

"My Mum always loved the trip out to Arranmore Island. We'll be following a narrow channel most of the way. See all those wee islands? And look. . . there's some seals." Tommy pointed and Tracey swung round, her hair lashing in all directions. She grinned, pink cheeked and red lipped.

"Mum claimed that on a sunny day, the trip was better than the actual Island. She said the difference between Donegal in the rain and the sun was the difference between watching a black and white television and a color one," Tommy continued.

"God that's brilliant! I so get what she means, especially the black and white part," Tracey said turning her face towards the grey clouds over head. She reached for his hand, hers cold against his skin. He took his other hand and wrapped it around hers.

Tommy heard a car horn blasting. He looked down at the loading ramp and saw Mickey's car with hands frantically waving from every window.

"Oh dear God, what are they doing here?" Tommy groaned.

"Looks like we'll have to share the day after all," Tracey said, but to Tommy's surprise she laughed. "It's not the end of the world. We still have our bikes."

What happened to the Jacuzzi plan?

"I can't believe they're taking the car over. Sure the pub is right beside the ferry slip." Tommy said. He forced a smile and waved down at them.

"Yeah, but the car and family deal is cheaper than four adults on foot." Tracey pointed at the tariff sign posted by the slipway.

"How bloody Irish is that!" Tommy grumped.

"Ach, now, don't get yer knickers in a twist," she said.

"I'll have to throw you overboard if you're gonna laugh at me." Tommy settled against the rail, leaning on his elbows. He put his hands on Tracey's waist and pulled her closer. Heat soaked through from her legs to his where they touched at the knees and lower thighs. It warmed him right through.

"Any chance you could stay at my place tonight when we get back?" he asked.

Tracey pursed her lips then bit the corner of her lip. She cocked her head and smiled up at him.

"Yes, I'd really like that." She leant in for a kiss.

Tommy cupped his hands behind her head, tangled in her hair. Her nose was cold where it pressed against his cheek, but her lips were soft and her tongue warm as it flicked against his. He pulled his head back and laughed softly, saying in her ear, "If we keep this up, I won't be able to cycle my bike!"

"Okay then," Tracey said, grinning, "So tell me more about dinner next week with your father." She rubbed her thigh against Tommy's erection. "He'd be really proud of you right now."

He laughed, then pulled back a safe distance. He needed to be ship-shape before the others met him on deck.

As the ferry moved off, Orla, Carla and Molly greeted Tommy and Tracey with hugs and hellos.

"The Jacuzzi was closed for maintenance, so we decided to come to Arranmore with ya," Orla said.

Mickey hung back, his face tinged green.

"Not good on boats?" Tommy asked him.

"Not after a skinful of beer the night before," Mickey answered feebly.

"Not to mention a big fry up the next morning," Carla added.

"Ah stop, would ya!" Mickey turned a darker shade of green.

"And don't forget the runny yolks on both of those eggs you ate," Orla said.

Mickey lurched for the side. Something in his hands clanged as he reached for the railings. His car keys dropped to a ledge about knee height as he emptied his stomach, the wind catching the vomit, flinging it back to splatter on his chest. The ship rolled and before anyone could grab for them, the keys slipped over the edge into the sea.

So much for a lovely afternoon with Tracey, Tommy though ruefully. Now they'd have to stick around, help push the car off the ferry and figure out how to get everyone home to Belfast.

Sunday, March 19th

CHAPTER TWENTY-NINE

In disbelief, Tracey looked over the railings into the gunmetal-grey waters sliding past the ferry. She looked up and saw a row of heads all doing the same. To one side of her Mickey stood, reeking of vomity alcohol. She felt her own stomach lurch so turned to face the fresh sea air.

"No point looking down there," Tommy said. "They're well and truly gone. Do you have spare keys?"

"Yes, but they are back in Belfast," Mickey said.

Although only a hundred and twenty-five miles away, the trip took about four hours due to winding mountain roads. Public transport for the route involved several bus changes, and the total trip would take less time than a flight from Belfast to New York. Tracey felt like shaking Mickey.

"Okay, let's start calling and get someone to bring them here," Tommy said, whipping out his phone. "Shite! No reception."

"We'll have to push the car off the ferry," Mickey said.

"I'll grab a sailor," Orla said, moving off.

"I think you call them crew," Tommy called after her.

"Whatever," she replied. "Meet you at the car."

"For God sakes, Mickey, go and wash that puke off. You stink," Carla said, holding her nose.

"And hurry," Tommy added, "The crossing only takes twenty minutes, and you're blocking all the other cars behind you."

Mickey cursed as he stomped off.

They met Orla and her "sailor" at the door to the car deck. He had long black dreadlocks tied at the nape of his neck. His dark skin looked like polished mahogany, and his teeth gleamed white as he flashed them a smile. He was very attractive, and Tracey wondered how a black guy ended up working on a ferry off the West Coast of Ireland. Certainly didn't look like a local.

"I can get you into the car, but I can't get it started for you, mate. You'll have to push it off the ferry to let the cars behind you off," he said in an English accent.

He set a tool bag down and took out what looked like an empty black pocket of material, and squeezed it between the door and the frame of the passenger side. He pumped a palm-sized bladder, and suddenly the door popped open.

Tracey and her friends cheered. At least they had the car open. Tracey fought off her irritation with Mickey. Bad luck happened. Getting pissed off with the poor sod wouldn't change things.

Around them, people returned to their cars. Tommy sent Tracey and Molly up to get the bikes and walk Wolfie off the ferry, leaving the others to push the car. Tracey was not sorry to go.

She pushed her bike up the ramp with one hand and held Wolfie by the leash in the other. An empty beach lay to the left and a road, dotted with little white houses, ran parallel above it. To the right, more houses formed a hub, with a shop, a pub and a post office. A road wound up the low hill from here. The boulder-strewn landscape played host to only the hardiest plants, heather and low trees. Tracey wondered how anyone had survived out here in the olden days when they didn't have the luxury of the frequent ferries to the mainland for supplies.

Tracey waited at the top of the ramp for Molly to wheel her bike alongside her.

"Look…" they both said at once and then laughed. Tracey liked feeling reconnected to Molly all of a sudden. They'd get through this hiccup.

They leant their bikes against their hips as they watched Carla steer the car while Tommy, Mickey and Orla pushed it off the ferry towards them, turning the air blue with their language.

"We'll have to leave the car here and push it back on the next ferry going home, if they'll let us," Mickey said, gasping.

"God yer man was gorgeous, wasn't he?" Orla said.

"Jaysus, the only black man in Donegal, and he breaks into my car!" Mickey laughed. He ducked as Carla took a swipe at him.

"Anyone any luck on the phone yet?" Tommy asked.

"Let's go to that pub," Tracey said, giving up any hope for a romantic cycle with Tommy. "And if there's no reception on the mobiles, perhaps they'll let us use their landline."

She took his hand as they followed Orla to the pub.

"What else can go wrong this weekend?" Tommy asked, sitting down at the table in the bar and taking out his phone. "Fuck! I've no network coverage here."

"Me neither," Carla and Mickey said together.

"Bloody hell. I'm on roaming. It's going to cost me a fortune!" Orla moaned.

They were all on roaming. Though parts of Donegal were further north than Belfast, County Donegal belonged to the Republic of Ireland, also known as the South of Ireland. Phone companies in Belfast were linked into the UK system. Tracey hoped she had enough money in her pay-as-you-go package to make enough calls.

"Okay, start calling then." Molly passed her phone to Mickey.

***

Forty minutes later, they still had not found anyone to drive the keys to Burtonport for them. In another thirty-five minutes, they'd have to push the car back onto the return ferry.

"I can't believe no one else is answering their bloody phone. My Mum can't drive this far with her bad back, but she's at the house with the keys all ready to hand over," Carla said. "The battery is getting low on your phone, Tracey." She tossed the phone over, and Tracey caught it, exasperated.

"I'll ask if I they have a charger," Tracey said, taking it to the bar.

Luckily, they not only had a charger, but they plugged it in for her. Just as she was about to walk away, the phone rang. The display showed Dermot calling. He'd not answered her calls all week, and *now* he phones her. Frustration bubbled inside her.

"What do you want?" she asked. "Make it quick. I'm on roaming."

"Where are you?"

"Donegal."

"What time will you be home tonight? I just wanted to talk to you."

"Right now, I don't know," Tracey grumped, but then found herself telling him about the drowned keys.

"Hang on a minute. I'll call you back." He hung up.

Tracey felt irritated that he'd passed it off. He couldn't do anything anyways because he couldn't drive, but she was curious as to why he wanted to ring her back. The phone hopped in her hand, and she answered straight away.

"Tell Mickey we'll be at Burtonport in four hours," Dermot said. He sounded excited.

"How? We?" Tracey asked, confused.

"Sheila's been teaching me to drive. She says a good long stint like this would be a good way to learn. She's happy to come with me and drive the bits I can't. I'll meet Mickey at the Lobster Pot. Okay?"

"No, no, no, no! Molly's here," Tracey hissed down the phone. "How the fuck do you think she'd feel if you turned up with fecking Sheila, and driving too, after the years she's spent pestering you to learn to drive?"

"I have to learn now. I don't want my baby born in a taxi, do I?"

"How fucking insensitive are you... you... you...argh." She hung up on him. Rage boiled through her. She didn't recognize this man; her brother was an alien to her.

Sheepishly, she joined the others. They were still discussing ways to get the keys from Belfast to Mickey. The conversation had turned to him staying the night and one of them taking the next day off work, though that wasn't going to work since they wouldn't all fit in the car with Tommy to get back to Belfast. Tracy felt bad that she'd vetoed the only solution.

Twenty minutes and no resolutions later, the phone in her hand buzzed again. Seeing it was Dermot, she got up and went outside.

"So lil' sis, simmered down yet?" Dermot had always said this when they'd rowed as kids. Now, it pierced through her fury with him and softened her, its familiarity like coming home to a place she missed.

She sighed.

"Wait – why are you doing this?"

"You're my sister. Mickey's my friend. I can help. Look, I know I've been a shit to Molly. I couldn't help that. I am sorry about it. Ever since I found out about this baby, my baby, I just want to do right by it."

What about doing right by Molly?

"Tracey, are you still there?"

"Yes, yes," Tracey snapped back. "So, why would Sheila do this?"

"Sheila is doing it because I asked her to," Dermot said. "She's not the evil dragon you'd like to make her out to be, you know. Plus, I promised her a nice dinner at the Lobster Pot!"

Tracey knew there was no other way. The Dermot who had been described by the girls last night was not *her* Dermot. She'd rather have him as her devoted brother. She could still love that man.

Maybe his leaving Molly is doing right by her in the long run.

"Oh fuckit – alright then. But this won't save you from the firing squad," she said. She knew she wouldn't be able to look Tommy or Molly in the eye as she walked over to break the news.

Sunday, March 19th

CHAPTER THIRTY

"Fuck away off! Are you serious?" Molly asked. "Really? Dermot and the trollop are the only ones who can help? What were you doing calling him anyway?"

Tracey's face flamed, and she fidgeted with the cuffs of her sleeves.

"He called me," Tracey said. "It's not my first choice either."

Molly tried to quench her infuriation with Tracey. Those bloody Duggans always stuck together. She'd have given anything to see Dermot, but not if he had that woman in tow. Evidently he didn't mind coming to Donegal with that bitch. Molly's chest burned.

"We'll leave for Belfast as soon as we get back. You might as well wait in the Lobster Pot Molls, while Tracey and I take the bikes back to the cottage. I'll come back down for you. Okay?" Tommy said.

He touched her elbow and bent down to look into her face.

Molly swallowed the lump swelling in her throat and nodded.

"I'm going back to Belfast with Tommy too," Orla announced as she folded her arms. "No way do I want to see Dermot, not after what he's done to Molly. The fecker!"

Molly took solace in the solidarity. She liked Orla's loyalty, even after the nasty words they'd exchanged last night. She had accepted that her friends had been trying to protect her by saying nothing about Dermot's drunken advances. At least she had chosen her friends more carefully than her husband.

"I need to get home for the kids," Carla said. "Do you think you could take me?"

Envy scalded Molly as she caught a glance shared between Tracey and Tommy. Tracey arched an eyebrow, and Tommy nodded. Tracey pursed her lips and tipped her head back exhaling.

"Okay," Tracey said. "I'll wait with Mickey and you three go home with Tommy."

"The boat will be here any minute. We gotta get that car on it," Mickey announced.

Weary with emotion, Molly trudged after the others back to the ramp. Tracey dropped back and kept pace with her.

"Molly, I didn't ask him to do this. I'm shocked that he even offered," Tracey said. "I don't get why that woman would bother doing this."

"Obviously she's the perfect fucking woman," Molly said bitterly.

"Not if she's low enough to steal another woman's husband," Tracey said. She linked Molly's arm.

"Perhaps she's trying to win brownie points with you." Molly's stomach rose to her chest at the idea of Tracey even talking to that bitch.

"She'll have to do way better than that. No matter what happens, Molly, you'll always be my sister."

The ferry horn blasted, making a reply impossible, which was just as well. Molly couldn't trust herself not to cry.

***

As much as she wanted to flee, to escape home to the sanctuary of her bed, Molly's curiosity taunted her. She wanted to see Dermot, see how he interacted with Sheila, and see how he coped driving.

It took them a nearly an hour to get the car back on the ferry, cross to the mainland and push the car off again and park it. Molly checked her watch. It was two o'clock . Where would Dermot be on the road now? Probably as far as Portadown. Molly wanted to rush the others, make them move faster so they could get on the road and away from here, but what if they stayed?

Tracey and Tommy cycled back to the cottage to retrieve the car. Molly followed everyone else into the Lobster Pot to wait. Another forty-five minutes ticked by.

Molly pictured the black Ford Ka pulling into the side of the road at the Ballygawley roundabout so that Sheila could get in and Dermot could take over the driving now that they were finished with the motorway. She could see how he'd have to change the seat position and adjust the mirrors. He'd look too big for that stupid wee car. He'd grind the gears and have "kangaroo" petrol as he got the feel of the clutch. Would he swear at Sheila? Molly decided yes. Sheila would be pissed off, and they'd be in foul moods with each other.

"Okay, the bus for Belfast is leaving." Tommy bounced in, jolting Molly from her daydream.

"Do you want to eat with us before you go?" Tracey asked them.

Molly held her breath. Go or stay? Which was worse – seeing and believing or imagining catching up with Dermot?

"I really need to get home," Carla said. "Sorry Mickey." She kissed him and got up and stood beside Tommy.

They left.

But not before stopping at the cottage to pick up their belongings. Time edged along another half hour. Dermot and Sheila would be crossing the border, closing the distance between them.

The car packed, Tommy locked the cottage, and they left.

Molly listened to Orla and Carla jabber about the kids, gossip about mutual friends, and laugh over old stories.

Oh, to not have a care in the world.

Tommy brewed silently at the wheel. He was probably pissed at having to leave Tracey behind. Molly certainly was. Tracey had promised that she'd come back with Mickey and have as little to do with Sheila as possible.

The cars would be meeting soon, if Dermot had taken the same road they always took.

"Sorry to be a pain in the arse, but that Guinness is just running though me. I need a pee stop," Orla said from the back seat. "No big emergency yet, but maybe stop at the next garage?"

"Sure, I could do with a bottle of water," Tommy said.

Fifteen minutes later, he pulled in at a garage at a crossroads. Orla dashed to the toilets while Tommy and Carla went to get snacks. Molly stayed put.

She watched a few cars pass, slowing for the traffic lights, some stopping level with her, then revving up and driving off.

Then suddenly she saw it in the distance. The black Ford Ka stood out as if surrounded by an aura. Her eyesight sharpened as she focused on Dermot driving towards her, the shape of his head and upper body behind the wheel unmistakable. Tension struck painfully at the base of her throat as the car slowed down, yet still approached.

Molly stared, glued to her window, unable to look away. The black-haired woman beside Dermot smiled as she placed her hand at the back of Dermot's neck. The car stopped, and Molly could see straight into it – could nearly feel the massage of the hand on her own neck. She felt sick.

The black-haired woman looked out her window. Her eyes scanned briefly as if looking for something, then locked onto Molly's gaze. Molly's stomach turned to ice. She glared back, willing every ounce of her hatred to fly from her eyes. The other woman's smile drizzled from her features, and her black eyes popped open before she swung her eyes away.

The lights changed. The Ford jumped forward. Clearly, Dermot still needed lots of practice with the clutch. Before it completely stalled, he got it sorted. As the car jigged off, the woman turned to look at Molly again, a cool sneer replacing the surprise.

Molly jumped as Orla pulled the car door open. Sweat cooled suddenly on her skin, and Molly shivered.

"Jaysus, are you okay? You look like you've seen a ghost," Orla said.

"I wish I had," Molly said, but decided not to share her encounter.

***

"I'm so sorry about the weekend, Molly," Tommy said as he drove the car down her street. Outside, the burnished sky had given way to deep blue. Orla slumped asleep in the front seat. They'd already dropped Carla home.

Molly pulled her mind away from the image of the black, sneering eyes.

"It's not your fault," Molly said. "Parts of it were kind of funny – like Mickey's face when the vomit blew back on him!" She shrugged a small laugh as she looked down at Wolfie's head in her lap and scratched him behind the ears. His tail thumped.

"Do you feel any better?" Tommy said.

"Sure. A wee bit."

Liar!

In the fading light, she caught his smile in the rear view mirror. She hadn't the heart to tell him how terrible she felt. Gloom settled on her, a suffocating shawl of dread. Molly retreated further into herself. The sickness in her stomach returned, and a fluttering sensation nestled in her chest as anxiety revisited its old haunts. The whole way home she could only think about Dermot hurtling towards Donegal, driven by the beautiful dark-haired woman in the black Ford Ka.

***

When Tommy dropped Molly off, the house stood dark and silent. Molly used to come in at night and see Dermot through the front windows, plopped in front of the goggle box. Usually he was too lazy to close the curtains, so the house would be lit up like a display in the Idea Home Exhibition.

Tonight the house looked ominous, abandoned. And why not? Hadn't it been? Hadn't she been? She took a deep breath and swung the gate open. Its familiar clatter sounded crass, too cheerful. She found the keys and opened the front door.

In the living room, everything was exactly as she had left it: tidy. In the old days, she would return home to a mess because Dermot spent the weekend without her to lift up after him. The sucking vacuum of emptiness extracted any of the energy that lingered from the trip.

Her breath quickened as she moved into the kitchen, searching, but not sure what for. She scanned the countertops. One cup of cold coffee sat by the sink. Her heart beat urgently, as if she expected something important to happen but didn't know what. She ran back out to the hallway and ascended the stairs two at a time, reaching the top breathless. She flicked the light switch to her bedroom. It threw a harsh glare on the room, transforming the two windows either side of the bed into black foreboding eyeholes.

Black glaring eyes.

She wrenched the curtains closed to block their stare. Trembling, she went to the closet. Slowly she opened Dermot's side. It still stood empty.

What had she been expecting? Sobs wrenched from her throat. In a frenzy of self-punishment, she opened all the empty drawers that had once been full of Dermot's belongings. She yanked the drawers out violently, not caring if she damaged them, and heaped them on the bed.

Spent of her fury, she collapsed onto her knees and curled her body, the rough bleach-stained carpet scratchy where her forehead touched it. She wept long, shattering wails, writhing on the floor, hacking in breaths between outbursts. Finally drained, she lay there exhausted. She found she could close her eyes now without seeing that bitch sneering at her, but she still felt seared by it.

She yearned to go back to the days when she was ignorant and blissful. Why hadn't she stopped then and registered "look, this is what it feels like to have someone to love and be loved?" She craved it back even though it had all been lies.

"Whatever I have done, God, I'm sorry. Just give me a chance to do it over. To do it right. Please God. Please!" she pleaded. She lay shivering on the carpet. Under the bed, she saw a dusty box. She recognized it at once. Her heart thumped. Did she want to go there? Could she bear it? She reached out her hand and decided that if she could reach it she would look at it.

Fully stretched, she still needed another inch. She dropped her arm. Her wedding album could wait until another day. Like her marriage, it could lie there, dusty and useless.

Wednesday, March 22nd

CHAPTER THIRTY-ONE

From her perch in the riverside restaurant, Tracey watched the Lagan water flow past the banks with a mesmerizing silkiness. She read the ripples on the water with a practiced eye. Eddies puckered and dimpled, outlining the main thrust of the flow. Further upstream, a battery of wavelets bore witness to a breeze lingering on the surface where the river banks curved and channeled the water in a different direction.

Tracey watched, with a mild kiss of envy, one of the university rowboats moving past her window, straight and true as an arrow, the crew working as one organism to propel their craft. She welcomed the pacifying effect of the river, glad that Tommy had chosen the Cutters Wharf restaurant for their dinner meeting with his Dad.

She hadn't seen Tommy since they'd left Donegal a couple of days ago. She was looking forward to seeing him, hoping that being with him would dissolve the guilt she harbored about Dermot. Perhaps just being with Tommy would set things back in perspective and help her to bring her world back onto an even tilt.

On one level, she'd been surprised by Dermot's helping them out by bringing the keys, yet Dermot had always looked out for her, helped her out, supported his mates. She'd dropped her frosty demeanor when he'd arrived in all smiles and tales of near misses in the car.

Mickey had greeted him with the usual, "Hiya."

Dermot shook his hand, and then moved to embrace Tracey in a gesture so fluid and familiar that it felt like coming home to a warm hearth. Dermot gave Mickey the key.

"I can't hang around," he said. "We're starving. I'm taking Sheila for a fancy meal, and she's waiting in the car."

Hiding like a coward, Tracey thought, though she was glad not to have to face her. Tracey would have done the same. What was the point in them meeting?

Dermot had seemed relaxed and happy. Tracey pushed guilt aside and warmed to his charm. She loved her brother. She loved Molly. She didn't have to take sides, did she?

"I'll see you next week, Tracey," Dermot said. "We need to talk."

Tracey swallowed the golf ball in her throat and nodded.

Dermot had punched her lightly on the shoulder saying, "That's my girl."

As he left, Tracey had felt loss drill through her. She missed him.

Now she sat in the Cutters Wharf with an eye on the door. No point feeling guilty. She couldn't change anything. Tonight she needed to focus on Tommy and his relationship with his Dad.

Her heart lifted when she saw Tommy open the door and hold it, allowing an older, stooped version of himself to walk in. She took a deep breath, lifted her hand and waved. *Here we go.*

"Dad, this is Tracey Duggan," Tommy said.

"I'm so sorry that my son didn't have the good manners to collect you, my dear," Tommy's father said as he reached to shake Tracey's hand. "In my day, young men collected their lady friends when they took them out to dinner."

"Dad, I explained in the car." A muscle flickered in Tommy's jaw.

"It's okay, Mr. O'Brian. I've a couple of messages to do after dinner, so I need my own car," Tracey said. "Thank you for being such a gentleman. I see where Tommy gets his chivalry from." She smiled her most twinkly smile at him.

"Sean. Please, call me Sean."

"Okay, Sean," Tracey said.

As the older man smiled, Tracey recognized Tommy's smile in the same crinkling around the edges of pale grey eyes, except the wrinkles fanned out into the blue veins mapping his temples.

"So you are one of the Duggans," Sean said as he sat down and opened his menu. "Anything to Dermot Duggan?"

"He's my brother." Tracey glanced at the menu.

"Ach, sure you know our Molly then, my niece. Dermot's a great fella too. Big into the football. I'd see him down the bookies from time to time. Good craic too, so he is," Sean said without looking up.

Tracey swallowed. Sean obviously hadn't heard yet.

Tommy cleared his throat. "Actually Dad, Dermot and Molly have broken up."

"What?" Sean looked up, his brow creased into a thousand folds.

"That 'great fella' has run off with another woman, gotten her pregnant, and our Molly is devastated," Tommy said.

So much for setting her world on an even keel. Did she detect a tone of triumph in Tommy's voice, having proven his father wrong? Tracey couldn't decide if she was more embarrassed at being Dermot's sister or more annoyed that Tommy had left the Duggans out to dry. So much for him not letting her down. She caught his eye and frowned, immediately mollified by Tommy's expression and pink flush. There was no nice way of telling anyone what Dermot had done to Molly, and it seemed petty to remind him that Dermot had saved the day by coming to Donegal with Mickey's keys.

Sean's mouth dropped open beneath the wrinkled brow. He closed it and opened it again, but didn't speak.

"I'm sure in your day young men didn't do that sort of thing either," Tommy said dryly, folding his menu closed. "I think I'll have the steamed Dundrum mussels for starters. Have you guys decided yet?"

Sean dove into his menu, making a growling sound as he cleared his throat.

Tracey welcomed the diversion. Her appetite had evaporated, but she made a decision, and they ordered their food.

"What did Aileen and Ben say? Has she even told her parents?" Sean asked.

"Aileen blamed Molly." Tommy's eyes blazed with anger as he continued, "She said she should have been able to keep Dermot happy and blamed her for driving him into the arms of another woman."

"Jesus, that woman!" said Sean.

"Poor Molly." Tracey felt deep sadness for her. "I didn't know that."

"Aunty Aileen does nothing but criticize her. Nothing Molly ever does is good enough." Tommy said. "I think Molly got on better with my Mum than with her own."

"She was so good to your Mother back when, you know…" Sean took a sip of water. "She was a great wee nurse. Sat up nights, brung us food and just..everything… She was a real wee angel."

"She really was," Tommy agreed. "We depended heavily on Molly."

"Aye, and she was there for me afterwards, you know, when I was left all alone." Sean stared at Tommy, who shifted position but kept his eyes fastened on his hands clasped on the table in front of him.

"Would she have him back?" Sean asked Tracey.

"Yes," Tracey said, "In a heartbeat."

"Thought so. That Molly one never held a grudge her whole life. She forgives people easily. Unlike some who'll hold on to past slights forever," Sean said.

Tommy rolled his eyes and sighed loudly.

"Molly is my best friend. I hate seeing her so upset. And I hate that it's my brother that has done this to her." She looked from Tommy to Sean and took a mouthful of water.

"I'm just saying that she's better off without him," Tommy said. "Dad seems to think that because he likes football and backing horses, he's a great guy."

Tracey inhaled sharply, mid swallow, triggering her cough reflex. Horrified, she sprayed the table with water before she was able to grab a napkin. The all-consuming tickle made her cough until she retched, forcing tears to her eyes.

No, no, no! How embarrassing.

Tommy patted her on the back, but she waved him away. She just had to ride this one out.

"Down the wrong way?" Sean said. "Give her some bread, Tommy."

Tracey waved that away too. She just wanted to breathe without spluttering.

"If you hadn't been being such a prat, she'd never have choked," Sean said.

"What?" Tommy said, puffed with incredulity, "You were the one being arsey, as usual."

"What do you mean? I didn't come here to be insulted."

"No, obviously you came here to be insulting!"

Angry, Tracey found her voice at last. She prayed that her vocal cords would hold up and not throw her into another spasm of coughing. "Stop it, the pair of you!"

Both men looked at her in surprise.

"You're both being prats!" she said.

Sean's jaw dropped open. Tracey ignored him and rounded on Tommy.

"That's no way to talk to your Da. Jesus, Tommy give him a chance. You've been getting digs in at him since you arrived. Knock it off."

"That's what I always…" Sean began.

"No, Sean, you two are as bad as each other from what I can see. If Tommy were gay, which he isn't, you'd be a bad father for ditching him. That's why Tommy is mad. It's not because you are accusing him in the wrong. It's because it shouldn't make a damn bit of difference. He's a good man. So are you. Now take the cloth out of your ears, spit the barbs from your tongues, and talk to each other like decent human beings." She shoved her chair back and stood up. "And speaking of spit, I'm going to try to clean myself up!"

Not caring if other diners stared, she stomped off to the bathroom with her heart hammering in her ears.

Her mascara wasn't as big of a mess as she'd thought it would be, at least nothing that a damp piece of toilet roll wouldn't cure. She came down from her adrenalin high with a thud. Her muscles quivered, and she felt sick. She could usually control her temper, but if she felt embarrassed on top of it, then she lost control. She wouldn't be surprised if she went out to an empty table.

She wasn't so naive as to think that a dinner together would fix Tommy's relationship with his father, but she expected Tommy to at least try to make some sort of effort. Instead, he'd only succeeded in needling the old man and pissing her off about Dermot.

She pulled herself together, taking one last look at herself in the mirror. Maybe she should just slide on out and go home, but she couldn't. She'd left her bag at the table. She had to face them.

As she approached the table, she saw Sean talking. He looked comfortable, gesturing calmly with one hand, the other resting on his wine glass. Tommy nodded and sipped at his water. Both men looked up at the same time and seeing her, they stood up. Tommy pulled out her chair for her, and she sat down. Both men sat too.

"I apologize for my outburst," she said mustering as much dignity as she could.

Tommy took her hand.

"I'm sorry," he said. "We both are."

Sean nodded.

Tracey's face burned as she choked back the swift rise of emotion.

"Perhaps we can all start again," said Sean. "I'm not sure I know how or where to begin, but I'm willing to try."

"Me too," said Tommy. "Are you okay, Tracey?"

She still didn't trust herself to speak. She nodded and picked up her fork and pushed food around on her plate. The men ate in silence.

"Maybe," Tracey said, finding her voice, "You should start with saying what you want, not what you don't want and not accusing each other of anything. Keep it simple and positive. Maybe you should go first, Tommy."

My counselor would be proud.

"I want." Tommy stopped. He screwed up his face and concentrated on his plate. "Okay I got it," he said. "I want my Dad back. I want us to be like we were before Mum got sick, friends, you know."

"It's just that I thought you. . . " Sean stopped.

Tension stretched in the air as Tracey waited for the same old lines to be recycled.

"Just tell us what you want Sean, as simply as you can," she said softly.

"I want that too, son."

Tracey exhaled the breath she'd been holding.

The old man smiled, his face a swath of corduroy wrinkles. The lights of the restaurant picked up the sharp glitter of moisture in both men's eyes.

Heartened, Tracey lifted her glass. "A toast – to finding a starting point."

Sean and Tommy clinked their glasses.

Thursday, May 4th

CHAPTER THIRTY-TWO

In the early days, Molly dreamed that Dermot came back to her and she, aloof, accepted him, but on her rigorous terms, which excluded football or socializing without her.

He would become the DIY guru and would love to stay at home and make things for the house and garden. They would spend their weekends fixing up their house or travelling to beautiful hotels and romantic camp spots. Of course, she would get pregnant and they and their seven children would be like a Belfast version of the Waltons.

Over the last few months, something fierce and bitter had come to roost in Molly's heart. She came to know raw hatred. She hated Sheila the most, then Dermot, and then herself.

She started back to work after Easter. The workdays dragged by, but not as much as the empty evenings at home alone. Today would be different, and she hoped that the break in routine would help with the monotony that had become her life. The pupils were off school to allow the teachers to attend a training day. A staff meeting in the assembly hall would start the day.

Molly needed papers from her room and used the few minutes she had left before the meeting to run down and get them. As she bent over to fish a folder out of a low cupboard she heard a soft thud on the window behind her. She'd heard it before and knew that it signaled the demise of a poor, disoriented bird. The large windows that ran along either side of her classroom gave birds the impression that they could fly straight through if she didn't decorate them with art work. Today the windows were bare. Usually, noise and activity when the kids were in the classroom scared the birds off.

Her classroom opened directly to the outside by a back door. She burst through it and scrabbled to find the bird lying below the window. The pigeon's head lay at an impossible angle. Molly knew that this one wasn't going to recover. That pitiful bird was just flying along then - whack! It never knew what hit it.

With tears blurring her vision, she picked up the poor dead creature and brought it inside just as the first few drops of rain began to fall. She placed it in a plastic bag but couldn't drop it in the classroom bin. The cleaners wouldn't be in today. It would lie there until tomorrow, and she didn't want to risk the kids seeing it.

She glanced at her watch. She'd no time left! Shoving the plastic-wrapped bird into her bag, she grabbed the papers and ran. Just as she reached the door of the assembly hall the school secretary approached carrying a bundle of folders and envelopes.

"Molly, a letter came for you today."

"Wow, I'm usually not important enough to get mail," Molly quipped as she waited for the secretary to riffle through her paperwork.

"Sure you are," the secretary said, smiling as she handed Molly a small white envelope before scurrying off.

Molly's heart stopped when she saw Dermot's handwriting.

Why is he writing to me at school? Maybe he wants to come back, and that witch won't let him!

She remembered the black sneering eyes mocking her from the Ford Ka on the way home from Donegal. She shivered.

"Come on," said a voice behind her. Her friend Laura, a primary three teacher nudged her. "Are you okay?"

"I don't know," Molly murmured and followed her into the hall. They made it the meeting with seconds to spare and found a seat in the back row. She should wait until later to read the letter, but to wait would be torture. Her blood rushed so loudly in her ears that she was sure everyone else could hear it.

Please let it be him begging forgiveness and wanting to come home.

Home – it was a strange idea since home for Molly described anyplace where she could be with Dermot. He was her home. The thought made her heart ache.

The Principal stood waiting for the teachers to come to order. After clearing his throat, he spoke into the microphone, which merely crackled. The IT coordinator fussed around with some wire and switches until the Vice Principal stood up and with an assertive voice, called the meeting to order.

Molly tore open the envelope. Would it be wiser to leave it until after school? How bad could it be? Nothing could be worse than his leaving. Perhaps it was good news. Maybe he wanted to come back.

"IN THE NAME OF THE FATHER." The VP spoke clearly and deliberately.

It was an old trick that teachers used on pupils. Starting the prayers commanded respect. By the end of the blessing all the teachers ended in unison with "Amen."

As the principal began to speak, Molly slid the letter out of the envelope. Laura gave her a quizzical look.

"From Dermot," mouthed Molly.

Laura pulled a face.

Molly shrugged and opened the letter. It was written on cheap paper with no address at the top. That amused her. She knew where he lived now anyway, but she liked that he didn't know that.

Molly could hear Dermot's voice, cool and disconnected, in the words.

Molly

You have been living in our house now for 2 months and I think that it is time that we divided up our joint assets. You need to file for divorce since the law says that I can't yet. You need to use the grounds of adultery. I think it will be best for both of us to get this sorted out so we can move on. I'm sorry I hurt your feelings.

I will have to stop paying my half of the mortgage once the baby is born.

Text my mobile with your solicitors name when you have it.

Dermot.

"Oh my God," Molly whispered, dropping the letter. She felt hot. Black spots rose before her eyes. The next thing she knew Laura was holding her up, preventing her from sliding off her seat.

"Molly." Laura's voice sounded anxious. "Molly. Are you okay? Let's get you out of here."

A few teachers looked round at the commotion of chairs moving at the back. A low rumble of voices travelled through the crowd.

Laura picked up the letter before dragging Molly out to the foyer and into a little interview room normally reserved for meeting parents.

"Here. Have some water." Laura gave Molly a glass of water from the tap in the corner. Molly took a sip and grimaced.

"Bad, eh?"

Molly wasn't sure if Laura meant the water or the letter. She nodded yes to both. "Read it." Molly said as she hugged her arms around herself.

"The bastard!" Laura said when she had finished. "Get a lawyer and sue the shit out of him."

"This isn't the movies. I don't even know if I could. And I don't want a divorce. I'm Catholic." Despair dripped from Molly's tone.

"Being Catholic doesn't change that! He left you. You should move on. Give yourself a chance to meet someone new. Someone who deserves you."

"I still love him," Molly said. "Oh God, I'd be the only person I know who's divorced. Me, a divorcee?"

"It's the twenty first century. People get divorced all the time now."

"Like who? Apart from me." Molly burst into tears.

"I'm sorry I was so abrupt, Molly. This is tough. Really, you should go on home," Laura advised. "I'll tell the VP you were sick. She'll understand. Do you need a lift? Are you okay to drive?"

"Yeah, no, I mean, I'm fine." Molly said.

Fine, fine, fine! Just keep telling them I'm fine.

She drove home in the rain, preoccupied with Dermot's letter.

Sorry I hurt your feelings! What a fucking stupid wanker!

She couldn't think of enough bad names to call him. Anger bubbled in her brain. Laura was right. He was a bastard and he deserved to suffer.

I'll give him hurt feelings, all right.

Thursday, May 4th

CHAPTER THIRTY-THREE

As March moved into April, the bobbing daffodils had turned papery, and their foliage gave way to slender-leaved bluebells. Sheila had blossomed in her pregnancy. Always aware of her appearance, she struggled with her expanding waistline. By the end of April, she had conceded to donning maternity wear.

"Is that all you are having for breakfast? Do you feel okay?" Dermot asked as he sat a plate stacked with toast beside her bowl of All Bran.

"Yes. It's fine. Don't fuss," Sheila said, wishing he'd hurry on to work and leave her with the morning to herself.

"Well, you are eating for two, or maybe even three. Is anyone kicking in there today?" He put his hand on her belly. When had her stomach become public property? Everyone wanted to touch it now. She shrugged him away.

"Don't even think that. One is plenty," she said.

"I wish you'd let me come with you to the scan today."

"There's no need. I don't see what all the fuss is about. It will be a blurry blob. You won't see anything." Sheila stood up, scraped the remains of her bowl into the bin and took a slug of coffee.

"Seriously, you need to eat more, and I don't think coffee is good for the baby," Dermot said, frowning.

"Jesus, Dermot!" Sheila slammed down her cup. "I'm fine. Let it go." She felt like a bitch as he got up quietly and put away his dishes. She had trained him well over the last few months, but now he flapped around her like a mother hen.

"Look I'll ring you at lunch time, okay?" he asked and then added softly. "You look beautiful, you know."

He moved towards her.

"Okay, okay," Sheila said, backing away. "Go on. You'll be late, and I'm not driving you today."

"Did you look at the baby names book? Will you find out if it's a boy or girl today?" Dermot pulled on his jacket, then looked out the window and took it off again.

"No and no. It's too soon." She pulled her cheek away from Dermot's quick kiss and resisted the urge to wipe at the wet splodge he left behind. She savored the quiet after the door closed behind him. Her ringing phone lifted her from her reverie. Elaine's number glowed on the screen.

"Hi. I just... wanted to wish... you luck... for the scan," Elaine gasped.

"Are you jogging to work right now?" Sheila asked.

"No...well yes... but not on purpose...I missed the bus." Elaine puffed the words, making Sheila laugh. "So, will you call me afterwards?" Elaine continued. "Is Dermot going with you to see the first pictures of his lovechild?"

Sheila cringed.

"Stop calling it that." Sheila immediately regretted her sharp retort and added more gently, "No. I made him go on to work. He's doing my head in asking me a hundred questions every day and trying to force feed me all the time. I'd be the size of a house if I ate every time he bugged me to."

"Ach, poor Dermot. It's so romantic. He's crazy about you."

In the background a bell tinkled, and Sheila checked the clock. Five minutes to nine.

"You've done a fabulous job keeping trim, Sheila, but really, is it healthy for the baby?" Elaine said.

"The baby gets what it needs," Sheila said, clenching her jaws together.

"Well, you look great. But then you always do."

"Thanks, Elaine. I'll call you later." Five minutes to herself. That's all she wanted.

***

The ornamental cherries in the gardens of south Belfast peppered pink petals onto the streets. Sheila took the opportunity of the sunny morning to walk to her appointment.

Her route took her through the Queen's University. Students, in the throes of preparing for exams, used the excuse of some sunshine to kick back a little. Some had even dragged their armchairs and sofas out into the tiny patches of front garden. Books - merely props for their conscience - lay on the ground as the kids soaked up the rays.

Students dotted the lawn outside the Lanyon building, too. Their pasty white skin soaked in the sunshine. Laughter floated across the lawn. They looked so free with their future glistening ahead of them. Envy stabbed Sheila. She shoved it away, not wanting to waste energy on that useless emotion. She should be going to get her travel vaccines. Elaine was booked to go to India for three weeks in August with a couple of other girls, leaving Sheila behind.

She felt cheated by the turn of events. She didn't want to be pregnant and certainly did not want to have a life shackled to her just yet, especially a helpless infant. Being tied to Dermot was stifling enough.

Most of the time, Sheila merely put up with Dermot. He did make her laugh, though, and she felt that in the future she might need the security of his being around. Even though she treated him with disdain, it only served to keep him coming back for more. Did treating them mean really keep them that keen?

Her appointment showed a normal, healthy baby. Sheila felt neither elated nor concerned. Whatever would be would be. Her midwife told her that the baby was due around the end of October —a date for her diary.

She left the hospital and began to walk home. The blue sky clouded over, casting a chill to the day. So much for the summer day the morning had promised. Sheila decided to hail a taxi. The cream canvas shoes she had optimistically donned that morning were not suitable for traipsing through wet streets.

The rain began while she was in the taxi, so that by the time she arrived in her street it bucketed down full pelt. Rain drops bounced up from the newly formed puddles. Sheila got out into the deluge and ran for her front door.

She saw something sodden attached to the door handle. She dashed over, hopping on tiptoes, futilely trying to prevent the hem of her jeans from wicking the water up her legs.

Three feet from the door she stopped, confused and horrified. Tied by its feet to the door handle hung a feathered body, bedraggled and headless. Dark red gobs oozed from the dead bird's neck. Some damp feathers stuck to the door, and dark red blobs lay on the ground. She covered her mouth, fighting the urge to both vomit and scream.

Sheila leaned over, and after a violent heave delivered her lunch into the shrubs. The stench of vomit soared up, causing her to dry heave again. Tears streamed from her eyes, and sweat broke on her body, despite the chill from being wet. Trembling, she reached for her mobile phone. With fumbling fingers, she punched in Dermot's number.

The answering service delivered its prompt for a message, but Sheila hung up. Terrified, she stood trembling in the rain, wondering what she should do.

She was afraid to go around to the back door in case worse awaited there. She shivered. The rain penetrated every layer of her clothing so it clung to her, restricting the simplest of movements such as raising her hand to place her phone back in her bag.

She inched toward the door. Should she call the police? Did this warrant such a call? Even now, people in this area were not comfortable with police because of the long and sorry history of the Troubles.

Dammit, where the hell was Dermot? What if someone was in the house? She looked up at the windows and decided that if someone had broken in, they wouldn't have needed to put the dead bird on the door handle. They could have simply left it inside on the table or, worse still, on the bed. She shuddered.

Rain pelted her, its intensity increasing as she stood there in a quandary. She needed to go inside. The bird's body lay directly over the key hole. She would have to touch it. She remembered the pair of nail scissors that she kept in her bag.

Digging deep, she found them, soaking the interior of her bag in the process. Taking a deep breath, she stepped up to the door. Her hands shook as she sawed the scissors through the cord holding the bird. When the final thread gave way, the bird's body dropped and landed with a plop at her feet, splashing blood and body fluids across Sheila's cream canvas shoes and jeans. She yelped in alarm and jumped back. Cursing at the ruined clothing, she put the key into the bloody keyhole and opened the door.

Sheila stepped over the bird and fled inside, slamming the door behind her. Gasping for breath, she looked around the hall quickly. Everything seemed to be in order. She walked through the apartment, briskly giving each room a cursory once over, though not sure what she would have done had she discovered anything out of place, or God forbid, anyone inside.

Satisfied, she flicked on the kettle and stripped out of her wet clothes where she stood. Still shivering, she loaded up the washing machine with all her clothing, including the canvas shoes, while the kettle boiled. She selected a hot wash, not caring if she ruined the clothes inside.

A sudden noise at the front door made her jump. She whirled around, grabbing a knife for protection, and a tea towel, in a vain attempt to cover her naked body.

Dermot opened the front door.

Sheila burst into tears and dropped the knife. She had never felt so lost and vulnerable.

Dermot ran to her.

"Why are you running around naked with a knife?" he asked.

"Oh God, Dermot," she gulped, "the dead bird! Didn't you see it on the doorstep?"

Dermot guided her to the bedroom, sat her down on the bed and grabbed her fluffy dressing gown, bundling her up in its warm folds.

"What dead bird?" he said, stroking her face with his thumb.

"It's on the doorstep. It was tied to the door handle. I had to cut it down to get at the key hole. Oh God, it was revolting. It had its head cut off, and its guts were hanging out of its neck!" she sobbed.

"Jesus Christ! When?"

"Just now. You must have seen the body on the doorstep when you came in."

"I didn't notice anything." Dermot looked bewildered.

"It must have rolled off." She marched from the bedroom to the front door and pulled the door open to show him.

It was gone. She stared at the door handle. Rain had washed away any feathers, and the doorstep was clean.

"It was here. I swear to God it was here!" Her voice rose with hysteria. She pulled back the foliage at either side of the doorstep to see if the bird's body had slipped down the sides but could not find it. The rain was still lashing down and causing water to run off the step. Dermot pulled her, still protesting, back into the hallway. He closed the door behind her.

"Dermot, I cut the bird down and it splashed blood all round my shoes and jeans." She stopped abruptly, realizing that the clothes were, by now, half way through a wash cycle. "Someone is messing with us."

Dermot looked at her, confusion in his eyes.

Sheila knew that he didn't believe her. What was going on? She was sure she saw the bird. But now it was as if it hadn't happened.

Thursday, May 4th

CHAPTER THIRTY-FOUR

Molly found Tommy waiting for her when she arrived home. She'd been derailed today. Tommy was just what she needed.

Wolfie stood in her garden on his hind legs with his front paws on the top of the gate, looking out at her. His mouth opened wide, his pink tongue lolling out the side. His tail wound to a frenzy as Molly's car pulled up. When she got out of the car he whined and wriggled, making the gate rattle at the latch.

"Wolfie, sit."

His master's voice brokered no argument, and the dog sat down, quivering, looking back and forth from Tommy to Molly, giving little whimpers and licking his lips.

"Laura texted and said you went home in a state — are you okay?" Tommy asked.

Molly lifted her bags from the car. She hugged Tommy and patted Wolfie's head.

"So you heard about the letter?" she said amid a jangle of keys. Tommy put his hand on her bags.

"Let me help you with that."

"No, no, no. It's okay. I've got it now." She presented the key and opened the door. Tommy clicked his fingers, and the dog charged in ahead of them.

"Home security device. If you have an intruder, Wolfie'll lick him to death," Tommy said, holding the door for Molly.

She managed a thin smile. She set the bags on the living room floor.

"Cuppa?" Molly asked. She walked into the kitchen without waiting for an answer.

Tommy followed her, pulling a giant bar of Galaxy chocolate from his jacket pocket.

"Crisis food," he said, sitting down.

She didn't deserve his sympathy, but she longed to wallow in it. *Deep breath. Don't cry.*

"I don't know what to do," she said. "He wants a divorce. He says he is going to stop paying his share of the mortgage. I can't afford to pay it all by myself. I don't want to sell the house. I love the house. I don't want to move. How can he do this? I'm his wife Tommy, his wife. He can't just end it."

"Molly, he has ended it. You need a solicitor, someone who can give you legal advice on your financial situation. I know you don't want to hear this, but Dermot is gone. You need to pick up your life and move on," Tommy said, his voice gentle. "Now, the house could be a problem if the mortgage is big. You bought the place twelve years ago. Even with the down turn in the housing market, you must have plenty of positive equity."

Molly shook her head, unable to contain her tears. "We extended our mortgage two years ago to build the extension to the kitchen."

"So, do you have any idea how much the house is worth now?"

"Well, it was supposed to put twenty thousand more onto the value of the house, but now that no one is buying, I don't know how that will work. But if I can't keep up the mortgage payments, then what can I do? Will the bank repossess me? God - I could lose it all!" Her voice rose in panic.

"What about your parents?"

"Mum is still of the opinion that Dermot will come back. She thinks that I pushed him away, that it's my fault for not being attentive enough to him."

"Christ, Molly, you know that's not true, and it's not fair of your mother to say it either. Jesus!"

Molly wondered how much of her mother's searing words were true.

"Molly, listen to me. You were a wonderful wife to Dermot. Any sane person would see that. Aileen lives in a fantasy world. Do not listen to her. What about your Dad, what does he say?" Tommy said.

If only she could believe what Tommy said was true. Strength drained from her, and she fought to keep some control.

"Dad doesn't say much, ever." Molly wiped her face with her cuff.

"Maybe they'll help you with the house. Your Dad hasn't retired yet. He may still have borrowing power."

"Or they may just expect me to move in with them." Her soul shriveled at the thought.

"No way, you can't do that. Let's get legal advice. I'm off every Monday. Set up an appointment for after school on a Monday, and I'll come with you. OK?"

"Oh God, I don't want to get divorced," Molly wailed and buried her face in her hands.

"Look, I'm going to get that cup of tea. Then we will sit down and calm down.

"There's water in the bowl for Wolfie," Molly said. The bowl sat permanently on her kitchen floor now that Dermot wasn't around to fuss about the dog visiting. "And I've got chew bars for him. Where did he go?"

The dog was too quiet.

Shit, shit, shit!

Molly bolted for the door as Tommy shouted, "Wolfie, come here boy."

They both arrived into the living room to see Wolfie lift his head out of one of Molly's bags. Feathers flew up around him in all directions, damp ones sticking to his face and ears. Red jellied globs hung from one side of the dog's mouth and skinny wee bird's legs stuck out the other side. Wolfie looked up, forehead wrinkled, eyes guilty.

"Shit! What is that?" Tommy said. "Drop it. DROP IT!"

The dog deposited the mangled bird onto the floor. Blood soaked from the open neck into the beige carpet. Molly ran into the kitchen. She grabbed a plastic bag and a roll of kitchen towels. How was she going to explain this? She had shocked herself today. When had she turned into this person? She blamed Dermot. The Molly who had been Dermot's wife would never have behaved as she had today.

Maybe if she confessed to Tommy he could help her make sense of her actions. He'd need an explanation now anyway.

"Dermot's letter just tipped me over the edge today," Molly said, trying to keep her voice from warbling. "I never saw myself as vindictive but when I thought about how Dermot has treated me..." She sucked in a breath and exhaled it as she scrubbed at the floor.

Remember, normal, not crazy.

"Jesus Christ! Molly, what did you do?" Tommy shoved the dog into the hall and stood with his back to the door.

"I – I just felt, like... a flame burning inside me. I wanted revenge. He should feel what I feel. The hurt. The anger. The panic. He's the one who did the bad thing, but I'm the one suffering – it's not fair! He has this cozy wee life now, and I'm all alone, and now he wants me to sell the fucking house." Her voice sounded louder than she wanted. Tommy didn't deserve to get shouted at. She took a deep breath and said quietly, "If Dermot died, I would be better off financially —I would at least own the house."

"Jesus Christ! Molly, don't say stuff like that!" Tommy knelt down beside her, took the bloody bag, and hugged her to him.

She felt the warmth of his body seep into her. She clung to him for a second, then pulled away, wiping the back of her hand across her face. If she had the connections, she could order a hit on Dermot. Did the paramilitaries do stuff like that? She wasn't even sure. Of course, she would be the number one suspect, and knowing her luck, would end up in jail.

"So where does this come in?" Tommy sat back on his heels and held up the bag. Molly sat back too, tore off a piece of kitchen roll and blew her nose.

"The pigeon crashed into a window at work. I didn't want the kids to see it in the bin, so it ended up coming home with me," she said.

"It smashed the window?" Tommy stared at the bag as if it might answer his question.

"Well, no. Its neck broke, but well...em, I did that. I- I cut its head off." She said the last few words in a rush.

Oh God, that sounds fucking crazy.

"What?" Tommy looked at her, his eyes wide open, his forehead wrinkled.

"Dermot is very squeamish. I wanted to put it through his letter box in return for the letter," Molly said, afraid to look up at Tommy again.

This confession only made her feel even crappier. Maybe she hoped Tommy would say something like, "Oh, that's okay. Sure wouldn't I do the same thing too?"

But Tommy was not driven mad with grief.

"I started with the idea of the bird in the letterbox. He really hates blood, so I thought I'd cut off the bird's head. Squishing it through the letter box, though, was a bit too yuck, so I decided to hang it off the door handle," Molly continued. "I used the knife we cut our wedding cake with. It wasn't the sharpest knife in the drawer, but then neither is Dermot."

She flicked her eyes up to see if Tommy had found that funny. His expression had softened, but he still looked like a priest hearing confessions.

Hacking off the pigeon's head had made a satisfying mess. She found some blue twine in the drawer. It too had seen better days, but it would do the job. She tied the twine to the bird's feet and then bundled the headless body into the plastic bag again. Blood and gore oozed against the inside of the bag.

She drove to Sheila's apartment. It took her a matter of seconds to hop out of the car, tie up the bird, get back in the car and zoom off, her heart racing. A few streets away, she began to regret her actions. Shame soaked her zest for revenge as she put some distance between herself and the bird. This was not who she was. This was something a demented person would do.

"I changed my mind about it, though," Molly said, looking up at Tommy, afraid he'd turn away, but he met her eyes, and she read pity.

"It was only coming up to lunch time. Everyone would be at work. So, I turned right around and took it down. The string had broken, and it was pissing down rain, so it cleaned away any mess. It was only there for about ten minutes or so."

"Good grief," Tommy said, shaking his head. "I sure am glad I'm your friend and not your enemy. How do you feel now?" He stood up and put a hand out to her.

"Stupid," she said. "Really. Fucking. Stupid. What if he'd caught me? What would I have said? Give this to your fecking solicitor?" She stopped. Tears welled up again, but at least she sounded less insane.

"Thank God you took that bird down. That could have gotten complicated." He nodded his head slowly, tipped her face up with a finger beneath her chin and smiled before saying, "At least no harm done, eh?"

Thursday, May 4th

CHAPTER THIRTY-FIVE

Concern tugged at Dermot. He'd never heard of hallucinating as a symptom of pregnancy before. Good thing he came home at lunch time today to see how Sheila's scan had gone. He'd been shocked to find her in the kitchen standing naked and shaking. It took him ages to get her to calm down and stop ranting about a headless bird. Finally she gave him the update on the scan.

Thank God, the baby was fine.

He made Sheila a cup of tea and brought it to her as she dried her hair. She looked cuddly in her big white fluffy dressing gown. He came up behind her and wrapped his arms around her, sliding one hand under the robe and bringing it to rest on the swell of her tummy. He nuzzled the nape of her neck, smelling the lingering fragrance of her shower gel. She smelled good enough to eat. He kissed her neck again and breathed in deeply. Sheila wriggled away from him as he got tangled up in her dryer and brush.

"Dermot, don't," she said, pulling away from him.

He sat on the bed behind her knowing that she was proud of how she looked. She simply needed space to fix her hair. He waited until she finished and turned off the dryer. Once more he stood up behind her and wrapped his arms around her, grinding gently against her with his hips.

"I love you, Sheila," he murmured as he bent his head to kiss her shoulder, trying to slide the robe off it.

"But you don't believe me," she said. Her remote expression reflected back to him in the mirror, cold, like the glass that forwarded it.

He held her gaze as dread dripped though his thoughts. He didn't want to argue. "What do you mean?"

"About the dead bird. You don't believe it." She turned to look straight at him.

He let out a long breath and folded his arms across his chest. He leaned against the dressing table, searching for the best words.

"Sheila, I just didn't see a dead bird. You came outside with me. There was nothing there. What am I supposed to think?"

"You are supposed to think that maybe I'm right. Instead, you think I'm making it up."

"I never said that." He didn't think she would make it up, but he had not seen any bird.

"So who would do such a thing? And why?" he asked.

"Molly."

"No way! She doesn't even know where we live."

"How can you be sure?"

"How could she? Even my family doesn't know."

"Why are you defending her?"

"I am not defending her," he insisted. Sheila's paranoia worried him.

"You are. I think she left a dead bird on the door handle. I stole her man, and now she is going to terrorize me."

"Calm down. Getting in a state is bad for the baby." Dermot tried to sound soothing.

"Don't fucking tell me to calm down!" Sheila roared at him. "What right do you have telling me what to do? Your crazy wife comes round with dead birds, and you treat me like I'm the mad one, and you stand up for her."

"I'm not standing up for her. I'm here… with you!" Dermot shouted Sheila down. "I chose you. You won. She is not my wife anymore. I've asked her for a divorce."

Sheila halted as if struck. "When did you see her?"

"I didn't. I sent her a letter and told her that she would need a solicitor and that I wasn't paying the mortgage."

"Really?" Sheila sat down on the edge of the bed.

Dermot hoped she would be pleased, but she seemed pensive.

"So when might she have gotten this letter?" asked Sheila.

"I posted it yesterday morning."

"So, she could have gotten it today. That's why she was mad enough to do this."

"Sheila, please. Listen to me. I know Molly's fucking psycho, and it's right up her street. I'll give you that but there was nothing there." Dermot spoke slowly and deliberately. "Let's look at this logically. Molly would be at work today. When could she have done this, even if she did know where we lived? And if she did, where is the bird now?"

"Dermot," Sheila said, matching his explanatory tone, "There is only one thing I know for certain. There was a dead bird hanging by the feet, headless, from our door handle today. I think it was Molly. What you choose to believe is up to you."

She stood up and walked into the bathroom. Dermot lay back on the bed and covered his face with his hands. He counted to ten. Perhaps this was a symptom of pregnancy he'd never heard of, but her paranoia frightened him. How well did he know Sheila really? Was it possible he had missed this? He thought Sheila had her shit together, but this was too weird. What did Sheila have to gain by making this up? It scared him more to think that she didn't make it up. He stifled the shiver that crept across his scalp. His biggest concern was that Sheila really believed her own crazy story.

Monday, May 8th

CHAPTER THIRTY-SIX

The floors creaked as Molly and Tommy beat their retreat from the solicitor's office. It was in an old building in the centre of Belfast, and its age lent gravity to the weight of the law practiced within. The fusty paper smell followed them as they clattered down the stairs and out into the street.

"Well?" Tommy said, shoving his hands into his pockets and hunching his shoulders at the first smatterings of rain.

"I'm more confused than ever." Molly had tried to soak in every iota of the solicitor's advice, but the woman had spoken in an alien language.

"A financial separation and not a full divorce?" Molly said.

"And that can happen as soon as she has all the details of your earnings and pension," Tommy said.

"Oh God, I have no head for money." Panic surged through her.

"That's the solicitor's job," Tommy said as they got into his car.

"Yes, but I still have to go through the damn filing cabinet to dig out the paperwork. Our filing system is a disaster." Molly felt depressed opening the filing cabinet, even when life went well. Now she couldn't bear the thought of it. Still, she did derive some hope from the fact that she could stall on getting divorced. The longer

Dermot was legally tied to her, the longer hope lingered that she could win him back.

"I think it went well," Tommy said, breaking in on her thoughts. "You have to split everything fifty-fifty, and it looks as though you could buy out his share of the house what with the low property values."

"I really can't see how that works. Maybe I missed something. Maybe you missed something. Oh, I hate all this." Molly felt desolate.

The window wipers squealed against the windshield until the rain shower fully opened on them.

Tommy drove the car in silence for a few minutes and then continued, "Have you called your Dad? Could he buy Dermot's half?"

"No, I haven't asked him yet."

"This is important. I really think you should ask him. Do you want me to ask him for you?" Tommy asked, his voice frosted with frustration.

"Good God, no! Are you nuts?" She knew he was right but she felt steamrollered. If her parents did buy out Dermot, they might hold it over her head. Her mother would bring it up every time she needed Molly to do something for her.

"Do you want me to help you find the documents you need? Tracey won't be home until after eight. We could order a Pepperoni Passion?" Tommy said.

"Well, it's the only passion in my life right now. Thanks Tommy, I think I'd like that."

They fell silent. The only sound beside the purr of the engine was the intermittent squeal of the wiper. Molly remembered all the preparation she put into her wedding day eight years previously. She'd embraced the planning and organizing, making lists, scratching out items and rewriting lists. She'd been thrilled to find a house and even excited getting a mortgage. Discussing money matters had been no problem back then. Unraveling all of that was not so nice.

By the time Tommy parked outside Molly's house, the sun had burst through again with such ferocity that the rain rose as mist from the road.

"The files are upstairs. Should I bring them down, or will we work up there?" Molly asked.

"Let's just work up there. I'll order the pizza now, though. I don't know about you, but I'm starving. I'll follow you up in a minute."

Molly pulled open the filing cabinet drawer and pages popped up at random angles. The hanging folders were labeled in roughly alphabetic order, with the first one having no letter at all. This was the "to be filed" file and as a consequence was stuffed full.

Molly sighed. This lot would have to be sorted first. She lifted out the pages, mostly bills, and began to place them in the relevant pockets. Her breathing quickened as a folder near the back caught her eye.

She reached in slowly and took out a letter written on jotter paper. As Catholics getting married in the church, they'd been required to attend a retreat before the wedding. Part of the retreat involved writing letters to each other. Her heart squeezed with pain, and she gasped in a sob as she unfolded the page. The paper crackled, brittle with age. She stared at Dermot's faded blue handwriting. The note was short but the words ripped through her.

My Darling Molly

I can't wait until our wedding day. You are the most wonderful thing that has ever happened to me. Thank you for putting up with me and my crazy family.

You are my home, my strength, my wings upon which I can fly and escape the fears and worries of my youth. I want to hold you forever.

With you by my side I can jump into the rest of my life knowing that you will always catch me.

I love you,
Dermot xo

Tears blurred her vision. Sorrow and rage surged through her together, a violent concoction, making her dizzy and nauseous at once. What happened to that boy she'd loved?

She gulped in air and struggled to breathe deeply. She couldn't bear to keep the letter, nor could she destroy it. The wardrobe in the study housed her wedding dress. Her white fairytale dress hung sheathed in a bag. She couldn't look at it. Just touching the plastic cover brought fire to her chest. With trembling fingers, she opened the bag and slid the letter in against the silky folds of material. Not wanting Tommy to see her so upset, she dashed down to the bathroom and quickly washed her face.

She returned to the study determined to stay focused on the task at hand. Still shaking, she put the bills into their appropriate place. She lifted out the file labeled "House". In addition, she needed the ones labeled "Wages slips" and "Pensions". The latter felt alarmingly light. That spoke volumes about her future. She took another deep breath. Thank God she'd stopped trembling. She hoped Tommy wouldn't notice her discomposure.

Where was Tommy? He was only phoning for the pizza, not making the damn thing.

"Tommy?" She called down the stairs.

"Yeah, yeah, coming now," he replied.

She could hear him saying goodbye to someone in a manner that spoke of more familiarity than a pizza shop warranted, even if they did eat a lot of pizza.

"Who was that?" she enquired as he walked into the room.

Tommy looked sheepish. His face colored. "Now, Molly, don't be mad, but…" He stopped, took a deep breath and, at her raised eyebrow, continued, "I phoned your dad."

"What?"

He flinched.

"I had to. I can't help you all by myself. I'm so worried about you," he said. "Molly, that whole thing with the bird… It's just… well you scared me."

"And phoning Dad is supposed to help?" She asked, incredulous, but her face heated up with shame at Tommy's mention of the bird. No wonder he was frightened. She was too.

"They are on their way over."

"Fuck me! Jesus Christ, Tommy. Are you trying to give me a nervous breakdown?" Molly could feel sweat trickling down her back. How would she face her parents? He'd backed her into a corner.

"Fine," she said, tight lipped. "But you know they drive me nuts."

They worked together, sorting bills, in sizzling silence for about twenty minutes before the doorbell rang.

"Well, it's either the pizza or the folks." Tommy tried to sound cheerful.

"Either way, I'll be left feeling bilious," Molly said.

Tommy went downstairs, and Molly crept to up the hall to her own bedroom and peeked out the upstairs window. A white car across the road sped off, spinning its wheels. The car looked familiar to Molly, but she was distracted by her mother's voice below.

"Good lord! There's so many yobbos in this neighborhood now really, isn't there? Ben, are you listening to me?"

Molly heard the front door scraping open.

"Hello Tommy. Aren't you looking handsome."

There was a silence that Molly guessed was her mother insisting on the European-style double-cheek kiss. Aileen picked this up from an Italian couple she met on her holiday in Galway. When she returned home she signed up for an Italian language class. All Aileen learned from it was how to pretend to be Italian, badly.

"Is she upstairs?" The voice faded as Aileen moved from the hallway into the living room. Molly's legs felt like lead as she descended the stairs. Her heart thumped as she entered the living room and prepared for the onslaught.

"Oh Molly, look at you! You're wasting away. You're far too skinny," Aileen said. "Men don't like skinny women."

Tommy scooped in a sharp breath like a verbal wince.

"Really, Molly, you need to eat. Is she eating, Tommy?" she asked, as if it were Tommy's responsibility.

"Well, actually there's a pizza on its way," Molly announced coolly.

"Pizza? That's hardly nourishment," Aileen said.

"Oh dear. I ordered enough for all of us," Tommy stammered.

Behind Aileen's back Molly smirked at Tommy as Aileen smoothly said, "That's lovely dear. You are so considerate. Isn't he considerate, Ben?"

"Ah huh," said Ben.

"My lovely nephew, you are just wonderful." She appeared to swell with pride as if it were all her doing.

The bell rang again. This time the pizza arrived. Tommy and Ben fought over the bill whilst Molly went and got plates, cutlery and napkins.

"Molly, do you have any white plates? You know I don't like to eat off colored plates. It makes the food look funny," Aileen said, sitting down at the table, waiting to be served.

Molly sighed and fetched the one white plate she had especially for her mother's visits. Her mother knew where Molly kept it, but went through what Dermot referred to as "the litany" each time she came over. Next, Molly would offer her something to drink. Aileen would say that she never drank with her food, then when everyone sat comfortable at the table she would decide to break her rule "just this once" and ask for something to drink. Then, of course, the water would be too cold for her sensitive teeth.

Molly set out glasses and a jug of tepid water. With everything organized, Molly sat down, and Tommy opened up the pizza and handed slices around. They chomped away in silence for a few minutes, and then Ben cleared his throat.

"So, Molly, Tommy tells me that Dermot has asked for a divorce."

Molly nodded, watching her mother fiddle with the hair just behind her ears. Her bracelets jangled as she twitched. Aileen's dark brown hair had a touch of grey. In an effort to hide it, she dyed her hair with a wash-in color that turned the grey areas plum.

Ben took the floor again. "I think you *should* divorce him."

Molly and her mother gasped in unison.

"He is a coward and a cheat and you are better off without him." Ben continued in a cool voice. He was never this opinionated. "I'll help you buy over his share of the house."

"What?" squawked Aileen.

"Look, Aileen, it's going to be her inheritance anyway."

"But we're not dead yet," she spluttered.

"No, but we can help her now, while we are alive." He glared at Aileen.

"Ben, we haven't discussed this," Aileen said primly.

"What's to discuss?" He stared her down.

Aileen opened her mouth as if to speak, then closed it again.

Molly savored seeing her mother put in her place. She felt a rush of affection for her father.

"Let me look over the paperwork first to see if I can help. You know I'll do my best. You are not in this by yourself," her father said.

The simple words brought fresh tears to her eyes, and not trusting herself to speak, she jumped up and hugged her dad. He patted her back and then pulled away, obviously unsettled by the affection.

When had she last hugged him? Too long ago, far too long.

"Where's my hug? It's my money too, you know," Aileen said.

"The hug was not for the money, Mum."

Sunday, July 30th

CHAPTER THIRTY-SEVEN

Molly couldn't move and hadn't been able to for some time. She had to get up and take Fran out for Sunday Lunch. Just taking a breath made her feel dodgy enough, never mind lifting her head. However, nausea was nothing compared to the horrible memory of what she'd said to Dermot last night after Tommy's thirtieth birthday party.

She cringed. Even that hurt her head, and a wave of sickness forced her to stand up and stagger to the bathroom, where she swayed as she stooped over, staring down at the water in the toilet bowl. A yellowy-beige ring of scum identified where the water met the air. A sour smell wafted up and tipped her over the edge. She heaved violently, filling the toilet with a putrid stench that perpetuated another gag reflex and another until she had emptied her stomach.

Weak and trembling, she lay on the bathroom floor. Her head thumped in tune to her heartbeat. She wished she were dead - not a new thought, especially at times like this when her loneliness bored a hole straight through her chest.

In the tree outside the bathroom window, the resident blackbirds sang back and forth to each other. The whole world existed in pairs; even the blackbirds mocked her single status. She often found herself staring at mothers walking down the street with their push-chairs laden with bags, coats and baby gadgets that Molly had no idea how to use. She envied them their dark circles under their eyes and their cranky children.

At least during the summer holidays she didn't have to make the daily appearance into school. Some mornings she got up, took a sleeping tablet and just went straight back to bed. As each day passed, she slipped further and further away from her old reality.

The house, or rather the mortgage for the house, now belonged half to her and half to her Father. Dermot, the bastard, had it all now: the beautiful woman, the kid on the way and the money. She had nothing. Her life felt empty, bleak and desolate. Dermot had done this.

Again she squirmed, thinking of the words she'd flung at him the previous evening, her embarrassment partly because she'd been so drunk, though not entirely her fault. She'd attended Tommy's thirtieth birthday party. He'd had the kind of party she thought Dermot would plan for her, only better. Whereas she would have been happy with the function room upstairs in McGinty's, Tommy's do was classier.

Tracey had pulled strings with a PR buddy and managed to get a private area room at Faze One, the newest and trendiest club in Belfast. The queues started at eight on a Saturday and Sunday evening, and you might stand for over an hour unless you knew the door staff. Molly had never been before. Belfast's "beautiful" people, whom Molly and Dermot would have sneered at behind their backs in a previous life, filled the bar. So Molly dressed up for the occasion. It was her first night on the town since Dermot left. She went all out in a coral colored silk dress from Karen Millen that her mother insisted on buying her for her thirtieth birthday. Molly had never worn it before and decided that she probably wouldn't again, although she had to admit that it suited her. Asymmetrical at the top, with one shoulder strap, it hugged her body and showed off her trim figure. The vibrant color made Molly's blues eyes flash.

She realized she'd been drinking too much when she heard herself verbally abuse a drunken old man trying to chat her up. Molly still wore her wedding ring. It irritated her that a guy would ignore the obvious "taken" sign. Worse still—he wore one too.

The party pumped in full swing around her, yet she felt isolated. She'd had enough and wanted to go home. She planned to slide off quietly without causing a fuss. This night belonged to Tommy.

Molly stood outside the club, a blue cashmere bolero folded over her forearm. Her joined hands held a sparkly blue sequined handbag that matched her peep toe high heels perfectly. The heels made her wobble as she walked. She noticed uncomfortably how men turned to keep her in line of sight for as long as they could whilst passing. She didn't want to be noticed by them. She was still Dermot's wife. Fortunately, it wasn't long before a taxi rolled up and stopped.

Relieved, she tottered forward but slammed to a halt as the front passenger door of the cab opened and Dermot climbed out. From the back door of the same cab emerged a very pregnant and positively blooming Sheila.

Molly stumbled back as though punched but mercifully, didn't fall over. It seemed to take a second for Dermot to register her. Alarm flooded his dark features, and he took a step towards Sheila, putting a protective arm around her.

"Molly," he said, unable to contain the surprise in his voice. "It's Molly!" he repeated, but turned, addressing his astonished observation to Sheila.

Sheila seemed thrown too. Dermot's words seemed to propel her forward, and with a strange half smile, she stuck out her hand saying, "Hi, I'm Sheila!"

Molly stepped back, and Dermot glared at Sheila as if to say, "Are you mad?"

Sheila's self-assured gesture lit a fuse within Molly. Fury flamed through her. With hedonistic delight, she gave in to it.

"You whore!" she bellowed. "You fucked my husband, yes, *my* husband!" Molly gestured wildly in Dermot's direction as a few people stopped to look.

Dermot stood, pinned to the spot.

"She fucked him and then got pregnant!" Molly addressed this to her spectators waving her arm as if introducing a circus act.

"Roll up, roll up, see the slut! Women, hold on to your husbands!"

Sheila shrunk close to Dermot.

"Let's go!" she urged him, her cheeks flaming.

"No, you fucking don't, you fucking tart! You'll stand right there and listen to what I have to say. You stole my husband, wrecked my marriage and my life, and you can just fucking stand there and hear me out!"

"Now, Molly, calm down!" Dermot backed away as he spoke, a combination of fear and embarrassment on his face. Molly had the upper hand. For the first time in her adult life she gave in to a full-on temper tantrum. It felt wonderful!

"Calm down? CALM DOWN?" she roared back. "Not fucking likely. That should be me, Dermot, and that should be my baby. I will never forgive you, either of you, for this, and I curse you." Molly spat in Sheila's face. "And your bastard. You will never have a happy day with that child."

That had been last night. This morning, in the cold, sober light of day, Molly thought her words over-dramatic and more like a line from a badly written soap opera.

"Not classy," she moaned to herself. She imagined them lying in bed together, intimate, laughing at her and her outlandish behavior. She cringed again.

How she got home afterwards was a mystery. She vaguely remembered Tracey leading her down the street by the hand, assuring her that Dermot and Sheila were not invited to the birthday party, promising her that they had shown up there by coincidence.

Molly fretted now that perhaps she'd tried to pick a fight with Tracey, but not for long. The nausea came back with full vigor now, and Molly pulled herself up over the putrid bowl for another exhausting bout of vomiting. Tears of despair fell from her chin and splashed into the toilet water.

She realized that maybe she wasn't as sorry about the content of her message as the cheap and tacky way she had delivered it. The corny parting line she ended with had seemed a great idea at the time, but it would make any B movie star weep in utterance. Molly managed to laugh at herself a little bit as she rolled her eyes, recalling her overdramatic grand finale.

"Mark my words. Revenge shall be mine!"

Sunday, July 30th

CHAPTER THIRTY-EIGHT

Sheila gasped desperately for breath. She tried to scream, but the sound froze in her throat. Lying flat on her back, she couldn't see with the glare of lights shining above the monstrous mound of her belly. She heard Molly's voice in the background absurdly calm, echoing and tinny.

"Is the whore prepped?" Hatred dripped from the words.

Sheila tried to move again without success. Her mouth opened in a scream that no one, not even Sheila, heard. Two piercing blue eyes peered at her from above the belly, sandwiched between a green surgical hat and a matching surgical mask. Molly's voice sang out, absurdly theatrical.

"Revenge shall be mine!"

As the mask slipped, the face changed into a growling husky dog, baring a barricade of teeth. The jaws opened wider to accommodate the huge belly beneath them. They snapped closed, tearing into soft flesh.

Sheila jumped up. Sweat soaked her nightdress. The images of her dream slunk into the recesses of her consciousness. She sucked in lungfuls of air as she scrambled back to reality. Her bedroom curtain's soft folds of fabric filtered the invading yellow hues of the street lights, the room soothingly familiar.

Dermot snored beside her. The rhythmical seesaw helped her to regulate her own breathing until it became less of an effort. As the creature inside her took up more and more space, she often found herself short of breath. Her own personal alien grew there, taking over everything, the distribution of fluids and minerals in Sheila's body, swelling her breasts, making them ache. It even dictated which foods she could and could not stomach. No matter how she tried, Sheila could not feel maternal. She did not dream of nursing, breastfeeding or playing with this baby. She didn't feel attached to it. She felt invaded by it, as if it belonged to someone else.

Molly's words earlier had struck a chord.

She believed Molly. That was the unnerving truth of the matter.

Later, when Dermot scoffed at Molly's display of rage, trying to melt it with his scorn, Sheila retreated to the bathroom to get some thinking space.

Molly was right. This should have been her baby. Sheila didn't want it and wasn't even sure she wanted Dermot. Yet poor, pathetic, enraged Molly managed to show Sheila that Molly had something that Sheila would never have. Love.

Molly loved Dermot unconditionally. It fuelled the passion with which she spat the words and her spittle at Sheila. Like a woman unhinged, Molly surrendered to her love totally, enduring self-destructing humiliation. Witnessing this boiling rage left Sheila cold, as if she wandered in an emotional tundra where to never experience great joy was also to never experience great pain.

Sheila had never been truly in love. She'd had a good time with Dermot, sometimes. He was not her every waking thought. She had never experienced the frenzy of wondering: would a guy she met ring her or not. She listened with distain to the tales of woe, carried in to work by her colleagues. Men who promised to call and didn't, who arranged dates and then did not show up. These females were distraught when guys chased them and then dumped them after sleeping with them.

None of it bothered Sheila. She was never let down, because she never cared. Men and women alike had described Sheila as being cool as a cucumber, as if it were something to be admired. This casket that surrounded her had protected her in the past, but now it felt as though she were being buried in it.

Molly had looked into Sheila's heart and discovered her truth.

You will never have a happy day with that child!

She shifted position, but she would need to get up and pee again before she could settle down to sleep. Wondering why she bothered to avoid waking the snoring heap of man, she slipped out of bed and found her dressing gown. Closing the bedroom door softly behind her, Sheila lumbered down the hallway towards the bathroom. When Sheila's mind turned to Dermot, her stomach twisted itself into knots. She didn't want to lose him. And she most certainly did not want to lose him to Molly. This feeling of ownership was primal, almost feline. Like a cat that tolerates its human to keep its food supply regular. Did she hang on to Dermot just to help her financially with the baby?

She felt agitated. There was no way she would get to sleep now, exhausted as she was. It was four in the morning. She was supposed to be meeting Dermot's mother this afternoon. She really didn't care if she met her or not, but Dermot had suddenly become all paternal, talking about family units and bullshit like that. What did people from dysfunctional families like theirs know about family?

Sheila went to the kitchen and made herself a fresh pot of decaffeinated coffee. No caffeine was one of the few concessions she made to pregnancy. The newspaper sat on the table. Sheila flicked it open and perused through it as she sipped her coffee. Saturday's edition usually had a good travel article. She read it religiously before meeting Dermot; back when she could travel.

The travel page featured a half-page photo of a beautiful white palace, the Taj Mahal, sitting alluringly beneath the headline "Enchanting India". Regret dragged through her. She should be there right now feeling the sun on her back and smelling the spices in the air, not sitting here in a cold kitchen watching the grey dawn battle forth.

Fear and dread filled Sheila as she realized she fully believed the words flung at her last night. Molly had cursed her. It was true. Already Sheila hated her life.

Sunday, July 30th

CHAPTER THIRTY-NINE

The ketchup bottle wobbled in the tray, threatening to land on the quivering yolks of the fried eggs snuggled beside the bacon and sausage. Tommy swore under his breath as he worked to turn the handle of the bedroom door with his elbow. Eventually, the door swung open.

"Good morning, Gorgeous," he said, setting the breakfast tray on the dressing table.

"Oh, I don't feel too gorgeous." Tracey groaned and stretched from beneath the covers. "That smells good," she said, perking up. "You have me spoiled rotten. I love it!" She sat up, grinning as she smoothed the duvet to receive her breakfast. "Are you getting in beside me?"

"We can pretend the butler brought it to us," Tommy said as he got into the bed.

"So what is the butler called?"

"Jeeves, of course."

"Not very original is it?"

"Keep your voice down. You'll upset Jeeves. We wouldn't want him spitting in our food, now would we?"

Tracey looked disdainfully at her plate. Tommy laughed.

"Don't worry," he assured her.

"I know, but it's just the thought. I'm feeling delicate enough already!"

"Well, what do you expect, drinking tequila shooters? I'll bet poor Molly is feeling as rough as a dog."

"She really had a tough night."

"God, how awful was it when Dermot showed up? What a dickhead," Tommy said. "I can't believe Molly thought we invited him."

"She knew we didn't. At least I hope so. My heart went out to her. She completely lost it. I nearly felt sorry for that Sheila woman."

"Are you serious?" Tommy said. "They have destroyed Molly. Her heart is broken, and the last thing she needs is her best friend taking their side."

"I understand what you're saying, really I do, but," Tracey took a breath before continuing. "It's just that…well… I miss him, Tommy. I can't imagine how much Molly must miss him. She is so in love with him. God, I can't imagine how I'd feel if you did that to me."

Tommy looked up from his breakfast sharply. They hadn't said the words "I love you," yet. Tommy had never said those three words to any girl. Well, any girl apart from when he was thirteen, and he'd kissed a girl he'd met at summer school. Her breath smelled of tootie-frooties, and she tasted sweet too. He couldn't stop thinking about her for a whole week. A whole week! That was a lifetime for a teenager.

When he told her that he loved her, she laughed at him and said in an annoyingly grown up way that he was too immature to know what love meant. As it turned out, she was right. Now, he knew. It meant being afraid, experiencing the twin extremes of pleasure and pain, feeling satisfied and complete when they were together, and empty and anxious when they were apart.

He didn't think Tracey would laugh, but terror gripped him at the thought that she couldn't say it back. He knew that she enjoyed being with him and that they had something special, but what if his special differed from hers? What if their definitions of love didn't match up? What if she wasn't able to reciprocate the sentiment?

Patience was something he had a ready supply of, until Tracey started talking about love without getting to the crunch of the matter.

"I know you wouldn't do that to me," she continued hastily. "You are one of the good guys. That's Molly's problem. She has bad boy syndrome. She is too besotted with Dermot to see that."

"Well, Dermot didn't just cheat on Molly," Tommy said. "He cheated on all of us, really. He was my friend too. I know what you mean when you say you miss him, but when I look at him now, I feel like aliens have abducted the real Dermot and left his outer shell. That man walking around with that pregnant woman can't be the Dermot we knew."

"Maybe when this dies down and Molly has moved on and met someone nicer, things will be different with Dermot," Tracey added hopefully, taking a bite of her toast and slurping some coffee to wash it down.

Tommy raised an eyebrow.

"It's just that the baby will be my first niece or nephew," she said. "It's not the baby's fault that its parents were such pratts."

She had a point, but that didn't mean he had to like it.

"I wonder why Molly never had kids," he said.

"Dermot said he didn't want them. She told me one day that she would love kids, but he had said no. It's so sad really the way things turned out."

"Why didn't Dermot want any children?" Tommy asked, amazed that Tracey knew all the answers, yet he had been so close to his cousin all his life. Girls discussed these personal matters.

"Dermot practically raised the rest of us, Tommy. Dad was useless and mum was bad with her nerves. He was a teenage dad in so many ways. I remember him sitting up with our Johnny when he had whooping cough. Dermot would have been only fourteen at the time. Dermot was the one we all ran to. He kept us together. Now it seems like he will drive us all apart."

"Has being part of a big family put you off having children?" Tommy said. This put them back in that ball park again. He felt nervous tension lodge in the pit of his gut. Tracey seemed oblivious to the direction of conversation and answered in a breezy tone, waving her bacon in the air before she bit into it.

"No, I think I'd like to have at least more than one, but certainly not a whole football team." She smiled at him as she chewed on the bacon. Did he detect a pink glow coming to her cheeks? Relief took the place of the tension that had crept over him. He reached for her hand and squeezed it, saying softly, "Me too."

He bent forward and kissed her, and she responded leisurely, her arms snaking up around his neck to pull him closer. There was a clatter from the tray as their shifting bodies upset it and one of the glasses of orange juice toppled, releasing its sticky contents across the duvet cover.

"Oh shite!" Tommy said, freezing. Tracey giggled, reached forward and grabbed the second glass.

"Jeeves will be very annoyed," she said.

"Step away from the bed," Tommy commanded. "Slowly. Put your weapon down on the bed side table. Careful. No sudden movements."

Tracey followed the solemn commands, unable to suppress a chuckle. She put her hands up.

"Okay. Okay. I give in." She laughed as he stretched across the bed and kissed her. The tray rattled threateningly, and he pulled away again, smiling at her woefully.

"We do have to get up now. What time are we due at your Mum's house?" he asked her.

"Oh, God, I nearly forgot. She wants us there by two. It's twelve now, so I suppose we need to get a move on."

"You take the first shower, and I'll get Jeeves to clean this mess up." Tommy lifted the tray and made for the door.

They had been invited to Tracey's Mum's house for Sunday Lunch nearly every week. Tracey was good at declining some weeks so that they could share their Sundays with his Father and also have some time to themselves. They hadn't been for lunch with Tracey's Mum, Carmel, in nearly a month, and Tommy had happily accepted her invite this week. They'd have dinner with his Dad on Tommy's actual birthday, which fell on Wednesday this year, though they'd celebrated with a party last night.

Downstairs, he loaded the dishwasher with the breakfast things and then headed back upstairs to change the bed before his own shower.

"Shall we stop at the off license and get your mother some of that rose wine she likes?" Tommy called into the bathroom.

"Only if you think she won't force me to have some too."

"Hair of the dog and all that."

"Okay then, but I won't promise to drink it." Tracey turned off the shower, and her hand snaked out and grabbed a towel. He gathered together the clothes he would wear for the day and left them on the freshly made up bed.

"Oh, you've made the bed already. You are a star, Tommy O'Brian." Tracey hugged him, the dampness from her towel penetrating his tee shirt.

"It's a dangerous business, you being so scantily clad," Tommy warned, hugging her.

She smelled zesty. Her skin glowed pink after the heat of the shower. She had her hair wrapped up in a white towel, the wispy tendrils that had escaped skirting along the nape of her neck. She looked scrubbed and brand new. She wriggled from his clutches and skipped into the bedroom.

"Hurry up, Tommy, time is ticking," she scolded.

***

Tommy and Tracey arrived at the Duggan's home at two o'clock on the dot. Tracey used her key to let them in and called from the doorway in a sing-song voice.

"Hello, Mum. It's just me, Tracey."

Despite the summer's warmth, the hallway held a chill. The carpet smelt musty, a smell that Tommy associated with this house. Carmel Duggan let the housekeeping slide. Certainly not like his mother.

"Hello, hello, hello, you two!" Carmel met them at the door to the living room. "Come on in. The dinner will be ready in about another fifteen minutes. Do you want a wee cup of tea? The kettle's just boiled there now. Here, give me those jackets."

She waited while Tommy and Tracey shrugged off their jackets. Tommy preferred not to relinquish his in the cold room but handed it over anyway. Rubbing his hands together, he sat down on the sofa.

"Is there anything I can help you with, Mum?" Tracey offered, following Carmel into the kitchen.

Their conversation drifted to Tommy over the plop and hiss of hot liquid bubbling in pots.

"No, Love, I think I have it all under control. Oh, maybe you could take the gammon joint out of the oven."

"Gammon joint? For just the three of us?" Tracey said.

"Oh, we have special guests coming today, so I thought I'd make a bit of an effort," Carmel answered.

"Who is it?"

"Well, it's kind of a surprise pet, just wait and see."

Carmel overdramatized most situations, but Tommy felt uneasy at the prospect of mysterious guests. As much as he didn't want to think negatively of Tracey's family, some of the younger boys had been run out of town by the paramilitaries for what they described as anti-social behavior. As far as Tommy could make out, they'd attempted to sell drugs in the wrong night club or street corner. He didn't relish making small talk with one of those little hoods. He didn't have long to wait before the doorbell chimed.

"Will you get that Tommy, please," Carmel called out to him.

Tommy got up, opened the door and froze.

Dermot and Sheila stood on the doorstep, looking equally stunned.

Tracey arrived at the door behind Tommy. All four stared until Tracey broke the silence.

"I swear Tommy, I didn't know they were coming," she said.

Tommy felt like his brain was being pressure cooked. Molly's gaunt face flashed in his mind. He was afraid he might explode.

"Tell your mother I'm not hungry," he said through clenched teeth. He strode forward, violently shouldering Dermot out of his way. Tommy hoped that Dermot would retaliate so he could vent his anger through his fists.

Sheila stepped back just before Tommy bulled through her also. Tracey shouted something, but a red mist of rage shrouded his ears. He didn't wait to listen to what she had to say. He stopped short at the car. No keys. He kicked the wheel hard.

"Fuck!" he spat.

A hand on his shoulder made him jump.

"Looking for these?" Tracey said. Her voice seemed measured, but fire flickered in her eyes.

He nodded and rubbed his hand through his hair. He should thank her, but anger still gripped his voice. She tossed the keys to him and marched to the passenger door. The car chirped as locks opened. They got in. Tommy checked the rear view mirror. Carmel's door was closed, Dermot and Sheila presumably inside. He floored the accelerator and swung out around a car dawdling in front of him.

Tracey jumped as Tommy blasted the horn.

"Jesus, Tommy, slow down, would ya?" She gripped the dashboard.

"He was going too slow. That's how accidents happen," Tommy growled back. But he knew Tracey was right. He fought the desire to frighten her more, to punish her with his anger.

"Pull over and calm down," she said in a quiet voice. "Please, Tommy."

Tommy gripped the wheel hard, turning his knuckles white, as he clamped down on his anger. He didn't want to vent it on Tracey, but what the hell was Carmel doing?

"Look, Mum's an eejit when it comes to Dermot," Tracey said softly, as if reading Tommy's thoughts. "She thinks she owes him for defending her against Dad. But fuck it -we all helped her. This is too much."

From the corner of his eye he saw Tracey's hand wipe her face.

Shite – she's crying. He felt like a right bastard. Tracey was as upset as he was. He'd walked off and not even considered her.

"I'm sorry about back there." Tommy realized that he was shaking. He drove the car over into a parking lot and stopped. "Are you okay?"

Tracey sighed and answered with a barely audible, "No."

It hurt Tommy to see her upset. He reached over and pulled her to him.

"Parents, eh?" she said sniffing, on the brink of tears.

"Can't live with them, can't get born without them," he said, hooking his finger beneath her chin and gently tipping her face up so he could look into her eyes.

She laughed, and his heart lifted. Her cheeks glowed pink as they rounded with her smile. He kissed her lightly on the lips. Then she frowned.

"What? Didn't like the kiss?" he asked, only half joking.

"No, you muppet, it's just the thought of having to go back home and face Mum again after storming out on her. She's just impossible to reason with."

"Well, I've been thinking about this for a while, actually." He pulled away, putting a little space between them. "Why don't you move in with me? You're there most weekends anyway . . . "

Before he could finish delivering the speech he'd had stashed in his head for weeks, Tracey lunged forward and grabbed him in a bear hug.

"Yes, yes, yes," she cried.

He kissed her slowly, tasting her mouth and teasing her tongue with the tip of his. Even with his joy, Molly's face haunted his thoughts. Dermot was always going to be a black smudge in their relationship. He hated that what they shared had begun in this atmosphere of betrayal and disappointment.

Bloody Dermot. . .

He pulled Tracey closer and kissed her harder.

"Boy, you are pleased about this, aren't you?" Tracey said pulling back a little.

"Ah, I think you're sitting on the gear stick, honey," he said, trying to shift them into a more comfortable position.

"Take me home," she said in a throaty voice. "What I want to do to you right now is not appropriate in a Safeway parking lot on a Sunday afternoon."

"I love you, Tracey." It just slipped out, and he couldn't catch it, couldn't reel it back in.

Her eyes widened, and tears glistened at their corners.

As Tommy felt her arms tighten around him, a current ran through them both, connecting them, as she at last spoke the words he'd been dying to hear.

"I love you too, Tommy O'Brian."

Tuesday, August 15th

CHAPTER FORTY

There was standing room only in Tommy's living room. He held another cardboard box in his arms and looked for somewhere to set it. Wolfie bounced in and knocked over a stack of boxes. Books spilled onto the floor, blocking the only walkway and stranding Tommy in the middle of the room.

"Wolfie, go lie down!" he roared. The dog walked over the top of the pile of books, skidded on their open pages and nearly did the splits.

"Wolfie, stay," he yelled.

The dog whined and looked at his owner with sad eyes.

Tracey appeared at the door with a frown that flickered to a brief smile before her eyebrows furrowed again. She reached towards the box that Tommy held.

"Holy God. There's no room to swing a cat in here, never mind a six-foot dog," Tommy said, giving Tracey the box.

"I'm so sorry," Tracey apologized. "I should have given half this stuff to the charity shop, but it's just so hard to let go of some of it. You just never know when you might need it again."

"Yes, whatever would we do without 'The Art of English'?" Tommy asked, holding up a battered textbook and nodding his head.

"Ok, that can go," Tracey conceded. "It's just the first time I've ever moved house really. I even lived at home for University. It's weird for me. We'll find somewhere for all this stuff, don't you worry."

Tommy wasn't worried. He knew that she was doing exactly the right thing. It was going to be perfect, even though her mother was upset. He'd asked Tracey to move in a month ago, and finally she'd ignored her mother's complaints and taken the plunge.

"I took the liberty of shopping earlier," Tommy said, moving towards the kitchen. He lifted a bag from the counter then returned to the chaos of the living room.

"I got something yummy and easy for tonight. Ta–da!" He pulled a Sainsbury's Thai food meal-for-two from the bag.

"Fantastic," Tracey said, balancing her box precariously on another and picking her way through the debris on the floor to Tommy. "I just lurve Thai food, and guess what?" She nuzzled her nose against his. "I just lurve you too."

Their kiss was interrupted by a clatter out in the hall followed by a thump, thump, thump as her kayak slid from where it had been propped against the wall and bounced down the last few steps of the stairway.

"Oops," she laughed. "Let me stick that out in the backyard, and then I'll help you nuke the dinner."

"How 'bout I open a bottle of wine, we leave all the mess, nuke the dinner and bring it to the boudoir?"

"I should have provided dessert," said Tracey, kissing him again.

"You are."

She laughed a throaty giggle as she nuzzled in against him.

"You are so naughty, Tommy; it's only seven-thirty."

The doorbell rang, blasting away their mood.

"Crap. Who can that be?" Tommy said, looking out the window. "It's Molly." He chewed at his lip. He really wanted to get back to "Dessert." He hated being so selfish, but Christ Almighty, Molly had the knack of souring any good thing these days. He caught Tracey's eye, and she gave him a questioning look. He shrugged and pulled the window open.

"Hey Cuz, what's up?" His throat caught when he saw her face. Black blotches of mascara smeared the red skin around her eyes, the only color in an otherwise pallid complexion.

What now?

She managed to say, "Sorry for disturbing you," before she burst into floods of tears.

Tommy raced to the door to let her in. Tracey followed close behind.

"Molly, calm down. What's happened?" he said, putting his arms around her and guiding her inside.

Tracey put her hand on Molly's shoulder and said, "You're okay now, just tell us what's happened." Tracey's brow furrowed with worry. She directed his gaze towards bandages on Molly's wrist poking out from beneath her coat sleeve.

Tommy's insides turned to ice. Had she done this to herself? *No, please God, not Molly.*

Tommy grabbed her hand and pulled up her sleeve. "Jesus, what did you do?"

Molly snatched her arm back. "It was an accident," She said backing towards the door. "I'm sorry Tommy – you guys are up to your eyes. God, I can't do anything right." Her eyes began to water as her face reddened and her chin puckered.

"It's okay, Molly," Tommy said gently. "Just tell me what happened."

"You think I did this to myself? I wouldn't do that. *Christ almighty!*" She turned to the door.

"I believe you," Tracey said, though Tommy wasn't sure she did. He knew he didn't. But Tracey remained calm, taking Molly's uninjured hand and spoke gently to her, "Grab a seat, and I'll make you guys tea," Tracey said, lifting a box from the chair nearest Molly.

"It's okay. Please, Tracey, sit with us if you want. Don't feel you have to go," Molly said. She reached out and rested her hand on Tracey's arm. A tear rolled down Molly's face. "Even if you won't be my sister-in-law much longer, you are still my best friend."

Tracey set the boxes down and hugged Molly.

Tommy cleared the last chair and a space on the table so that they could at least see each other before he sat down with them.

"So, Molly, what happened?" he said.

"Oh God, I feel terrible," Molly said. "I was supposed to call in with Fran this morning, but I felt so crap when I woke up I took a tablet and went back to bed. I didn't get up till five this evening, and I went round to her house, but there was no answer. The house was dark and the curtains were still open. I looked in through her front window, and I could see her lying on the ground." Molly squeezed her eyes shut, shuddered, then took a deep breath before continuing.

"Oh my God," Tracey gasped. "Was she. . . "

"Dead? No – but I didn't know that then. She was facing away from me, and I could only see her top half because she had fallen in through the door from the hallway," Molly continued. "Jesus Christ, poor Fran had fallen down the stairs. I don't even know when. She could have been lying there all night and all day. And it's my fault."

Tommy handed Molly a tissue as she sniffed. She took it and wiped her eyes, then blew her nose.

"How is it your fault?" Tommy asked.

"I should have called round sooner, found her sooner, maybe even prevented her from falling, but I didn't. I slept all day."

"But you weren't feeling well," Tommy said.

"No, I wasn't sick," said Molly. "I said I was feeling crap – in here." She pounded her chest. "I took a sleeping tablet." Molly hung her head.

"How many?" Tommy asked in a gruff voice.

"Only the one." Molly looked up, her eyes wide open. "No, I'm not suicidal."

Tommy stared at her arm. She followed his gaze. Tracey cleared her throat but before she could speak Molly jumped in again.

"This." She held up her hand. "This was an accident. I called an ambulance but couldn't just stand and wait and leave Fran lying there. I thought she was dead. I couldn't wait, so I broke the glass on Fran's front door to get in, and I cut myself."

"And Fran?" Tracey asked, barely audible.

"She was breathing, thank God. But only just. I never knew a person could be that color. Her skin was mauve. But the worst was her leg. She was lying right on it."

"Oh my God," Tracey said.

Tommy exchanged a glance with her. The color had drained from her face too, but Tommy had trouble picturing what Molly described.

"How do you mean?" he said.

"It was bent up behind her, with her foot at her head." Molly stopped and looked up at the ceiling and drew in a breath. "She was lying on it, and it bent backwards under her."

Tommy fought nausea as Tracey exhaled through her teeth beside him. Molly raised a shaky hand and tucked a curl behind her ear.

"I can't get the image out of my head. Oh God, poor Fran."

Sobs took over Molly, and Tracey folded her up in her arms. Tommy's heart went out to his cousin. What an ordeal. No wonder she looked so haunted.

"And how's Fran now?" Tracey asked as the two girls pulled apart.

Molly shook her head slowly.

"When the ambulance man lifted her, she groaned and said, 'Anthony, is that you?' and I thought she could see him in the afterlife or something. I swear, I thought she was going to die there and then. I was in bits. But the ambulance man said she was delirious with the pain, and they gave her an injection. Then they took both of us to the hospital. I got four stitches, and Fran was still unconscious when I left."

"That's so awful for you, you poor pet," Tracey said.

"How are you feeling now? Any better?" Tommy asked.

"I just can't do this. Every time I think of Fran lying there and me sleeping next door. I can't bear it." Molly ran her fingers through her hair leaving some of the curls standing like wispy horns on top of her head.

In the past Molly had been the strong one in the family. After Tommy's mother was diagnosed with secondary bone cancer, Molly took care of them all. She didn't get bogged down in the miry mantle of emotion like he and his Dad had. Molly brought them homemade food several times a week and comforted his mother in ways his own suffering prevented. She was as deft at holding a sick person's hand as holding a bed pan and would unflinchingly support his mother's head while she vomited. Before his mother moved into the hospice, Molly changed the beds and gently moved his mother's wasted, aching body to more comfortable positions. In the hospice, Molly kept the bedside vigil with Tommy and his father. She organized the rest of their family and friends, timetabling visitors during the day and night, giving Tommy and his Dad a chance to rest.

She sat with Tommy and his father as they held on to Caroline in her last moments. Molly helped them guide their beloved mother and wife through that last door, and comforted them as they wept when Caroline left them.

Tommy couldn't have had a better sister.

But now Tommy was at a loss. Molly's all-consuming sorrow cast a black cloud on everything she did and the company she kept. It ate her up, and he didn't know how to stop it. Molly had morphed from the confident, fun-loving girl that helped everyone else into a creature on edge and unsure of her place in the world.

Tommy took her hand in his, pulling it from her face so he could look her in the eye. "Molly, do you remember when I came home from the hospital after Mum was diagnosed?"

Molly nodded.

"Do you remember what you told me when I said I couldn't bear it, that I didn't know how to keep going?"

"Yes, that God makes the shoulders for the people to carry their burdens." Molly looked straight into Tommy's eyes, her startling blue eyes, unusual and crisp, delivering a punch of their own. "When God let Dermot walk out on me, God left with him."

Tommy took a sharp breath. Molly's clarity at that moment chilled him. He and Molly often talked about faith. They believed and trusted in a higher being, not necessarily a God of the fire and brimstone variety marketed by the Catholic Church of their youth. Tommy derived great comfort in this belief when his mother died and often felt that she watched over him from a better place. Molly's words showed Tommy a cold, barren landscape, peppered with fear and desolation. She needed God. They all did.

"Molly, you don't mean that."

"Don't I?" Her ferocity made the hairs stand on the back of his neck. "Before we got married we did a course, provided by the Catholic Church. They told us that a husband and wife's love for each other is an expression of God's love on earth. So tell me Tommy, what does this say about the way God loves me?" She swallowed, as tears spilled down her face.

"God does love you, Molly, He does." But Tommy didn't know what to say to convince her without sounding contrived and stupid. There were no buttons on faith. You could not switch it on or off at will. Tommy thought it would be cruel to point out to Molly that if she didn't believe in God, she ought to have no dilemma about getting a divorce. Being Catholic in Belfast, even these days, was about more than just believing in God.

Molly pursed her lips and blew something between a snort and a sigh.

"I suppose you're gonna tell me too that we're all God's children and that He loves us all – even poor old Fran whom He condemned to a life of loneliness before throwing her down a flight of stairs and leaving her lying there 'til she was found by some lazy neighbor? Huh?" Molly said, ending in a high pitched squeak, as tears engulfed her once more.

"But how do you know Fran was lonely?" Tommy said, confused. Fran always seemed dapper and cheerful any time he'd met her. A woman full of gusto, she always left him smiling, feeling good about life. Not his definition of lonely by a long shot.

"Of course she was lonely. She lost Anthony when she was about my age. She never remarried. She must have been so lonely without him." Molly dabbed at her eyes with a tissue.

"Oh come on Molly, you don't need a man in your life to be happy," Tracey said.

"Says the woman who's just moved in with her boyfriend," Molly bit back.

Tracey's cheeks flared crimson. Tommy wanted to touch her, hold her hand, give her some kind of comfort and support, but if he did, Molly would see it as taking sides.

"Maybe I'll make that tea now?" he said, desperately hoping for a distraction. Tracey shook her head, her face still stricken, and Tommy suspected that she didn't trust herself to speak yet.

Molly replied with a tight lipped, "No thanks," and kept her eyes down. She fiddled with her bandage and drew a deep breath. "I'm sorry, Tracey, but I'm not in the mood to be preached at about girl power and how we don't need men. I want a family, or at least a life partner. Someone to face the world with. I want to grow old with someone, share jokes with him, laugh at our wobbly bits. I need a man in my life, and I don't want to be old and fall down the stairs and have nobody care."

"Someone did care for Fran," Tracey said. "You cared, Molly. You were there for her eventually. You did save her life you know."

A cloud seemed to lift from Molly's eyes; her face lightened ever so slightly.

"I suppose you could say better late than never, but I should have been there that morning," Molly said.

"But you still don't know when she fell, do you?" Tracey pressed on bravely. Tommy felt awash with love for her as she continued, "I mean if she didn't fall until lunch time, it might have been a good thing you did hold off or she'd have to wait until your visit the next day."

"Good point," Tommy said. "Molly, just wait and see what Fran says when she wakes up. Don't consider the worst case yet. You've had a terrible shock. If you need to stay here tonight..." He didn't finish the sentence.

"Look, I've spoiled enough of your evening, guys," Molly said. She looked a lot less haunted, but Tommy felt as though she were itching to be gone.

"Have a lovely what's-left-of-your evening. Thank you both for being there," she said, getting up quickly and moving towards the door.

"Keep us updated on Fran. I'll say a wee prayer," Tracey said. "And lay off the sleeping tablets. Those things aren't to be taken lightly."

"I know, I know," Molly said curtly.

She hugged Tommy, and he squeezed her back saying, "Tomorrow, okay?"

"Okay." And Molly left. Tommy found her departure a relief.

Tracey and Tommy waved Molly off as she drove her car out of the street. Even though it was a warm July evening, Tracey shivered. Tommy understood why. Loneliness emanated from Molly like cold air blasting from an open freezer door.

He pulled Tracey closer to him.

Sunday, September 3rd

CHAPTER FORTY-ONE

Sheila planted her feet wide apart to lower herself into the armchair. Dermot laughed. Boy, was her belly huge! She shot him a stony glare. He switched on his puppy dog eyes and smiled. Sheila flicked her hair back and sighed, focusing on the television.

He still found her extremely attractive. The curves of her breasts and belly excited him. Sometimes her hands and ankles swelled up at the end of a long day in the beauty salon, but she kept herself in good shape. She astonished Dermot when she started yoga.

"If I can't work out properly, then this will have to do for now," she said. She had continued with her jogging until her belly and boobs had gotten so big that they bounced too much. Dermot took pride in how refined Sheila looked. She always dressed nicely and kept her figure trim. Once Tracey got to know her, he hoped that they'd be as good friends as Molly and Tracey were.

Molly's behavior when they bumped into her almost a couple of months ago had shocked him. Admittedly, her fiery display tugged at something primitive in him. It turned him on, and several times he'd had erotic dreams involving Molly being very commanding and very dressed in black leather. Even the thought of it made him hard.

He glanced at Sheila, now planted in the armchair watching the news.

"So, did you get your thirty minutes of exercise today?" he said in a low voice, trying to sound seductive. Sheila considered sex as exercise.

"Yes," she answered, not even looking in his direction. He got up from the sofa and sat at her feet, taking one in his hands and gently massaging the ball of her foot.

"That's lovely." She groaned with delight. Heartened by this success, he slid his hand up her leg massaging her calf muscle.

"I know what you're up to, my dear, and I'm telling you now it's not going to happen," she said. Dermot dropped her foot.

"Oh, Sheila, come on. I'm really horny." he pleaded. She looked down at him, her forehead scrunched into a frown.

"You really know how to woo a girl. That's a right royal turn off ... whining about being horny."

"Oh, give us a break. We never shag these days."

"I'm seven months pregnant. I'm bloody knackered!" she said.

Dermot got to his feet and wandered out to the kitchen.

"Hey, what about my other foot?" She called after him.

"Fecking do it yourself!"

"You drive a hard bargain, Dermot Duggan," she called after him. Hearing a note of humor in her tone, he smiled to himself.

"So do we have a deal, if I finish the massage?"

"Maybe later. Maybe. But I am really tired, and I do have to work tomorrow." She looked up at him as he walked back into the living room.

She did look tired. Her big doe eyes begged him for understanding. He melted and sat back down on the floor at her feet, teasing her by nearly lifting her other foot and then stopping.

"One in the bank for Saturday morning then?" he negotiated. She nodded, smiling coyly.

"Oh alright then," he said, laughing. "You win." He picked up her foot. "So when are you leaving work?" he asked.

She sighed. "I want to work as long as possible. Maybe right up until the birth."

"Oh, so you can have longer maternity leave?" Dermot nodded his head knowingly. He had overheard a couple of girls at the office discussing maternity leave, and he'd picked up this little tidbit. Sharing this now made him feel like a modern, clued-in sort of guy.

"Not really, no." Sheila avoided eye contact. "I'd like to go back as soon as possible too."

"What?" Dermot looked up at her, incredulous. "But, but, but what about the baby? Surely you need time to recover, and then who's going to look after the baby?"

Dermot had just assumed that Sheila, as a modern mother, (who went to yoga, for Christ's sake!) would want to be all earthy and connected to her baby.

"The crèche can take the baby at eight weeks." She looked at him, then said in a rush, "Look, Dermot, I know I kinda let you think we had it all figured out, but I'm really not the baby type. I thought I'd change my mind closer to the baby's arrival, but I haven't. Not one bit. If you want to spend all day changing nappies and wiping up goo, be my guest. I'd rather work and spend most of my wages paying someone else to do it."

"Are you serious?"

"Absolutely."

"Aren't you going to breast feed?" he asked.

Sheila snorted and pulled a face, then added "No way! That's gross."

Dermot's mind swung to Molly, who had begged him for a baby; Molly, who would have taken as much maternity leave as she could, to look after and care for their baby, babies; Molly, who had wanted a big family.

Now that he was having a baby, he looked forward to it. He had brushed away all his anxiety about bringing up more kids. He'd done it before in much more dire circumstances and with little or no financial backup. Maybe he'd been a fool. It didn't matter. Fate dealt a hand that he had to play out, and he knew he couldn't go back, no matter who wanted him to. He was having a child with a beautiful woman who didn't sound as though she wanted it. Maybe this was a form of punishment for turning his back on Molly.

"I really think you should take maternity leave," he said. "This is a new life, a little person. A baby needs a mother."

Sheila exhaled loudly through her teeth and rolled her eyes.

"I'm serious," he continued. "You'll feel differently once you have it." The new life that pulsed inside Sheila made him feel different already. It had crept over him gradually, making him see the world through the eyes of the son or daughter that Sheila carried. He watched out for play parks near where they lived, listened to people's stories of their day-to-day lives, and watched the news, wondering how he could protect his son from the drug culture springing up around them. He thought about how he would warn his daughter away from bad choices in men. Men like his father who made his childhood a battleground littered with daily struggle. Men like him, who could callously break a woman's heart and walk away.

"Maybe," Sheila said, yawning at the same time. He didn't reply, knowing that his words would be ineffective right now. He would fight this battle stealthily and not push it too far just yet.

Handling Sheila required skill. She still baffled him. That intrigued him and bound him to her. Deep down, he acknowledged that Molly was a much better person than Sheila, but that ship had sailed. He happily pursued the challenge that Sheila presented, hoping that by the time he tired of the chase, he would have broken through Sheila's Ice Queen Veneer and connected with the woman beneath it.

All women were soft and mushy beneath their surface. He had thawed out plenty of frosty prospects in his time and had them chasing him before they knew what hit them. There were two exceptions to this.

Molly had never been cool. In fact he'd been drawn to her warmth like a traveler to the hearth. She gave him the strength he needed to deal with his father and face down his dysfunctional parents. They had worked as a team, him needing her comfort, her needing his need.

Then he met Sheila, the one he hadn't melted yet. And now here he sat at her feet, at her command. The irony of it made him smile wryly to himself.

"What are you smiling about?" Sheila asked.

"Oh, nothing. I was just lost in thought," he said.

"So share."

"I never massaged Molly's feet, you know." Dermot sensed Sheila stiffen at the name. This surprised him. He hadn't thought of her as the jealous type. Was this a chink in the Veneer? He met her eyes, her face tense and guarded.

"Of course, you have much better legs."

Did he sense her relaxing? It amused him that she would be jealous of Molly. Shelia, the victorious, who held all that Molly wanted, with the green-eyed monster on her back. Didn't she know she had nothing to fear? Women were so damn complex.

He hoped the baby was a boy. That way he'd at least be able to figure out what the rascal was thinking in his teenage years. As for girls - they were pretty and stole their Daddy's hearts, and Dermot was not a guy who was used to women breaking his.

Sunday, September 3rd

CHAPTER FORTY-TWO

It unsettled Sheila when Dermot spoke so nonchalantly of Molly. Sheila shifted uncomfortably. Her back hurt and usually when it got this bad only a warm shower or bath would soothe it. She welcomed the idea of an early night. Weariness dragged her down. Even though it was only the start of September, dread tugged at her as the birth of the baby loomed closer.

The twentieth of October, the doctor predicted, though he warned her that first babies tended to come late. She tried to negotiate an elective caesarean section, but the doctor told her that natural was best, stating that a c-section took longer to heal. That, and the idea of a scar, made her think twice.

"I'm going on up to bed. Don't wake me when you come up, OK?"

"I'll be up after the sports results." Dermot nodded towards the TV belching out the day's news.

He's so pathetic.

The thought ricocheted through her head so loudly she wondered if she had in fact spoken the sentiment aloud. She turned to look at Dermot before she left the room.

"Night," he said, without looking up from the TV.

She closed the door softly behind her, feeling guilty at her aversion to him. Maybe after the baby was born, and she wasn't encumbered with pregnancy, she would be able to rekindle some affection for him. She knew she didn't want anyone else's hand on him, and certainly not Molly's, but she expected that her jealously and feelings of possession also carried with it some semblance of love.

Sheila moved on autopilot to the drawer of her bedside table. She pulled out a picture frame wrapped in an old tee shirt and took it with her into the bathroom. She locked the door behind her. As she ran the bath, she sat on the edge of it and unwrapped the picture, staring yet again at the blue eyes blazing out from behind the glass. Molly.

Sheila found it hard to get the tortured woman she had encountered that warm July night out her head. It seemed unreal that Dermot and Sheila had been invited to his mother's house for lunch the very next day. Sheila wasn't sure why she had elected to go. She knew that she could have escaped it by saying she felt unwell. Dermot was such a simpering idiot when it came to the baby that she could wrap him round her finger with a whimper.

Sheila yearned to feel the same way about Dermot as Molly had, before he had been such a shit to his wife. By going to his mother's house, Sheila hoped to get an insight into Dermot that abolished her image of him as a spoilt child, who liked getting his own way no matter who he hurt.

Sheila nearly had heart failure when Tommy opened the door. She had spotted him the night before, and Dermot had mentioned that he was Molly's cousin. She couldn't help but admire the attractive fair-haired man. He stood a couple of inches taller than Dermot, and she cringed inwardly at Dermot's lame attempt at being cocky before he scuttled out of the way of the more athletically built Tommy.

When Tracey stormed out after Tommy, Sheila envied Molly for the second time in less than twenty-four hours, jealous of how these two people could so passionately defend her.

There it was again: the "P" word. Why did she think of Molly and link her to passion in nearly a violent capacity?

Sheila could not think of a time when someone had ever stood up for her. She had never needed it. She'd always stood up for herself. Now that she was cast as the evil-other-woman she didn't feel like standing up for herself. She had taken something that wasn't hers to take, and now she was vaguely sorry.

Sheila's curiosity about Molly had spiked when she perused Carmel's collection of pictures of her children and their loved ones in a dusty cluster on her sideboard. When Dermot went to the bathroom and left Sheila alone in the living room, while Carmel finished dinner, Sheila spotted a picture of Molly and Dermot standing in what looked like a football terrace.

Molly wore a red Clintonville football top over a black sweatshirt with a scarf wrapped around her neck. They looked cold, but happy. Molly's blue eyes stared out from the photo frame. Sheila picked it up for a closer look, mesmerized by Molly's eyes. They were the truest color of pale blue Sheila had ever seen.

Sheila slipped the frame into her voluminous leather tote bag and turned to look nonchalantly out the window into the grimy street outside as Dermot had returned to the room.

Sheila studied the picture often, fascinated by Molly's expression in the photo, captivated by the bare innocence in Molly's blue eyes. A hunger lurked there too, nearly lupine in nature, yet demure. These eyes spoke of trust, of ambition, of an intensity that threatened suffocation.

Sheila sat with the picture in one hand and her other hand on the mound of her stomach, wondering if the thing with the baby would happen again. A few seconds ticked by and then thump, the baby kicked her hand. Not a flutter like it had the very first time six weeks ago when she'd sat on the edge of the bath like this for the first time staring at the picture. Sheila's heart beat faster. Lately, the movement in her belly had become stronger, more violent. And it only happened when she looked at Molly's picture.

Sheila quickly wrapped the picture up in the tee shirt again, and the baby went quiet. Her heartbeat returned to normal, and she promised herself, as she had last night and every night before that for the last few weeks, that she wasn't going to look into those eyes ever again.

Tuesday, September 19th

CHAPTER FORTY-THREE

Gold, amber and bronze danced in a dappled mosaic from the surface of the water. Tracey loved autumn, when there was still warmth in the water and color on the trees. This, together with the setting sun, bathed the world around her in an ochre glow.

"So what did you think?" she asked Tommy as they pulled the topo duo kayak up from the river to the parking lot. She prayed that he loved it as much as she did.

"Well, I've got blisters on my thumbs that will sting like hell at work tomorrow."

"Oh dear, I never thought of that," she said, disappointed. Her thumbs had hardened calluses where the paddle rubbed. "So you didn't like it?"

"No, I did, really I did. I just need to practice and toughen up." He beat his fist off the buoyancy vest over his chest making a satisfying "thwack."

"So you'll come out again?" Tracey said delighted to have him as a kayak buddy.

"I might even join the club," Tommy said as they lifted the boat onto the roof bars of her car.

"Really? That's brilliant. I'm so excited. We can go on all sorts of trips. It'll be class!" She threw her arms around him. God, she loved him so much. His companionship made her life so rich. Sometimes she felt like she was going to wake up and discover it was all a dream, that at any moment this happy bubble she existed in with him would suddenly burst.

"Me too, God don't strangle me! I'll be feck all use as a crew if I'm asphyxiated," he said chuckling as he hugged her back.

They had just finished changing and tying the boat to the roof rack when Orla rang. Tracey could hear Tommy making arrangements to go to the salon. He caught her eye and made a thumbs up sign, then turned it down. She shrugged and gave him the thumbs up. Sure she didn't mind.

"So what's up?" she asked when he finished talking to Orla.

"The big numpty has forgotten how to cash out the new register, and she thinks she's screwed the whole thing up. She has a knack of banjaxing every computer she touches. Do you mind swinging by so I can fix it for her? I'm supposed to be going to the suppliers in the morning, and she has clients first thing, so if we can sort it now that would be good."

"No problem," Tracey said.

It took them thirty minutes to drive to the Castlecourt multi-story car park and another five minutes to walk to Clippers. As they rounded the last corner, they stopped dead in their tracks, stunned by the sight in front of them.

"Oh shit, no!" Tommy said and started running.

Panic rose in Tracey. Two fire engines flanked the building that housed the salon. Firemen laid hoses on the street and policemen trailed yellow tape from lamps to fences. Blue lights flashed in windows and puddles. A crowd of people stood watching at each end of the street, held back by yellow tape.

Tommy pulled Tracey with him as they pushed through the crowd, glancing anxiously at each other. Tracey could not find words; fear trapped them in her chest. They reached the edge of the crowd and scanned the faces of the people watching.

"Can you see her?" Tommy asked. The edges of his words curled with panic.

"No!" Tracey cried. Thick black smoke pushed out from under the door of the salon and billowed from an upstairs open window. "Orla!"

Tommy ducked beneath the yellow tape. Tracey's legs felt like noodles. She wanted to run after Tommy, but she froze to the spot.

"No, Tommy!" she managed to call out. But he didn't stop, swiftly closing the fifty yards to the building. A fireman rushed towards him. Tracey couldn't hear what he shouted over the sudden roar of sirens as more engines arrived. Tommy frantically pointed at the building. The fireman shook his head and tried to turn Tommy around.

Orla would have no chance. Already, red and orange glowed from deep within the building. A loud bang caused onlookers and firemen to duck. Tommy pulled away from the fireman and sprang towards the salon.

"Tommy, no!" Tracey screamed so hard it left her throat ragged.

Tommy had nearly reached the salon when the sprinting fireman grabbed his arm. Two policemen joined him in dragging Tommy back from the fire to a police van. Tracey's heart bounced in her chest as she scrambled through the crowd. She fumbled with her phone trying to ring Orla but her phone was switched off - or burning. Tracey reached the van and ducked reflexively as two more explosions inside the salon blew out the windows and shattered glass rained down on the pavement where Tommy had stood wrestling with the fireman moments earlier.

"Hairspray, it's just cans of hairspray. We have to go in there," Tommy pleaded with the policeman bundling him into the van. "There's someone in there, please!"

"Sir, we have to clear the area. I can arrest you for hindering fire-fighting operations." The policeman spoke with a calm authority.

"Tell him!"

"It's true, there's someone in there." Tracey struggled to hold back her sobs as sorrow turned to despair. Tommy ran his hands through his hair as the policeman spoke into a radio before turning back to them.

"We are doing everything we can," he said. "I understand you're upset, Sir."

"Upset? Of course I'm fucking upset!" Tommy bellowed.

Tracey placed her hand on Tommy's arm as the policeman drew himself up to his full height.

Emotion thickened Tommy's voice. "Look, please my best friend is in there. We have to do something. . . "

"Sir, the situation is beyond our control. A suspect device has been found at the rear of the building. I'm sorry but we have to withdraw the fire crews and allow the building to burn until bomb disposal can deal with the device."

"But my friend is in there. You can't just let her burn." Tommy pushed past the policeman, wild eyed. The policeman grabbed his arm and twisted it up his back, holding him in a vice like grip.

"Let me go," Tommy roared.

Tracey moved towards Tommy, torn between helping him and helping the policeman restrain him. She felt a tug at her sleeve and turned to shrug the hand away. Orla stood beside her. Pure joy exploded at her temples.

"Orla! You're okay. Tommy, Tommy look – it's Orla – she's alive!"

"Of course I'm alive, ya fuckwit." Orla's glistening eyes belied her jocular words.

The policeman dropped Tommy's arm. Tommy scooped Orla up in a bear hug. Tracey hugged her arms around herself, watching them through a flood of tears before joining in the reunion. They pulled apart, and Orla looked over at the policeman with a wide smile.

"You're not really gonna arrest him are ya?" she asked.

"What happened?" the policeman countered.

"I left the salon right after I talked to you, about a half an hour ago, to go buy cigarettes, and when I came back there was all this commotion. You tell me what happened?" she said.

"Jesus, Orla, you're the only one I know of who can claim that smoking saved your life," Tommy said, sounding hyper. Tracey too felt ridiculously overjoyed now that Orla was okay. Tracey grabbed his hand, and took hold of Orla's with the other. Orla looked down at their joined hands and gave her a quick smile. Tracey felt lightheaded with relief.

Tommy looked back at his burning business and his features darkened.

"Fuck that," he said his voice raw. "All that work, and fucking saving money, and for nothing." His hands trembled. Tracey understood his feelings.

"Well, now that your friend is safe, can I take it you'll be no more trouble?" The policeman asked.

Tommy nodded.

"Are you the business owner?" An approaching fireman asked Tommy.

Tracey noticed the fireman and the policeman exchange nods.

"I am." Tommy ran his hand over their joined hands. Tracey watched his throat bob as he swallowed hard. There wasn't much of a business left.

"I'm Station Commander Joe Smith. I need a word with you about the possible cause of the fire." He pulled out a note pad before continuing. "Bomb squad is dealing with a suspicious device at the back of the building. I'm sorry, but we can't fight the fire until we get the all clear."

Tracey squinted tears from her eyes. Tommy had worked so hard for this place.

"Do you have any enemies? Is there any reason why someone would want to burn down your business?" the Station Commander asked.

"No—" Tommy began.

"Oh, my God! Yes!" Orla cried out.

They swung around to face her.

"It was Kieran," Orla said.

"How can you be so sure?" Tracey asked as she clenched her teeth against the quick rise of bile.

"Is he still driving that white Subaru with the black door?" she asked.

"I've seen that car around here," Tommy said. "He broke my headlights back in March."

Oh Christ!

Tracey prayed that Tommy wouldn't blame her, blame their relationship, and worst of all, end what they had together. She squeezed his hand. His hand tightened around hers as Orla said, "He pulled out of that alleyway and went screeching past me as I walked to the shop."

Saturday, October 6th

CHAPTER FORTY-FOUR

Tommy picked his way through the charred interior of the salon by torchlight. The windows had been boarded up in the days following the blaze. The aftermath of the fire hit Tommy in waves. One minute he'd be weak with despondency, all that hard work literally up in flames. Starting over seemed such a huge chore. Then he'd be fired up with rage at that bastard Kieran Quinn. The stupid fucker could have killed someone.

The fire department had returned the following day with the police to carry out their preliminary investigations and establish a cause. Tommy had been eager to come down and see the extent of the damage but had not been allowed access to the building until the forensics work was finished.

"Two weeks!" Orla had exclaimed when he told her, "Sure, on CSI they get it all done in a matter of hours."

As Tommy wandered through the rubble, he wondered what his hurry had been. Everything about it depressed him. He couldn't salvage any of the furniture or appliances, and the hair products had helped fuel the fire. Just a stinking charred shell remained standing, fit only for demolition. He'd poured everything he had into this business. Orla had given up a good job to join him, and now neither of them had any money coming in. The insurance would not pay out until the criminal investigation concluded and the guilty party sentenced. That could run into years. The dole was a pittance, but he'd have to live on that until he got this back up and running – or he could give up and find a job. The idea of such failure nearly broke him. He swallowed hard and focused on what he was going to say to his father.

Sean had called the previous evening and taken Tommy by surprise when he asked to see the place. Hope ignited in Tommy, and he'd decided that he would ask his father for a loan to get the business restarted while he waited for the insurance to pay off, if the insurance did payoff. He'd been getting on better with his father since he'd introduced him to Tracey. Still, his heart rate accelerated and disturbed the butterflies in his stomach as he thought about asking him for money.

"Hello? Tommy?" Tracey called from outside.

Tommy rushed outside to meet her, glad to escape the smell of burned chemicals. The October air smelt fresh and alive. He squinted as his eyes adjusted to the glare of the low hanging sun as it threw beams of golden lights between two banks of cloud, glinting off the modern glass buildings and giving warm hues to the stone of the older ones.

"You look like you've been 'down pit'," Tracey said giving a Yorkshire accent to the last two words.

"Everything you touch in there is black, and it gets everywhere," he said, using his sleeve to try to clean his face. "How did the bail go?"

"He didn't make bail," Tracey said and smiled.

Some of the pressure lifted from the load on Tommy's mind. He felt much safer with Quinn behind bars. It also lent weight to his insurance claim. The police had found a broken window at the back of the salon and blood on the shards of glass. The DNA had matched Kieran Quinn's. They had a watertight case against him.

"Did they say when the trial will be?" Tommy asked. His heart sunk as Tracey shook her head.

"No. But be prepared, love." She took his hand, but he turned his head away.

If he met her eyes and saw them full of concern and sympathy, he might just break down in tears. He clenched his teeth together as she continued to speak in tender tones.

"It will probably be months before they get him to trial. The insurance company may not pay out until they know the outcome. "

"I can't wait that long. I need the cash now, today. And even at that it took me weeks to get set up, and the building wasn't like this when I started the first time." Rage turned his stomach acid. He didn't want Tracey to think he was mad at her. He kissed her hand.

"You don't need to stay here," she said. "You can get new premises. Maybe the landlord will let you out of your lease."

"Even so, I still need about ten grand to get started again. I don't have it. I-I. . . everything's gone, unless Dad pulls through," He turned and walked away so he could wipe his knuckles across his eyes without her seeing him.

"Not trying is losing. You two have been getting on better lately, right? What have all those fishing trips been about?" She caught up with him and turned him around to face her. "It's not been about feeding us with fish, now has it?"

He couldn't help smiling. They never caught anything worth taking home.

"When he gets here I'm going to make myself scarce. Okay?" Tracey smiled up at him and for a second he felt strong. He could pull this off.

"Great. . . " Tommy did not relish asking his father for money. The banks were not in a lending mode these days. He had no other choice – unless he gave up his dream of having his own place.

"Hello, Son," Sean said.

Tommy spun around, nearly knocking Tracey over. She stepped back and winked at him, then turned to his father.

"Sean, it's good to see you. I'm going to grab us all coffee. Want one?" she said brightly.

Sean's face lit up, the wrinkles creasing further, forming a smile as he nodded. "That'd be lovely thanks. Just black for me."

She waved at Tommy."I'll be back in a minute."

Tommy stood beside his Dad. They watched her disappear around the corner.

"She reminds me of your mother. You're lucky to have her," Sean said in a quiet tone, turning to his son. Tommy read concern in his father's grey irises. The crinkled folds of a smile had rearranged themselves into concerned furrows. His heart lifted. His dad was on his side, and it felt good.

"I know," Tommy said, flicking at the button on the torch, "Would you like a tour?"

"Go on then."

Tommy answered his father's questions about Kieran Quinn and the court case as they picked their way through the salon.

"He's a bad one. I'm glad Tracey had the gumption to leave him for you. I'm just sorry that it led to this, but whatever you do, don't be blaming her, son. She's a good girl, and it's not her fault," Sean said.

"I know. Don't worry, I haven't been thinking that." His Dad's advice heartened Tommy. He liked this side of his father.

It's a miracle – father and son actually agree on something.

Sean bent to pick up what looked like a chair and came away holding the metal frame, leaving the rest floating to the floor in a drift of ashes. He sneezed.

"Careful. This can get you coughing." Tommy swung the beam of light around the room and then let it rest on his father's face.

"Jaysus, are ye trying to blind me?" Sean stuck his hand up in front of his face.

"Sorry," Tommy said, pointing the light at the floor. "Have you seen enough?"

"Aye, let's get outta here."

They emerged into the light before Sean spoke again.

"I'm sorry about your business. Really I am. I know you worked hard at this."

"I wish you'd come to see it before. . . before this." Tommy didn't know where to start.

"Me too. I wanted to."

"You did?" Tommy couldn't hide his astonishment.

"I needed a cut and shave." Sean didn't make eye contact.

Tommy struggled to read him.

"I'd have come to the house, Dad," Tommy said. A nugget of hope germinated within him.

"Well, actually, I was hoping Orla would do it."

Typical – so much for getting his support.

"I see," Tommy said. "Well she'll be happy to do a home job now that she's out of work."

"And you're on the dole too?" Sean paused and looked at Tommy.

Now or never.

"Dad," Tommy began. He cleared his throat. "I need help. Financial help."

"How much?"

"About ten thousand. Enough to get started again. I'll pay it all back."

"Would you consider going back to school? I'd pay for it. You know you can still think about the financial industry, math's and accounting haven't changed that much since you did you're A-levels. Though the economics A-level might be outdated," Sean said.

Tommy struggled to keep a grasp of his temper. He had been on that career path before his mother got sick. Helping her during her illness had shown him how much he needed to work with people not spreadsheets. The thought of returning to that made him feel like he'd swallowed a block of lead.

"No. I'm thirty years old. I'm not going back to school," he said. He tried to keep his temper on a short leash, but it strained to run free. "I knew you'd say no. I don't know why Tracey even thought you'd help me."

"Tracey thought I'd help you?"

"Yes, Dad. Don't sound so incredulous. It's not that preposterous you know – some fathers do help their sons." Bitterness crackled in his words.

"But I won't. . . "

"Look, don't worry about it. I know you didn't want me to be a hairdresser because of some homophobic voodoo you believe in. I won't ask you again."

"It's just that I don't have. . . "

Tommy interrupted him again. "Ach Dad, just go, please. I don't want to argue with you, and this had been tough enough. If you say you don't have the money then you don't. I'm sorry to put you on the spot. Please go, before I lose my temper and say more than I want to."

"Fine, you're upset," Sean said backing away with his hands up. "When you've calmed down, we'll talk some more." Sean turned and walked away, not waiting for an answer, which infuriated Tommy even more.

Sean had to get the last word and turn it around to make Tommy look bad. Tommy fumed as he listened to his father's footsteps fade. He leaned back against the wall and bent forward, resting his hands above his knees. He took a couple of deep breaths, but he couldn't get rid of the sour taste in his mouth. If only he hadn't gotten his hopes up.

"Tommy, are you okay?"

He felt a soft hand rubbing his back.

"Where's your Dad? What did he say?" Tracey asked. She set the coffee tray on the ground.

Tommy straightened up and opened his arms. She moved to him and he enveloped her.

"He said he won't give me the money. He claims he doesn't have it. He has it when he wants to turn me into a stockbroker though." To his extreme embarrassment, Tommy burst into tears.

Tuesday, October 24th

CHAPTER FORTY-FIVE

Fran sat forward in her hospital bed and pressed closer to the mirror, opening her eyes wide. She placed her hand at her hair line and pulled back, then let go and watched the folds of skin gather again.

"Look at how wrinkly I am," she said. "I'm like a blood hound. A right old hag!"

"Ach, don't be at it," Molly said, smoothing the bed covers and wheeling the tray table out of her way. "I think you're beautiful. Every line on your face reflects the joys and sorrows of your heart. Laughter-lines, tears – think of each line as a diploma in wisdom earned over the years."

Fran set down the mirror and looked up at Molly.

"When did you get to be so damn clever?" she said.

Molly shrugged and handed Fran a box wrapped in silver paper patterned with the words "Happy Birthday" in a variety of pink fonts.

Fran's mouth formed a tight "o". "You remembered," she said, her voice wavering.

Molly looked away, unable to bear the tears that gathered in Fran's eyes.

"Well, I know it's at the end of October, but you won't tell me which day, so I picked today." Molly smiled as Fran's chuckled amid the crackle of wrapping paper.

"Ha!" the old lady said. "So much for diplomas in wisdom." Fran held up the pot of Olay anti-wrinkle cream.

"And when you get out of here, we'll have a big party too," Molly said. "Now that the cast is off and you can manage with the walking frame…"

Fran looked away and cleared her throat.

Molly felt her scalp prickle. "What's wrong Fran? Is your leg still sore? Are there more complications?"

"No, child dear, no. It's just. . ." Fran's gaze met Molly's. "I've decided to sell the house."

"What? But where will you live?"

"Loughview Manor."

Molly's mind reeled. Loughview was the old people's home. No one ever moved out of there unless they were packed in their own wooden box. Dermot's grandmother had spent three years mentally trapped in dementia and physically trapped in Loughview. The poor woman had hated it and tried to escape every chance she got. She cried and begged them to take her home with them when they visited her.

"No. I'll look after you. You can't go there." Molly's mind flashed forward to herself forty years from now. Is this how women without families end up? Shoved in a home because no one cares for them?

"Don't argue with me. It's all been arranged. I can't stay here forever, and I need help. More help than I'm willing to take from you. You have your life to live."

"But it's only been ten weeks since your accident. I know it's a long time to be in a hospital, but that's only because you got that infection. Aren't you over that now?"

"Yes, but. . ." Fran began.

"But nothing. Most people your age would have needed a new hip, but you didn't. The home is for old people."

Fran harrumphed.

"No, I mean really old people," Molly continued. "The doctors said you'd walk with a limp. So you won't win Dance with the Stars, but you can have a normal life."

"I can still have a normal life in the home," Fran said, her grey eyes steady, locked onto Molly's. "I can come and go as I please. You can visit as much as you want – we can still go on day trips if you'd like. But I'll not have to worry about falling down again and hurting myself and having no-one to help me."

Heat flooded Molly's face.

"Child dear, my fall was not your fault," Fran said. "And it's not fair on either of us to have to worry about it. Okay? I'd like you to be with me on this. Are you?"

Molly gulped. She nodded but looked down, keeping her eyes, hot with tears, from Fran's scrutiny. The winter ahead threatened to close in cold and empty. Molly missed having Fran next door and had looked forward to cozy chats by the fire after school. But now... She wiped her face with the back of her hand.

"It's parents' night tonight. I have to go early." Molly hated having to leave early after having heard of Fran's plans. She stood up to leave. "Whatever you want, I'll support you." Her voice sounded stronger than she felt.

***

The woman had such bad breath that every time she spoke, Molly suppressed a wince. She shifted back from the awful woman in front of her and glanced around. Parents sat on hard chairs, set out in rows in the middle of the assembly hall, waiting to talk with the teachers sitting at desks around the perimeter of the room. Her line grew by the minute. She had a caseload of sixty children tonight, and she was only on number five.

"You're the only person that says anything bad about my Petey," the pong in front of her droned on. "All his brothers and sisters love him, and he's no bother at home. He never gets into trouble, not even with his Da. . ."

Molly didn't care.

". . .and he's so good to his wee brothers. . ."

God, there were more of them to come through the school. She'd managed to gain some composure between Fran's visit and arriving at the school, but now she felt her temper sliding from her grasp.

". . .his football coach says Petey is the most talented. . ."

This meeting was pointless.

". . .top of the league. . ."

The mothers of the Peteys of this world would never listen to her.

". . .man of the match. . ."

It was all bullshit.

"Mrs. Fitzpatrick," Molly cut in sharply. "Peter is one of the most ill-mannered children I have ever taught. He has no respect for himself or other people. He delights in thwarting authority and is constantly pushing behavioral boundaries. It is totally unacceptable and it is affecting the progress of other individuals in the class!"

Molly stopped to draw a breath, but she felt her eyes popping, sensed her nostrils flared. Mrs. Daly, the teacher stationed at the next conference table looked up at Molly's raised voice and frowned.

Mrs. Fitzpatrick leaned in so close that Molly could see the black heads in the creases of her yellowed skin. "So what exactly are you saying?" The stench of stale booze and cigarettes oozed out with every word.

Molly stood up violently enough to knock against the table and slop water from her glass all over her notes. She heard Mrs. Daly's sharp intake of breath, but the locomotion ran at full steam now.

"I'm saying, Mrs. Fitzpatrick, that your son is a little shit! He is a spoilt wee bastard, and all the teachers here dread the day they have to deal with him. I hate parents like you who lay the blame at everyone else's fucking feet. Wake up and take responsibility, you stupid bitch, your son is a delinquent and will most likely end up in jail!"

All around her, stunned teachers and parents stared with mouths hanging open. Her blood rushed in her ears. Molly turned and thrust her own chair out of her way. She ran to a fire escape door and shoved the handle hard. An alarm sounded as she launched herself outside, slammed the door behind her and ran around the side of the building to the parking lot.

She sat outside in her car, gripped by an insane urge to laugh as she pictured Mrs. Fitzpatrick's face. Hysteria gripped her as she pictured the school principal fussing over Mrs. Fitzpatrick, exercising damage limitation.

Molly thought of all the times in the staff room when they discussed what they would really like to say on parents' night, laughing and comparing it to what they did say. "Disappointing result" coded for disastrous result and how "satisfactory" was anything but!

She'd really done it this time. With shaking hands she turned the key in the ignition. As she drove out of the car park, she saw her friend Laura come racing out the door waving both arms, but Molly could not stop. She needed to get home before she completely fell apart.

As she opened her front door, Molly heard the phone ringing. She refused to answer it. She heard the Vice Principal identify herself politely and say, "Molly I know you are under a lot of stress at the moment, and we, the senior management committee, think you should take the rest of the week off. Please call the school tomorrow so we can have a chat about this, and how we can move forward from here. Thank you, goodbye."

Molly plopped down on the sofa in the living room. Was she suspended? Schools were all about pleasing the parents. Perhaps the school would wriggle out of this. It was hard to sack a teacher these days, but could they strongly encourage her to leave? Would they paint her as some sort of basket case?

No hard task there. I am a basket case.

She wasn't sure if she heard the voice aloud or just in her head.

"I'm totally loopeee!" she shouted and laughed until she started crying. Fear pierced her. She foundered in a cold dark place that she didn't recognize. She pushed herself up off the soft sofa and trudged upstairs. She didn't bother to wash her face or even brush her teeth. She went straight to the bedside cabinet and took out her newly-filled prescription of sleeping pills.

They were the only thing besides alcohol that induced sleep, and even they were becoming less effective. Tonight, she'd take two. Her head hurt from the nervous buzz that had built all evening. She could compliment her sleep with a little pain relief. She fished out her stash of co-dydramol left over from a bad backache she'd had a year ago. They were good "zonking" out agents too. She held the four tablets in the palm of her hand and stared at their white chalkiness. Maybe this was too many? Four little white tablets would be fine. Tonight. A one off. But not every night. Same goes for "effing off" parents. Once wouldn't hurt.

***

Molly heard Laura's voice. Then the answering machine beeped, and Molly drifted off to sleep again. Twice more she heard the answering machine beep and scold, but the shackles of sleep dragged Molly back to the promised place of bliss.

A while later, Molly heard Laura's voice again, accompanied with a series of loud bangs. Molly groggily looked at the clock. The red digits blazed out "6:00". It was still dark outside.

"Someone better be dying!" Molly called as she struggled out of the bed and threw on her dressing gown. What the hell did Laura want at six in the morning? Molly opened her bedroom window and stuck her head out.

"What?" she snarled. "Why are you here at this time of the morning?"

"Jesus, Molly. Thank God you're okay!"

"Of course I'm OK. What's going on?"

"When you didn't turn up for work I was worried and then no one heard from you. . ."

"What do you mean work? It's only six in the morning. What are you on about?"

"Molly, it's six P M!"

"What? Shit! Wait a minute, let yourself in. I'll be right down." Molly flung a key out the window to Laura and raced around the room, finding a pair of jogging bottoms and a sweatshirt to pull on. There wasn't much she could do about her wild hair, so she scraped it into a loose bun. Her mouth felt foul. The metallic aftertaste reminded her she had taken two sleeping tablets. No wonder she'd slept the day through. Her heart pounded as she thudded down the stairs. This was the stuff of nightmares. Next thing she'd be turning up at school naked, if she still had a job.

"Oh God, you scared the life out of me. I was worried sick! What the hell is going on with you?" Laura scolded, but Molly recognized a rant fuelled by concern.

"Look, Laura, I need a coffee, do you want one?" Molly moved into the kitchen and Laura followed her.

"Eh no. No coffee for me." She shook her head. "So where have you been?"

"In bed." Molly flicked on the kettle then looked around at her friend, surprised that the answer wasn't more obvious. Should she confess to having taken extra sleeping tablets?

"Are you on drugs, Molly?" Laura asked the question slowly, her voice stern. That answered Molly's query. Best not mention the tablets in case someone tried to take them from her, or tell the doctor and stop her supply.

Molly rubbed her hand across her face in a gesture of exhaustion. She sat down at the kitchen table with her head in her hands.

"Look, Laura, I just had a few nights in a row that I couldn't sleep and that's why I was so short tempered last night."

"Short tempered!" Laura interrupted, her voice rising an octave. "That was a damn sight more than short tempered!"

"Yeah, whatever," Molly brushed it off with a wave of her hand. She knew they'd get to that later. "The school rang last night and told me to take the rest of the week off, so I didn't set an alarm last night and I slept in."

"Slept in by half a day!"

Molly shrugged. "I had a lot of sleep to catch up on."

"And the thought of losing your job on top of whatever else that has been keeping you awake didn't keep you tossing and turning?"

"Look, what's with the cross examination?"

"You're acting weird. Look at what happened last night. What the hell were you thinking?" Laura stood next to Molly, hands on hips, looking down at her.

"It was obvious what I was thinking. Same as what everyone else was thinking. What I'm thinking is not a problem. What I say seems to be. Ha! I certainly spelt it out to Ma Fitzpatrick." Molly cracked a grin.

Laura's features softened. Mirth threatened to lighten her features, but she gained composure.

"Molly, what's happening? Tell me please." The gentle tone of Laura's voice undid Molly. She struggled to find words to clothe her living hell in a way that Laura might understand. Her tears spilled over, ran down her face and dripped off her chin.

"I miss him so much." Molly's voice wavered as she struggled to stop her face from wobbling. "Everything reminds me of what I haven't got. Every song on the radio; every movie; every breath I take. Oh God, how pathetic. That sounds like the words of the song."

Molly gave a snuffly laugh, trying to jolly herself out of the wretched position she found herself in. She felt her grip on sanity weaken again, and the fear it dug up overwhelmed her. She abandoned herself to weeping, unable to speak.

She felt Laura's arms go round her shoulders. Her body shuddered as she wept. Laura tightened her grip and rocked her back and forth, making soothing shushing sounds as if comforting a child.

Molly had cried alone many times, too often to count: in her bed, dampening the pillow case so she had to turn it over to find a dry patch to sleep on; sitting alone at the kitchen table, staring at dinner for one; hunched over in the bath, letting tears drop into the soapy bath water until it went too cold to stay in.

Rarely did she have comfort from another human being as she cried, and its release was bittersweet. The consolation relaxed and warmed her, but loneliness would sweep into the vacuum Laura's withdrawal would create. Molly mourned the times she'd cry alone in future, and Laura hadn't even released her yet.

"Molly, you need help with this." Laura pushed Molly back so she could look her in the eye. Tenderly she brushed stray curls out of Molly's eyes, attempting to hook them behind her ears. They disobediently unfurled, working their way back to where they started.

"I'll talk to the VP tomorrow and we'll get you counseling, okay?"

Mute, Molly nodded.

"You take your time off Molly, and then, when you come back, you'll be a whole new person." Laura smiled.

"A whole new person," Molly echoed.

Saturday, October 28th

CHAPTER FORTY-SIX

Condensation dripped down the inside of the glass along the front of the coffee shop, creating a crazy map of rivulets. A tide of noise, the clatter of voices and crockery, hit Tracey and Molly when they opened the door. The coffee shop smelled of damp hair and clothing.

Tracey wondered if she'd made a mistake taking Molly here. She felt bad for neglecting her lately, but she'd her hands full trying to help Tommy through the trauma of the fire. Molly's depressing gloom exhausted Tracey. She knew her friend's heartbreak, but she wondered when Molly would start to count the blessings in her life. She was a beautiful young woman, wounded now, but with a lot of love to offer some lucky guy. It was a pity Dermot passed that up so readily. His baby was due soon. Curiosity about her new niece or nephew gnawed at her when her mind drifted to her brother.

She snatched another glimpse at Molly, feeling guilty for even thinking about Dermot and the baby with Molly so close by. Molly's face was closed and hard to read. Tracey sighed. There was a time when they could nearly speak each other's thoughts. Molly had retreated somewhere that Tracey couldn't follow.

But Tracey knew that she too had become guarded. She couldn't tell Molly about how she loved being with Tommy or describe how much joy he brought to her life. Knowing this love, she understood the depth of Molly's pain. Tracey only had to imagine losing Tommy to feel it sting. They'd only been together months now, not years like Molly and Dermot.

She'd banked on some retail therapy lifting both their spirits, but with the coffee shop this busy, her hopes for a quiet chat with Molly evaporated. They'd be lucky to get a seat, and Tracey could sense Molly's growing agitation.

Slowly they inched up the queue. Molly shifted her shopping bags from one hand to the other and then turned to Tracey saying, "If you give me all the bags, I'll go find a seat, and you could order the coffees. Here's some cash." Molly began digging into her pocket.

"Oh don't worry, my treat," Tracey replied with forced cheerfulness. "Good idea. Skinny café latte, right?"

"Please, and could you get me one of those chocolate covered shortcake fingers? They're in the basket by the till, not one of the tray bakes."

"I know the one." Tracey handed over her bags, and Molly went scavenging for seats. Tracey got to the counter and ordered the drinks and picked out the biscuit for Molly.

Molly found a table with four seats right by the door. Just as Tracey set down their cups, another cup was placed opposite hers.

"Do you mind if I sit here?" a guy in a suit asked. He looked too smooth and acted over confident, but she had no choice. She raised an eyebrow at Molly, who did not seem overjoyed either, but they couldn't begrudge him the last seat.

Mr. Slick, as Tracey christened him in her head, sat down, setting his brief case on the chair beside him. Molly sat without making eye contact with the guy, and Tracey prayed that he wouldn't try to make small talk.

The girls chatted together ignoring the stranger, who had become engrossed in his mobile phone.

"So, Orla has invited us all to a fancy dress party on Halloween night. Will you come?" Tracey asked.

Molly furrowed her brow.

"What night is Halloween?"

"Tuesday night" answered Tracey and Mr. Slick in stereo. Molly and Tracey stopped talking, not wanting to engage the guy. He flashed a toothy smile as he lifted the chocolate covered shortbread bar from the table, unwrapped the snack, took a bite and set it back down.

Alarmed, Tracey looked at Molly, who stared open-mouthed at the biscuit. Her face like thunder, she glared at the man, then made eye contact with Tracey. They rose to leave. Picking up their bags of shopping, Tracey got to the door first. She turned back in time to see Molly lean over the table.

"People like you sicken me, bullying other people and just taking what you want!" Molly reached down, picked up the bar, took a huge bite out of it and threw it back down on the table.

The guy sat motionless and watched her exit the café.

"Good for you!" Tracey said as Molly ran up beside her. "Did you see the look on his face?"

The girls laughed as they headed to the car. Tracey set down her shopping and put her hand in her pocket to get her keys. A hot flush tore up her cheeks.

"Oops!" she said, as she pulled the chocolate covered shortbread bar from her pocket.

"Oh God!" Molly cried. "I thought the one on the table was mine!" Her blue eyes looked around her wildly. "Quick, get in the car in case he follows us!"

"Not likely! He probably thinks you are one hell of a nut-case. I don't think he'll be following you." Tracey fumbled with the keys, clumsily unlocking the car door.

"Oh my God, what must he be thinking?" Molly groaned. "I can't believe I just did that!"

"Oh it's okay. Where's your sense of humor?"

"I left it in the café. I thought I was funny taking a bite out of my own chocolate bar but this? This is…"

"Hilarious?" Tracey suggested, laughing.

"Just hurry up and drive. Get us out of here!" Molly pleaded.

"Okay, okay, we're going!" Tracey pulled out at the first gap in the traffic. "So, as I was saying before we were so rudely interrupted."

"By a guy eating his own chocolate bar," Molly added as she burst into tears.

"Hey, come on now," Tracey said, wondering if she should pull over. "It's not that bad."

"But it is," Molly said, wiping her face with her sleeve. "I just can't seem to control myself. Look how I lost it last week at the parent's night."

Tracey nodded her head. "I've been thinking about that. Do you want my two cents?"

Molly shrugged and sniffed at the same time. "Can't hurt," she said.

"These are all good signs," Tracey said.

"Aye, right."

"No. It means you haven't given up. You're fighting back. You had me worried a while ago."

"The wrists, right?"

"Shit yeah." Tracey felt the connection between them humming again. "Promise me you'd never do something like that."

"Jesus no way, I mean – yes, promise. Suicide is selfish. I'd never do that to you or anyone I love," Molly said. "But I still don't see how cracking up at people is good."

"You're going through the anger stage of grief," Tracey explained. "It's normal, and it's healthy. You shouldn't bottle it up."

"I don't think I am." Molly waved the biscuit in front of her.

Tracey looked over and caught a glimpse of a lifted eyebrow and a smirk hovering on Molly's lips.

"Good. You're getting mad at men and maybe even Dermot?" Tracey glanced over, trying to read Molly's expression as it changed and the smile drifted from its contours.

"So, does that mean I'll start to feel better soon? Because this all still sucks like. . .like. . . fuck it! Like a big sucky thing."

Tracey couldn't decide if Molly sported a smile with a mock frown or the other way around, but the old Molly floated close to the surface.

"According to my therapist you need to feel and acknowledge the anger," Tracey said, encouraged.

"You're still going to counseling?" Molly asked.

"Not so often now. But it really helped. You should go," Tracey said.

"Laura from work suggested it too. I think I will." A ghost of a smile haunted Molly's lips.

"Good girl, and what about the party on Tuesday? Tommy needs something to lift his spirits." Tracey said.

"Still no word from his Dad about helping him out?"

"Ah you know that pair – stubborn and stubborner. So will ye go?" Tracey pushed.

"I don't know . . ."

"Oh come on. No ifs, buts or maybes. You're going," Tracey said.

"Alright. Anything for a quiet life," Molly said, sighing.

"Tommy and I will collect you on Tuesday night at eight O'clock. Okay? We'll get a taxi from your place. I won't take no for an answer." Tracey looked over at Molly, who was lost in thought and staring out the window. Maybe she'd pushed her too far. "Okay, Molly?" she persisted.

"Okay," Molly mumbled.

Tracey pulled up outside Molly's house. Her heart flooded with pity as she watched Molly standing at the gate. Her shoulders slumped as she dropped her bags and fumbled with the latch.

Tracey jumped out of the car and ran to help. On impulse, she hugged her, saying, "Love you, Molly!"

"You too, Tracey," Molly said, looking puzzled.

Embarrassed, Tracey lightened her tone and chirped, "We'll see you Tuesday then?"

Molly nodded.

Tracey got in her car and drove off, glancing in her rear view mirror to see Molly waving from her front door, still looking bemused.

Tuesday, October 31ˢᵗ, Halloween

CHAPTER FORTY-SEVEN

The old folk sat around the edges of the recreational room of the Loughview Home in stiff armchairs. An undertone of chemical floral scent suggested an over-use of air freshener. Washed out pastel green walls and beige and brown carpeting made the room look drab to Molly. Blinds on the windows lent a clinical edge. The T.V. blared in the corner, the ad for some car promising a flashy lifestyle to the buyer, brandishing a life now unattainable to them. Molly spotted Fran dozing in a chair at the far end of the room. As Molly approached, Fran's eyes blinked open, and her face crinkled. Amid the swath of wrinkles, Fran's eyes glittered with delight.

"Molly!" she cried. "How lovely to see you, child-dear. Would you like to see my room? I even have a view of the Lough. Not that you can see it at night, but during the day it's lovely."

As she spoke, Fran struggled to her feet using the walking-frame in front of her. Molly wasn't sure how to help her up. Pulling seemed too forceful, and lifting would be awkward. Fran stood up before Molly could decide.

"Now child dear, if you'd carry my handbag, that would be lovely." Fran lifted the walker and placed it a few inches away from her, then shuffled up to it.

"So, how are you?" Molly asked. She hefted the bag onto her shoulder. "Jeepers, are you carrying gold bars around in here?"

"Just a few bits and bobs," Fran said. She led Molly down a corridor with cream walls and shiny beige linoleum floor. Molly was surprised that the place did not smell of disinfectant. She expected it to be just like a hospital, yet noticed homey little touches, like watercolor paintings on the walls.

"There's painting lessons if we want them. Some of them are quite good, aren't they?" Fran said, nodding in the direction of Molly's gaze.

"The um-patients did these?" Molly said. She wasn't sure what to call them, and the only other word she could think of was "inmates".

"Oh yes. And the residents," Fran's eyes twinkled as she stressed the word, "did all the flower arrangements too."

"Seems like you'll be busy then." Molly looked at her friend and smiled. Tension slithered from her brow.

"Me? I couldn't paint a moonless night in a cave, me." Fran chuckled. She stopped at a door, then moved to the side as a shrunken old man followed his walker down the hall.

"Hello, James?" Fran said.

"Eh?" The man raised his head and focused on Fran. His features softened and his eyes were transformed from dazed to delighted. He put his hand to a device at the back of his head. A piercing whistle made all three of them wince before he was able to shut it off. "Sorry, these hearing aids are giving me gip. How are you, Fran?" he said loudly.

"I'm fine," Fran replied, matching his volume. "This is my friend, Molly. She used to be my neighbor."

Molly shook the grey and mauve mottled hand he offered. The strong grip surprised her, but her heart stung. *Used to be my neighbor.*

"Ach, you're a pretty young lass. Must be something in the water in your street, eh?" he said, dropping Fran a wink.

"Go on, away o'that will ya," Fran chuckled turning pink.

James shambled on past the door.

"Was he just flirting with you. . .with us?" Molly asked.

"What passes for flirting when you're ninety-two," Fran said turning the handle on the door. "Dirty old bugger," she mumbled, still grinning.

Molly had to laugh as she followed Fran. The room was decorated in muted pink and grey. A metal bed with hydraulics, pedals and levers lay against one wall. In the corner, a little sink unit stood with a mirror above it, and a counter ran from the edge of the sink under a window. A vase of pink roses stood in front of the window. There were large drawers below the counter, beside this a large floor-to-ceiling wardrobe.

"I was going to bring you flowers, but I also wanted to see if there was anything you needed. You know, like pajamas?" Molly said.

Fran sat down in another stiff armchair Molly hadn't noticed tucked in behind the door.

"Don't worry, child dear. I got those from an admirer." Fran winked.

James? Molly wondered. Good grief, it didn't take him long, but then she supposed at ninety-two you don't have time to waste.

"Child-dear, the expression on your face is priceless! But seriously, I have everything I need. It's just good to see you. Your presence is present enough."

Molly felt her throat tighten. Fran was such a trooper. She made moving to a home seem bearable. Molly saw herself forty years down the line, perched in the same upright armchair. Hot tears filled her eyes.

"Ach, what's the matter, child-dear?"

Over-come, Molly hiccupped the first few words, "Just seeing you here. You should be at home." She wiped at her tears with her sleeve.

"Child dear, life is full of changes. In fact, change is the only constant thing in life. It's nothing to be afraid of."

"But I am afraid."

"Afraid of what?"

"I'm afraid for you being unhappy here. And afraid of being alone all the rest of my life and then ending up in a home, like…" Molly stopped.

"Like me?" Fran said gently. "I'm less alone here than I would be at home. I'm making loads of new friends here."

Molly heard the familiar old chuckle and looked at Fran.

"After I'd mourned Anthony, I had to move on," Fran said. "Just like you must. Don't think I've lived all my life pining for Anthony. In fact, I'll tell you a secret. I found out at his funeral that he'd had an affair."

"Oh my God!" Molly gasped.

"Oh yes, Saint Anthony, savior of little girls, had been a naughty boy." Fran's voice sounded briefly brittle, then she smiled and grabbed Molly's hand before continuing in a gentler tone, "But I got over it."

"How?" Molly said. "I don't think I can ever get over Dermot. It's just too much, too big. I can't. . ."

"Child dear. How do you eat an elephant?"

"I don't know," Molly said, wondering if Fran was a little senile.

"One bite at a time." Fran's face furrowed into swaths of wrinkles and smiles.

Inside Molly, something clunked into place, like a gear on a bike suddenly catching the cog. She laughed, imagining Fran with a knife and fork carving an elephant leg. But it made her think.

"Well, I haven't been missing all that football on the telly all the time. I can watch what I want now. I go to bed when I like and never get wakened up with his snoring," Molly said. Anger still smoldered as she nudged up against it. She remembered what Tracey had said about how her anger at the Parent Teacher meeting and at the man in the cafe was a sign that she was on the mend. "I've managed the mortgage and the finances," she continued. "That's the first few bites, so even less of the elephant left to eat. Maybe it's not impossible."

Fran nodded sagely. "I think you're getting the picture, child dear. It comes slowly, but there are benefits. After his life insurance paid out, I never wanted for anything my whole life, God bless him. Had a lot of fun, too."

"But didn't you get lonely?" Molly thought of the dark evenings of winter approaching.

"Sometimes, at the beginning, but I met other people to love. I never told you about the six months I spent in Paris with the handsome musician, or about the invite to emigrate with the dashing American sailor." Fran smiled, throwing her face once again into a merry fold of wrinkles. "Just because I didn't remarry doesn't mean I became a nun."

Molly flushed pink, not sure where this was going, or if she wanted to hear it.

"I've had a great life. And I reckon more to come, please God. But before I go, I'm looking forward to spending time in this peaceful place being catered for. Your needs change as you get older.

Now, you probably get bored quickly and time drags by. I remember that. But when you get to my age, time speeds up. It feels like I sit down for breakfast every twenty minutes! Child dear, it's time for a rest." Fran sounded as though she'd only just discovered this. "Might even take up painting."

Molly tried to identify the pleasant sensation she felt. The delicious taste of anticipation, of looking forward to the future infused within her. She felt as though she were marinating in possibilities for the first time. She'd get counseling with the help of the school, like Laura had suggested, and she'd climb back from this. That shithead Dermot Duggan had not beaten her.

They both looked up at a soft knock on the door. An attractive man in his thirties with a shock of red hair and brilliant green eyes stuck his head round the door at Fran's invitation to enter.

"Hello, Nurse Mackle. This was my neighbor, Molly," Fran said.

"Ach, I've heard all about you, Molly. I feel like I already know you. Call me Charlie," said the man, extending a hand to Molly. His green eyes held hers for a second as they shook hands.

Molly felt a tingle at their touch. Confused she dropped his hand but not his gaze. It felt warm and kind. "Nice to meet you, Charlie," She said after what seemed like far too long to her.

"I just wanted to check if you wanted your tea in the canteen or up here? Would you like a cuppa, Molly?"

"Ach, that would be lovely, thanks," Fran and Molly answered together, and then laughed.

"Stereo!" Charlie said, and gave them the thumbs up and left.

"What a nice man," Fran said. "Single too."

Molly felt herself pinken, but she liked how her heartbeat sped up a touch.

"How do you know?" Molly said.

"I asked him yesterday."

"What? You, like, just up and asked him, just like that?"

"Well, I'm too old to be beating around the bush."

"Fran, you're not suggesting..." James was one thing, but Charlie?

Fran threw her head back and laughed, her mouth thrown open so Molly could see her denture plate.

"No, child dear, no! I've plenty of men friends my own age to flirt with here. But I'd like to be around for your next wedding day, seeing as how I missed the practice one."

Ha – a practice marriage! Dermot was a prick. Her best revenge would be to forget him and get out and have fun, perhaps starting with a nice man like Charlie.

"So if he asks for your number, or even just finds it lying around?" Fran arched her brow, lifting a cascade of wrinkles on her forehead.

"Fran, you are incorrigible," Molly laughed. "A tonic – but incorrigible."

"What are you doing tonight?"

"No! I'm going out to a fancy dress with Tracey and Tommy tonight."

"Have you decided on what you are dressing up as?"

Molly folded her arms and chewed her lip before answering, "You know what? I just decided. I'm gonna dig out my *practice* wedding dress and go as the bride of Frankenstein!"

"But it's supposed to be make believe – you did marry Frankenstein," countered Fran.

Tuesday, October 31st, Halloween

CHAPTER FORTY-EIGHT

"You are not seriously going to wear that are you?" Sheila said. She needed to pee every twenty minutes. Ten days overdue left her over-wrought and uncomfortable. She just wanted this baby out of her.

Yesterday morning she'd burnt her huge belly on the hot kettle as she reached into the cupboard above it for a cup. Stretching her arms had caused her pajama top to ride up, exposing her bare tummy to the searing metal. The flash of pain on her skin made her yelp, and she jumped back, dropping and smashing the cup.

Dermot, sitting at the kitchen table snoozing over his cornflakes, had jumped up.

"Is it time?" he asked, lifting newspapers and patting down his pockets.

"No," Sheila said, "I just burnt. . ."

"We need to get you to the hospital," He said finally pulling his car keys from a pocket.

"No! I'm okay," Sheila shouted. "I just burnt my belly."

He stopped and stared at her. "Oh shit. Are you okay? Should we go to the hospital anyways?"

"I'm fine, but could you just take a look?" Sheila pulled up her top.

"Holy shite!" Dermot said.

"Fuckit, get me a mirror," Sheila said as Dermot stared at the wound. "NOW!"

Sure enough, an angry red mark splashed across her skin, and Sheila could make out the beginnings of a blister. She applied cold cloths for most of the morning to cool the pain and avoid scarring. Dermot had taken the day off work, claiming that he was traumatized by the event. Sheila dreaded how he would react to the birth.

He attempted now to cajole her into some kind of festive mood. "Oh, come on – it's Halloween! The neighbor's children will be coming around trick or treating. I want to scare them. They love that sort of thing. We always did it!"

Sheila twitched at the reference to his life with Molly.

"Never mind," he said, setting down the grotesque mask and hairy hands he had intended to wear. "I'll just give them some sweets when they come."

Sheila felt guilty. It was an emotion she was tired of, but somehow Dermot triggered it in her. He was so enthusiastic about this baby that neither of them had wanted to begin with. At least one parent would welcome its arrival.

Dermot pushed her to pick names. Sheila didn't care. Her only stipulation was that they should be short and phonically spelt. They had agreed to wait until the baby arrived to see how it fit the names they liked. So far Sheila didn't like any. She still thought of the thing she was carrying as "it".

Sheila felt the urge to pee again. As she stood up to make her way to the bathroom, she felt a sharp tug in her lower abdomen and warm flood down her legs. Her first thought was that she wet herself, but there was too much fluid. Then pain doubled her over, and she folded up with a grunt that forced the air over her vocal chords in a loud "Ouf".

"Oh my God!" She could breathe again once the vice grip released her abdomen. "I think my waters just broke!"

Dermot jumped to attention. "Let's get you straight to the hospital." Have you your bag packed?"

"It's been packed for two weeks."

"Where is it? I'll go get it. You sit there. Don't move."

"It's in the bottom of the big wardrobe in the bedroom. To the left hand side. A small, grey suitcase." Before Sheila finished, Dermot was halfway up the stairs. She heard him thud-thud into the bedroom.

After a few seconds he called out, "I can't see it Sheila. Where did you say it was?"

"Try the other left!" she called back, rolling her eyes. Men could never find anything. She heard him pounding down the stairs. He burst into the living room triumphantly waving the bag.

"I got it!"

"Where was it?"

"Where you said it was," he said, sheepishly grinning at Sheila. She started to smile back but another contraction gripped her abdomen. Pain squeezed the breath out of her. She couldn't believe how much it hurt already. Wasn't it supposed to build up to a crescendo and then – pop - out comes a baby? She wished she'd paid more attention in ante-natal class.

Dermot grabbed the bag and his car keys in one hand, and put the other arm protectively around Sheila, supporting her as she walked. She felt grateful at that moment that Dermot was there, happy to let him take charge.

Even with only a short drive to the hospital, by the time Dermot pulled up at the maternity admittance, Sheila was in tears. The contractions tore through her in agonizing streaks that frightened her. Even though she'd had nine months to prepare, this birth caught her by surprise. She'd hadn't expected this pain, this helplessness.

Dermot jumped out and ran around to help her.

"Don't cry, sweetheart." He tried to soothe her. "We are at the hospital now. You are in good hands. You'll be okay."

Sheila couldn't stop crying. Torrents of emotion hammered at her. Fear chased out any attempt to gain control. Vulnerability permeated her with a sense of unreality. She, the ice queen, was now torn asunder with pain and terror. Sheila fought for control of her breathing, trying to bring the air in through her nose and out through her mouth. Or was it the other way around? Nothing quenched the rising tide of panic. Her heart pumped blood through her veins so hard they pulsated in her neck. With a desperate gulp of air, she heaved herself out of the car, to her feet and walked to the entrance with Dermot supporting her.

"Concentrate," said Dermot gently in her ear, as if he were reading her helter-skelter thoughts. "Think of a quiet, beautiful place."

Surprise jolted her out of the escalation of her terror. She leaned into him, enjoying his tenderness as they waited while the automatic doors swung open like welcoming arms. Sheila, suffering the onset of another contraction, eagerly entered the embrace. The pain of the next contraction was all-consuming. She felt as if two huge hands were reaching around her womb and wringing it out like a wet rag. She squealed.

"Oh God! Are you okay?" Dermot said as he ushered her to a chair in the waiting room.

"No I'm not!" Sheila screamed at him. "Are you fucking stupid? This is your fault. I hate you."

As she was wheeled into the ward, she heard a nurse saying to Dermot, "Lots of women say stuff like this during labor."

But she meant it. She wanted him to vanish as the pain took over again. In between contractions she conceded that Dermot was of some use, rubbing her back and getting her ice cubes to suck. But as pain and pressure built to a crescendo, each contraction worse, longer and closer together than previous ones, Dermot was more a hindrance than a help.

When the midwife examined her, Sheila was already seven centimeters dilated.

"I want an epidural!" Sheila demanded as she sucked in the gas and air to no effect. "Just take the pain away. I don't care how you do it. I want this damn baby out of me! I should have had a fucking abortion!"

She heard Dermot gasp. Fuck him and his "I'm going to be great father" bull shite. Sheila bent over a pillow to open the vertebrae so the epidural could be administered. She wished she could roll back time and never meet Dermot, never get pregnant and certainly not be sitting here in undignified agony. She could not keep going for a minute longer.

Tuesday, October 31ˢᵗ, Halloween

CHAPTER FORTY-NINE

An early firework bloomed neon pink against the inky black night. The bang made Molly jump. She'd never get used to the sound - too much like gunshots. Rain lay in puddles on the ground, reflecting the lights of passing cars. As Molly looked out the living room window, different colors bounced around her, cast by nonchalant TV images. She spiraled backwards in time, hoping to find answers to questions she feared would never be answered. What had she done wrong? What could she have changed? She revisited times when she and Dermot were close, intimate in more than just the physical sense. But this time she looked with a mind that wanted to learn, with a heart that wanted to change and with a view to her own improvement. Dermot was not her problem nor ever would be again. She turned off the TV and marched upstairs to get ready for the Halloween party.

She sat on her bed and clutched her wedding dress to her. The smell of the perfume she'd worn that day wafted up, releasing memories that pulled at her heart. She remembered how excited she'd been sitting in the car with her father on the way to the church. She could still see the people all waiting for her as they arrived, and even now her heart rate increased as she remember looking up the aisle and seeing Dermot waiting for her, so handsome.

I can do this.

She gulped down a glass of wine she'd brought up to the room, hoping for some Dutch courage.

I will do this.

She drew in a deep breath and peeled off her clothes. With her recent weight loss, the dress fit perfectly. She pulled up the zip and remembered Tracey doing it for her, dressed in her bridesmaid's dress. Molly smiled. Maybe she'd be in a bridesmaid dress soon, pulling up Tracey's zipper. She hoped so. She went to the mirror to have one last nostalgic look before she ripped it into her Halloween costume. What would Call-me-Charlie, the nurse with the green eyes, say if he saw her now? She did look good.

Music. She needed music. She turned on the radio beside the bed. Pink's "So What?" blasted the opening lyrics. Molly turned up the volume and punched the air. Joy, power, strength all pulsed through her as the beat caught her. She sang along, grabbed the hem of her dress and tried to tear it, but she needed scissors to start it. She danced over to the dresser and found a pair as she bopped. Just before she snipped the material, she hesitated. What was she doing? This dress had cost her a fortune. Could she really destroy it?

The chorus rolled around again. She loved the bit where the singer called her husband a tool. Dermot was a tool too. She snipped the white satin and pulled. It gave easily and she continued to dance and shred, singing along and finding meaning in every word. When Pink's song finished, another came on. It wasn't one she knew. She turned down the volume a little and poured herself another glass of wine drinking it more slowly, savoring the buzz it produced. She shredded the dress more carefully now, trying to make it a little sexy and arty by baring a leg and having the tatters form points. Even with all the ravaging, the dress still looked good. The image of the dusty wedding album beneath the bed drifted into her mind's eye. Not worried about dirtying her dress – it would add to the desired look later – she lay on her tummy and used the scissors to pull the album within reach.

Her heart beat sped up as she flicked through the book. The smiles seemed fake now and the poses staged. Jesus Christ, she'd been such an idiot. She'd completely lost herself in this fantasy of her and Dermot. Despite the great "love" she'd been mourning, she realized that there were whole chunks of Dermot that she couldn't stand.

Molly stared at picture after picture; the one on the altar with the priest, the two of them in the doorway of the church gazing into each other's eyes, them with all their immediate family members and the multitude of Duggans crowding out Molly's side. In each one, Dermot was perfect. He hadn't allowed her to keep photos that didn't flatter him, regardless of how she looked. She picked out one where her eyes were closing, making her look like the village idiot. Well of course she was, she'd married fucking Dermot!

Next time she'd find a better man, someone not so in love with himself. Someone who was kind and sensitive and who loved her the way she wanted to be loved. It would not be that hard to do better than Dermot Duggan. She had a lot to offer the next lucky guy. She had her own place, a career, and a good figure. She twirled once again in front of the mirror and placed her tiara and veil on her head. She looked like a princess. Yes, she could afford to be choosey the next time. She'd be as loving and loyal, but this time to a man who deserved it. She remembered how she'd felt looking into the nurse's green eyes and realized she'd never felt that before. Not even with Dermot. Yep, she was a rock star.

Molly strode to the window, opened it and flung the book out Frisbee style. The corner of the album hit the frame, skewing the trajectory of flight. The album flopped to the left, down onto the flat-roof of the bay window below and caught on the guttering.

"Typical!" Molly said. She opened the window fully and leaned out. She could nearly reach the book. If she could just flip the corner of it she'd be able to flick it down into the front yard. She pushed herself out further, balancing on her pelvis. She needed another half inch. If she could just stretch her arm that little bit more. The muscles pulled and strained as she tried to lengthen her fingers, her wrist, her arm.

The sky flashed green and pink, but that didn't prepare Molly for the loud pop. She flinched, overbalanced and slid out of the window, head first. Desperately grabbing for the guttering at the edge of the flat roof, she missed and got her arms tangled in her dress. She hurtled towards the ground, her arms free again but flailing. The crown of her head struck the concrete. The snap of her neck registered in her ears. Pain thundered behind the sound and roosted at the apex of her skull. She wanted to lift her hand to rub it away, but she couldn't move, couldn't even feel her hands.

The sound of water trickling down the spout from the guttering made a tinkling, bright sound. It made her think of diamonds, flashing in sunshine the way her engagement ring had sparkled when it was new. Fran's eyes had sparkled tonight when she'd given Molly the gift of hope.

Images and ideas clashed as she struggled to discern them but decided they were not worth the effort. She gave in to the floating sensation.

The pain receded gently, like a tide going out.

Tuesday, October 31ˢᵗ, Halloween

CHAPTER FIFTY

The pain melted away. Her legs felt dead, weird even, but Sheila was so relieved to have respite from the pain that she welcomed the paralysis. At the business end, the midwife told her that she was now ten centimeters dilated. She looked at the midwife dully.

"I want you to push for dear life!" the midwife said.

The thought of pushing, of doing more work, horrified Sheila.

"Come on. You can do it." Dermot took her hand.

She looked at him smiling at her, doing his best to support her, and she hated him; loathed him. But he was right. She needed to get this baby out so she could get some sleep. She pushed hard for twenty minutes. It was the most physically intense work she had ever done.

As she heard a baby crying, she knew her job was done. She was aware of the midwife and nurses working on her. They had to wake her up to tell her that her baby was a girl. Sheila had no energy to smile even if she felt like it. They tried to make her hold the baby, but she pointed to Dermot.

Give it to him. It's his fault.

And she drifted off to sleep.

Tuesday, October 31st, Halloween

CHAPTER FIFTY-ONE

The waistband of the skirt dug into Tommy's side. The gusset of the nylon tights he'd hauled up his legs, hung below the hemline of the short skirt of the nurse's outfit for the fancy dress party. The costume did not come with shoes, so he wore his trainers instead. They did nothing for the hairy legs encased in black nylons that wrinkled around the ankles and stretched to breaking point near the waist band.

"Sorry about your nylons." Tommy did not feel in the least contrite as he stood at the top of the stairs waiting for Tracey to look his direction.

"Oh, you big eejit! Go back in the bedroom and I'll help you fix those," Tracey said as she followed him up the stairs. "You need to work from the toe up, stretching it evenly," Tracey said, kneeling down and tugging at the fabric around his ankle.

"Oh that tickles!"

"Stop wriggling or I won't help." Tracey glared at him, or rather, her face paint glared. She was dressed up as a "sexy" devil in a red mini dress and thigh-length red boots, topped off with a headband sprouting light-up horns. She'd drawn flames at her temples coming from the corners of her heavily outlined eyes. The whole effect achieved a very dramatic, sexy look. Tommy intended to be a very bad boy himself later, if these damn tights didn't strangle him first.

"What time did you tell Molly we'd pick her up?" he asked glancing at the clock on the bedside table.

"At eight. Ten minutes ago!" Tracey pulled at the tights faster. "We'd better get a move on."

"What is she dressing up as?"

"I don't know. I didn't want to push it. She didn't really want to go at all."

Downstairs Wolfie howled, making Tracey jump.

"It's okay, he does that with fireworks. He can hear them even when we can't. We should take him with us to go get Molly. Then we can drop him back and get the taxi from here. That way he gets to spend more time with us. Those bloody bangers scare the shite out of him."

"But we'll be really late for the party," Tracey said.

"Eleven o'clock is late for that party. Come on - it's easier to come back and leave the car here. We won't need to go get it tomorrow then." Another crescendo of howls erupted from downstairs. "Oh, poor Wolfie."

"Oh, alright then," she conceded. "Now stand up so I can fix your crotch."

"Pardon me?"

"No time," she said sternly. "Don't even think about it!"

***

Wolfie whimpered in the car the whole way to Molly's house.

"He's not usually this bad," Tommy said.

Tracey bent round in the front passenger seat and tried to placate him. "Shush. It's okay, pet."

It didn't help.

"Enough, Wolfie," Tommy commanded as he pulled up in the street at Molly's gate. He let the dog out and Wolfie made a beeline for the front gate, nosing at it impatiently. He whined louder with his tail tucked between his legs. Tommy opened the gate, and the dog pushed through so it clattered violently against the wall. Yelping and whining, he ran past the front door, past the overgrown rose bush and stopped by a bundle of white material on the concrete path.

Then Tommy saw her. He flew to Molly's side. Confusion collided with disbelief. What was she doing lying on the ground in her wedding dress? Molly lay on her stomach with her head twisted around so her eyes stared over her shoulder, the angle weird and improbable. A veil tangled in her curls, a red sticky mess, and fluttered weakly in the wind where it caught on weeds, the ends still white. The dog whined and pawed at Molly's hand, then dunted his nose under her arm as if inviting her to pet him.

"Oh my God!" Tracey reeled against the front door, her face frozen in shock.

"Molly, no! Please no." Tommy tried to remember first aid. He'd done it years ago, but it lay in his mind like a faded rag. He could see that Molly wasn't breathing. He grabbed her hand to search for a pulse. Nothing.

Clear the airway.

He turned her on her back but her head lolled. The veil got in his way. He pulled it off and flung it away. He put a hand at the back of her neck, desperate to support it and do no further damage, but frantic to clear an airway so he could bring her back. As he straightened her neck, he felt bones grind beneath his fingers which were now slick with her blood. He fought the urge to vomit, swallowed, then covered her mouth with his and blew.

Nothing happened.

He forced himself to think. His mind raced. His own breathing was shallow and ragged. Behind him he could hear Tracey moaning. Having slid down the wall into a sitting position on the ground, she sat rocking, her arms wrapped around her body.

"Call an ambulance!" He flung his phone towards her. His voice jolted her into action, and he could hear her weeping on the phone, begging for help. He turned his attention back to Molly.

Tilt back the head.

That's why there was no air moving. Hope flickered as he tilted Molly's head, adjusting it against the halo of black blood puddled around it. It felt loose. As it wobbled he cringed. Her skin seemed grey even under the orange street lights. Her blue eyes stared into forever. He blew into her mouth again.

Her chest expanded.

Hope flared, and he blew again several times until he became light-headed himself. Kneeling up, gasping lungfuls of air, he put his hand on her chest and pushed.

It can't be too late, it can't be. COME ON!

He felt her body yield under his pressure and tried again. Nothing about her changed. Frantically, Tommy tried to breathe into her mouth again.

Still nothing.

"Tracey," he called. "Come and pump her chest. Hurry!"

As Tracey pumped, Tommy forced air into her lungs. He couldn't give up. Each breath could be the one to wake her up. Still pressing on Molly's chest, Tracey keened. The sound of her wailing spurred Tommy on.

Please, Molly. Please come back.

Beside them the huge dog whimpered.

The first guy to reach Tommy gently tapped him on the shoulder and said "I'll take it from here." Tommy moved away. He gathered Tracey in his arms. His face was wet with tears. He couldn't stop them.

Tracey murmured over and over, "Oh God. Please. Oh God. Please."

Tommy could hardly breathe, never mind speak. He felt the pulse of every blood vessel, every muscle stretched tight, every sense on overdrive – the smell of blood, the taste of adrenalin, the dampness of tears – all there as a background symphony to the pain pounding at the base of his throat. Still desperately hoping, he watched the doctor arrive on scene and approach Molly. She nodded to the nearest co-worker and looked at her watch. Tommy convulsed into a sob and clutched Tracey.

She can't be gone.

Wolfie gave a soft high pitched whine, lay down beside her and laid his head on her hand.

Wednesday, November 1st

CHAPTER FIFTY-TWO

A thunderclap of emotion awakened Dermot's psyche. Fear and love rubbed sparks between each other as he gazed at his newborn daughter in his arms. Love swelled for this tiny creature. He saw a resemblance to his own father in her red wrinkled features, and as her hair dried, it showed up blond and curly like that of her Aunty Tracey. This tiny miracle embodied ancestry intertwined with the promise of immortality.

She was the most beautiful being he had ever seen.

Fear clutched equally at his heart. She was so tiny, so defenseless. His protective instincts climaxed at her mewling. He wanted to shield her from the ugliness in life. He never wanted her tainted as he had been by events beyond his control. He had to be a better man to be her father because she deserved that. She should have a world of love, and yet here she lay, barely one hour old, and her mother slept without wanting to look at or hold her. Even his mother, who had borne ten children, had sat proudly holding her youngest after the delivery. Joy glowed from her as she had embraced that baby as, Dermot was sure, she had the previous nine. So how could Sheila be so cold after giving birth to this cherub?

Dermot glanced over at Sheila. She was exhausted. Perhaps he shouldn't judge her so harshly. Everyone was unique, and if Sheila's approach differed from that of his own mother, then that was all right.

The baby stirred in his arms, and he gazed down at her again. He wondered how he would ever get anything done now that he had her. All he wanted to do was look at her; drink her in with his eyes. He wanted to absorb every flicker of her eyelids and twitch of her cheek. He watched in awe as she flexed a wrinkled red fist, fingers unfurling one by one, then curling up again like a shy sea anemone struck by a shadow. With great reluctance he gave her up to the nurses who wanted to bathe and feed her. They suggested that he go and inform the family of the joyful news.

Dermot headed to the doors of the hospital to get better cell phone reception. Beyond the glow of the hospital lights the night pressed in, black and oily with more rain about to burst from the clouds at any moment. Dermot shivered and pulled his jacket round him and took out his phone.

His mother lifted the phone on the second ring.

"Mum, I'm a Dad!" His voice thickened with emotion just by putting it into words.

"Well, what is it?" she asked.

"A beautiful girl!"

"Weight?"

"Seven pounds and four ounces."

"Good size. Congratulations. What is she like?"

"Mum, she's the image of Tracey! Even down to the blond curls. She's gorgeous." Dermot reckoned that his voice must sound strange as emotion strangled him.

"Oh Dermot, that's wonderful. And how is Sheila? Did she have a bad time?"

"Yeah. She's sleeping now though. They are washing the baby."

"The Baby! Have ye no names yet?"

Dermot laughed at her astonished tone. "Not yet, Mum, but you'll be the first to know. Now, Grandma, go get your beauty sleep. We need you all rested up for babysitting!" Laugher rang in his voice, now as it got stronger again.

"Okay Son. Good night and God Bless."

Sheila's mother's phone rang seven times before it switched to the answer phone. He left her a message. He decided to text Tracey, mainly because she wasn't taking his calls at the moment, and at

Halloween, she was most likely out partying by now. He punched out a message. Simple words, telling Tracey she was an aunty and that he hoped that their differences could be overlooked so Tracey could get to know her beautiful niece who looked so like her. He realized he had burnt many bridges with his affair and now hoped his daughter, the new love of his life, would not suffer as a result.

He sent messages to several more of Sheila's friends and realized sadly that he didn't have many people to tell. It would be crass to send one to Tommy, though in days gone by, Tommy would have been the first person he'd have thought of. Dermot had no friends anymore.

His phone rang. Sheila's mother, he thought. As he lifted his phone to answer it, he saw Tracey's number in the caller ID. His heart lifted with joy. She was welcoming the baby! Heart racing, he answered the phone.

"Tracey?"

"Dermot, where are you?" Her voice sounded low and urgent, hardly effusing with joyful congratulations.

"I'm at maternity hospital. Why?" he asked. Fear squirmed behind his breastbone.

"Where?" she asked.

"The front door, but..."

"Stay there. I'll be with you in five minutes. Don't move, Dermot. Wait for me."

"Are you at the hospital?" he asked, but she had already rung off. Why was Tracey here? Had his mother been able to get in touch with her already? But then, why did she sound so desperate on the phone?

He saw someone run along the side of the building from the direction of the accident and emergency entrance. A long black coat flew out behind her as she raced toward him. Under the coat he saw flashes of red boots. Despite her heels, Tracey crossed the distance between them quickly. Her face was smeared with makeup and tears, eyes red, skin white and taut. She threw herself into his arms.

"It's Molly," she sobbed. "She's, she's. . ."

"She's what?"

"Dead!"

"What?"

"She's dead. We found her...she was..." Tracey started crying.

Dermot stared down at the tormented eyes of his sister, unable to grasp her words.

"I...what...how?" he stammered.

"The police think she fell ...or maybe jumped, from her bedroom window and broke her neck. We couldn't help her. Tommy tried but...Oh God, Dermot, she's gone!"

"Suicide?"

The word walloped Dermot in the gut. He doubled over, gasping for breath. Tracey supported him, guiding him to the wall where he slumped against it.

"No," Tracey said, "she would never, she promised me..."

But guilt battered him. Lips quivering, perspiration popping on his forehead, he tried to compose himself. Beside him Tracey cried. Heaving sobs shook her entire body. He pulled her to him and held her as anguish and grief swallowed them up.

Wednesday, November 1st

CHAPTER FIFTY-THREE

Sheila stared out through the gap in the curtains onto the darkness. The only light came from the front doors of the maternity hospital. The baby's cries rang in her head, repetitive, nearly mechanical. Sheila tried to find a pattern in the sawing noise of the cry. The gasp of the baby's breath at the end of each cry kicked in the recovery as the lungs expanded. This fuelled the next climaxing crescendo which waned out as the lungs emptied, and led into the momentary quiet as it drew breath again. Dread dragged at her heart. She wasn't cut out for this crap. Hot tears spilled down her cheeks, but their release did little to dampen her desolation.

She watched the man in the light of the door talking on a cell phone. Sheila recognized the tilt of Dermot's head and wave of his hand. She figured he was spreading the news of the baby. From the bottom of her field of vision she saw a woman run up to him. He staggered and then clumsily embraced her.

Sheila gasped. The light from the lobby illuminated the woman's blonde curls. He was hugging Molly. Blood rushed in Sheila's skull. He was going to leave her with this wailing creature, go back to his old life, and she could do nothing about it. She boiled with rage, watching as he took the other woman's face in his hands and looked intently into her eyes. She nodded at whatever he said, and then they hugged again. He let her go, wiping his face.

Wiping away lipstick?

"Dirty bastard," she spat through gritted teeth. She wasn't surprised by his betrayal. She was fuming that he would do this to her, and literally leave her holding the damn baby. She was better looking than that drab Molly, even at nine months pregnant. With all his talk of loving her, Dermot knew an easy ticket when he saw one. Wasn't that why he'd hooked up with her in the first place? Molly was too needy for him, but a mother and baby were even needier.

The curtain around the cubicle swished back, and Dermot appeared. He went straight to the cot and scooped the baby up. It stopped wailing. Its eyes rolled in its head until they met Sheila's and then they steadied, staring at her. Sheila pulled her gaze away and looked up at Dermot. His face was white, eyes stricken, hands shaking. Ha – at least he felt bad leaving her.

"I saw you outside with her!" Sheila snapped.

Dermot raised his hand, devastation etched into the very gesture as he closed the open palm and dropped his arm around the child.

"Molly's dead." He rasped the words out.

"I saw her, at the door, with you!" Sheila yelled. What was the liar playing at?

"That was Tracey," Dermot said through clenched teeth, "My sister."

Sheila let the information settle into the whirlpool of her emotions.

"What happened?" she asked, forcing her voice to be gentle.

"It sounds like …" He drew another breath as if the next word was so momentous it required all his effort. He dropped his head, and Sheila had to strain to hear.

"Suicide."

The word hung in the air between them. Sheila could almost see the black letters wavering, like smoke, stretching from Dermot's mouth to her face. It blasted away her fury. She felt a void of emotion. As if, to change into one set of emotions, like clothes, you had to discard the first. Stripped bare, guilt wrapped its gauze around her.

"No." She breathed more than voiced the word.

"Yes," Dermot said simply. "Jumped from a window."

"When?"

"A couple of hours ago."

The baby coughed. Sheila's gaze shifted numbly to the dark-blue eyes that looked straight back at her, wise and accusing.

Two hours ago this baby was born, entering the world as Molly's soul left.

***

Sheila's first morning as a mother dawned dismal and gloomy. Pewter clouds hovered low in the sky, threatening to empty their contents on the damp streets below.

As the epidural wore off, Sheila felt pain in places she only vaguely knew existed. Dermot sat beside the bed feeding his daughter. He had taken over this task once the nurse realized that Sheila was not going to do anything else but sleep. Dermot didn't look as if he had slept at all. His face had the grey pallor of the overtired. His reddened eyes sunk into mauve sockets beneath a furrowed brow. Sheila watched him smiling down at the baby. The baby gazed back up at him, and they seemed to be locked into a world of their own, together and cozy. Sheila felt excluded. He should be looking at her that way. Hatred for the baby burned through her. As if sensing her eyes upon him, Dermot looked up at her.

"Don't feel guilty," he said.

"Guilty? Why would I feel guilty?" She felt her cheeks flame.

"I know you didn't mean it when you said you wished you'd had an abortion. Don't feel bad."

"I don't."

"She needs a name," he said.

"So give her one." Tension thrummed between them. Sheila knew she should care but couldn't manage to.

"Have you any preferences?" Dermot's voice sounded gentle, patient with her, but she didn't feel like helping him bridge the gap between them.

"Nope." She kept her face blank.

Dermot swallowed. "I like the name 'Cara'," he said. "It means 'friend' in Irish."

"Sure." And with that Sheila's offspring had a name. She closed her eyes again, hoping that Dermot would go away and take the child with him. Instead, she could hear him shuffling, getting up from his chair. She sensed him approach the bed.

"Sheila," he said, "Please, look at your daughter. Look at how beautiful Cara is."

Sheila opened her eyes. The baby's face was directly in front of hers. It wriggled in the grip of Dermot's hands, tiny arms flailing, head lolling. The baby opened its eyes and from the pink face two orbs of blue stared back.

"She has blue eyes!" Sheila said, alarm filling her voice.

"Yes," said Dermot, warmth in his voice, "all babies have blue eyes when they are born."

"But hers are so blue. How can she have blue eyes when we both have brown eyes?" Hysteria tinged her voice. Dermot looked at her quizzically.

"Brown-eyed people can have blue-eyed babies."

"She doesn't look like my baby. She's not how I thought my baby would look." Sheila hadn't given much thought at all to the baby, much less how it would look, but the creature before her was an alien. It had nothing that she could identify as "Sheila". Daughters should be like miniature versions of the mother. Her baby should have thick black hair and dark brooding eyes, not this wispy blonde covering on its skull and those flashing blue eyes.

This baby looked more like Dermot's wife than its own mother.

Sheila caught her breath.

The baby's eyes opened, and Molly stared straight back at Sheila, then smiled slyly. Dermot's wife had died at the moment of this child's birth. Sheila's hair stood on end. Goosebumps raised the skin on her arms. Fear snapped and fizzled in her gut.

Oh my God! She knows I know!

"Take her away," Sheila pleaded. Panic filled her voice, her body felt drenched full of cold horror. "I don't want her near me!"

Dermot stepped back, looking wounded and shocked. He cradled the changeling protectively.

"What's wrong, Sheila?"

"Nothing. It's just..." For a wild moment she almost told him then thought better of it as they both looked at her with wide eyes, his brown and bewildered, hers blue and accusing. "I'm tired, really wrecked!"

"I'm going to talk to the nurses. Maybe they have something that can help you."

"No!" Sheila could tell by the suspicious look on Dermot's face that she had reacted too quickly. She tried to manage her tone to sound less frantic, less crazy. "I don't want to bother them."

Dermot stood up, seemingly placated.

"I need to use the loo," he said. He laid the baby down, glanced at Sheila and then at the baby again. He pulled the blanket around her and gently tucked it in. He lingered, looking at it, then finally bent down and kissed its forehead before walking out of the cubicle.

Sheila tried to catch a grip of herself. Further down the ward another baby yowled. The baby in the cot in Sheila's cubicle turned its head slightly and stared at Sheila with its all-knowing, blue eyes. Helplessly, Sheila met those eyes, transfixed.

Wednesday, November 1st

CHAPTER FIFTY-FOUR

Tracey shivered as the undertaker's men lifted the coffin from the hearse and placed it on the shoulders of the men who loved Molly most. A huge crowd gathered at the O'Kane's family home in Suburban Belfast. Parked cars lined the streets, and the mourners gathered at the gates, watching the men carry the coffin into the house. Tracey wondered who all these people were and how they knew to come so quickly.

Tracey recognized some of Molly's colleagues. Four of them stood back from the mouth of the driveway, glancing awkwardly around them as if unsure of their role there. They smiled a nervous greeting at Tracey, and she acknowledged them with a nod, feeling like she'd never smile again.

Laura appeared at Tracey's side. Tear stained and drawn, she took Tracey's hand.

"She thought the world of you, Tracey," Laura said, her voice hoarse with emotion.

"You too, Laura," said Tracey, unable to derive any comfort from the words.

"I'm sorry, Tracey. Really sorry. I was going to get her some help, but I was too slow. Oh God!" Laura covered her mouth with her hand as tears spilled down her face. Tracey hugged her, clinging to her to impart some comfort even though she herself was impervious to it.

"We were all too late" she whispered. "All of us!" The girls broke.

Tommy, Sean, Ben and Mickey carried the coffin up the front steps of the house, planting their feet carefully and working to keep their balance. The Undertaker buzzed around them, quietly issuing directions so that the men worked in synchrony to bring Molly's coffin gently to rest on the stand in the parlor.

Ordinarily, Tracey hated the concept of a posh second room that was rarely used. Most people used it to store dust-catchers and trophies of a bygone era, but now Tracey appreciated it. Earlier that day, Tommy and Mickey had cleared all the large furniture out of the room and lined one wall with chairs. As was custom, they set up a little table with candles and some holy water. They used a white sheet to cover the big gilt framed mirror above the marble fireplace. The room looked stark until the coffin was placed there. The undertaker waited until all but his assistant had left the room, then closed the door behind them.

The mourners filed into the family room. A posse of female relatives and neighbors went to the kitchen to begin the two-day tea making. Tracey joined them, trying to avoid both the small talk in the other room and thinking about the undertaker setting up Molly's corpse. Soon they would view the body, encased in white nylon satin, lying as if sleeping, her blue-white, waxy-skinned fingers intertwined as if in prayer and draped with rosary beads. The rosary beads she'd had since her first holy communion, childish looking with their shiny pink beads.

Kettles boiled and women cut sandwiches. Loaves of bread, filled with sandwich filling but not yet cut, lined the shelves in the fridge. Already the pantry held a mountain of pastries and buns. Trays stood ready, set up with cups and saucers.

Tracey moved to the sink, itching for something to occupy her, desperate to stop tuning in to the hushed conversations brewing around her. When she'd attended wakes before she'd wondered why bother with such a massive catering. Now she welcomed the distraction. Some of those wakes in the past had even been quite a social occasion. If the deceased had lived a full long life, a wake could be good craic. Not in this case.

"It's terrible, isn't it?" wheezed one heavy woman sitting by the table.

"God, imagine. . .you know, doing that," replied a younger woman with heavy makeup, perhaps a second cousin of Molly's. Tracey wasn't sure.

"Ach she was desperately unhappy since that husband of hers left."

"It's always the women who suffer."

"Ach aye, but to do that, you know. . .Will the priest even bury her," the old woman pressed her lips together hard and pulled her head back so that her face ended in a multitude of chins.

"They will. They changed that years ago, thank God," the young woman replied.

Tracey glared at them, but they were so engrossed in their gossip they didn't notice. She moved away, afraid she'd lose her temper and cause a scene.

"I heard she did it on purpose," a man behind Tracey was saying to another. She didn't dare turn around.

"You mean it was. . .?" replied the other.

Tracey could hear him tutting before he said in a whisper, "Shocking. That Dermot one will just have to live with himself now."

She clenched her fists so hard she felt the bite of her fingernails into her palms. They'd all have to live with themselves now. Besides, who had started this gossip? The police never said it was suicide. They said Molly had fallen, and Tracey believed them.

She lifted a tray of tea, hoping to escape the kitchen, the gossip and the dire judgments on her brother. Tracey missed Dermot acutely. He'd been the one she always turned to, the father figure when their own father lay comatose on their sofa, soaked in his own urine. Dermot was the one who cleaned him up when everyone else recoiled at the thought of touching him. But in the last eight months, Dermot, too, had evaporated.

Tracey carried the tray, clinking and rattling, laden with cups of weak tea wobbling in saucers, into the family room. Robotically she murmured "tea." Equally mechanically, people lifted saucers, slopped milk into them and heaped spoonfuls of sugar into the grey liquid, muttering a muted, "Thank you."

In the parlor the priest led a round of the rosary. Tracey stood in the hall between the front door and the parlor door. She couldn't bring herself to join them. Molly lay there cold and forever gone, and Tracey hadn't worked up the courage to see her yet. The rhythmic tones of the priest's words answered by the people in the room drifted out into the hall, a somber music.

Tracey pulled open the front door and slipped out. The front yard had a tiny eight-foot-square lawn bordered by roses. Along the hedge, a little garden bench looked inviting. She realized how clever this spot was. She couldn't see the street past the rose bushes. Tracey sat there a while, savoring the smells of the damp soil, the cawing of the crows in the trees above her and the cool air plucking at her skin. A car stopped in the street, and car doors clunked open.

"I'm telling you, child-dear, it was not suicide."

It was Fran! Tommy had left earlier to go get her. Tracey sat still, hardly breathing, as Fran continued. "It's all claptrap. She just fell. I was talking to her only an hour beforehand. She was in the best form I've seen her in months."

"She'd been really erratic this past while. Her moods swung really black. And she was in her wedding dress. . ."

"It was Halloween," Fran interrupted. "She was going to be Bride of Frankenstein."

"That's a bit of a stretch."

Tracey stood up. "She's right," she said, louder than she meant to.

"Holy Mother of God!" exclaimed Fran. "You nearly gave me heart failure."

Tommy handed her the walking frame he'd been wrestling from the back of the car, and she leaned on it heavily.

"Sorry, Fran." Tracey met them at the garden gate and swung it open for Fran. "But she is right about Molly. She didn't kill herself. She'd never do that. She promised me."

Tommy raised his hand to signal stop. "If it helps you to believe that, fine, but don't deny facts to shift the blame from your brother."

"What? You think I'm saying this to protect Dermot?"

"Don't even say his name to me," Tommy said.

"You aren't being fair to Molly. Do you really want everyone to think she committed suicide? It makes her look stupid, selfish, like a silly wee girl. Fran, tell him." Tracey swung around to face Fran.

"People will believe the juiciest story they can pump from most situations. People aren't who matter." Fran edged her walker towards the house. "I know she had turned a corner for the better. She was going to be fine. It's just one of life's tragedies. I'm going to miss that girl. She really was an angel, and now she's with them. I'm telling everyone who'll listen, what a wonderful girl she was."

Tommy looked at the tips of his shoes. Tracey wanted to scream at him. Instead, she touched his arm and said, "See now?"

Fran hoisted her walker onto the door step and then turned to look at both of them. "And now is neither the time nor the place for you two to be arguing. You need each other. And Tracey, I need to see Molly's mother. Would you mind telling her I'm here, please?"

Tracey's face burned with shame.

"Of course, sorry," she mumbled, but she noted that Tommy said nothing and kept his head bowed.

Molly's mother was in neither room. Tracey went into the kitchen. Her own mother, having taken on the role of Commanding-Officer-of-tea-making-operations, filled a large water heating urn.

"Mum, have you seen Aileen?" Tracey asked.

"I think she went upstairs, but that was about an hour ago," Carmel answered, brushing her hair back from her face before plopping her hands onto her hips and surveying the kitchen with an air of authority.

"Annie, don't be bringing out those buns yet. It's too early. Take these sandwiches out first," she directed. Tracey marveled at the etiquette upheld even at a wake.

Especially at a wake.

Why would anyone care what they ate and in what order? Perhaps it was good that people were forced to care about the minutiae. Otherwise it would be tempting to stop caring about anything at all. It would be bliss to turn it all off and feel nothing for a time.

"I'll go just upstairs to check on Aileen."

"No problem, love. I think we have things under control here."

Tracy's feet sank into the thick carpet on the stairs. Her footsteps muffled by its plushness made Tracey feel as though she were ascending stealthily. She cleared her throat so as not to startle Aileen and to signal that she wasn't snooping.

There were three doors on the landing. Two were wide open, one showing the bathroom, the other a bedroom decorated in muted creams and beiges giving the room a tranquil air. Tracey fleetingly thought of lying down and drifting off, but she knew that her racing mind would drag her back to harsh reality.

Tracey approached the closed door. Her pulse quickened, and her tummy fluttered. She wasn't that close to Aileen. If she found her crying privately, they both would be embarrassed. Emotions tumbling through her chest, Tracey lifted her hand and knocked.

"Come in," Aileen's voice, clear and collected, rang out from the room. Tracey opened the door a crack and popped her head around it.

"Fran's here, Molly's neighbor. She'd like to see you."

"Okay, thanks, I'll be down in a minute, but I could do with your opinion," Aileen said, looking up and smiling. "Come on in," she prompted. "I was just looking for a picture of Molly. Something from her happier days. Something that has her, well, you know, smiling."

Tracey swallowed the flame of emotion that flared in her throat. She understood Aileen's need to make it all seem normal even though there was nothing normal about burying a thirty-year-old woman.

Girl.

Despite her age, Molly always seemed to Tracey to be a girl— sweet, naive and young at heart. Tracey sat down beside Aileen and glanced at what she held. It was a picture of a baby – one of the hospital ones that are taken only hours after birth.

Aileen gave her a sad apologetic smile.

"It's her baby picture."

"It's beautiful!" Tracey stared at the blue eyes in the photo though not really recognizing her friend. "We may need something a little more up to date though." The smile hung in her voice as the tears sprung to her eyes.

"I know, but I don't want to use this." Aileen passed her the next photo. Molly's beloved smile blazed out from the glossy paper. She wore her wedding dress and poised to throw her bouquet. Tracey could picture the flowers rotating as they moved through the air. She remembered squinting against the sun before she lifted her hand to snatch the flowers to herself. Everyone had thought it hilarious that Tracey, the girl whose relationships barely lasted a month, caught the bouquet. It had been such a happy day. How did it all end up like this? Too overcome to speak, Tracy shoved the photo back at Aileen.

"Actually, Tracy, I was hoping you would get these copied for me. Just a color photocopy would do – I just want to keep them in my handbag for a while, and I'm afraid of damaging the originals. Could you do that for me?" Aileen put the two photos in an envelope and handed them to Tracey.

"Sure." Tracey half gulped the word out, anguish engulfing her. She put the precious photos in her jacket pocket and stood up.

"How could she do this to me? Stupid, stupid girl," Aileen said bitterly.

"Who? What?" Confusion blistered in Tracey.

"Suicide. . .so. . .so selfish. So typical!" Aileen spat.

Anger burst through her so violently that Tracey tasted it, sour and bitter in her mouth. "It wasn't suicide, and to say it is a disservice to Molly," Tracey said. She forgot the hushed funeral tones as she continued, "Molly was too smart to try to kill herself by jumping from the second story of a building, for God sakes. Who'd do that? Can't you see that? If she'd wanted to kill herself, there were far easier, more reliable ways. She had a pile of sleeping tablets she could have used. Or she might have cut her wrists, or driven her car into a wall. Seriously, do you really think Molly would jump willingly from her bedroom window, risk breaking her leg and not doing the job right?"

Tracey stopped for a breath.

Aileen's face crumpled as she whispered, "Do you really think so?"

"Yes," Tracey said gently, awash with pity for Aileen. "It was just an accident. A tragic, tragic thing."

What did it matter? Molly was still gone. Gone, never coming back, never cracking a joke, never laughing again.

"I'm sorry. She and I. . .we just never. . . I never. . ." Aileen gulped back a sob and took a deep breath before continuing, "I pushed her hard. I wanted the best for her. I loved her."

"I know," Tracey said.

"I just wished I'd told her."

"She knows, Aileen, she knows now."

"Does she? It's my punishment. I deserve it. No, don't try to comfort me." Aileen whipped her hand back as Tracey tried to take it. "You're a good girl, Tracey. Molly was so lucky to have a friend like you. Go on. I'm okay. Just get me those photocopies, please."

Without trusting herself to say anything more, Tracey fled from the room to the bathroom next door. Locking the door, she sat on the floor with her back to the door and let the tears fall. She pulled her knees to her chest and lowered her forehead to them, sobbing quietly. She should be down there like Fran, standing up for Molly. Tracey ached for Tommy – missing him now that he'd pulled into a shell. With the first gush of emotion spent, she stood up, went to the sink, washed her face and drew in some deep breaths in an effort to pull herself together. It was only the beginning, and she didn't know how she was going to get through the next few days, never mind face living life, without her best friend.

"Oh Molly, Molly, Molly," she groaned. Sorrow hollowed her out. How could somewhere so empty ache so badly? She pressed her hand over her chest and took a couple more deep breaths.

She felt the envelope in her pocket. One task at a time, she decided. Go get these photocopied. Then come back and make more tea.

Wednesday, November 1st

CHAPTER FIFTY-FIVE

Despite the comfort of the big bed and fluffy duvet, Dermot didn't find oblivion in sleep as he'd hoped. After the last few days, he wasn't sure if fatigue made him over-emotional, or if he'd be feeling this odd even if he weren't so dog tired. Mentally he tried to shake himself, but any energy he mustered drained from him when he thought of Sheila's frosty attitude towards his daughter. Too exhausted to even be angry, Dermot tried to piece together his thoughts.

Molly is dead.

Lonely images of the woman he once loved floated through his head, marinating in guilt. What could he have done differently? Stayed with her feeling trapped and unfulfilled? That grim scenario may have resulted in his own suicide via the bottle, like his father, the man he was determined never to become. Though hadn't he treated Molly every bit as badly as his father treated his mother? Whilst he hadn't left Molly for the booze, he had abandoned her nonetheless. Any opportunity he may have had to put things right had died with her.

What about the house? The divorce proceeding were not finalized so was he still Molly's next of kin? Did the life insurance policy pay out on suicide? Shame drenched him. How could he think of profiting in this? God! Was he that evil? Self-hatred flushed through him. He wondered if this was how his father felt when Dermot had witnessed him drunk and crying into his whiskey. As he drifted in a haze that wasn't quite sleep, the endless stream of questions took on scenes, the characters jumbled up and merging. Molly and his dad both crying and reaching for him, seemingly one entity that looked like neither but which Dermot recognized anyway.

Then Cara, his beautiful daughter, crying in Sheila's arms until Dermot lifted her. She stopped crying and looked into his eyes, but she became so heavy that he couldn't hold her.

When he looked down again, Molly lay in his arms wearing her wedding dress, smiling up at him, love written all over her face. But such was the drag on his arms, he had to let go of her. As he dropped her, she fell into a huge black hole, and though Dermot tried to reach for her, he was too slow, too tired, and his arms wouldn't move. As the black hole swallowed Molly up, silence washed through Dermot, jolting him awake.

He cried, sobbing and broken, for the first time in years. He gave in to despair, letting it rack though his psyche, ricocheting off past emotional traumas and resurrecting demons long buried. Like a storm, it passed, leaving him feeling ravished and fragile.

Sleep was not an option.

He tried to focus on Cara, the one shining light that existed in his life. Would Cara like football? He daydreamed about taking her to football matches, dressed in matching his-and-tiny-hers team colors. He'd put red ribbons in her hair too. She'd be adorable. He couldn't wait to bring her home tomorrow. Two nights in the hospital was enough for Sheila. The doctor declared her "disgustingly healthy for a woman who had just given birth," so Sheila and Cara were being discharged around noon, after one final doctor's round on Thursday morning, leaving Dermot all day to prepare.

Though it approached ten thirty in the morning, the sun hadn't penetrated the grey clouds that clung to the horizon. With limbs of lead, Dermot dragged himself to the bathroom and stood under the shower, hoping the flowing water would infuse him with some vigor. Again his mind drifted back to his daughter in the hospital cot. He felt energy spark deep within him as he considered her and the miracle that she was, a miracle that he could love another human so deeply and so unconditionally. He didn't know her, had never communed with her, yet just holding her in his arms that first moment he was lost to her. Forever.

Dermot gave the apartment a quick tidy. Sheila would find fault no matter what he did. If he had the place gleaming, but missed one little spot, that was what she would focus on. Best give her a choice of things to moan about. He assembled the cot and the changing station, set the bottles and sterilizer out on the kitchen counter, and arranged the miniature white clothes on the bed. The place was hygienic, and you could at least see the coffee table after he'd cleared away nearly a week's worth of newspapers, stacking them on the kitchen table for recycling later. By mid-afternoon, Dermot had done all that he was going to do in preparation for the homecoming.

With time on his hands, Dermot wondered if he should go to the wake. He didn't want to cause a scene, but Molly deserved his recognition, albeit too late.

Outside in the street a slight breeze sprang up, shuffling leaves and litter in lazy circles where the intersection of garden walls and house generated wind eddies. The air smelled damp, of mildew and autumn. Dermot welcomed it, hoping it would clear his head as he shoved his hands in his pockets and set off for Molly's mother's house.

At a brisk pace, Dermot figured it would take him about half an hour. Even with his lack of sleep and mental strain, the walking released feel-good endorphins and stirred up latent energy. His qualms about visiting the wake house dissolved with each step. After all, he had known the entire family for a very long time. Surely they would interpret his gesture as a symbol of respect. It would be harrowing to see Molly. Was the coffin open? How would he feel seeing her lying there? When his father had died, he found it hard to reconcile the waxen face with the image of the man in his head.

What would he say to Molly's parents? If he said, "I'm sorry," did that sound like he assumed responsibility? Was he responsible? If so, did he want the world to know it? What would that achieve?

Was the trite "Sorry for your loss" an insult? Surely that said "It's your loss not mine," and did that point too keenly to the fact that he had left Molly? His stride shortened as doubt infiltrated his good intentions. He was now only one street away. If he kept going to the corner he was committed. He'd be visible from the house. He toyed with stopping, turning around and running. Suddenly Tracey appeared from around the corner and halted, open-mouthed, looking at him.

"Hey Sis," he said, delighted to see her. She'd understand. She was the closest person to him, and she knew him better than he knew himself sometimes.

"Jesus Christ! What the hell do you think you are doing here?" Her anger surprised him.

"I-I just want to pay my respects. I feel, well, it's just so, I don't know," he mumbled to a stop.

"You can't go there. It's just not appropriate. Everyone, well you know, everyone thinks. . ."

"Thinks what?" Suddenly inflamed by the hint of accusation, Dermot's voice rose. Tracey's face flushed.

"Thinks that Molly killed herself because of you," Tracey said.

Dermot inhaled sharply.

"She didn't. It was an accident," Tracey continued.

Dermot felt his heart rate slow, but his limbs felt shaky, as if he had bubbles in them. "So, you don't think...?"

"Don't flatter yourself, Dermot." Tracey's voice carried a hard edge. She avoided his gaze and folded her arms, rubbing her hands up and down her upper arms. Dermot shivered too.

"So come back with me, to the wake. Tell them." Dermot placed his palms on her shoulder. Tracey whipped her arms apart and dislodged his hand.

"Don't be stupid. You can't just turn up and claim innocence. Do you want to cause a riot?" Spittle flew from her lips, her face crimson and crumpled.

"But you said," Dermot said, confused.

"I said she didn't kill herself. I did not say she wasn't dead because of you! If you hadn't left her, hadn't played the field, she'd never have turned to the drink. It was the drink that did her in, Dermot. Just like Dad – except you could have stopped it this time!" Tracey's hand flew to her mouth, her forehead wrinkled above her raised eyebrows.

Dermot stood stock still, gutted. The air around him seemed heavy, and he felt suddenly hot. Sweat popped on his forehead, and he could feel his underarms moist. Tracey blamed him, just like everyone else.

"But I didn't think she'd do this."

"That's your problem. You never think! You rush in head first and decide later if was it wise or not," Tracey said.

"You never complained when I was getting Dad off your case or any of those waste-of-space boys you dragged home. Like that one who just burned down Tommy's place, eh?" Dermot shot back.

Tracey's face melted in a sea of tears.

"You bastard! As if things aren't already horrific, you want to go up there to the wake and rip to shreds the people who really loved Molly with your pathetic excuses. It's just selfish – pure selfish. But then what's new about that?" She took in a breath and changed tack, "And where is your whore now anyway?"

"In the hospital. With your niece." Dermot's quiet retort stopped Tracey in her tracks. She dropped her head and stood shaking it. She lifted her hands out to the side in a helpless gesture. Her words still stung him. The worse part – she was right.

"Do you really blame me?" he asked gently, aware of wetness seeping into his eyes. Tracey kept her head lowered.

"Does it matter who is to blame? Molly's gone…" Tracy's voice cracked and Dermot rushed to her and as he put his arms around her, he felt Tracy give in. Her body shuddered as she sobbed. Tears sprung from his own eyes, yet his pride taunted him, making him hope no one would see them embracing and crying together. Was this what he had been seeking by going to the wake? Release? Shared misery? An unburdening?

Tracy pushed him away and looked up, her face a tangle of hair and tears.

"Don't go to the wake, Dermot, please, for everyone's sakes." She sniffed and dug into her pocket, producing two tissues. She handed one to Dermot.

She's still looking after me.

"I really need to go." She backed away.

"No! Please, Tracey. Don't go!" His voice, forced violently into action, sounded high and absurd. He needed her. They had always been each other's champions.

She drew a deep breath, her face closed. "Leave me alone!"

He reached for Tracey's elbow, but she shook him off and broke into a run.

Isolation swallowed him. Once more silence rang in his ears, reminding Dermot of his nightmare. Dermot felt cast off. He wasn't ready to be on his own with this. He had been going to the wake to escape his own demons, but now saw that it would cause pain to the one person left on this planet who loved him.

"I've been such a shithead," Dermot said out loud, abhorred at how many times he'd run away from Molly in the past few months in exactly the same fashion. Considering how insecure she was, he realized that he'd been criminally selfish and unfair. He thought of the night he'd gone back to get his clothes. Her eyes had brightened and her face had flooded with hope when she'd opened the door and found him standing there. He'd smashed that hope as surely as if he'd smashed his fist into her face. He should have been gentler with her.

He thought of how he'd left her at the hospital after she'd gotten bleach in her eye. He imagined her coming out, expecting to find him. Perhaps she'd have had that same hopeful expression, blue eyes beneath eyebrows drawn together, shifting to puzzled, hurt, abandoned. He should have had the courage to face her, face Tommy, face all of them. He would have, if he'd been in the right.

He stood with his chin on his chest. His shoulders humped up around his ears and he closed his eyes tight, hoping to quench the fire he felt burning at the base of his throat. Slowly he relaxed his face muscles, letting daylight filter in. That's when he saw the fresh, clean envelope on the ground, just where Tracey had been standing. Dropped by Tracey, he realized.

Slowly, as if arthritic, he bent down and picked it up, staring at it, wondering if he should open it. There was no name on it, so he decided it would be okay. In case it wasn't Tracey's. How else would he return it to its rightful owner? The flap was not stuck down, so Dermot fished the contents out, and stared at the pictures of Molly. He looked into her eyes as she gazed out from her wedding picture. Once again, pain seared through him quickly fading to a dull ache.

"Ah Jesus, Molly, why did you have to go and do that?" he murmured to the picture. He sniffed.

Tracey must have dropped these. Hope ignited. He could take these to her and maybe she could see her way to reconciling with him. He needed Tracey to help him sort through his own head. Maybe she still needed him, like the bad old days with Dad. He expelled air in a long loud sigh. Slipping the envelope into his pocket, he headed home.

Thursday, November 2nd

CHAPTER FIFTY-SIX

Sheila stood on the doorstep of her apartment waiting for Dermot as he fumbled with the house keys in one hand, the loaded baby carrier in his other. He smiled as he opened the door and said, "Home at last!"

But it would never be the same place again, invaded now by this alien creature. Sheila hated it, all of it. The apartment, the baby, Dermot and even the way Dermot ignored her overnight case and brought the baby in, lifting it up and saying in a sickeningly honeyed voice, "Welcome home, Cara. This is where you live."

Sheila followed them into the bedroom and slung her case between the wall and the laundry basket. Hospital stink clung to everything she'd packed.

"This is Mummy and Daddy's room. And here's your cot."

Sheila shut him down with a withering stare.

"I'll just give her a bottle. Are you hungry?" Dermot asked.

"No. I had lunch in the hospital." Sheila left them in the bedroom and tried to escape to the living room. She needed a bigger apartment.

At least he'd stopped trying to cajole her into fussing over the child. The baby crinkled its wrinkled old-man's face squealing in protest when anyone but Dermot lifted it.

Sheila sat in an armchair and stretched her legs in front of her. She wanted to go to bed but didn't have the energy to get up. She had barely five minutes to herself before Dermot joined her with the baby and its feed. Whenever he cooed into the pink face, its cheeks worked dragging the milk from the bottle. Dressed in a pink all-in-one and with its pink skin, it reminded her of a giant pink leech. The baby's eyes stared right into Dermot's. They were locked in a staring competition, a notion Sheila would have found laughable but for the hairs that stood on the back of her neck. The child vied for Dermot's attention continuously. Even though Sheila could hardly stand Dermot anymore, she refused to lose him to this little monster.

As the bottled drained, the leech's eyelids became heavy. Dermot held its chin between his thumb and forefinger and rested its chest against the palm of his hand. He tipped it from its lying down position to sitting up. A couple of rubs to its back and the pink leeched belched. A dribble of curdled milk dripped from its lips. Sheila felt her gorge rise.

"Good girl," Dermot cooed as he wiped the leech's mouth.

Within seconds it lay sleeping in his arms.

"You look done in," said Dermot softy. "I'll put Cara in her cot, and you can have a wee sleep too. Is there anything you want me to get you?"

"No, thanks," she answered, sodden with weariness. "I'll just sleep now."

She went to her bedroom and changed into a fresh pair of pajamas. The bed linen was freshly laundered, to her surprise, and she tumbled into the softness.

***

"Wah!"

"WAH!"

"WAAAAAAAAAAH!"

The sound shattered the air. Yanked from a deep sleep, nauseous with weariness, Sheila didn't know where she was or what the hell made that God awful sound.

The baby!

Fury surged in her as she lifted the pillow beside her. The bedroom door opened and the shadowy figure of Dermot moved swiftly to the cot.

"Shush now, you'll wake your Mummy!" Dermot whispered. At the sound of his voice, the crying changed to a plaintive bleat. Sheila put down the pillow, wondering why it had been clenched so tightly in her hand. She felt dizzy.

"Too late for that – I'm awake now," she spat through gritted teeth.

"Oh sorry, I just put her down and walked out to go to the toilet. I thought she was fast asleep." The child's wail droned on, a backdrop to Dermot's words.

"Just take her away from me. Anywhere, I need sleep. Take her for a walk or something."

"But it's cold!"

"Well, that's what blankets are for." She all but added the word "Idiot!"

"I'll bring her down to the supermarket. Is there anything you need?"

"Sleep!" Sheila snapped.

Dermot bundled the baby up, fussing unnecessarily, changing the nappy which had only been changed an hour ago and causing the child to cry more.

"Right, we're away!" he called cheerily from the doorway.

Sheila grunted.

She lay for about half an hour trying to get back to sleep, but she'd been jerked awake so suddenly she found it impossible. She needed some herbal tea. She dragged herself to the kitchen and flicked on the kettle. She spotted Dermot's jacket on the floor. Irritated, Sheila stomped over and scooped it up. A white envelope flew out of the pocket, slapped against the kitchen wall and landed propped against the skirting board.

Sheila nearly ignored it, too exhausted to be bothered, but she liked order, and the envelope lying there defiled the harmony she needed. She trudged over and picked it up, folding the offending jacket over her arm.

The envelope contained stiff paper, the kind photographs were printed on. Curiosity bit through her fatigue, and she pulled the contents out. Shocked, she dropped two photographs onto the kitchen counter. Two images blazed up at her - Molly and a baby.

Hollow blackness crept through her chest. Why did Dermot have a photo of Molly in his pocket? Why was there also a picture of the leech? When did he take it? Sheila had chased the photographer who visited the ward. She hated those "first photos of baby" that parents forced on their family and friends.

Flames of rage licked through her. How dare they photograph the leech when they were told they couldn't? Wasn't there a law against it? But then, that idiot Dermot probably did it.

The bastard! Everything was his fault. If she'd never met him, she wouldn't be lumbered with this horrible child.

Sheila looked again at the picture of Molly in her bridal white. She noticed the perfectly plucked eyebrows and the French polish on the thumb nail of the hand wrapped around the bouquet. Molly's face spoke clearly of love, an open trusting look, the look of a fool.

A sour taste developed in Sheila's mouth. She swallowed, her throat tight. Why did Dermot have this? And why did he have a picture of her baby in the same envelop as the picture of his dead wife? Was this some kind of black magic?

"I'm being ridiculous," Sheila said to the empty kitchen.

The kettle came to the boil and switched itself off with a click. Silence filled the space around her. Her hands shook, and she knew that she must think straight, but her eyes kept straying to the pictures. Her friend Elaine always talked about voodoo and reincarnation. She often said that if someone had even a strand of your hair or a finger nail clipping that they could cast a spell on you. Sheila had dismissed it as nonsense, but were these things possible? And if they were, what or why would anyone want to cast a spell on her and her baby?

Coldness crept through her as she thought back to that awful day she found the dead bird hanging from the door handle. It definitely was there, yet it disappeared when Dermot went to look. It was Molly's black magic. Perhaps it was the start of the spell. Molly might have even broken into her apartment, stolen a hair, something. A shiver wriggled up her spine and set her scalp tingling. Molly had cast a hex to ruin her experience of motherhood. Sheila shuddered as she remembered the words Molly flung at her outside the night club.

You will never have a happy day with that child.

She felt relieved. That was why Sheila didn't feel any love for her baby. It wasn't her fault. Molly made her hate this baby.

The boiling kettle switched itself off. The noise snapped Sheila back to reality.

No it's all crazy. Who would benefit from such a spell? Besides, these things aren't real.

Her mind returned to the first and most basic question. Why did Dermot have a picture of Molly and the baby in the same envelope? Cold fear crept through her as she remembered her realization that first morning in the hospital. Was it only yesterday? It felt like a hundred years ago.

The leech was Molly!

Molly was fanatically in love with Dermot. Molly killed herself and then came back as the baby Sheila gave birth to. This way she could stay with him. He did love the child to distraction. The photos provided some conduit for her soul.

Sheila breathed heavily. Panic coursed through her and she sat down feeling weak and unsteady. Dermot was in on this. The pictures were in his pocket. He knew.

Sheila heard a jangle of keys and Dermot's voice cooing at the front door. She moved to the kettle to finish making her tea, hoping the routine chore would settle her. She had the kettle in one hand and the photos in the other when Dermot entered the kitchen. He set the baby carrier on a chair by the kitchen table, humming happily to himself.

"What the hell are these?" she demanded.

"Oh!"

"So?"

Dermot explained in a rush of words, "I bumped into Tracey, and they dropped from her coat pocket. I picked them up to give them back to her. They aren't mine."

"What is Tracey doing with a picture of our baby?" Sheila's voice increased its pitch even as she tried to modulate it. So, Tracey was in on it too. Sheila set the kettle down haphazardly on the pile of newspapers and magazines that always gathered in the middle of their kitchen table. She ran her free hand through her hair and tried to pull herself together. Glancing up, she saw Dermot's confusion. If he was pretending, he was a pretty damn good actor. Maybe Molly and Tracey had done this together.

"This!" she hissed, waving the picture of the pink leech in his face. She fought the rising hysteria, gulping for deep breaths of air. "When did you take a photo of the baby?" she demanded.

"I didn't, not yet."

She gasped. Was he denying it? She felt weak and powerless. Here she was, sleep deprived and terrified. There had to be a simple explanation, her mind screamed.

"The photos in your jacket, of the baby? When?" She struggled to be coherent.

"That's not Cara. That's Molly. As a baby!" Dermot said.

Sheila drew a sharp breath. They were identical! This leech creature really was Molly, reunited again with Dermot.

"No!" She threw the photos on the floor and turned to the leech. She pulled the blankets and hat off it, flinging them to the ground and picked up the baby under its arms and held it out from her. Its head lolled back and its eyes rolled open, blue and unfocused.

"Sheila, stop," Dermot pleaded.

"See," she screamed. "Evil. It's evil!"

"Sheila, stop!"

"Can't you see? It's her? It's Molly." Sheila brought its face close to hers. "I know what you're up to, you little parasite. I won't let you get away with it."

"Jesus, Sheila, be careful!" Dermot put his hands up to the leech, cupping its head and back.

Sheila held on, shoving the baby closer to Dermot's face.

It wailed.

"She'd do anything to be with you," Sheila hissed.

He tried to take it from her. Sheila stepped back, nudging the table.

"Careful, the kettle. . ." Dermot said stepping towards her and nodding at the table.

She looked around. The kettle rocked on the pile of newspapers and then settled. She sensed him close in on her again, and before she could react he'd swiped the child out of her arms. Its wailing downgraded to a hiccupping cough. Dermot nestled it closer to him, wrapping shielding arms around it.

"No!" she yelled. "You're in on it too."

She flung a hand out and struck the kettle, sending it flying towards Dermot and the baby. Dermot swung around, protecting the child as a gush of scalding water hit him in the back. His screams joined with the baby's.

Sheila froze. She watched the monster howling, morphing from a man and a baby into a two-headed demon that squealed through her kitchen. Then her legs gave way, and she curled up into a ball against the wall, covered her face and screamed too.

Thursday, November 2nd

CHAPTER FIFTY-SEVEN

Tommy needed air. It was all over now, the wake, the funeral, but not the grief. As he let Tracey and himself into their house, even the dog greeted him quietly. Tommy felt as though he hadn't drawn a breath since he'd first seen Molly lying on the ground.

Already dead.

Still warm to the touch.

If only he could inhale deeply and dispel the dread that dragged through him, but Tommy could not remember ever feeling this bleak. This pain accompanied by a desolate weariness he recognized now, not only in himself, but in Molly's parents.

He'd had to tell them the news. At the hospital. In the middle of the night. In the harsh glare of clinical lights. Where he could see his words splintering them as he spoke. The four of them had sat swaddled in sorrow and confusion, a strange sight with himself and Tracey still in their Halloween costumes. Through Aileen's wail and subsequent sobs, Tommy could hear Ben repeating three words in wondrous disbelief, emphasizing a different word each time.

"*Molly* killed herself?"

"Molly *killed* herself?"

"Molly killed *herself?*"

Tracey kept repeating "No, no, it wasn't like that."

But it was exactly like that. She killed herself because of Tracey's bastard brother. He had killed Molly as surely as if he'd pushed her himself.

The family had gathered at Molly's mother's house this morning. Tommy felt as if his heart would burst when they closed the lid on the coffin. He would never again see her smile or hear her laughter.

Tears flowed freely down the mourner's faces as the men carried the coffin from the house and up the street to the hearse which waited at the junction with the main road. It was a mark of respect to carry the coffin, the distance a measure of how much the deceased was respected. The hearse crawled along behind the slow procession, until everyone had had their chance to show that they too had loved Molly and would miss her.

Tommy had struggled to compose himself throughout the funeral service that was so similar to the one they'd had only a few years ago for his mother. There was a larger crowd here now, weighed down by the sorrow of a young life tragically ended.

In the graveyard, the family had sobbed outright when they lowered her coffin into the ground. The finality of the soil thumping on the wood reverberated though the headstones and dissipated in the rustling branches overhead. It had been a fresh autumn morning, charged with energy. Large clouds raced across the sky, chased by a brisk wind that buffeted the ravens about the big oak trees in the graveyard. The crows had opted for walking. Tommy wondered why he even noticed these things. Molly would have noticed.

Back home, in that vacuumous space left when the crowds clear and people return to their normal lives, Tommy could barely lift his head. He played the events of the past four days over in his head, wishing he could turn back time - just get to Molly before she jumped. It played out like a movie reel he couldn't change.

Tracey came in from the kitchen with a tray. Wolfie trotted quietly behind her.

"Here, have some ice cream, I can't look at another cup of tea or sandwich." Tracey handed Tommy a bowl and a spoon.

"I've no appetite," Tommy said. He looked up, and she pushed the bowl toward him.

"Me neither, but just try some. Ice cream is always nice." She smiled as if coaxing a child, then took his hand and placed it so it supported the bowl. He could feel the chill through the ceramic.

"It's just comfort food, Tommy," she said.

Tommy lifted the spoon to his mouth - what kind of food could give them comfort now?

Once started, the ice cream disappeared. Tommy still felt hollow, but the taste of too strong tea had been replaced by sweet vanilla. He looked at Tracey. She had black smudges beneath her eyes and her pale skin, almost startlingly white, made her blue eyes flash. She was beautiful. Something happy welled up in him. Thank God he had her, this strong brilliant woman who knew what he needed even when he didn't.

They set their empty bowls on the floor at their feet and turned a blind eye to Wolfie, who mooched over to lick out the remnants. CSI started on the TV. The opening scene showed a young woman lying face up in a fountain. Her black hair fanned out behind her in the water and her eyes stared from her pale face, way past seeing the brightly lit Vegas night. Tommy reached for the remote. He changed the channel, but he not could stop his mind from replaying the moment he found Molly. He lifted a hand to blot an escaped teardrop. He felt Tracey's hand on his arm, a gentle squeeze, a soft sigh.

Tracey's cell phone rang. Her eyes widened when she read the caller ID.

"Shit!"

"Who is it?" Tommy asked. Wolfie began to whine. If she didn't turn off the noise, he would break into a full on howl.

"It's Dermot," she said.

"Don't answer it!"

Tracey scowled and silenced it, just as Wolfie broke into full song. Tommy hushed him and the dog settled down, thwacking his tail off the floor a few times.

"I don't like doing that," Tracey said. She set the phone on the coffee table.

"He's a waste of space."

Tracey shifted slightly away from him but kept eye contact.

"Don't, Tommy. Just don't," she sighed wearily, "He's still my brother. Maybe you don't understand that because you don't have one. No matter what they do, they are always connected to you."

"Well, today we buried the closet thing I ever had to a sibling because of your brother."

Tracey recoiled.

"The police said that she'd fallen from the bedroom window, that she'd been intoxicated, and that no foul play was suspected," she said. She picked the ice-cream bowls off the floor and stood up. She took a step towards the kitchen.

"No foul play? Oh, come on," Tommy pleaded. "It was all foul, stinking rotten and foul. Molly was so destroyed by Dermot that she jumped. It's so fucking obvious."

"She didn't do it!" Tracey roared back. "Don't be so blinded by hate. She fell, fell, fell. You can't blame Dermot for that. Only Molly is to blame, she got drunk and fell out the window. All Molly, just Molly, and if you have to be angry at someone, be angry at Molly 'cause I sure as hell am!" She fired the bowls on to the floor, turned and ran out into the hallway.

Tommy sat frozen to the spot, listening to her sobs as she thumped up the stairs. He felt like a right shithead. Why was he arguing with her? Did it matter that they believed different things? Tracey knew Dermot's faults every bit as much as he did, but she could find forgiveness in a way that was alien to Tommy. He was stubborn, and he knew it.

Tracey's phone rang again. Tommy saw that it was Tracey's mum.

"For Christ's sakes!" Tommy said to the dog. Wolfie stopped his howl and folded up again on the floor. Tommy brought the phone up to Tracey.

She lay face down on the bed, her hair a tangle over her face.

He sat down beside her. "You okay?" he rubbed her back.

She rolled over. Red rimmed eyes full of pain sought his. She sat up and reached for him and they clasped together.

"I'm sorry," he whispered into her hair.

"Me too." She tightened her arms around him. "I love you. Let's not fight."

"I love you too," he said turning her face to his and kissing her forehead and then her eyelids before releasing her. "Your mum called," Tommy said, handing her the phone.

"Do you mind if I call her back?"

"Go on," Tommy said. Poor Tracey tried to look after everyone.

"Hi, Mum," she said. "Oh, my God!"

What now?

Her forehead furrowed in a frown as she listened to a lengthy saga from her mother's side of the call. Tracey interspersed "Oh God!" with "Oh no," and "How awful!" and finished with "I'll come now and get you. I'll be there in ten minutes." She hung up and turned to Tommy.

"I have to go get Mum and take her to the hospital. Dermot's been scalded with boiling water."

"Why do you have to go?"

"You know Mum. She doesn't like to drive at night."

"Why doesn't she wait till the morning?"

"She has to take the baby home. Sheila can't look after it."

"What? Why not?"

"She's had a nervous breakdown!"

"What! *She's* had the breakdown? But she's the one who won the guy and is having the baby and well, shit, Tracey, everything's sweet in her garden. I don't get it."

"According to Mum it's some kind of post-natal depression or psychosis or something. Apparently she threw a kettle over Dermot because she thinks that her baby is Molly!"

"Holy shit! Are you serious?"

Tracey nodded. She covered her mouth with her hand and looked at Tommy with wide eyes.

"What kind of a crazy bitch is she?" Tommy asked.

"The kind that gets taken away by the men in white coats, according to mum. The baby has no one to look after it."

"God, I wish Molly were alive for this," Tommy said. Was the world going completely mad?

Tracey began gathering up her keys, coat and handbag.

"So you're really going?" Tommy asked.

"I have to."

"No, you don't. You've got other brothers and sisters. Let someone else do it. Just tell them, 'No'. Your mother can get a taxi. Why does everything have to revolve around Dermot fecking Duggan?" The dog slid under the table in the corner. Tommy took his voice down a notch. "Don't go to him. Please, Tracey. I need you." He felt ashamed admitting it.

"Don't do this, Tommy. It's not about choosing one over the other. There's more than just Dermot now. Mum's in bits. Her nerves-"

"-are bad," Tommy said, finishing her sentence. "They're just using you."

"Of course they are - they're my family. We all use each other, otherwise what's the point of family? We all need each other. All the time. But Tommy..."Tracey's eyes beseeched him. "...right now the new baby needs me the most."

"That crazy slut's bastard to an adulterer is more important than us?" Tommy hated the words as soon as he said them.

Tracey stood in the open front doorway. She paused, then turned to Tommy and said quietly, "Yes."

"You're not serious?" Tommy took a step towards her. She stepped out over the threshold.

"Oh for Christ's sakes, don't get all Victorian Irish Catholic on me. It's the twenty-first century. This shit happens. Has always happened. I thought you were more liberal minded than that, Tommy. He made a mistake. She made an even bigger mistake, evidently."

"I don't care. I never want to see that baby. Don't bother coming back here with it," Tommy yelled back.

Tracey sucked in a breath, closed her eyes, and when she opened them again, they were glittering.

"They all made mistakes – Dermot, Sheila and yes even Molly, but you're going to blame an innocent little baby? Grow up, Tommy!"

She slammed the door behind her. Tommy stood looking at the closed door. The rage that had pounded through him burst like a balloon. His ears rang with the silence that followed. He ran to the door and opened it, hoping that Tracey would still be there, but not knowing what he would do if she was.

The wind howled. The tree branches rattled, and the phone lines hummed as air sang through them. Leaves and litter swirled and tumbled along the street in the wake of Tracey's car.

Thursday, November 2nd

CHAPTER FIFTY-EIGHT

"Oh my God! She's so tiny. Just out of the packet!" Tracey said, amazed by her niece. She closed the door of the hospital family room behind her, shutting out the noise from the ward and walked over to her mother. "She's beautiful!"

"I know. She's the image of you as a baby," Carmel said, holding her granddaughter.

"You know, Mum, I can see how it would freak Sheila out having such a fair baby with her and Dermot both so dark," Tracey said.

Her mother had given her a confusing account, but the whole story would have to come from Dermot.

"You know it's not that uncommon, sure our Frankie has red hair and your Dad and I are both dark. Look at you, for that matter. That Sheila one is off her rocker. Every time I think of what she did to our Dermot, oh God!" Carmel's eyes teared up and her chin wobbled. "Oh what am I gonna do now?" she wailed.

"Shush, Mum, you'll wake her." Tracey reached for her niece, snuggling her into the crook of her arm as she gazed down at her. She'd fallen in love with her already. If only it could have been Molly's baby. How happy a time it would have been. Tommy would be at her side – Tommy. She felt sick to the pit of her stomach. Was he lost to her now? He'd been so good about the fire and not blamed her, but this. . . Sorrow pierced her joy about the baby.

It would be the end of their relationship, if he couldn't accept the baby. And why would he? He'd lost the closest thing he had to a sister because of this innocent little girl's birth. How could a mother abandon this beautiful wee thing? Tracey hugged her closer, a protective instinct taking hold.

The doctor came into the room. Tracey and Carmel turned to her.

"How's Dermot?"

"He's in a great deal of pain."

"Oh Holy God!" Carmel said putting her hand to her mouth.

"Well, we've given him medication for that. He has third degree burns down his back and left thigh."

"Mother of God!"

"Shush, Mum, will you let her talk."

"Sorry but, oh my God! Will he be scarred?" Carmel's hands shook and she clasped them together at her breast.

The Doctor nodded. "There will be permanent scarring. He will require postoperative care at home. Is there someone who can do that?"

"Oh Jesus Christ," Carmel wailed.

"I'll look after him," Tracey said. She supposed she'd be moving back home again. Tears threatened again, and she swallowed them back. Her mother couldn't cope, but Tracey wondered if she alone had the strength for this. She missed Tommy already. How lovely it would be to rest her head on his shoulder and have him put his arms around her - around her holding Dermot's baby.

Tracey felt sick at the thought of Dermot's skin scarred. She didn't know what to say when she went in to him. She was afraid of her reaction. What the hell had happened? Did Sheila really do this to him?

"Doctor," Tracey tried to modulate her voice. Still it wavered. "What is happening to the baby's mother?"

"We can't discuss that with you. You can go in to see Dermot. He can talk, but he'll find it painful to move. Try to keep him calm."

The doctor led them down the ward to the last alcove. A blue curtain gave the bed some privacy. The doctor pulled the curtain back about a foot and gestured for Carmel to go in first. She hugged the babe in her arms a little tighter and took a deep breath. Before Tracey got there, she heard a hoarse whisper as Dermot greeted his mother.

"Look at the state of you, son. What did that mad woman do to you?"

"Mum!" Tracey hissed.

Carmel moved aside, sobbing, and dabbed at her eyes with a hanky. Tracey heard a deep sigh from Dermot and she turned her head towards him. Her stomach flipped over and her whole body cringed, dragging everything inward as though she'd sucked a giant lemon. He lay on his stomach, his head turned to face them. Most of his back and thighs were swathed in gauze that had an ominous looking yellow fluid soaking through it. Dermot saw her and filled up with tears.

"Tracey," he sobbed. "Thank you for coming."

Tracey gulped back her own emotions.

"Of course I'm here."

"I called you... but. . ."

"Hush, I'm here now," Tracey soothed, ignoring the stab of guilt. "Do you want to tell us what happened?"

"Oh God, it was awful!" His words faltered between sobs as he worked to control his breathing. "Sheila just went crazy. She thought the baby was Molly. I had pictures. The ones you dropped yesterday."

Tracey nodded. She'd searched for those damn pictures for hours.

"And then Sheila threw boiling water round you?" Tracey asked, horrified.

"Something like that, yes." His eyes flicked away.

"So where is she now?"

"She's at the psychiatric unit being treated for post-natal psychosis. It's not her fault. It was triggered by giving birth. It causes hallucinations and paranoia. It's a really rare condition, worse than post-natal depression. She went into a stupor after I got scalded. I managed to call an ambulance, and they treated her for shock, but then she started again going on about the baby being evil and having to be stopped, and they admitted her after that." He stopped, drained.

"So where was Cara while all this was happening?" Carmel asked.

Dermot shuddered then gasped with pain. "I was holding her," he said.

Tracey could barely hear him. She cringed at the very thought of the hot water hitting the baby.

"And what about you?" Tracey's voice was tender.

Dermot sniffed. She could see him battling tears.

"The pain medication is taking the edge off. My career as a Speedo model is over though." He tried to joke, but Tracey knew that his vanity would cause him to suffer. "I don't know what I'm going to do. It's all so hopeless. Sheila, the baby, everything. Oh God!" His body shuddered as he sobbed. The pain made him gasp. "I feel like I'm looking into a big black abyss. It's all so hopeless. I think I know how Molly must have felt." His voice was bleak. It opened a dark pit for Tracey.

"Oh God, Dermot, please don't start down that road. It's never so bad that you should do. . . You have Cara. Molly felt..." Tracey stopped herself. She didn't want to burden anymore guilt onto Dermot.

"She felt that she had no one." Dermot finished the sentence for her. "I see that now. I'm so sorry, but it's too late. I was such a shit to her. Too wrapped up in my own stuff. Too selfish."

Tracey couldn't speak. They'd all been wrapped up in their own stuff. Her throat constricted, and she could barely breathe. Sorrow, forceful and all encompassing, held her in a rigor-mortis-like grip. Her next inhalation released something in her, and her brain rebooted.

"True, Dermot." She hadn't meant that to sound so cold. She tempered her tone. "But she did have people. We were there, Tommy and I; we just didn't know what she needed. That's no defense, just the truth. She should have asked for help. And you need to ask for help," she added in desperation.

"It's all my fault. All of it. The only good out of this is Cara, and even her wee life is blighted. My poor baby." His tears flowed again. "But it gets worse. The social services have been here already. With Sheila in the loony bin and me so badly injured, they want to take Cara away from me."

Thursday, November 2nd

CHAPTER FIFTY-NINE

When Tommy heard the knock on the door an hour later, he felt sure that Tracey had come back. Maybe she'd listened to reason, his reason. He wondered why she just hadn't let herself in, and he hesitated. Perhaps she had the baby with her. The knock echoed in the hallway again.

"Tommy? Son, are you there?" Sean's voice called through the letterbox.

"Coming, Dad." Tommy answered, relieved and disappointed at once. He'd not spoken much to his Dad since that day he'd asked him to lend him money at the salon.

"Come in," Tommy said opening the door.

"Thanks, son. Is Tracey home?" Sean asked.

"N-no," Tommy said. His tongue felt too big for his mouth.

"That's okay. It's you I came to see." Sean moved into the living room and Tommy followed, grappling for composure.

Sean took off his coat, folded it over the back of the armchair and sat on the sofa opposite.

"Tea?" Tommy asked.

"First, I wanted to give this to you," Sean said handing over an envelope.

"What's this?" Tommy said taking it.

"Open it."

Tommy lifted the flap of the envelope and slid out a slip of paper, a check. He turned it over and gasped.

"Ten thousand pounds, but I thought you said. . ." Tommy began.

"No, son. I never said no. I just needed to see if I had it all, that's all. You can do what you like with it."

"Even re-open the salon?" Tommy asked. He didn't dare hope. There was bound to be a catch.

"Yes. After seeing Ben and Aileen, I realize how precious you are to me. I nearly lost you once, Son; I will never make that mistake again."

For a moment Tommy couldn't trust himself to speak. He placed his hand on his father's shoulder and squeezed it.

"I want to apologize." Sean rubbed his hands together and cleared his throat before continuing. "I should have accepted you. . ." Sean cleared his throat again.

"I'm sorry too. Thanks for this." Tommy held up the check. "It means. . .it means. . ."

"It means you'll do me proud, like you always have done."

Tommy swallowed. "I'll pay back every penny, with interest."

"It's not a loan. I'm giving it to you." Sean's wrinkled face folded into a smile. "So maybe I will have that cup of tea after all. Where is the lovely Tracey anyway?"

"Ah God, Dad, I think I've really screwed this one up."

Sean followed Tommy into the kitchen as he made them a cup of tea and told his father what had happened to Dermot and Sheila.

"Molly is dead because of that baby. I can't, I just can't look at it."

Sean shook his head and said, "And I thought I was the stubborn one. Tracey's right about the baby. It is the innocent one. If you love Tracey like I think you do, then some day that wee ba will be to you what Molly is to me." Sean's voice caught on Molly's name.

Tommy ran his hand through his hair and grasped the nape of his neck, pulling his head down. His face muscles quivered as he fought back tears. He took a deep breath but couldn't speak. He had nothing new to say.

"Unless," Sean continued, "you do what I did and allow stubbornness and ignorance to take away from you the potential for great happiness. Go after her Son. No problem is too big if you love each other. Just take it as it comes, a little at a time. You don't have to accept Dermot too. Just Tracey, just for now."

Tommy put his hand on his father's shoulder and looked over at the check where he'd set it on the counter. If his father could get past his prejudices, then so could he. He pulled the strength up from deep down in his gut as he said, "You're right, Dad, so right."

He lifted his jacket and keys.

"Where are you going?" Sean asked.

"The hospital."

***

Tommy stood in the burns ward outside the cubical where Dermot lay. He'd been told to wait further up the ward, but he could hear Tracey's voice from behind this curtain. The staff didn't notice him relocate to a plastic chair further down the hall. He tried not to eavesdrop. He didn't think he could have cared about Dermot, but when he heard pain, sharp and glittering, in his old friend's voice, pity stirred.

"I can't let them take Cara away," Dermot was saying. "I've done everything wrong since the day I met Sheila. This is one thing I have to do right."

"Shush, now, don't be upsetting yourself. Mum and I will look after Cara. Look, she's as snug as a bug in her granny's arms," Tracey said.

Sorrow wrapped around Tommy. Tracey had already written him out of the equation. It would not be enough to beg her forgiveness. He'd have to man up and accept that baby.

"No, I'm her father. I'll look after her," Dermot said. Tommy heard him gasp. There was a rustle of fabric and he could hear Tracey's mother mumbling but couldn't make out the words.

"I deserve this, I suppose. I was such a bastard to poor Molly. I'm so sorry."

The sobs reached a place in Tommy's heart that words couldn't. He felt sorry for Dermot, who had to deal with loss *and* guilt, a caustic combination. Tommy had decided what he needed to do even before Tracey spoke.

"Family forgives. You must forgive yourself too. And Cara has us now too. Molly's hurt is over. She wouldn't want us all hating each other, making each other suffer more. Forgiving each other is not forgetting her, but we do need to focus on our wounds. Physical and otherwise. You're my big brother, Dermot," A small intake of breath belied the sob she suppressed. "I love you, and I need you. We'll get through this."

"What about Tommy?" Dermot asked in a small voice.

Tommy held his breath.

"I don't know." She sounded bewildered.

Tommy stood up. Three steps took him to the cubicle. He pulled back the curtain. His eyes sought out Tracey. Confusion and alarm spread across her features.

"I do know," he said, reaching for her hand. "I know that I love you, and I'll do whatever it takes to keep you."

Tears spilled out of Tracey's eyes.

"If you'll have me, that is," he added in a rush.

"And what about Cara?" Tracey asked, nodding towards her mother holding the baby.

He pushed his lips together, and nodded. "Whatever it takes."

She threw her arms around his neck. He squeezed her tightly to him. He closed his eyes to savor the moment. When he opened them again, he looked over at Dermot. They held each other's gaze for a long second. Understanding flowed like an electric current. Tommy knew they had a long way to go, but with Tracey by his side, the journey would be bearable and the destination worth it.

THE END

ABOUT THE AUTHOR

Byddi Lee grew up in Ireland. In 2002 she took a sabbatical from teaching and traveled round the world for two years, writing blogs about her adventures as she went. She returned to Ireland in 2004 and resumed teaching. In 2008 she and her husband moved to San Jose, California where she made writing her new career.

Besides being a novelist, Byddi is also a Master Gardener. She writes a blog on life as an Irish gardener and traveler living in California called, "We didn't come here for the grass."

CPSIA information can be obtained at www.ICGtesting.com
Printed in the USA
LVOW04s1322040515

437156LV00023B/346/P